COUSINS

Also by Suzanne Goodwin

SISTERS

COUSINS

SUZANNE GOODWIN

St. Martin's Press
New York

Library of Congress Cataloging in Publication Data

Goodwin, Suzanne.
  Cousins.

  I. Title.
PR6057.O585C6 1986   823'.914   86-1740
ISBN 0-312-17057-2

First published in Great Britain by Severn House (Publishers) Ltd.

First U.S. Edition

10 9 8 7 6 5 4 3 2 1

PART ONE

Autumn – 1932

Chapter One

They were lying in the orchard grass which was long and coarse and should have been cut three months ago. Inslow always forgot the orchard on purpose. You couldn't use the lawn-mower there, the ground was uneven with many slopes and bumps. He considered a scythe, which he could use to perfection, beneath his dignity; did they think he was a farm worker?

Elizabeth lay uncomfortably with her head against the trunk of an apple tree. Peter was flat on his back. Above them the spreading tent of leaves had not yet begun to crisp and turn, but it would be any minute now, she thought. She never needed bonfire smoke to tell her autumn was on the way; she felt the seasons in her veins.

Peter said nothing for a while. He had kissed her once or twice and she wished he would do it again. She was always wanting her cousin to touch her these days. And when he did, lightly and chastely, her inexperienced body melted. It was very disturbing.

He lifted his head, looked at her, and dropped into the grass again.

'You're very quiet, Liz.'

'I like being quiet.'

'Not you. So what is it?'

'I was thinking something pretty boring.'

'Bore on, then.'

The sounds of deep Devonshire country were all about. Innumerable hidden birds chirped. Insects whirred. A bee went loudly by.

'Well?' said Peter, yawning.

'I was thinking we've been here too long, and Uncle asked you to go with him to the Bowdens at four, to talk about buying new stock.'

'You're right, that *is* boring. And stop being my conscience.'

'Someone has to be.'

'Stern daughter of the voice of God. Duty. Tennyson.'

'Jiminy, do I sound like that?'

'All the time . . .'

His voice slurred and she knew he was going to sleep.

He lay half hidden in the grass. She moved closer and saw a lock of hair had fallen across his forehead in a curl. It hurt her, that curl. His round face was horribly endearing. The mouth which had kissed her just now was relaxed, thick-lipped, turning up at the co. .ers. Sleep brought indifference to his handsome face.

She shifted again to sit upright. She was tallish, not beautiful, with dark hair which curled at the edges and odd slanting eyes with little flaws in the iris, like freckles. Her skin had an olive tint, which people who did not know her might think came from Italian or Greek forebears. Elizabeth liked her swarthy skin and freckled eyes. Many of the Bidwells, back to Tudor times, had one or other of these characteristics. Most things about her were Bidwell. Her figure, strong and straight, her mouth like Peter's with thick lips, her short nose. She was not impulsive and could be pig-headed – as her ancestors had been. She was often blunt. Peter disapproved of that, saying that speaking your mind was usually a mistake.

Away from the overgrown orchard of apples, cherries, plum and walnut trees, were the gardens of the house. There was a paved rose garden, fine lawns, herbaceous borders, yew trees, lavender bushes, and – at the top of the sloping velvety grass, shaded by a venerable sycamore, was Merriscourt. Bidwells had lived on this hill, a few miles from the sea, for hundreds of years. Their land was red sandstone which formed the remarkable crimson ploughlands and brilliant cliffs – which in summer rose above an indigo sea – of

4

southern Devon. The family, from the military class, had come to the county in the 1580s and liked what they saw. The hilly, coloured, up and down countryside, the tumbling rivers and moors blazing with furze, the soft air and soft rain. In 1585 they bought and pulled down a medieval manor and built in its stead a Tudor house. Part of the old chapel, in the form of a single arch, still remained and led incongruously to the stables. The Bidwells, destroyers and builders, raised or felled a succession of houses all called Merriscourt. There was stone on their land which they quarried and used for new wings, stables, outhouses, boundary walls. From their own woods came the oak for floors and beams and panelling.

The family thrived and by the eighteenth century had become a kind of territorial aristocracy, their handsome manor a meeting place for Bidwells who now lived from Dawlish to Bovey Tracey and Newton Abbot; the land was fertile and so were they. But it wasn't until mid-Victorian times that a William Bidwell created the Merriscourt where Elizabeth and Peter now lived. William, a man of fashion, hired the most notable Victorian archictect, demolished much of the Jacobean house and built a high main wing to Merriscourt in the elaborate gothic style. His taste ran to stained glass, the carved figures of medieval kings at the heads of stairs, vaulted ceilings, and living rooms and bedrooms with the air of church interiors. The only surviving wing of the Jacobean house was joined to the Victorian enormity. The house was a mish-mash, yet it had a kind of harmony. Grey stone and red brick, irregular cobbled courtyards, mullioned windows. Its personality was as feminine as Devonshire was. It had no austerity or sadness. It was a serene house and in a way an isolated one.

Elizabeth knew her family history as a Catholic knows his religion. The portraits on the stairs, in the dining room, or poked away in dark corners, many with eyes like her own, stared out at her like old friends. Colonels and lawyers and squires; not a hero among them. There wasn't a single ances- tor whose exploits were told with pride. The Bidwells had

5

never been affected by the deep Devon passion for the sea. The family had a tradition of soldiering which continued, off and on, and in the Civil War they'd fought for King Charles . . . . but no more bravely than hundreds of other country squires. They either disdained or disliked reckless courage – which explained their lack of any kind of title. Their best talent was undoubtedly caring for their estates and marrying heiresses. The Bidwells were simply a stout part of an unmoving and stable society, rooted in the red soil of one corner of provincial England.

Elizabeth often wished her cousin were as tough as their ancestors had been. Speaking of the Devon gentry, the great Queen Elizabeth called them born courtiers. Now there was one trait, the only one, Peter *had* inherited. He had an indolent, irresistible charm. Having loved him all her life, and now half in love with him, she sometimes thought he was in the wrong place. How well he'd suit modern society, charming troops of servants, breeding thoroughbred horses, winning motor races at Brooklands. Now, in 1932, the depression had been going on for two dreadful years, there was unemployment and poverty, hunger marches, civil unrest. But there still seemed to be many rich people whose antics were described with relish in the newspapers. Peter would fit into that alluring, despicable life.

But then where would I be? she thought. She could imagine being nowhere but here at Merriscourt. Which, had she been a boy, would have been hers.

Her father had been the elder of two sons. In the last years of Edwardian peace Richard Bidwell had brought his young wife to Merriscourt, where their daughter Elizabeth had been born. War came. Elizabeth could only faintly remember her father, whose photograph in uniform was on her mother's dressing-table. Dolly Bidwell rarely spoke nowadays of her husband. And in her daughter's mind he had become a myth. He had joined Kitchener's army in 1914, fought the bloody battles on the Somme and stayed in that sector. The war went on, killing men in hundreds of thousands, advancing and retreating a few yards, a few blackened yards. Richard survived for three terrible years. In the spring of 1918 he was in the 2nd battle of the Marne when the British and French lines joined. A few weeks before the Armistice, in northern France not many miles from where his regiment had first fought, he was killed by a sniper.

His brother Garnett inherited everything.

Losing Richard was terrible for Garnett. He himself, invalided out of the Army after Gallipoli with a recurring fever, had come back to England still ill. He returned to Merriscourt where Dolly had been caring for his small son, for his wife died in childbirth. Dolly took Garnett, too, under her wing and nursed him devotedly. All four, the frail man and his boy, the young woman and her daughter, were together when the news came that Richard had been killed.

On that very morning, Garnett asked Dolly to stay at Merriscourt and make it her permanent home, as she'd done until now. He could not cope alone.

Dolly took the change in her fortunes with philosophy. She had been spoiled as a girl, her father had been lavish and, as she occasionally told Elizabeth, she had 'wanted for nothing'. He had settled a handsome sum on his only child when she married. But he had been a self-made man who liked money to move, to be earned and spent, and it never occurred to him to invest his daughter's settlement, tie it up and consequently give the girl an income. He simply made over a large sum which Dolly and her young husband began to spend. They redecorated the old house. They enjoyed themselves. They went to stay in Paris, where Richard bought his young bride Parisian gowns embroidered with beads, and flame-coloured ostrich feather fans. The money drained away as it does when it is not watched over. In a few years, to the Bidwells' surprise, it was almost gone.

On her widowhood, due to an entailed estate, unthinking extravagance and a young husband who never planned to die, Dolly had almost no money. But she was unselfishly fond of Garnett and more interested in looking after him than worrying about herself. She had none of the resentment of a taker for a giver. Her fondness and gratitude showed by the way she invested her brother-in-law with a sort of halo. She was the most feminine of women, and it was this quality, vulnerable, soft, amorphous, which caused Garnett to beg her to stay.

She also took on his only son. That was no fine gesture of kindness – Dolly had loved the child the moment she set eyes on him. She'd always preferred men to women and her love for Peter replaced all she might have lavished on her lost husband. She adored Peter when he was four years old, and when he thundered through the house in thick school shoes, an ungainly twelve. She admired him when he was a self-conscious youth of sixteen, and as he grew taller and older and more enchanting, Dolly sat and marvelled.

Elizabeth didn't mind. She loved him too. The only one of the Bidwell quartet to have inherited the family's practical head, she thought it fortunate that her mother was so devoted to Peter. It meant harmony.

Perhaps Dolly loved him too much. Everybody has a heel of Achilles, and with her it always had been Peter. Her face changed when he came into a room. She liked his graceful male figure, his drawling voice, his facetious jokes. She admired his expensive clothes and instinctive sense of fashion. His dark, fine hair was never shaved, Army-style, up the back of his head to show his scalp but expertly cut and becoming; he wore a well-trimmed moustache. His shirts were exquisite, and the Savile Row tailor, who had made clothes for the family since the year dot, knew Peter was a perfectionist. Peter Bidwell was interested in pretty women, clothes, horses, gossip, and the look of things. And when he wanted something, he got it.

Except once. He had always wanted, longed, to go into the Army and make it his career. The Army was in his blood, and his grandfather had been a colonel in the Royal Devons. When at public school he took it for granted that he would be going on to Sandhurst. Garnett said no. Poor Peter had to listen to his father querulously advancing argument after argument. Peter must remain at home, he said, to help with the estate which he would eventually inherit.

Peter surrendered. Elizabeth was shocked.

'How feeble you are, haven't you any guts? If you'd really wanted to go into the Army you would have dug your toes in.'

'I did want it. I still do. But how can I leave the old man with the estate hanging round his neck like an albatross?'

'He's got the bailiff, for heaven's sake! Oh, do stop looking so hangdog. I don't know why Uncle's so set on having you to help. We could have perfectly well managed without you.'

'*You* could. But he'd never allow you to do much, Lizzie. And besides. . .'

'Besides, Merriscourt does not belong to me.'

'Of course it does. You should get half.'

'I won't get a single twig as you know perfectly well.'

She shifted her ground.

'Perhaps it is a good thing you aren't going into the Army, actually. Uncle isn't looking at all well.'

He laughed. 'Oh, nonsense, he's only got a cold. What a contrary woman you are – one minute packing me off to Sandhurst and the next, because my father sneezes, you chain me to Merriscourt like a farm labourer.'

'I would if I could.'

Although her uncle owned everything and she and her mother nothing, Elizabeth felt protective towards Garnett, and uneasily sorry for him. His health had been permanently weakened by the fever, he walked with a stoop, he had gone prematurely grey. At 48, he looked over 60. And he was so anxious. She knew too well that tone of voice, irritable with worry, which rose and cracked.

Peter had only a father, Elizabeth a mother. Garnett and Dolly Bidwell might never even have been friends if family relationship, and tragedy, had not pitched them together. Dolly admired strong handsome men and Garnett was afraid of women. His own pretty gentle little wife was a ghost, as Richard Bidwell was. Merriscourt was occupied by two

9

tribes, one exclusively male, the other female, linked by treaties.

From a very early age, the children were sternly told to be quiet in the house. Garnett's name was used as a candle-snuffer to extinguish high spirits. 'Sh. Your father is worried,' Dolly would say. Or 'Elizabeth, lower your voice. Remember your uncle.' Peter, with the ruthlessness of a child, once said, 'Father's always worried,' and gave a mar-tyred sigh.

Now Peter was twenty-six, Elizabeth twenty-one, and what had changed? Peter had sacrificed his career for his father's sake, but did nothing to relieve the burdens which each year bent Garnett's back a little more.

In the tall grass, Peter stirred and opened his eyes.

'I've been asleep.'

'Imagine that.'

He looked drowsily at his watch, then sat up with a start.

'Why didn't you wake me! Is that the time?'

Springing up, he brushed the grass from his trousers and ran a hand through his hair, thinnish and soft and unlike his cousin's which was as thick as a pony's mane. He put out his hands and tugged her to her feet. As she was thrown forward towards him she thought they were going to kiss. They didn't.

'There'll be ructions, damn it.'

'You'll talk yourself out of them.'

'Come on,' he said, and they began to run.

The French windows into Garnett's study were open, and, casting a speaking look at her, Peter vanished. She heard a complaining voice.

'Where have you been? You're very late.'

'I was looking at the orchard, sir. Inslow has forgotten to cut it again. I really must have a word with him.'

Elizabeth went indoors, up the elaborate carved staircase, with figures of kings and queens at its base and top, and along a passage to the room she used as a study. Here there was a rickety ancient desk, the leg of which was propped up with a wedge of blotting paper, two or three chairs, and some

10

sentimental engravings of children, ponies and collie dogs from the old nursery.

She worked in the poky room at village hall accounts, she helped to organise jumble sales or whist drives for local charities, and did any minor job for Merriscourt which her uncle grudgingly allowed. At present she was sending out the invitations for two Christmas parties which he gave every year, one for the tenants, the other for the parish. There were many Bidwell traditions at Christmas. Cutting the holly, for instance; she and Peter and Inslow went to the woods a week before Christmas and always brought home a barrowful. Years ago, quarrelling violently with Peter during holly-cutting, Elizabeth had shouted the immortal war-cry:

'Pass me the billhook, please, Inslow, 'cos I'm going to cut off Peter's head.'

Carol-singing was a Christmas pleasure too. Peter and Elizabeth, the butler Marchant and a troop of giggling maids, tramped across dark fields by torchlight to sing outside the farms. Doors were flung open and the singers welcomed into smoky kitchens. But Elizabeth's favourite of all was what happened every Christmas Eve, when the farmers went out into their orchards to pour quantities of cider over the roots of the prime apple trees. Toast sops dripping with cider were balanced on bare branches. Peter and Elizabeth always went to the ancient ceremony, and joined in the song:

> Here's tu thee, old apple tree,
> Be sure you bud,
> Be sure you blow.

She was busy drawing up the tenants' list now when there was a tap on the door. It was Kathleen, youngest of the housemaids, who had the habit of going the colour of a beetroot when either speaking or spoken to. She came into the room quite puce.

'The Mistress says to tell you tea's ready, Miss Elizabeth.'

'Thank you, Kathleen. Just coming.'

The girl disappeared like a rabbit.

Elizabeth's mother was seated on the sofa, pouring tea. The drawing-room at Merriscourt was the most gothic of all William Bidwell's creations; no elaborate and romantic detail had been omitted. There was linenfold panelling, a doorway shaped like the arch in a church, marble kings and queens wearing crowns and holding sceptres, a fireplace of magnificent size, carved with leaping stags. Most dramatic of all were the high stained-glass windows. These represented the Arts of Music. Four white-clad copper-haired girls drooped respectively over an organ, a viol, a harp and a recorder. Above their heads were branches heavy with brilliant birds and fruit.

The afternoon sun, slanting through the windows, threw blue and crimson patterns on the floor.

Sitting down, Elizabeth stretched her legs and looked critically at her feet.

'Peter's very rude about my shoes, Mother.'

They both regarded the polished leather brogues.

'Take no notice, my child. Did you tell him that I chose them?'

'Of course I did. He said you should be ashamed of yourself, shoes were meant to be seductive, and he was going into Exeter to buy me some.'

Dolly's laugh ran upwards in a pretty scale of notes.

'Never refuse a present. We can always change them.'

Elizabeth's mother was a small person. Her little hands wore a number of diamond half-hoops, her little feet shoes as uninspired as her daughter's. Her nose was handsome, her dark eyes bright and wary as a bird's. She laughed easily. As a girl she had been much admired by men for her gaiety, her frills and her eighteen-inch waist. She had daringly bicycled in Battersea Park, and worn out her slippers by dancing all night long. She had been spoiled and flattered, ogled and proposed to. She had a warm heart and was a snob.

The other branch of the great Bidwell family which had once spread across South Devon had lived at Bovey Tracey before the 1914 war and had looked very much down their noses at the suburban girl Richard had brought back from London as his wife. Dorothy Allen's father owned a grocery business or, as the Bidwells put it, was in trade. He was very generous when his only child made a classy marriage. The Bovey Tracey Bidwells said it was a *mésalliance*, and approved of the wedding settlement.

Dolly had been impressed by her husband's relatives and eventually the Bovey Tracey group accepted her in a patronising way. But the war decimated that family. Unmarried sons were killed. Daughters married and left for the colonies. Now only one great aunt remained in England. She lived at a hotel in Bloomsbury.

The strange power that sex sometimes gives to a young woman did not last for Dolly Bidwell. When she became a widow it evaporated like scent from a bottle smashed on a stone floor. But she still knew how to be clever with men, and she often wished that Elizabeth did. Watching Dolly as a girl skilfully coping with her many admirers, her father had once remarked that a woman could have one of three gifts – 'Beauty, brains or tricks,' he said, 'and the greatest of these is tricks.'

It was a surprise to Dolly that her own child did not seem to have even one.

During tea, Dolly was rather quiet. It seemed that she had something on her mind. Finally she picked up a letter which was lying on the tea-table.

'Have you heard your uncle mention his cousin George Westlock?'

Elizabeth had noticed the letter; it was of a kind she remembered very well at school. They arrived for girls whose parents were on the other side of the world, in India or Ceylon or Malaya. The letters, on thin paper with many darkish stamps, always brought drama. Sometimes fits of hysterics. Once one of Elizabeth's friends, receiving a letter from her mother in Ceylon after a year, had been sick.

'Westlock isn't really a cousin, is he? Once removed or

something. But I know the one. He sends that Christmas card every year.'

She giggled.

Years ago Peter had nicknamed Westlock the Cousin from Calcutta. A regular soldier who had served in India for years, Westlock's only existence for the cousins was the card which arrived punctiliously every year weeks before anybody else's. It always looked the same as his previous cards, with a regimental crest and firm handwriting wishing them all a merry Christmas. He might have been an old friend. And every year Elizabeth wondered why he bothered.

'The usual card from the Coz from Calc,' she would say.

Her mother was fidgeting with the letter and Elizabeth said suddenly, 'I bet I can guess what's in it. He is coming home on leave, and wants to see you and Uncle. People always start to be interested in distant relations when they're due to come back to England. Very obvious.'

'Scarcely a distant relation. His grandfather married Great Aunt Bessy's sister.'

'That's sounds extremely distant to me. Go on, Mother, break the bad news. He's landing on us for a weekend. I trust it won't be longer.'

Dolly was re-reading the letter.

'I don't know how long he wants to stay. Yes, he has some leave due.'

She put down the letter again and said musingly.

'It will be strange to see him again after sixteen years.'

'I suppose you've completely forgotten what he's like.'

Dolly did not answer. She rarely thought of the past because when she did it hurt her. And the present was what she enjoyed. But curiously enough she recalled George Westlock very well – a fair, soldierly young man of a type she admired, with rugged good looks and an eye for a pretty woman. She remembered the first time they had met. Richard had been on leave. One of those hectic, pleasure-packed, sex-enchanted London leaves. They had stayed at a great hotel which no

14

longer existed, a huge place on the river not far from the Savoy. Dolly recalled the rows of Allied flags hanging outside, the marble entrance hall, the lofty Egyptian pillars, a bedroom with an open fire. Richard had taken her to musical comedies every single night of his leave. After seeing a play, their heads still full of songs, they dined late, danced, and went back to the fire-bewitched bedroom to make love. How long ago it was. She could scarcely remember the lovemaking, although she still played on her piano every one of the songs . . .

On an afternoon during the week, in a London where there was not a man to be seen out of uniform, they had gone to a *thé dansant* given in some Duchess's Mayfair house, in aid of the Red Cross.

'George Westlock told me when I saw him at the club that he may be there,' Richard said. 'He's by way of being a second cousin. I'm sure you'll like him, dearest.'

'What makes you so sure?' asked Dolly coyly.

'All the girls do.'

'Then I shan't.'

Richard like his Dolly provocative.

'Contrary Mary. Just you wait and see.'

She first saw George Westlock when she and Richard were seated at a table in the ballroom; the band played waltzes, footmen served tea. And there was a good-looking young man whom Richard pointed out to her. He was dancing with a girl who couldn't take her eyes off him. A thin girl with a cloud of dark hair and a bony, intense sort of face.

'Why, that's the Earl of Bagot's daughter, Lady Priscilla,' said Dolly who was a devout reader of the *Tatler*.

'Trust George,' said Richard.

Westlock saw them and when the dance ended came to join them for tea after taking his partner back to a crowded table. He was young and lively, in his mid-twenties, with a thatch of short fair hair and an easy laugh. Dolly couldn't help liking him in spite of the fact that within five minutes he asked if he could bring Lady Priscilla to meet them.

15

'She's with that dragon of a mother but I know I can extri-
cate her, and she's dying to come over.'

Westlock had been charming to Dolly, but when Lady
Priscilla arrived, his interest was concentrated on the young
girl and not the young wife. How he flirted, paying his companion a teasing provocative kind of attention. How taken
with him Lady Priscilla had been, fixing huge dark eyes on
him in a quite shameless way.

Alone that evening, Richard said, 'Something going on
between those two.'

'You can't mean –'

'I most certainly can.'

Dolly looked shocked.

'I can see the idea of his sleeping with that girl has made
you twice as interested in young George.'

'Richard! What a thing to say.'

'True, though.'

They met Westlock again during the week by chance, at the
Gaiety Theatre, with Lady Priscilla in tow. A year later when
Richard managed a few days of his leave in Devon, George
paid them a flying visit. He took a great fancy to Merriscourt.
Richard and he went shooting, the two men were out for
hours, and that night her husband told her with amusement
that 'the Priscilla affair is still going strong.'

'Did he *tell* you, Richard?'

'Yes, he did, and don't you ask any more questions, you
naughty girl.'

Dolly came back with a start. To today. Her own middle
age. Wartime London, wartime Merriscourt, the way Richard and George had coaxed her to play the entire score of *Chu
Chin Chow* after dinner, men's voices laughing, her husband's
handsome face, faded into ghosts. All gone. All done.

And here was young George, young no longer, coming
back into her life.

Elizabeth, seeing her mother's reverie, had been silent,
absently stroking the airedale who put his head in her lap and
gave one of his sighs. Her mother, with a shake of the head as

16

if banishing her thoughts, asked if she wanted more tea. Elizabeth said, prompting, 'So he hasn't said if he wants to stay a weekend or a week?'

'No. And there's another point. About his god-daughter. He writes to ask if he can bring her too. Sylvia Ashton. Apparently both her parents are dead, poor things. John and Fay. I can't believe they're gone. Isn't it tragic?'

'Mother, I have never heard of them.'

Detecting flippancy, Dolly frowned.

'George introduced us to them during the war. He and John Ashton were in the same battalion in India – posted back to fight in France, in 1917 I think it was. Your father and I liked the Ashtons so much. Fay was a pretty little thing. John became Colonel in India eventually, after they went back in peacetime. It seems he was killed in some awful riot in Peshawar. George imagines we read about it in *The Times*. And now poor Fay . . . scarcely three months ago. She never looked strong.'

Elizabeth did not feel it reasonable of her mother to expect sympathy about two complete strangers.

'So what's happening is that the Cousin from Calcutta is bringing an orphan in tow and wants her to stay too.'

'I told you. She is his god-daughter.'

'She isn't a Bidwell, though.'

'But he is a member of the family and I cannot possibly say no,' said Dolly, in the prissy voice of someone pointing out a social rule which her daughter should know very well. 'In any case, I do not want to. It will be a pleasure to see George again.'

'I know I sound inhospitable, but I'm blowed if I can see why we should put *her* up.'

'It won't be for long. She's about eighteen, apparently, and he's keen for her to be presented at Court next spring.'

Elizabeth was nettled. Most of her friends in the county had been to Court – satin dresses and three little feathers – but her mother had no money for such an expensive caper, and would not have dreamed of asking Garnett to pay for it. It was an unspoken rule between mother and daughter that Garnett should be asked for the least, the absolute least that was necessary. He would have been exasperated had he known of their countless economies and self-denials.

'So the Calcutta Cousin is coming over to launch her as a deb on the hunt for a husband. Getting her off his hands fast.'

'Don't be crude, Elizabeth. I've told you about that before.'

'But you've often said yourself that girls are presented for just that reason – a shove to help them nab a man.'

Dolly was very put out. Her daughter's slang grated.

'It is generous of George Westlock to want to do things for the girl. And they're very much looking forward to coming home.'

'Home! How sentimental. How long is it since *he* clapped eyes on the white cliffs of Dover?'

'People in the colonies always refer to England as home.'

'Well, it isn't. Anyway, we're straying from the point. Must you ask Uncle if they can stay?'

'Of course. I'm looking forward to seeing them too,' said Dolly, giving her daughter a quelling look.

Dolly went to her brother-in-law's study that evening before dinner, as she wanted to speak to him privately. He rose as she came into the room, and remained standing until she was comfortably settled. His manner to her always had a tired gallantry. Dolly's to him was a mixture of affection and respect.

She explained about the letter and gave it to him. He read it slowly.

George Westlock wrote with aplomb, saying he was only too conscious of the great gap of time since he had seen either Garnett or Dolly. He was writing now because they were his only surviving relatives in England, even though the relationship was a distant one. He knew he was asking a great favour. He went on to the subject of the Ashtons.

'Of course you'll both remember them. John was a magnificent soldier – it was an honour to serve under him. I'm sure you read about his death in that riot last year. You can imagine the terible loss John was to the regiment and to us all. The blow was fatal to poor Fay. This country never suited her, and she shouldn't have stayed here year after year, but John couldn't get her to go home regularly as the other wives do now. Naturally, she went to the hills, but that wasn't enough. Her health was poor and since John's death much worse. The doctors did all they could but she had no strength left. It was a double tragedy.'

He went on to write of their daughter Sylvia, just eighteen. She'd been educated in the north of England but all her childhood, and the last three years, had been spent entirely in cantonments. He, George, was the only person even slightly connected with her – the girl had no living relatives of any kind. As her godfather, he felt responsible for her. He had a long leave due, and planned to arrange for Sylvia to be presented next spring. He also wanted a chance to look up some old friends . . . he would be so deeply grateful . . . a week or two in Merriscourt . . . a wonderful way to start their stay in England.

Garnett put down the letter.

'What do you think, Dolly?'

'It's up to you, my dear.'

He brooded a little.

'No. It is up to you. You will bear the responsibility for the guests.'

She looked a trifle self-important.

'George is a relative. I think we must say yes.'

'I agree. Shall I send the cable, or will you?'

When she heard the verdict, Elizabeth made a face. She was not best pleased. But she never wasted time on arguments when a battle was lost and kept her opinion to herself.

Peter came lounging into her study one evening in late October and stretched out in a chair near her desk.

'Be careful, Peter, you're much too heavy for that chair.'

'Must you have firewood to sit on?'

He leaned back and the chair creaked in pain.

19

'Have mercy on the poor thing. Uncle says it's eighteenth-century and you can tell by all those little painted shells along its back. I'm fond of it.'

'Oh, all right.'

He went over and sprawled in an upholstered chair which was too small for him, a little stuffed Victorian thing without arms, once used for a nursing mother.

'This so-called cousin from Calcutta and some female he's got in tow. I call them a damned bore.'

She raised her eyebrows. When she'd told him about George Westlock he had made a joke, but now she realised he had not been paying attention – or not realising the implications of the news. Now he'd thought about it, and was annoyed. When things happened which were not as he wished, Peter was pettish. He made a trumpet shape with his lips as if soundlessly whistling.

'You're in a bad mood,' she said.

'So should you be. You can't tell me you're delighted that Aunt and Father have decided these people can dump themselves on us.'

'Of course I'm not. I feel the same as you do. It's a bore. But they'll only be here a short time, there's nothing we can do about it, so why not have a bit of philosophy?'

'God, you're a prig sometimes. I don't want to have a bit of philosophy, as you call it. Why should I? I resent people we don't know cluttering up the place. And you can bet your boots that we'll be expected to dance attendance. Can you see my father doing the honours? Aunt Dolly will be in her element, sending you and me on errands for them. I can just hear her. God, what a prospect.'

She knew that if she said anything cheerful, pointing out that the visitors might prove amusing, or that she and Peter might even like them, he'd become more irritable. With a 'I can see *you're* going to be a lot of help,' he flung out of the room.

He was absent from the house a good deal after that. His excuse was real enough, he was looking for a new horse. His own thoroughbred, Baynard, a good jumper whom Peter had hunted for years, was getting on, and Peter had decided he needed a cob more suited to the steep hillsides and ground often pitted with ditches. But buying a horse, just the thing he enjoyed, had become a dreary puzzle, for his father had put a limit on the amount Peter could pay. An unrealistic limit, Peter complained to Garnett and later to his cousin. 'Father,' Peter said in a disagreeable voice, 'becomes more miserly every week.'

The reverberations from a lack of money were like a gong ominously sounding in the distance. Elizabeth often heard them, and wondered that her mother and cousin did not. As owner of Merriscourt, Garnett was landowner, employer of labour, magistrate, head of the family, and the man to whom everybody looked for their needs. Hard times had come three years ago and seemed to be getting no better. There had been a fire at Little Crediton which destroyed a barn and one of the labourer's cottages. Mercifully the family escaped, but what was being done to the blackened remains of the cottage and the barn? Riding by, Elizabeth saw no signs of rebuilding. There were other problems. Ploughed land was being turned back to rough grazing – only a quarter of Merriscourt's land was under tillage now. Tenants left. Her uncle's face grew more worn, and young Ferrers, the bailiff, was simply pompous and incompetent. Elizabeth couldn't stand the man, why didn't Garnett sack him?

Her uncle's troubles were always custom and tradition. When his old bailiff Ferrers died suddenly, it simply did not occur to Garnett not to give the post to the son. Young Ferrers had been training for it. But the decision was a disastrous one, for the young man was incompetent, a concealer of mistakes and worst of all a procrastinator. When Elizabeth, who knew a lot about the estate, asked him what had been done about this or that problem, Ferrers gave the invariable answer, 'Don't worry, Miss Bidwell. It will all be done when the time is right.'

Once when he dished out this fatuous reply she snapped,

and when, pray, was the time *wrong* for a leaking roof?

She found these days that she was thinking more instead of less about her uncle and his worries. She caught his anxiety as one might catch a cold. She hated to think of him mewed up in his study with that ass Ferrers as his only help. Or going round the estate listening to Ferrers and his excuses. She began to nag and encourage Peter by turns about his father. It did not work. Poor Garnett still asked his son to come with him to visit the farms, still invited him into the study sometimes. Oh Uncle, she thought, don't you yet know what Peter is like?

Sometimes she marvelled that Garnett had actually mated and produced the fascinating son who so disappointed him. It seemed impossible that her uncle had ever been to bed with anyone, let alone the mild dark-haired girl in the portrait in his study. When Elizabeth glanced at the big bowed figure at the head of the dinner-table, she couldn't imagine him capable of making love. I suppose, she thought – the idea of sex came to her too often lately – nobody can imagine anybody else doing it.

Peter was sulking, Garnett worried, Elizabeth concerned, but the fourth member of the family was in excellent spirits. Dolly Bidwell did not get much in the way of change and loved it when it came; she began to look forward to the visitors arriving. She consulted with Marchant, the elderly butler, and together they went into the Jacobean wing to choose two pleasant bedrooms. Dolly was quite excited when a cable arrived saying that Westlock and his goddaughter had 'taken ship from Calcutta'. Later postcards arrived from Port Said. She showed the garish things to Elizabeth and smiled.

'I didn't tell you, did I, but there was quite a scandal over George Westlock during the war. In society, that is. People said he was having an affair with Lady Priscilla Bagot.'

'Who's she?'

'Never show your ignorance, my child. She was the Earl of Bagot's daughter. Your father and I met her once with George in London. The girl was completely infatuated with him.'

22

'Why didn't she marry him, then?' Elizabeth was faintly interested. She always imagine that nobody slept with anybody out of wedlock during the Great War.

Dolly looked pitying.

'Society people don't marry out of their class. I expect she was ordered to give him up. I must say he was attractive in those days. It will be interesting to see how much he's altered. The more I think about it, Elizabeth, the more I'm convinced that some new faces at Merriscourt are just what we need.'

Elizabeth wondered why a goose went over her grave.

Chapter Two

It was in character for Garnett Bidwell to decide after receiving another cable, this time announcing the visitors' arrival date, that he would go to meet the ship at Southampton. He asked Dolly if she would like to accompany him, and she jumped at the chance. Peter said he would go too, which Elizabeth thought generous, considering how he felt about the invasion. His father was dismissive.

'They don't need a crowd. Your aunt and I are sufficient family.'

Elizabeth thought that her mother and her uncle travelling up to London and then all the way to Southampton was excessive. She remarked during dinner that she supposed George Westlock was perfectly capable of getting to Devon without help.

'They've come by sea half-way across the world. The last hundred miles or two won't exactly be an ordeal.'

Garnett looked annoyed.

'I will not have members of the family arriving without somebody to greet them.'

Elizabeth was only just stopped from saying for the twentieth time that Westlock was merely something like a second cousin by her mother's expression. Dolly forbade people to argue with Garnett, she said it was bad for him.

It occurred to Elizabeth as the meal ended that she was being very obtuse. Of course, with her uncle and mother out of the way, she'd have Peter to herself.

Garnett and Dolly left the house too early for their London train. They invariably had to wait at least twenty minutes on the platform at the start of any journey. They climbed into

Garnett's Hillman car, with Bernard, the elderly groom, sitting upright in the back, Dolly's hatbox on his knee. Bernard would have preferred to act as chauffeur, but Garnett never allowed anybody to drive him. The groom was going to the station so that he could bring the car back.

Dolly, looking unfamiliar in Londonish clothes, a dark coat with a big fox collar and a small tricorn hat, was excited at the idea of the trip. Her dark eyes shone like a blackbird's and, as the car turned the corner, she waved a suede-gloved hand from the window.

Elizabeth listened to the Hillman roaring down the lane – her uncle drove too fast. It was a contradiction in a man timid with women, nervous over his estate, reticent, shy, that in a car he behaved like a racing driver. Local farmers were none too keen on his car's noisy appearance in roads which had been made for pack-horses a century or more ago. The lanes and by-roads, with high ferny hedges, were curved and dangerously narrow, and it had been known for village women (*not* on the Merriscourt estate) to encourage their children to pelt the Hillman with stones. Once there were tintacks on the road. 'Why can't we *ride*?' Peter would plaintively say to his father. But Garnett liked cars better than horses.

When the car had gone, Elizabeth went indoors. There was no sign of her cousin. It was late in the morning, the French windows were wide open, she could smell and feel the autumn. If I can't ride with Peter, I'll go alone, she thought.

Walking along the terrace, she turned under the chapel arch into the stable yard. With Bernard absent, she saddled up her stocky white pony, automatically checking for signs of wear on girths, stirrup leathers and reins. As a child, Peter had taught her that accidents can be caused by broken saddlery, and although she trusted Bernard, she still checked. He'd be cross if he knew, she thought. She rode off towards the woods.

Like all the oldest houses in the district, Merriscourt was on high ground; its gardens sloped, the orchard fell away, and so did the hazel woods where she and Peter used to play as children, or ride along the bridle paths on their ponies. The woods had been mysterious to the cousins then. There was an overgrown stone quarry beyond the woods where Peter had found the fossil of a trilobite. There were two leafy ponds for sailing boats, a sand pit whose steep red sides were full of martins' nests. Years ago she and Peter had seen two weasels in the sand-pit, playing a sort of hide and seek, peeking out, vanishing, bobbing up again and chittering at each other . . .

Nothing could keep the cousins from the woods. In winter two pairs of wellingtons stood in the scullery, mud-splashed, waiting to be pulled on the moment breakfast was finished. In summer old Inslow, he'd been old to them even then, taught them to build a house of bracken which he called a cubbyhutch.

All Elizabeth's childhood seemed somewhere in the woods. She and Peter had found the paw-marks of badgers, had caught glimpses of the snake-like form of a stoat moving like lightning. Once they'd seen a stag. And on a certain night of high summer they had secretly crept from their beds, tiptoed down the back stairs, and run all the way to the woods by starlight. Inslow, little knowing what he'd started, had said it was the month for the nightjars.

'They nests in the heather and feeds on moths at night,' he said. 'Them is mystifyin' birds. The Master said they come all the way from Africa, but they only stay a handful of weeks here. Why do they come?'

Elizabeth was desperate to listen to the nightjars, and Peter agreed to the escapade for fun. They ran into the woods, found the place Inslow had described, and crouched on the ground, waiting what seemed an eternity.

At last it happened. First came a single churr. Then, gradually, from one end of the woods to the other the nightjars began to call and to answer. Their song rose and fell, long drawn, with a sudden change from the harsh churr-churr to a liquid cadence pure as a curlew's note. It sounded as if there were scores of Inslow's mystifying birds. As the children sat motionless, Peter pinched her arm. Birds as big as bats had begun to wheel overhead, they could hear the flack-flack of their wings as they hunted for moths.

'Oh, they're better than nightingales!' she exclaimed, as they yawned their way home.

'You just say that because there aren't any nightingales in Devon,' said Peter. But even he was excited when the path through the woods was lit by the greenish-white of glow worms.

She remembered the nightjars as she rode down the same path through the bracken.

The autumn was too lovely to waste; she did not want to return home but rode on for a long time. Yellow leaves like sovereigns spun down now and then. Sunbeams slanted through the trees. At last the woods ended, and she rode into a lane which dropped and climbed and dropped, as all Devon lanes did in a country as uneven as a choppy sea. High on either side were the hedges, broken now and then by a sprouting holly tree or a barred gate. The pony was in his slow mood, he'd changed from a trot to an amble. She only turned his head for home when the sun went in and the air started to get chill. She'd forgotten that she had had no lunch.

Peter was in the drawing-room, his legs almost in the flames of a fresh-lit fire, a habit of his. He turned and looked at her lazily. She had pulled off her hat and thrown it on the chest in the hall.

'You look like Mad Moll. Go and comb your hair.'

'What a fuss. Why should I?'

'Because you look better when you do.'

Laughing and annoyed, she went back into the hall, carelessly did her hair in a mirror framed with carved angels, and returned to her cousin.

'An improvement,' he said.

She did not rise to that.

'It's hot in here. Why didn't you come riding? It was wonderful in the woods.'

'I wish I had. Father made me promise to talk to Leslie

Ferrers. Imagine, Liz. There I was, sitting at my father's desk, and there was Ferrers droning on, I thought he'd never stop talking. How can anyone be so tedious?'

'Ferrers find it easy. What was he talking about?'

Peter shrugged.

'Putting up the rents of the Crediton cottages from two shillings to two and sixpence. I said no. The rest of the droning was Ferrers giving his reasons for all the things he hadn't done.'

'And he said they would be when the time was right.'

'Yes. We had a lot of that.'

He lost interest in himself as temporary landlord.

'Come and sit. Your cheeks are all red. It must be that fresh air. Do they feel hot?'

He leaned over and put his hands on either side of her face, brought her closer, and kissed her.

She shut her eyes, feeling as if she were driving over a hump-backed bridge. Her stomach dropped. He stopped kissing her.

'There are times when one might almost say you're pretty.'

'Oh thanks.'

'Except that your nose is quite comic.'

'My eyes are good. Admit that.'

'If one likes eyes with freckles. I know, I know, old William Bidwell had them too. I'll say that before you do.'

'So I have the Bidwell eyes.'

'Why is that something to boast about?'

She said nothing because he began kissing her again.

'Yes,' he said, finishing the kiss, 'one way and another you're rather sweet.'

'Ugh. How sickly.'

He laughed.

'Now that is something you are not. There are girls one knows who could be called distinctly sickly. Never you.'

The logs made a busy licking sound. To her faint surprise, she heard the rain. A gust blew against the high windows. This was what she wanted. To be alone with Peter. She was silent, thinking, does he love me? And, as uneasily, do I love him? She was afraid that she did. She was still a virgin, but so were all the girls she knew except her friend Topsy who had married three years ago when only eighteen. Topsy never talked to her about sex – how Elizabeth would hate it if she did. Unmarried, well-bred girls were always virgins. They were freer than their mothers had been and were allowed to go out alone with young men, but there were rules. Elizabeth kept and preferred them. At a hunt ball a few months ago a man had kissed her, thrusting his tongue into her mouth and Elizabeth, who had never once experienced such a thing, thought she would be sick. Only her upbringing, politeness even in disgust, stopped her from wiping the wet embrace off her mouth and slapping his face.

As a child wandering about the farm or in the fields she had learned the facts of sex, seeing animals engaged in what she considered a curious business. She was not very fascinated at the idea – she was too busy living. When she grew up, it was girls whom she saw, not gripped and mating with men, but floundering in love like creatures caught in quicksands. *She* never experienced that, and Topsy once said Elizabeth was taking a long time about it.

'You're sure to fall in love one day and probably then you'll be worse than the rest.'

'And what about you?'

'Oh, I'm another story,' said married Topsy.

Young men liked Elizabeth. She rode and danced well, there was something seductive about her curving figure, olive skin and slanting freckled eyes. They inclined to fall for her. This was invariably followed by a stream of sentimental letters and telephone calls. Her mother and cousin teased, and Elizabeth laughed with them. She extricated herself from importunate invitations. Eventually the young man would cool, to her relief. She liked her beaux, and loved none of them.

Now serenity and indifference were gone. She felt restless and sad and even when she was happy, heartache wasn't far off. The emotion she had begun to feel for her cousin, the man she'd known all her life, troubled her; it was almost absurd. But there it was. She wanted to be near him, to be in his thoughts and heart, his soul, even. She wanted to exist *in* him, and how could that be unless they married?

The firelight flickered unevenly, lighting Peter's round, broadish face. His dark Bidwell hair was not thick and plentiful like hers, but rather dry and she wondered if he might go bald early; she felt tender at the thought. His chin was cleft. If he grew a beard it would divide into two tufts like the beard worn by their Tudor ancestor Aden Bidwell, whose portrait on a cracked wood panel hung in Garnett's study. But there the resemblance ended. The man staring out of the dark picture had toughness and brutality; he was strong. The Bidwells for hundreds of years had been thrusting, shrewd men and this showed nowhere better than in their talent for marrying heiresses.

That was what Peter should do.

It was 1932 and Merriscourt, like Devon and like England, was vigorous no longer. Once the estate and its county had flourished together. Merriscourt's lands were richly prosperous and Devon not only thrived with her magnificent agriculture, but in fisheries and mines, woollens, weaving, lacemaking. All gone. All lost. The county now was a place of static towns in an abandoned countryside. Each year more tilled land was made over to rough grazing, or left to the yellow bushes of the furze. The only new money coming to the county was from holidaymakers staying in the seaside towns or bare-kneed hikers on the moors. When Elizabeth rode through Little Crediton, it shocked her. It was silent and peeling. The market had gone years ago, and now there were only dusty cats and flies buzzing in the windows of tumbledown cottages.

Her uncle's back bowed under adversity. Peter lazed. The Bidwell blood, she thought, has thinned and yes, he ought to marry money.

But could she bear it if he did? *She* was penniless. Couldn't

30

she, though, bring Merriscourt other necessary things?'
Imagining herself at Peter's side, she thought, my blood's still
thick, I could keep up, face any problem, I could be the tough
side of Peter. But why should I think he might actually marry
me? Perhaps he doesn't love me. I suppose he's had lots of
mistresses, she thought, using the word from nineteenth-
century novels. The idea excited and repelled her.

She had been quiet for a long time, and Peter suddenly
leaned over and kissed her again, pressing his mouth against
hers so hard that his moustache tickled her upper lip. The kiss
went on a long time.

'Sit on my lap.'

'I'd feel such a fool.'

'Come on. I want you to.'

'Someone will come in.'

'Who? The parents are safe in London and I told Marchant
to give himself and the maids an evening off.'

'Did Marchant faint? Uncle doesn't approve of extra evenings off,' she said. She felt shy.

'Have you ever seen Marchant surprised at anything? He
boomed something about calling on the vicar. I didn't believe
a word. Either he goes to a gambling hell in Teignmouth or to
see some crook about selling off our vegetables . . . come
along, Lizzie . . . '

He scooped her into his arms. She felt weightless. Helpless.

'Yes, you *are* sweet,' he said, setting her down on his lap
and turning her face to his. For the first time he lingeringly
kissed her with an open mouth. She hadn't guessed how beautiful it would taste.

The Cousin from Calcutta plus godchild were due to arrive
from London with Garnett and Dolly at the end of the week.
Interest had begun to ripple through the sleepy old house.
The stout and ponderous Marchant, butler to the family since
the Great War, addressed his group of maids and gave instructions. The two rooms must be aired and made ready. The
head housemaid, Ada, went clinking to the linen cupboard

31

with her bunch of keys. The visitors would be sleeping in the Jacobean wing, a low rambling part of the house far prettier than the main Victorian building. Fires must be kept burning in both rooms for three days before the visitors arrived. The rooms had not been occupied for months.

Early on the morning the family were due to return, Garnett telephoned. He asked for Peter, who had disappeared with the gamekeeper immediately after breakfast. When Elizabeth explained, he sounded put out. Would Peter please meet the train, he said, speaking in his usual meticulous fashion when giving Elizabeth any instructions, rather as if she were half-witted. He repeated the train-time twice.

'There are too many of us to fit into the Hillman as well as the luggage. Ask Peter to arrange with Haywards to bring their largest station taxi to meet the train. They can take the trunks and so on.'

She meekly agreed, adding – for she was curious – 'How is everybody?'

'Perfectly well. Do you wish to speak to your mother or your cousin George?'

He sounded even more put out at the idea, and she hastily said no. When she had rung off, she regretted not having had a chat with her mother to hear the news. How tired Garnett sounded. It must be years since he had been to London, let alone also travelling to Southampton and back.

There was no sign of Peter at lunchtime. He was often away for hours when he was out with the gamekeeper, but she had reminded him yesterday evening that the family were coming home today. By late afternoon, still no Peter. She began to feel annoyed. She could just imagine her uncle's face when the only person waiting on the platform was herself.

She ordered the largest Morris from Haywards to meet the train and fetch the luggage, waited until the last minute, and finally backed the Hillman out of the garage. Damn Peter. He'd stayed away on purpose.

Merriscourt was miles from the main road, down winding lanes which already in early winter had become nearly impassable. After recent heavy rain, the lane leading downhill was slippery and shiny with red mud. Elizabeth drove carefully, reflecting that her uncle wasn't going to miss the spattered state of his car as well as the absence of his son. Peter was infuriating. What possible reason could she give for his not turning up? It was so rude of him. In any case, she thought, why do I have to defend him? Because I always have, I suppose.

Teignmouth looked shabby in the afternoon mist. She tried to see it with foreign eyes. The houses lining the road had not been painted, the Depression had smeared them with a dingy hand. She did not want to notice that the little town, admired since Georgian times, looked down-at-heel. She wanted the Cousin from Calcutta to admire everything Devonian. But how could he, she thought, driving past a dirty-looking pub on a corner.

In Bidwell fashion, she was early at the station, bought a platform ticket, and walked on to the familiar platform thinking that at least the GWR looked smart. After India, they won't be able to help being impressed with our railways. The GWR served Devon and all the west of England and it had real, luxurious style. The men who worked for it boasted that the trains were incapable of being late. And it was as safe, they said, as the Bank of England.

The white wooden roof of the station was fresh and newly painted, the iron seats were a glossy dark green. Even the metal advertisements on the walls, for Virol and Singer Sewing machines, were regularly replaced and hadn't a sign of rust. Elizabeth knew every corner of the station. She had stood on the platform in school uniform, a black velour hat crammed down over her ears, trying not to cry at the start of how many school terms?

Her cousin was usually on the platform too – he went back after she did, and so accompanied her mother to see Elizabeth off. Three or four other girls from school caught the same train, and as it moved out, Peter did not only wave to *her* but as enthusiastically to all the other girls squeezed into the open window. They admired him. 'Aren't you lucky, having him for a cousin?' they used to say.

The signals turned green at last. There was a low rumbling in the distance which grew and grew, and then, in a cloud of steam flecked with smuts, in all the drama of its huge presence, the train roared in, drawing up with a deafening hiss.

Doors swung open, passengers descended. Porters pushing hand barrows bustled up to collect suitcases and heavy trunks. Elizabeth walked up the platform looking for the family – but where were they? She saw no tall stooping figure of her uncle, no short be-furred silhouette of her mother, no unfamiliar arrivals with them, organising too much luggage. The last door slammed, a whistle blew, and the great monster began to move . . .

She stood watching the train go, filled with anxiety. It was utterly unlike her uncle not to be here. She was sure he had never missed a train in his life. She still couldn't believe they had not been on the train. A voice said,

'Miss Bidwell? Sorry, did I startle you? I am George Westlock.'

The man was in Army uniform. He smiled, his teeth white in a face so darkly tanned that to English eyes it looked extraordinary.

'Where is the family?' She had no idea how sharp her voice was.

'Held up, I'm afraid. They are catching the next train. I am the bearer of messages and apologies.'

'Are they all right?' She was still very sharp.

'Oh, right as rain. Look, do you think we could get some tea? Then I can explain.'

'I'll drive you home.'

'Oh, we don't want to spend the next two hours driving back and forth, surely? Their train's due at half-past six. Is there a reasonable hotel in Teignmouth?'

After rearranging the taxi from Haywards for half-past six, she found herself driving him through the town. She did not like either the situation or the man who had bustled her into doing what *he* wanted. So this was the Cousin from Calcutta. He was fortyish and looked it, of medium height and far shorter than Peter, but squarely and strongly built. His face was broad but thin and not unattractive despite the tan which, when she had first seen it under the platform lights, had a dull greenish tinge. His hair, very short Army hair, shaved at the sides and the back, was brownish gold. He had almost invisible fair eyelashes and slightly bloodshot blue eyes. He wore his khaki with a sort of panache.

Elizabeth turned into the entrance drive of the hotel, a small pillared Georgian building set back among damp lawns and facing the grey line of the sea. The wind was blowing and it was cold.

The hotel shone with lights, and when they went inside, her companion immediately ordered tea. In the near-deserted lounge a coal fire was going out. Westlock rang for the porter and asked him to make up the fire. The man practically saluted, jumping to do as he was bid. What a manner, thought Elizabeth, regarding Westlock. I suppose it's Indian Army.

The visitor, too, was looking at her with the same curiosity that she felt for him. He saw a dark girl with hair tucked into a tight felt hat, the brim hiding her eyes. She wore country tweeds, and looked well-bred and unremarkable.

The porter made up the fire generously, and hammered a piece of coal into flame. He looked pleased at what was apparently a large tip. Westlock held out his hands to the small blaze.

There was one of those pauses between strangers. This was the man, she thought, glancing at him, whom her mother had known when he was young during that tragic and forgotten war. He did not look old enough to be nearly her mother's contemporary, he had that curious spring and dash she had sometimes noticed in men in the Services. It was as if they had entirely different rules which made life not bearable but positively exciting. His face at present was serious, but there was a fan of laughter lines round his eyes.

'I'm sorry about the family not turning up,' he said. 'Sylvia's fault, I'm afraid. She got it into her head this afternoon that she needed to do some more shopping.'

'Then why didn't my uncle telephone me again?'

'She was hurrying them. They are supposed to be on the next train, but I wouldn't put it past her to wheedle them into another night in town. You're still perplexed, Elizabeth. May I call you that?'

'Of course. And yes, I am. I can't imagine Uncle agreeing to shop with anybody. He doesn't even go to his own tailor.'

'Stays the same shape and writes for a new suit? The best way. He did look a trifle flummoxed over the shopping. But he's so good-hearted, I daresay he took pity on her. And your mother was tremendously kind. I'm afraid I was the one who made a getaway.'

'You're Miss Ashton's godfather. You must have known the family for a long time?'

'Best man at her parents' wedding and all that. My oldest friends.'

She knew that she ought to say something kind about the tragedy of losing both those friends. But she did not feel a responsibility of sympathy. It piqued her that he had cheerfully abandoned *his* responsibility, and left her mother and uncle in London with that god-daughter, while he sat enjoying his tea.

'It's good of you all to put us up. I look forward very much to seeing Merriscourt again. Has it changed?'

'It doesn't.'

'I'm glad. One can't say that about India.'

She said in surprise that she had always understood India to be a place which never changed, a country of very ancient tradition and deep religion.

'That's true, and those don't alter. But the English have in all kinds of ways. Let me give you an example. They've simply stopped bothering to learn Hindi. When new people arrive, it doesn't enter their heads to take lessons. We ground away at Hindi for years. Then it's curious to notice how they

36

don't use old Anglo-Indian slang now. You hear people boast that they don't understand words like tiffin or pukka these days. Quite out of date, even in the Army.'

'I suppose one must change with the times,' she murmured, thinking what an inane remark it was.

'It probably takes courage not to,' he said. 'Talking of the Army, didn't your mother say that your cousin had hoped to go into the Service. What made him change his mind?'

'He felt he should stay at Merriscourt and help his father with the estate.'

He was too well-bred to raise his eyebrows but Elizabeth, always thin-skinned about her cousin, was certain that Peter was being silently judged and misjudged. And by a man who had not yet met him and knew nothing of the circumstances. I suppose he can't think that anybody wouldn't choose the Army, she thought.

Poor Peter. Who so longed to.

'I came to Merriscourt once during the war,' he was saying. 'I suppose you must have been about three years old. Trotting about busily. I wish I could remember more of the visit. Sylvia keeps asking me about it and saying she can't imagine life in the English country. Of course she went to school in Northumberland, but she was in India as a child, and for all the long vacations, and apparently detested school. She certainly doesn't know a thing about Devon.'

He was very easy and sociable. She supposed that manner, it had a certain confident charm, was part of his Indian life. But she felt that both she and Merriscourt were being calmly taken for granted, and she resented it. Her first objections made to her mother when his letter had arrived were still there in her head, made worse now she had met him. And so she felt incapable of somehow introducing the unmentioned and terrible subject of his friends' deaths.

'Sylvia was sorry to leave India, of course,' he said dryly. 'She has been the centre of the gay social whirl there for some time. It's a place for enjoying yourself when you're Sylvia's age. But you'll understand that she couldn't stay.'

37

Here was the cue. She took it carefully.

'What a dreadful thing. To lose both her parents.'

'Indeed. But her father was away a good deal with the regiment, you know. And poor Fay, her mother, had been ill for many months; her death was expected.'

'A tragedy, though.'

'Yes. But Sylvia is eighteen and young for her age, with a strong sense of self-preservation, thank heaven. I don't know if you've heard of the Anglo-Indian ritual on board ship? When a ship is returning home, and one isn't going back to India, one throws one's topee overboard just as the ship sails out of Port Said. Sylvia pitched hers over with a vengeance.'

She could think of nothing to say.

'Your mother's been getting on with her like a house on fire,' he added, smiling.

He said nothing about himself, for all his ease of manner, and she knew that he was reserved. Well, so was she. Peter's grace always seemed to her to be given too soon and too often. Like his hand waving to the girls as the school train moved out of the station, it was depressingly impartial.

She telephoned Marchant to explain that they were meeting a second train, and was told that her cousin was not yet home. He can't be still out in the woods, she thought, it's almost dark. She supposed he had gone to see one of the many girls with whom he kept up a kind of running flirtation. She had another rush of annoyance; *he* should be here coping with the Cousin from Calcutta.

The hotel lounge had begun to fill up with guests who had come in from afternoon expeditions. Westlock suggested they might 'take a turn by the sea.' Out of doors was dampish. The pavements scintillated, the lamps along the parade were a necklace of white circles. In the distance to the right was the Ness, a tall red headland crowned with dark green trees. Crossing the road, they took the paved causeway which ran between the railway and the sea. Ahead, the railway vanished into one of Brunel's tunnels bored into the cliffs. Out at sea stood the Parson and the Clerk, two curiously-shaped detached rocks, haggard by wind and tide. The sea wall dropped more than ten feet to the dark sands. Elizabeth had seen waves in rough weather hurl themselves against the wall, but now the tide was far out. An unbroken white line of low waves was running in steadily with a continuous mild roar. The air was salty. Beside her walked this unknown man with his incongruously sunburned face, saying nothing. She thought – if only it were Peter.

Eventually Westlock halted under a lamp to look at his watch.

'Alas,' he said, 'time to turn back.'

It was her second visit to the station in two hours, and she thought what a waste of time the afternoon had proved. Her curiosity about the visitors was quite gone. She'd met her second cousin and now the train was bringing the other half of the invasion. From now on for weeks, Merriscourt's quiet would be broken, and both her and Peter's independence of movement gone. It was going to be all boring smiles and clichés.

When they heard the distant sound of the approaching train, she noticed that her companion stiffened. She glanced at him from under her eyelashes, thinking that he was like a hunting dog, a pointer, freezing into stillness when a bird has fallen. He stood watching the line in the direction from which the train would come. And there it was, roaring towards them, as huge and powerful as its predecessor, rendered dramatic by showering red-hot sparks into the dark, and stopping with its huge sigh. Westlock hurried forward.

Elizabeth saw her uncle at once, handing out her mother. Then he turned to help a girl from the train just as Westlock caught them up. Elizabeth saw him sketch a salute – and the girl put out her arms. They almost ran into an embrace.

She walked up slowly to join them.

'There you are, my child,' cried Dolly gaily. 'But where's Peter? George explained why we caught the later train, didn't he? We've had such a happy time. Well, Elizabeth, here she is. This is Sylvia.'

The girl standing beside Westlock put out a gloved hand. She gave Elizabeth a smiling, almost conspiratorial look, as if to say, '*We're* the only young ones.'

She was fair and pale and startlingly beautiful.

Chapter Three

Elizabeth's first impression on the station platform of a fragile, ethereal beauty was wrong. Sylvia Ashton was certainly exceedingly good-looking but she was also talkative and lively and often behaved like a schoolgirl. She was very young. Her face was heart-shaped, her chin pointed like a kitten's, and in contrast to the bloodshot blue of her godfather's eyes, hers were like forget-me-nots. Her movements were also kittenish, soft and darting, and when she spoke to people it was as if she touched them with a velvet paw. Were there claws? There was no sign of anything sharp in Sylvia Ashton.

Dolly spoiled her from the moment of their arrival when Sylvia, opening her eyes at the stained-glass windows and marble kings and queens, exclaimed in admiration at everything in the house.

'What a topping place, Mrs Bidwell! There's nothing to touch it in Calcutta.'

Elizabeth doubted that but saw it was kindly meant.

Peter arrived deliberately late on the first evening, coming into dinner as the first course was served. He greeted George Westlock pleasantly, and when Sylvia was introduced to him, she gave him a society smile which had an indifferent radiance. Apparently that impressed him. He set himself out to be charming to the girl.

Garnett was kind to her, but after they settled down in Merriscourt, made his escape. He was no man to enjoy being with the young, particularly young women. But nobody else avoided Sylvia.

It was quite obvious to Elizabeth that the young girl had decided to make a friend of her, and she herself could

41

scarcely refuse; she was quite taken with Sylvia. When they went for walks in the wintry country, accompanied by Merriscourt's three grateful dogs, Elizabeth asked Sylvia about India. To her country-bred ears the stories were very strange. There was a hugeness and glitter about them, they had the quality of scenes from a musical play at Drury Lane – painted backcloths of temples with solid gold roofs, elephants whose wrinkled skin was decorated with patterns of lilies, chains of marigolds hung round your neck for welcome, lotus flowers. Elizabeth often went to hunt balls and sherry parties, but when Sylvia described a ball it was at the Taj Hotel where two thousand guests were in fancy dress, the fountains were coloured like rainbows, 'and everyone behaved as if they were two years old, including *me.*' The parties had names. There was the Bachelors' Ball, given by bachelors and grass widowers 'who are really rich', and the Gloom Club, to which everybody went dressed in elaborate mourning. There were balls where the guests dressed in babies' clothes, bibs and bonnets. To Elizabeth it sounded as if enjoyment was organised on a vast, a frantic scale.

Sylvia chattered about cocktails which were now the rage, and the necessity of going to Gimlet Parties to wile away the long mornings. The waiters wore sashes and turbans and served trays of oysters.

'Oysters! In the Indian heat?'

'Did you think we'd fall dead from poisoning?' said Sylvia, laughing. 'They're brought from Karachi in cold storage. One must have oysters with champagne cocktails.'

'Must one?'

Sylvia had the grace to giggle. Now, she said, she'd tell Elizabeth something funny. Just before leaving India, she had been invited to a swimming party. 'We were all on one river bank, and guess what. On the other the herdsmen were washing their camels.'

The journey home was her favourite theme. The P & O liner was like a luxurious floating hotel. There were Tudor rooms and Renaissance rooms, a ballroom which turned into a night club after midnight, and a music room where George taught her to play mah-jong.

'George says I'm good at it because you mustn't lie, but you mustn't *absolutely* speak the truth either.'

Elizabeth noticed that there wasn't a single mention of Sylvia's dead parents.

A few days after her arrival, a battered trunk was delivered to Merriscourt by Carter Paterson. It was carried up to her room by the gardener and the groom, both of whom gave the impression that the trunk was filled with bricks. They set it down with relief.

Sylvia stood looking at it dubiously.

'You will help me unpack, won't you, Lizzie?' She had taken to using Elizabeth's nickname. 'Unpacking is no fun alone. I know I'm not staying here very long, but I have to sort things out. I shall need your advice – you can tell me which clothes are all right for England, and which aren't.'

'But are you sure you want me? I should have thought it would be better for Ada to help you.'

Ada, the starched head housemaid, was under Sylvia's spell, like the rest of the staff, excluding Marchant.

'Oh, Ada can put away later,' said Sylvia carelessly, and Elizabeth heard the echo of a girl accustomed to half a dozen people waiting on her.

The girls spent an afternoon emptying the trunk; it smelled of sandalwood. Sylvia knelt on the floor, the tray of the trunk beside her, and pulled things out one by one, throwing them round her on the floor or up on to the bed. There were enormous numbers of things. Dresses of brilliantly coloured silk, accordian-pleated like fans, in turquoise, orange, a gleaming yellow, a vivid pink embroidered with silver thread. Big straw hats were wreathed in Parma violets. White parasols had long tassels. There were blouses so finely tucked it seemed impossible they could have been hand-made. Everything was embroidered, and on the corners of every one of dozens of handkerchiefs was a big elaborately curled 'S'.

'Do you like this?'

'Is this any good?'

'Isn't this a hoot? I'll never wear it again, it was for the Babies' Party. Here's my bib with "Diddums" on it. And my frilly bonnet.'

She frowned over most of her clothes.

'You must have seen all those rules in the *Tatler*, Liz. I expect you know them by heart. Two inches below the knee for sports suits, four inches for tailor-mades and eight inches for afternoon dresses. Oh dear, think what a lot of work it's all going to be. We weren't so strict in India.'

'We aren't in Devon.'

Sylvia laughed merrily, as if at a good joke.

At the bottom of the trunk she pulled out a heap of clothes tied with white ribbon.

'Poor darling Mummy bought these,' she said. 'Last year. Knickers! Fluffy on the inside, like the ones we wore at school. She said when we came home I'd get stomach-ache if I didn't wear them.'

It was the first time she had mentioned her dead mother. She pushed the knickers back under discarded clothes, a tennis racquet and two badminton racquets.

After a moment Elizabeth said, 'We were so very sorry – to hear you'd lost your mother. Of course we didn't know her. But Mother and Peter and I do feel for you.'

'That's kind,' said Sylvia in a voice which until now had never sounded brittle. 'She was fun. Thank goodness for old George, I can't imagine what would've happened if he hadn't been there.'

She gave a slight shudder.

'You must be very fond of him.'

Sylvia's face lightened.

'I have to be, don't I? I owe him everything. He gets so cross when I say that, he absolutely loathes gratitude. Of course he's always been part of our lives, you know. I never remember when he wasn't. It's like that in India. Men who don't marry sort of adopt other people's families. My father

44

admired George, he said he was his idea of a soldier. And Mummy depended on him. George is very dependable.'

She shut the lid of the trunk and sat on top of it.

During the first days after the visitors' arrival, Elizabeth found herself responding to Sylvia's light overtures; she was pleased to be pleased with Sylvia. And her early prejudice against George Westlock faded – she had been wrong about him. He was a different kettle of fish from her cousin, and the traits in Peter which stirred her were noticeably absent in George. He had none of that extraordinary charm which struck Elizabeth to the heart. But there were things about George. She began to like the rugged line of his face, the sudden way he laughed, his very masculine presence, and something else, a reaction to herself. Despite his obvious devotion to his god-daughter (he was always, so to speak, at her service), Elizabeth felt that he also liked *her*. Now and then she actually felt that he quite admired her.

One afternoon when Sylvia was taken off by Dolly 'to pay some calls, my child', and Peter was out, having heard of another possible mare, George came into the drawing-room. He found Elizabeth on her knees by the fire, combing the long black ears of the spaniel Chloe. Bob the airedale sprawled close by. The mongrel half-spaniel, Bill, was asleep. The girl knelt in a sea of dogs.

'That looks a tricky operation,' he said, watching her. 'Does the poor animal hate it?'

'Bitterly. But her ears are disgusting. I washed them in a basin of soapy water – the dirt! Now it's the tangles. Most of them are burrs. I do try,' went on Elizabeth, holding one long curly ear and pulling the comb gingerly through it, 'not to hurt her.'

George gave a smile, as if at a private joke.

He sat down in his manner so unlike Peter's. He never sprawled.

The silence was broken by an agonised yelp and Elizabeth's '*Sorry!*'

45

'I've been making a tour of Merriscourt,' said George, 'Your pictures especially.'

'Oh, stop looking as if you're being hanged, drawn and quartered, you fool,' said Elizabeth, releasing the dog who, tail between legs, rushed from the room.

They both laughed.

Elizabeth gave him a friendly look.

'I didn't answer about the pictures. Did you like them? My uncle is fond of them.'

'Not you?'

'I never really think about them. They're part of the walls. When I was small I used to be afraid of one at the end of the passage near your room. A woman with a white face, Arabella Bidwell, eighteenth century, with pearls. She stares so. I suppose people can't help being interested in their ancestors. Vanity, do you think?'

'Curiosity. Am I going to turn out like her or him.'

'I thought of that. Arabella looks a trifle mad. But there is one Bidwell, Charlotte Lucy, early Victorian, whom I'd love to resemble. She looks as if she treats life as a marvellous joke.'

'Perhaps you will.'

There was a little pause, and then he said, with a curious ring in his voice, 'There are family traits one does devoutly hope not to inherit.'

She looked up curiously.

'Who do you mean?'

Almost immediately she blunderingly added, 'I shouldn't have asked that.'

'It's no secret, Elizabeth, your uncle and mother probably heard all about it. I never concealed it when I was younger. Ancient history now, though. My father, he died years ago, was not a man I would like to resemble in many ways. He treated my mother badly, ignored her and took her for a fool. He was a Victorian to his finger-ends . . . isn't it curious,' he added, 'one is taught that it's a duty to forgive the past. I imagine that I do. Yet when he comes into my mind, I can only remember that he made my mother miserable. She is

46

dead too, so the past really is gone. It was your Merriscourt pictures that set me off this afternoon.'

Reacting to feminine interest and sympathy, he began to tell her something of himself. He had been attracted by painting since he was a boy. He'd learned to paint 'poorly' at Eton but had excelled in the history of art, and had begun to collect one or two pictures even when still at school. His parents lived in Berkshire, and when scarcely fifteen he and his mother went to house auctions together, sometimes returning truimphantly home with spoils – a pencil drawing, a little water-colour. Neither of them had any idea how the boy might use this odd gift in his future. Perhaps he could start a gallery? Certainly his father, after George had left university, would be able to afford to set him up. At sixteen, George was coolly informed that he was to go into the Army.

'My father, it seemed, had arranged everything. He had seen the Headmaster, I was to be put into the Army Class, and from there go on to Sandhurst. And that was that.'

'Didn't he even consult your mother?'

'Oh no.'

'And you had no choice?'

'I certainly didn't. When I tried to explain about my taste for painting, about which he had literally no idea despite my mother and I discussing it in front of him, he looked as if the table had started to talk. The long and the short of it was that I was ordered to toe the line.' He shrugged. 'I had no money and nor did my mother. And that was an obstacle you couldn't ride over in 1905.'

'Or now either.'

'That can't be true, Elizabeth.'

'But it is. The opposite happened to Peter. He *longed* to go into the Army but Uncle stopped him.'

He looked at her very attentively.

'I'm sorry.'

'Oh, I'm sure my uncle wasn't harsh, like your father,' she said earnestly. 'He couldn't be. But the result was the same, he got his own way. He put Peter into the position where he

47

simply couldn't say no to his father. He had to give up his career for him. And for Merriscourt, if I'm going to be fair.'

'Mm,' he said. 'So things don't change while parents have the purse-strings.'

She thought for a moment or two and then murmured, 'And yet you seem a born soldier to me.'

'Good.'

'But –'

'But you have to be a blockhead not to be affected by the best in the Army as well as the worst. I settled down. I pegged away at it. I made friends. And at twenty, after leaving Sandhurst, I was sent to India. God, it was an exciting place to be. I can't pretend my father ruined my life, can I? But he did treat me, while he had the power, like a chattel, as he treated my mother. That's the trait I prefer not to see in myself.'

'And do you still regret, a little, not having had your gallery?'

'Stop being so kind,' he said, laughing. 'Of course I don't. But seeing those water-colours of Arabia, that series on the second floor, suddenly reminded me that I nearly bought two very like those. Life in the Service is not conducive to collecting anything. I have a few paintings, mostly in packing cases. None near as good as yours.'

'I feel rather guilty. I've never actually looked at them properly.'

'Come with me later and I'll show you my favourites.'

Just then Sylvia and Dolly came into the room, exclaiming over the cold, ordering tea. And breaking the mood as if it had been made of glass which they trod underfoot.

George never did go with her to look at the water-colours. She went alone, weeks later, and thought them haunting. And wondered why she had never thought so before.

She felt differently about him after that. Sometimes they exchanged a glance or a smile during mealtimes, but they never happened to be alone. His time was taken up by Sylvia, or occasionally by Garnett who seemed very fond of him.

But it was Sylvia who claimed the most of George. He was

48

always on hand if she needed him and Garnett actually lent them the Hillman so that George could drive her into Exeter or Teignmouth. Sylvia's way with George was that of a child certain she would get attention. The soldierly man with his handsome sun-tanned face, the girl in a green coat with a fur hood which he had bought for her on a recent shopping expedition, were out together a great deal. Once from her bedroom window Elizabeth saw them in the garden, walking round the brick paths or between the yew trees, deep in talk. She rather envied them.

She was interested in Westlock. She saw him as a paradox, the man of action with unexpected attributes, a love of painting, an unhappy boyhood. He was not all of a piece. Once, when she was looking for her airedale, she went down the corridor in the Jacobean wing and passed George's bedroom; the door was open and she glanced in. Bedrooms spoke of their occupants. Sylvia's did. But George's said nothing about the man who slept there. There were no photographs in those leather frames beloved of travellers, no clock which had fussily ticked away the hours in Indian heat, not even a pair of shoes. On the dressing-table were two ivory-backed hairbrushes. That was all. But the windows were wide open, far wider than anyone in Merriscourt opened them in wintertime. The icy air of early December had taken possession.

'Luck, my father liking the Coz from Calc,' remarked Peter to Elizabeth one morning when they were alone. 'It takes the weight off my shoulders for a change.'

'I've never noticed them weighed down.'

'Now don't start on that. Admit I'm behaving beautifully.'

'You're pleasant to Sylvia which is a mercy.'

'I quite like her, to my surprise. I thought she was sure to be a Colonial bore.'

Elizabeth was relieved that he had taken a fancy to the girl, it would have been very inconvenient if he'd remained sulky. He was affable to Sylvia. The cousins took her riding and Sylvia turned out to be an excellent horsewoman. She was amused when Peter complimented her.

49

'In India, I'm only average.'

Sylvia had her successes and failures. It was to be expected that Garnett would more or less ignore her, but it was unusual for Marchant, the family's elderly butler, not to be more taken with someone like Sylvia. He was an admirer of young and beautiful women to whom he paid exaggerated respect. But Sylvia was apparently not his type. On the credit side was Ada, the head housemaid and usually thin-lipped and disagreeable, but only too eager to do anything Sylvia wished.

As for Dolly, she was plainly captivated.

'I know we are not related, my child, but you must call me Aunt Dolly.'

'I'd love to.'

They were two of a kind. They liked to talk about clothes, enjoyed magazines and never read a book; they preferred men to women and if there was not a man about, made do with each other.

'Sylvia,' said Dolly to Elizabeth one day, 'reminds me of myself at her age.'

Dolly's conscience did not trouble her about her own daughter. Elizabeth had never been jealous of Peter, and now rather approved of her mother's admiration for Sylvia, which Dolly did not bother to hide.

'My aunt has turned into a slave,' remarked Peter one morning when he and Elizabeth were riding. It was raining and although invited, Sylvia had refused. The lane was muddy, the cousins rode with bent heads, needlepoints of rain pricking their cheeks.

'She does seem rather fascinated,' said Elizabeth.

'And how about you?'

'She's nice. You think so too, don't you?'

'She's attractive,' he said critically. 'What about the Coz from Calc?'

'He's okay,' she said, after a pause.

'But pretty slavish to her too? Does that annoy you?'

He looked at her mischievously, hoping to get her to rise.

'My dear Peter, I wouldn't mind if he fell on his knees

every time she came into the room, like Queen Elizabeth's courtiers. She's jolly lucky to have a godfather like that. How long do you suppose they'll stay?'

He shrugged.

The single telephone, Garnett would have preferred none but he had been ill recently and the doctor insisted, was in a draughty corridor near the kitchen. The light was some distance away and at night one could scarcely see. When the telephone rang during the winter afternoon or evening, Sylvia took her torch, in the shape of an owl with the eyes made from two electric bulbs. With the owl as company, she settled down to enjoy calls which were always for her. There were invitations from people to whom Dolly had introduced her, calls from shops and calls from young men she had met at local parties. She laughed a good deal. Elizabeth wondered how soon her uncle, who thought the telephone a shocking waste of money, would demand that the owl should be extinguished, particularly when the longest calls were made by Sylvia herself. But nothing of the sort happened, and when Elizabeth came into the house, she constantly heard the distant sound of Sylvia on the telephone. She wished Merriscourt could settle back into its silences again.

Crossing the hall one morning before going out with the dogs, Elizabeth heard another and unfamiliar sound. It was her uncle laughing. She recognised the answering voice as George's. She stood for a moment, feeling uneasy. It should be Peter in the study with his father, making him laugh so pleasantly. Oh, Peter, Peter, you don't even try, she thought. George does effortlessly what I've begged you to do. She whistled for the dogs.

There was a scurry of claws on parquet, and her handsome black and brown airedale, Bob, came rushing round a corner in the company of Bill, black and white with tattered ears. Chloe, the pure bred spaniel and her mother's favourite, was in the kitchen, getting fat.

'We'll go without her, shall we, old boy?' Elizabeth said to Bob, who wagged his tail.

51

There were hooks screwed into the carved Victorian panels behind the front door. Recently the wood round the hooks had begun to split. Nobody but Peter had noticed this, and when he said the panels ought to be repaired, Garnett was annoyed. So the splits were getting worse. Riding crops hung there, and old umbrellas; there were luggage straps, discarded scarves and caps and many dog leads. Elizabeth selected a lead and wound the thong round her wrist. The study door opened.

'I'll be most interested to come to the Bowdens' farm this afternoon, sir. Three o'clock on the dot,' said George.

He might have been speaking to his superior officer. Muttering something in a friendly tone, Garnett went back into his study and shut the door.

George looked across the hall at her.

'Taking out the dogs? May I come?'

It was mid-December now, and leaves lay glued by the rain to the paths and on the lawns. The scent of winter was strong. Soon it would be holly-cutting time.

'Do you know, I'm still not used to England after four weeks or more. Look at the day, it's so dark. I think what I miss is the colour and the light.'

'But I thought the Indian light was blinding,' said Elizabeth, springing to the defence of her beloved Devon. 'We pride ourselves on our landscape keeping its colour in winter. It isn't like the north. Uncle took us to stay in Yorkshire one winter. I can still remember that everything looked bleached out with the cold, all greys, blacks and white. Now just admire that lichen,' and she pointed to the trunk of an oak, where lichen shone in emerald and russet.

'Not bad.'

'Oh, very grudging,' she said and laughed. 'I thought Anglo-Indians all preferred home, as you call it. Sylvia said people get dewy-eyed about England, longing for muffins by an English fire or tennis on the lawn and the chime of the stable clock!'

'Yes, I know those conversations only too well. But Sylvia's only talking about one side of English life in India.'

'She makes it sound fun.'

'Polo and fancy dress parties. They *are* fun. But there's far too much petty snobbery, and an absurd importance attached to protocol.'

Elizabeth stayed in interested silence and he went on. 'India has a curious effect on people who serve there; it seems to bring out the best and the worst in the British. There's a lot of dedication to the job. People in the Army and the ICS give their lives to it. But there's the snobbery, literally feuds about the wrong places at dinner. All that is pretty repellent.'

'Not the country, though. I should think one could fall in love with it?'

'Oh yes. Men do.'

'And the women?'

He smiled, and she noticed the laughter lines.

'I'm afraid they're the ones hankering for the stable clock.'

Since coming to Devonshire he had stopped wearing khaki, but somehow he managed to transform his clothes into a kind of uniform. They were kept in speckless condition, and there was something in the way he wore them and in the way he walked. Elizabeth noticed the difference between his strong swinging stride and Peter's negligence.

'Could you hold the gate open?' she said. 'I must put Bill on the lead. The gamekeeper would plug him full of pellets if he caught him hunting.'

'What about the big dog?'

'Bob's too clever to hunt when Pyne is about. Bill,' she added, snapping the lead on the mongrel's collar, 'has no brains.' George looked at the animal who strained against the lead, rushing forward, only to be tugged back again.

'Dogs are like people. Some know the score by instinct and some never learn it. Talking of the score, I don't expect you could recommend me a London hotel, could you, Elizabeth? Your family stayed at Brown's when we arrived, but it's a bit above my sights, alas. I'll be in London three or four days.'

'My great aunt lives in Bloomsbury at the Imperial and Royal. Rather stuffy but quite pleasant.'

53

'What a good idea. Your mother and I were talking about Great Aunt Bessy – I'd love to see her again. She's the link I have with your family, you know.'

'She'll be delighted to see you. She loves relations.'

'I'll ring and book my room. I'm off tomorrow, by the by.'

'When are you back? By the end of the week?'

'Oh, I'm sorry. I didn't make myself clear. I'm leaving Devonshire, Elizabeth. I've trespassed on your kind hospitality too much already.'

She was so surprised that her mouth fell open and he couldn't help laughing.

'But you're on your long leave – I thought it was months before you had to go back to India.'

'I'm not going back to India.'

'Goodness. What a shock for you. Where has your regiment been posted?'

'It's still there,' he said. 'Didn't Sylvia tell you my news? She's not the world's expert at things to do with other people. I've written to my colonel to say I've decided to leave the Army.'

She couldn't believe her ears.

'I'm retiring,' he said.

'*Retiring*! But you're still quite young. You're a born soldier, it's written all over you.'

'Thank you, Elizabeth. You told me that once before. But there's no point in talking about it. My army career is over.'

She was about to exclaim, to go on with the conversation, but she saw something in his face that stopped her. She had the feeling that it caused him pain to talk about his decision, and – for all his courtesy – he did not regard her as a friend who could ask such things. To her own surprise, she found that she herself was hurt.

'I'm going up to Scotland for a while,' he went on. 'I have some old friends in Skye who've asked me to stay. Look, can't I take Bill? He's pulling your arm out of its socket.'

'I'm used to him, thanks.'

She spoke rather brusquely, still occupied with what he

had told her. They continued in silence along the muddy path between the trees. A thought suddenly struck her.

'But what about Sylvia? You said you wanted her to be presented. Is that all cancelled too?'

'Oh no. That's still on. I've spoken to your uncle. He's been good enough to say she can remain with you here for the present.'

Elizabeth walked into her mother's bedroom before luncheon; Dolly was at her dressing-table, doing her hair.

'Did *you* know George is going tomorrow, Mother?'

Dolly picked up a suede buffer and began to polish her nails.

'Of course. To Skye, and very beautiful it is I gather, but the Scottish weather's bad. They could get snowed up.'

'Nobody told me he was giving up the Army.'

Dolly wore the air of somebody very much in the know. Oh yes, she said, it was a big decision for him, but after all he had spent so many years out East . . . he hadn't said anything, but she had the feeling that he wasn't all that strong.

'Look at your poor Uncle. He was never the same man after he fought in Gallipoli.'

'George looks as strong as a horse to me. The point, Mother, isn't what *he* is doing, but what he's doing about *her*.'

'I presume you are speaking about Sylvia,' said Dolly coldly. 'Naturally your uncle and I have said we'll take care of her. It's the least we can do.'

'So he's landed her on us. I call it a bloody cheek.'

Dolly slowly put down the nail buffer.

'That is quite enough. And don't show that ill temper of yours downstairs, if you please. It is George's last day here and I wish him to enjoy himself.'

The airedale was waiting for Elizabeth outside the bedroom. She touched his bony curled head and he pressed against her. She was bitterly disappointed in George and consequently angry with him. He wasn't the man she had thought him. She went up the steps which led to the Jacobean wing. Sylvia's door was ajar.

Like Dolly, she was at her dressing-table, but attended by Ada whose grim face was smiling until she caught sight of her mistress's daughter.

'Will that be all, Miss Sylvia?'

'Yes, Ada. You're so clever with my hair. Thank you.'

Ada creaked out. Of all the Merriscourt servants, she used the most starch. When she buttoned her apron straps, they made sounds like pistol shots.

Sylvia turned with a smile to Elizabeth. The gas fire roared on the far side of the room but the air was cold. Sylvia wore a thin lilac-coloured dress, showing her arms and falling round her knees. The skirts were short and she wore flesh-coloured silk stockings.

'I was very surprised to hear that George is leaving the Army,' said Elizabeth, without preliminary.

'So was I,' was the airy reply. 'He was in Daddy's regiment forever. I mean, my whole lifetime. And before that in Mespot. George is forty-two!'

She gave a little scream of laughter.

'My mother says his health is not good.'

'Oh how sweet. Aunt Dolly thinks it a miracle anyone survives in India. George is perfectly all right. He was wounded ages ago on the North West Frontier, but everybody is eventually! Maybe he's using his health as an excuse, though he'd never admit it to me. I'm certain he's staying in England to see me presented. However, at present he's off to the Tuckers. They have a teeny castle called Ashnacraig. George adores Scotland and the Tuckers as well. Her, anyway. She was an old flame, Priscilla Tucker, she has a title – an Earl's daughter or something. I met her once in India. One of those horse-faced women with a mass of thick black hair. I couldn't see the attraction – golly, she must be nearly forty herself. So now you'll only have me,' finished Sylvia with a radiant smile.

There was a festive dinner for George's farewell: two pheasants, and apple crumble with clotted cream. The conversation was lively, even Garnett made some jokes. After the meal the three men spent so long over their port in the dining-room that Sylvia became thoroughly annoyed.

'Considering he's going tomorrow, he's the limit.'

'Won't he be back soon from Skye to fetch you?' said Elizabeth. Shrugging crossly, Sylvia said she had no idea, and he was only going to Scotland to hang round Priscilla Tucker.

'Is that Lady Priscilla?' asked Dolly, with a gleam. Sylvia said an indifferent yes.

'He'll be back in good time to see you presented, my child,' said Dolly, going to the piano. She began to play a waltz. But the music, lilting, enticing, did not dispel Sylvia's scowls.

George, Peter and Garnett eventually appeared and the moment she saw them, Sylvia sprang up, linked her arm into George's and made both young men sit on either side of her on the settee. She teased them in turn, laughing and joking, miraculously recovered.

Elizabeth drank her coffee and listened to her mother's music; she'd known the little waltz all her life. *Why* was George leaving? The ignoble thought came into her mind that perhaps he was broke and this was an ingenious way of getting Sylvia's lodging free.

The family gathered in the hall next morning early to bid him goodbye, while Marchant supervised the Army trunk being heaved down the staircase and out into the car. Garnett called George into his study for a last-minute word in private. Dolly, wearing her fresh morning look and her pearls, waited to give George a goodbye kiss.

'Don't forget,' she said, as George emerged from the study and came to her, 'that you promised you will write to us.'

Sylvia and Peter had decided to go with him to the station, and Dolly, giving George a motherly smile, went out into the drive towards the car. For a moment Elizabeth was alone.

George took her hand and gripped it. He made no move to kiss her, but looking at her with intense bloodshot blue eyes he said, 'Look after her for me.'

He walked out and she heard the car start.

Unreasonably, she wished he had not gone.

Chapter Four

'Tea. Lovely,' said Sylvia, coming into the drawing-room where Elizabeth, Peter and Dolly were gathered round the fire. It was late February. George had been gone for over two months, and although he wrote regularly to Sylvia (and occasionally to Dolly), all that Sylvia reported was that Skye sounded too dismal and she was glad she wasn't there.

Sylvia was above all things adaptable. She stumped off in wellington boots to look for snowdrops in the woods with Elizabeth. She rode and hunted with Peter. Muffled in furs, she and Dolly drove in the Hillman to Exeter to shop or to call in for tea at the houses of Bidwell friends. Yet a few months ago her life had been spent under a pitiless far-off sky. Across her bedroom ceiling had scuttled spiders the size of coffee saucers, and once her ayah had found a cobra sleeping in Sylvia's riding boot. Now the soft Devon rain flushed her pale cheeks, and she was even prettier than when she had stepped off the train on to the Teignmouth platform.

Sitting beside Dolly, she accepted a crumpet and began to eat it as delicately as a cat.

'English tea. Do you know, Aunt Dolly, people actually serve it in India. I've eaten crumpets with the thermometer at a hundred and twenty or whatever it is. Sizzling, like the crumpets.'

She took the limelight unobtrusively, but she took it just the same. Peter sat watching her.

'Aunt . . .' said Sylvia, 'I don't suppose I could ask a simply tremendous favour?'

'And what is that?'

'Well . . . you know I've got to meet that awful Lady Chedworth next Thursday?'

Dolly nodded, brightly interested. She and Elizabeth had heard a good deal about Lady Chedworth who was to present Sylvia at Court. Yet Sylvia had never set eyes on the lady. The curious arrangement had somehow been managed, through Army connections, by George.

It was a problem for any girl coming from abroad, with no relative who had previous been to Court, to become a debutante. Finding someone to present her was difficult but possible, through much enquiry and personal recommendation. Such ladies existed, willing for a fee (practically accepted as a favour) to accompany young girls to the Palace to make their curtsey.

Sylvia, when speaking of her unknown patroness, always affixed 'ghastly', 'dire' or 'awful' in front of her name.

'I'm dreading having to meet her,' continued Sylvia. 'And I know you kindly wrote to Brown's for me to stay there, Aunt Dolly, but you did say you weren't too keen on my going to London by myself, although girls do these days. But I'd be eternally grateful if you *could* come too. I didn't like to ask but now, well, I am asking. Lady Chedworth might be bearable if I had my aunt with me.'

Dolly looked positively delighted.

'Of course I'll come. I should have suggested it myself.'

'Oh, will you? You're so kind.'

'Perhaps I should come too,' put in Peter, in a teasing voice. 'You both need a man to look after you.'

Dolly gave him a long-faced look of disapproval. Much as she loved him, the last thing she wanted was her nephew sharing the fun.

'You know perfectly well, Peter, that your father has already asked you twice to look over the accounts with Ferrers.'

Peter groaned.

'So how can you come gadding up to London?' said Sylvia, looking at him with a mischievous face. An elf in Grimm, and not a well-wishing elf either.

Peter sprawled in his usual way close to the fire. The

59

February afternoon was very cold, but the great arched gothic room was intimate. The grimacing carved figures round the fireplace, the stained glass dark against the winter night, the panelled walls and crowned figures, seemed to be part of a warm kingdom with the fire its mystic centre. But Elizabeth knew that Sylvia had changed the very heart of the house. It was as if nobody, mutely, understood anybody else since she had come. She had brought a different language, and – learning it – the other three had forgotten how to speak their own.

While Sylvia and Dolly talked, Elizabeth could not stop herself from looking at her cousin. He leaned back, his eyes shut, but she knew he was not asleep. She wondered with an intense hunger what his thoughts were just then. And shuddered from knowing that they would hurt her.

It was bitterly cold and half snowing when Dolly and Sylvia alighted from the train at Paddington. The difference from Devonshire was a shock. They had left home on a soft damp day, with a slight chill perhaps, but with the bulbs beginning to peer out of the earth. The London streets were icy. Dolly shivered in her Persian lamb coat and Sylvia, wrapped in a high-buttoned creamy coat already marked from smuts during the train journey, declared, looking from the taxi window, that she was never going to be warm again.

'Only a few more minutes, my child,' said Dolly, in her little tone of patronage. 'Brown's is always most comfortable.'

Living up to its reputation, the hotel had a large fire burning in the entrance hall. Dolly walked up to it and warmed her gloved hands. She heard Sylvia impatiently telling the porter to be careful with her hatbox. Dolly thought the girl's manner with servants a trifle Anglo-Indian and decided, not for the first time, that she ought to speak to her about it. Later, when they were shown to their rooms, Sylvia, still pinched with cold, made a tiresome scene, declaring her bedroom too small and too dark. Dolly, who had a larger room, did not join the argument. Much as she admired her adopted niece, and pleased as she was to be acting as a debutante's chaperon,

Dolly did not intend to be involved in such complaints. Sylvia's room was adequate, hers was pleasant, and age took preference. Garnett did happen to be paying for the expedition.

She left Sylvia in the corridor, throwing her eyes up to the ceiling in an exaggerated fashion and demanding to see the manager.

'I need a little rest after the journey,' murmured Dolly.

She shut her door, lit the gas fire, took off her coat, arranged the pillows on the bed and rang for tea. The meeting with Lady Chedworth was not until six. She could still hear Sylvia's voice, muffled through the door, but it seemed to have dropped a tone. Later there was silence.

Dolly drank her tea and dozed.

The hotel telephone rang.

'Aunt? It's me. Are you all right?'

'Perfectly comfortable, thank you,' said Dolly cautiously.

'Wait until you see my room, it is absolutely vast! A sort of bridal suite. And what do you think, the manager sent up a vase of yellow roses. It was difficult to keep a straight face.'

Dolly wasn't at all sure she approved of Sylvia's triumph. Invited to do so, she did not go and admire the new room before going down to the cocktail bar just before six.

She found Sylvia sitting in a large leather chair. She looked point-device, her black silk dress a perfect fit, perfect length, her hair gleaming without a curl out of place. She was a little work of art. But for once she seemed nervous.

'What do you think the old gorgon will be like?'

'Now, Sylvia, I'm sure she isn't old and why should she be a gorgon?'

'Because she gets paid for dragging people to the Palace. What a job.'

'Things aren't easy these days even for the aristocracy,' said Dolly sententiously. 'I daresay she's fallen on hard times.'

'Of course she hasn't. She charges a fortune. You should have just seen George's face when he saw how much it was going to cost. But he said he still wanted me to be a deb. All the girls are. One can't *not* be.'

She had forgotten that Elizabeth had never been presented and Dolly pretended to forget too.

'Peter and I looked the Chedworths up in Debrett,' continued Sylvia, fidgeting. 'Paragraphs about them but they're all dead and she hasn't any children. Oh Aunt . . .' her voice fell to an alarmed whisper, 'I do believe that's her!'

Two pairs of eyes, one dark, one blue, stared at a tall, ill-dressed woman who had just come into the bar. She looked bad-tempered and, worse, provincial. She said in a loud drawling voice to somebody behind her, 'No sign of Eddie, of course. That boy has the manners of a crossing sweeper,' and went out again.

Sylvia gave a long sigh of relief.

'Imagine if it *had* been. What agony.'

Her voice trailed, for a woman was approaching them. Small and elegant, wearing dark green and a tiny cocktail hat in the shape of a wreath of green felt leaves. She gave them a quick smile.

'Mrs Bidwell? Miss Ashton? I am Honoria Chedworth.'

Dolly ordered sherry and Lady Chedworth asked if she might have a White Lady. During the interview, which lasted half an hour, she drank three White Ladies as if they were tennis lemonade. She was composed, spoke fast, and was just a little grand.

She explained that she could present two girls in the case of their mothers being abroad or, as with Sylvia, 'if they are no longer with us'. Sometimes the parents were divorced and then, of course, she was needed since divorced people were not received at Court. Luncheon parties for the season, she said, began in March. The mothers gave the luncheons to exchange names and addresses, don't you know, for the debutante's various parties which began in April. The cocktail party for each girl came *before* the girl's balls.

Honoria Chedworth spoke quickly but with great precision, like an officer instructing raw lieutenants. Some of the

62

balls were given in country houses and then accommodation had to be arranged for girls invited. 'One knows various families,' said Honoria, waving a hand which held a jade cigarette holder. 'Your ball will naturally be given in London. We will talk about that later.'

While she described the coming three months, Honoria Chedworth summed up the aunt in brown velvet and the young person in black silk who was to come under her practiced wing. She knew about young girls. She had launched trembling creatures who would have given the family diamonds to escape the parties and the preening and the agony of talking to vapid young men. She had also taken the daughters of South American millionaires to the Palace. They had a cool confidence, even while falling into deep curtseys in front of Royalty. Within weeks of coming out, they invariably became engaged to young Chileans or Venezuelans as rich and passionate as themselves. 'Why,' Honoria often asked herself, 'did they bother with me?' But bother they did, and she charged them four times the fee paid by the parents of English girls.

She had met Anglo-Indian girls before. They were daughters of the Services, and she'd noticed that they were the ones who occasionally had divorced mothers. One wondered about society in India. Honoria, *in loco parentis*, set many little white satin-clad ships bobbing out on to the street of London society.

She did her job better than other impecunious baronesses. She didn't fool herself. What the girls wanted was to find husbands, and that was what their parents wanted too. The old dance invented by the nobility in the eighteenth century had scarcely changed, apart from the arrival of foreign virgins among the white-clad troops. Husbands were hunted, and every time one of Honoria's girls collared one, she regarded it as a rider does a rosette at a hunter trial. Honoria's memory was crimson with rosettes.

'Your godfather wrote to me from Ashnacraig,' she said, finishing her third cocktail. 'Aren't the Tuckers dears? He tells me your nineteenth birthday is in June. We might give your ball on that date. Quite an idea.'

They planned Sylvia's next visit to London. Honoria took it for granted that Dolly would be with her and Dolly complacently agreed. Taking out a tiny white diary, Honoria jotted down dates, then put the diary away in her embroided handbag.

'That's all nicely settled. I shall look forward to your being one of my girls this season, Sylvia.'

She called her by her name already, as a Head Mistress might a new arrival.

'You'll need to be very fit, there are so many late nights! So see that you get as much beauty sleep as possible beforehand,' she added, laughing at her own joke.

'There's just one thing, Lady Chedworth,' said Sylvia modestly.

She really is very handsome, thought Honoria, maybe she will catch somebody worth having. The Hibbert boy is rich, and there's Mitcham's son, of course . . .

'It's about your fee,' said Sylvia.

Dolly was appalled.

'My dear child, I scarcely think –'

'That has all been arranged by Captain Westlock,' interrupted Honoria coldly. 'You have no need to bother your head about it.'

'I'm so *sorry*, Lady Chedworth. Apparently my godfather didn't exactly explain. You see, it isn't his money, it is mostly what my father left me. And I did think your fee was a little – well – high. I was talking to Jossy Tremayne in Devon last week, you presented her last year, didn't you? And she only paid . . .'

The rest of the conversation struck Dolly dumb. Money had embarrassed her since she was a girl. Thanks to Garnett, she had never needed to worry about it, and thanks to her own generous nature she had refused to ask him even for money to launch Elizabeth in society. She was too proud and too kind. She expected Lady Chedworth to be as shocked as she was

64

and probably, in an aristocratic way, to be quite rude.

Nothing of the sort. Lady Chedworth remained cold but unmoved, Sylvia appealing but firm. She apologised a good deal. She might have been asking a small favour of an old family friend.

Without blinking an eyelash, Honoria accepted a fee far lower than the one she had named.

When she had said goodbye to them, and taken a taxi back to her house behind Harrods, she wasn't exactly sure why she had done this. She ought to have told that young baggage to take ship back to India.

She found herself laughing.

Chapter Five

Sylvia's future apotheosis, feathers and all, took up most of Dolly's time after she and her adopted niece came home. There were many expeditions down the hill to Teignmouth or further afield to Exeter. The telephone rang constantly. Now and then it was necessary for Sylvia to go to London alone for dress fittings. It was agreed that she should stay, for economy's sake, at the Bloomsbury hotel, the Imperial and Royal where Great Aunt Bessy, the only survivor of the other branch of the family, now permanently roosted. Bessy was delighted – she liked a new young face and Sylvia's connection with George, whom she had met in December, made her almost a Bidwell.

Whenever Sylvia arrived back from London she brought more cardboard boxes with her, and lately it was Dolly, not Elizabeth, whom she invited to help unpack and exclaim over the contents. Dolly was fashion conspirator, and Peter had become escort and chauffeur. He drove Sylvia obligingly up and down the hills, still in the spring sun rather slippery with crimson mud.

Preparing for her debut, Sylvia resembled a glittering circus figure dressed in tinsel from head to toe. She seemed to Elizabeth to pirouette in every room in the house, as well as dancing in Dolly's head and through her conversation. Escaping, Elizabeth fled to Topsy Rolles.

Topsy, her best friend, lived half an hour's ride away in a large Georgian mansion, and whenever Elizabeth trotted up the well-kept drive and turned into the stables, she was sure to find Topsy with the horses.

'Good. I keep ringing you. Permanently engaged,' said

Topsy on a windy March morning when Elizabeth appeared on her fat pony. Wearing her usual uniform of breeches and silk shirt, Topsy gave instructions to Josh, the groom, and led Elizabeth into the house.

'I need coffee, do you?'

The Rolles house, Whitefriars, built on the ruins of a medieval priory, was in its usual impeccable order. The Rolles family had three times the number of servants as had Merriscourt and it showed.

'David's out,' said Topsy. David was her middle-aged husband, a bluff man, wealthy, important, a JP, a magistrate, and given to travelling round the county. He was much in demand and his presence carried weight.

'It's weeks since I saw him,' said Elizabeth, who did not approve of her friend's attitude to her husband and thought she could at least pretend some wifely affection.

Topsy was not listening. They sat by the fire in her favourite room apart from the stables, a small white parlour in which the horse, in old prints and small oils, in trophies, cups, statuettes and mounted silver hooves, figured somewhat ludicrously.

When coffee arrived, Topsy drank a large cupful and demanded news. She was a big, broad-faced, handsome blonde girl, with the ample figure of a barmaid and the lineage of a thoroughbred. As Topsy Treby ('what a name') she had been the richest heiress in Devonshire and a catch. Her father John Treby, who had died three years ago, had owned more than five thousand fertile acres, farms and entire villages. At school Topsy, popular and carefree and wonderful at sports, had worn the aura of a girl destined for great things. A year after leaving school, scarcely eighteen, she married David Rolles. His land marched, as it was called, alongside the Treby acres and like John Treby he was rich. He also happened to be fifty-five.

'Topsy, it's impossible! You can't marry a middle-aged man you don't love.'

Elizabeth had been aghast.

Topsy shrugged.

'I don't love anybody, so why won't David do? Anyway,

Daddy's set on it and when he's made up his mind . . .'

Elizabeth loved her friend and continued to argue, but without a hope of success. Everybody knew that the Honourable John Treby was a despot. He was a short, thin, red-faced man, a somewhat brutal rider, liked by an impressed county – just – dedicated to his land and to Whitefriars. His wife had died years before, probably, said his enemies, from fright. Certainly the bold and reckless Topsy was afraid of him. He behaved to his only child as if she were a very young and raw sub-lieutenant in a battleship of which he was Admiral. He ruled and ignored her. Topsy cared for him, was awed by him, did as she was told and managed, God knew how, to love him and to stay cheerful. But then she saw very little of him.

During a year-long engagement, occasionally meeting the future bridegroom and struck each time by his middle-aged appearance, Elizabeth went on trying to persuade Topsy to refuse to marry him.

'Can't argue with Daddy,' was the philosophical reply.

Elizabeth tried another tack.

'It isn't only rotten for you, it's worse for poor David. Why should he be saddled with a girl who doesn't love him?'

'Oh, you sentimental old thing, you. David's mad about me. You should hear him maundering on. Most embarrassing. And he goes scarlet when he kisses me. Sometimes I think – aha, a heart attack.'

'Topsy, you're being dreadful.'

'No I'm not, I'm being sensible. I can't go against Daddy. I never have and it's too late to start now. Anyway, all this stuff about marrying for love. Love doesn't last, I'm told. I'd as lief marry scarlet old David. It's rather nice having him about. Like a big elderly sheepdog.'

One spring day Topsy was disguised in a robe of white taffeta, her milkmaid face behind a veil of priceless Honiton lace in which she had been christened, and John Treby led her up the aisle. Elizabeth was the only bridesmaid; she thought she'd never attended such a strange wedding.

The county talked about it for months. Then the subject gradually lost its shock, its symbolic quality of crabbed age and youth. Finally, it was simply accepted. A year after his daughter was married, John Treby was killed on the hunting field.

If it occurred to Topsy, shattered and grieving, that she need never have married David Rolles, she did not show it. She genuinely mourned the father she had been afraid of; David Rolles was very kind to her, and her good health and high spirits returned.

Topsy had now been married for nearly four years. She looked blooming. She was the same girl who had played hard tennis and lacrosse, shared all her sweets, her pocket money and her secrets. But Elizabeth felt shy when they were out riding one day and Topsy said, 'Sex is a big disappointment, I can tell you. Now *there's* a lot of fuss about nothing.'

She looked at Elizabeth from under the brim of her hat.

'Want to know the hideous details?'

'I don't think so. Poor David. If he knew you're willing to tell!'

'But he does it, doesn't he? All right, I won't put you off before your virgin knot's untied. You've got it all ahead of you. But take it from me, it's a bit of a bore. Puff and blow, thump and grunt . . .'

Now Topsy poured second cups of coffee and turned her rosy face to Elizabeth.

'I saw your beloved cousin chauffeuring Sylvia again. Hasn't he better things to do?'

'He's very good-natured.'

'Come off it, he's smitten. I can't say I like her any more than you do.'

'But I do like her and don't tell me I don't or I might start believing you.'

'There's a silly remark, either one does or one doesn't. If she were in my house, I'd trip her up. What about the Cousin from Calcutta? Do you miss him now he's gone?'

'Surprisingly, yes.'

And it did surprise her that George came often into her thoughts at Merriscourt. She had gone up to look at the Arabian landscapes again, and staring at the rocks, the sand bluish in a curious light which made it seem like water, the veiled figures, she had remembered what he had told of when he was young. Yes, she missed him.

'You probably miss him because he hung round Sylvia and now all she's got to work on is Peter. I'll tell you something. When I met George that time, I thought he was sexy. Something about the eyes.'

'Rather bloodshot eyes,' said Elizabeth perversely and Topsy roared with laughter.

'I'm not sure you're a good judge of men, Liz. Remember the time you had a crush on the vicar at school? Which reminds me that there are some new arrivals locally (not a vicar and family). One of them thirsts to meet you. Now you look interested. Well. I'll tell you. David brought some people for drinks the other night called Anstey. Nouveau riche, David says. Harold Anstey's big and fat and looks important. He's Anstey Garages and all that implies. She's astonishing, even fatter and is rather like a good-natured woman selling herrings on the quay. No, that's not exactly right. She's more like a dear old milch-cow, the kind that blows at you over a gate. Only she's hung with diamonds. Their son came with them . . . rather nice . . .'

This was Topsy's word for any man she found attractive.

'You've made a conquest there. Ted Anstey, the son, has seen you about and asked me twice if I'd introduce him.'

Nobody can resist hearing that someone wishes to meet them.

'What's he like?'

'Bigger than Peter and very different in style. Your cousin's so languid, isn't he? This one looks ready to go. Built like a rugby player, with a big chin and grey eyes and laughs a good deal. At all my jokes. His parents are mad about him. The milch-cow in the diamonds looked at him as if he'd descended from heaven. He isn't nouveau like his parents, by the by.'

'Why did David bring them to meet you?'

'Because Harold Anstey's just moved here, and one of the first things he did was to give David a fat cheque for the Farmers' Institute. And guess which house they've bought. Remember Broad Oaks?'

Both girls laughed. Broad Oaks, built in the twenties on land not far from the Dawlish cliffs, had stood empty then. Empty houses fascinated the schoolgirls. They hoped for ghosts. During the holidays they had trespassed into Broad Oaks' overgrown gardens and once, finding a hole in a shutter, climbed into the damp house and frightened each other.

'They're vulgarly rich,' said Topsy with relish. 'And David says Harold was one of the lynx-eyed few who took to motors before the war. He messed about with steam motors and electric ones, and opened a garage in London in 1908 or something. He made a mountain of money during the war, I bet he was a profiteer. His wife was Plymouth-born which is why they've moved here, I suppose. And anyway he's started a big garage and a repair works and sales place, huge great showrooms, in Plymouth. He's got a chain of garages and showrooms in places like Sussex and Hampshire. You should just see the Anstey Daimler. One imagines the Prince of Wales.'

A few days after this conversation, Topsy telephoned to invite Elizabeth for sherry to meet 'guess who?'

Sylvia and Peter were out, Dolly at the vicarage, and Elizabeth accepted the invitation with a certain mild curiosity. Topsy had invited a number of other friends, her elderly husband was bustling about hospitably and came over to kiss Elizabeth. He was fattish, kindly, and reminded Elizabeth of a headmaster. He had bushy eyebrows which met in the middle, and always twisted them comically when he saw her.

'How's our young bridesmaid?' he would say, as if the wedding had been last week.

Topsy, gesturing, disappeared into the crowd and returned dragging a young man by the arm.

'Here she is. Ted Anstey. Elizabeth Bidwell. I'll leave you both to it.'

She vanished again.

Elizabeth and the young man looked at each other. He was not embarrassed.

'I've been looking forward to this for weeks,' he said, giving her a look of unconcealed admiration.

To be admired by a good-looking young man was not exactly repulsive and to be listened to with ardent attention was new. She smiled at him. Topsy was right, he did look like a rugby player, he had big shoulders and a figure made for athletics. His face was handsome in a regular, undramatic way, with a straight nose and a firm chin. His thick wavy hair was brushed back from his forehead, and his expressive grey eyes had lashes like a girl's. They had scarcely talked for five minutes when he asked if he could see her again.

Dolly was not pleased when, on returning home, Elizabeth told her about Ted Anstey.

'Just because Colonel Rolles finds these people useful and they have long pockets does not mean you have to go out with the son,' said Dolly.

Her mother's snobbery got on Elizabeth's nerves. She had never liked it. Why should Dolly be a snob? She had come from Streatham, her father owned a grocer's shop, she was quite as jumped-up, her own phrase, as the Ansteys.

Elizabeth knew her mother would not be welcoming to Ted Anstey when he came to Merriscourt to fetch her, and on the evening he was due she listened for his car and darted out to meet him when she heard it drawing up in the drive. He arrived in a magnificent-looking Alvis sports car, dark green, a two-seater which even she, who preferred horses, knew must have cost a lot of money.

He had asked her to dine at Teignmouth's only smart hotel and then to go to a film. But to her surprise, he did not drive her straight to the hotel, but turned the car near the promenade and drove to the sea front; he parked facing the sea. The evening was dark and a moon was rising. The sea was flat calm and as he wound down the window, she heard the sigh of waves.

'Elizabeth. May I call you that?'

'Of course. Don't be ridiculous.'

'Yes. That's what I am.'

He shifted, putting a heavy arm along the top of the seat behind her and turned to look at her. As she met his eyes, her heart sank.

'I want to tell you something important. Listen. Please. It's just that – well – I know it sounds far-fetched but I saw you before I met you at Topsy's this week.'

'Why is it far-fetched? Topsy told me you'd seen me.'

'That's not it. You came into the hotel one night last November with a man. You walked into the lounge and you looked so beautiful. You were wearing blue. Or was it brown?'

What is he babbling about? she thought. It must have been that evening I had tea with George Westlock.

'Elizabeth,' he said again, very solemnly, 'the minute I saw you that night I knew – I knew – I thought, there's the woman I want to marry.'

Elizabeth's heart which had been sinking low enough now fell to the floor of the car. Was this young man actually proposing marriage when they'd met once at a sherry party and been together this evening for quarter of an hour? It was pitiful. More than that, it was extraordinarily disappointing. There was no challenge in it. They might have been children at a party, and he'd walked up to her, extending a sticky hand and saying, 'Will you be my best friend?'

Elizabeth found herself taking refuge in some pretty worn-out clichés. She said that of course it would be necessary for them to know each other better. Ted fervently agreed. She also said that she was touched at what he had told her, which was not true – he had actually made her feel rather uncomfortable. But when she remembered their conversation later, she realised with amusement that never at any point had she told Ted Anstey that it was out of the question for her to marry him. The truth was that he simply wasn't a man she could imagine herself accepting – ever. But on that first evening what happened was that she developed a kind of collector's instinct about him.

Here was a big, handsome, admiring young man who told

her that he had fallen in love with her. She was very flattered, and she thought she would rather like him as a companion. One could not only have Peter in one's life, particularly a Peter who was behaving as Sylvia Ashton's chauffeur.

She began to see Ted quite often after that and she enjoyed herself. She grew to like him. He was so good-natured and good-tempered, so glad to be with her, so easy to amuse.

Peter liked his cousin's new admirer from the start. The two men were very different, but they were both sociable and had one particular interest in common, they much enjoyed talking about cars. When Dolly found her nephew being pleasant to Ted Anstey, she was reasonably polite to him but she did not approve of Anstey in the least. Elizabeth, wearing dark silk and a little fur jacket, went off to dances or films or dinner with Ted, and as Peter saw her leaving the house with her new admirer, he was pleased. He wanted her to have a good time.

He still felt his old easy fondness for his cousin, but she did not affect him as she used to do. Until a few months ago, Lizzie had been the strongest influence in his life. He was sorry for his father and guilty about him, but he did not respect him. Worse, although he did not realise it, in his heart he had never forgiven Garnett for refusing to let him to go into the Army. The act had been one of crude selfishness and Peter had no intention of even pretending an interest in the estate.

Standing in his life, a physical embodiment of conscience, had always been Elizabeth. He complained that she reproached him for dodging his duty, but if she didn't tell him uncomfortable truths, who would? Aunt Dolly doted on him. The county girls with whom he flirted were a charming frivolous lot, and so were the girls he slept with. They were not from the county, for one did not sleep with one's friends' sisters. He went to bed with shop girls, secretaries, barmaids sometimes. He was sexually experienced but did not need it all the time. The game itself, kisses, pressing a girlish figure in the sexy satin dresses they wore, stirred him and left him wanting more. He liked that.

In a moment of unthinking sexuality he had embraced his cousin and the effect on her had been so strong that it had worried him. This girl, half sister, wholly friend, changed under his touch. The strong one, she weakened. The sure one, she grew uncertain. She altered and trembled and he knew he ought not to touch her again but couldn't help himself. He marvelled that her familiar figure excited him. He wanted her and knew that she ignorantly wanted him . . .

Peter was used to success with women but had no smirking self-satisfaction at giving the girls a treat. He simply liked women and preferred them to men. He liked their scents, their voices, their silken legs, their habit of touching his sleeve. He liked older women such as Aunt Dolly with her fits of shrewdness and prescience and her love, warm as a thick sweater. He liked – he loved women. In return for this they telephoned him and wrote to him, patted the seat beside them so that he would sit close, smiled at him, ran towards him and some of them stripped naked to be in his arms.

For a while, despite an obscure alarm, he was pleased at his effect on his cousin and had times when he thought he might marry her. She'd boss him about, but she would make him happy. People said first cousins ought not to marry and that the children of such a close blood relationship could suffer, but he thought that impossibble. He and Elizabeth were strong and healthy. There were all kinds of reasons why the marriage would work. It wasn't particularly exciting, of course. Elizabeth looked quite sexy, and he guessed that when roused she could be passionate, but she had no surprises. He preferred enigmas. His cousin was like Devonshire, a landscape beautiful, fertile, and very very familiar.

He had been easing into the inevitability of that marriage when, coming into the dining-room one winter's night, destiny held out a pale hand.

Did Sylvia know how complete a conquest she had made? He trusted not. He knew his cousin realised it unconsciously, as a dog smells death or thunder. He struggled not to fall into the perilous rushing flood of emotion. He kept away. But

Sylvia sought him out, soon learning her way round the big house and popping up with a triumphant smile.

'I have a silly idea you are avoiding me,' she said, appearing one morning in the cobwebby gun room at the top of Merriscourt's Victorian turret.

'Oh, I run away from you all the time.'

'I don't see why. I'm very nice.'

She was dressed for a walk in a thin, high-collared coat with frogging.

'Have you joined the Army?'

'A tailor in Calcutta copied this from George's undress uniform. Does it suit me?'

'Everything does.'

'Oh good.'

But after she'd gone he forgot what she had worn or how she had looked. He never remembered a word she said. Sylvia had come into his life like an apparition. Before she was there he had been content enough, finding a way to please himself inside limits at Merriscourt, going to stay with friends, hunting. Pretty girls ran after him. And at home another pretty girl, his cousin, companion, conscience, was there, the girl whom he had been half-disposed to turn into his wife.

'Ever till now, When men were fond, I smil'd and wonder'd how.' A simpler man than Angelo in *Measure for Measure*, Peter was struck down in the same way, with astonished pain.

When he and Elizabeth had been children, she had once dropped the family thermometer on to the brick floor in the kitchen, and among the slivers of broken glass the mercury had glittered. They had been fascinated by it.

'Let's try and scoop it up,' he said.

First with a finger, then a teaspoon, Elizabeth attempted to capture the tiny silver globes. They split into two. Four. Eight. The stuff fled from being touched and lay shining and daring her to try again.

That was Sylvia. When he wanted to be with her, she darted away. She divided her smiles and talk among others.

She appeared and disappeared. When he did occasionally have her in his hand, so to speak, he tried to get her to talk about India. She had no gift of description and Peter, with difficulty, discerned through her careless words the country she had left behind . . . ruined temples where gigantic statues of the gods glared down . . . dust storms filled with dragonflies. From such a place, so unimaginable, this enchanting girl had come. And now sometimes she trudged beside him through the woods, saying it was much nicer *here*.

'Soft and damp. Good for the complexion. No horrible sun.'

'You wait until summer. Devon can be really hot.'

She burst out laughing.

When Peter woke every morning his thoughts rushed at once to the room where she slept – or to which she would return if she was away. He lay and longed for her.

He had never bothered to look into the future, and when Elizabeth often said it was necessary to do that, he disagreed.

'How can one plan more than a week or two? Anything could happen.'

'Now what? You sound as if you expect something extraordinary.'

Sylvia was away again in London, this time without Dolly who had regrefully decided to stay and look after Garnett, in bed with a bad cold. The spring weather was having the tantrums. One day sunny, one day rain and cold winds. Peter was restless as the day went by. The last thing he wanted on a dull dreary afternoon was to sprawl by the fire with his aunt and cousin. Merriscourt without Sylvia was nothing. He was bored and out of sorts. But when he went into the drawing-room, nobody was there but Bob, Elizabeth's airedale, who wagged his tail and went back to sleep.

Peter threw himself into a chair by the fire. The room was so quiet that he could hear Ferrers talking on the telephone to one of the tenants. Listening to the bailiff's conceited voice, he had the old familiar guilt that *he* was not helping his father and taking the weight off those bowed shoulders. But hadn't

Aunt Dolly said his father had stooped ever since the war?

Dolly came in just then, accompanied by the mongrel and the sentimental spaniel Chloe. She looked pink from a cold afternoon walk, and rang for tea. Marchant arrived, carrying the silver tray, which he placed in front of her, lighting the spirit lamp under the silver kettle. Like many fat men, his movements were deliberate and rather graceful.

'Ring if you wish for more hot water, Madam.'

'You mean you know I shall drink the whole tea pot, Marchant. I expect I shall. Thank you.'

Marchant bowed gravely and went out.

'What a treasure,' said Dolly, pouring.

'Old rogue,' said Peter.

She smiled. But thought her nephew looked depressed. It was almost April, and soon the debutante merry-go-round would begin in earnest, and apart from being invited himself to London for one or two of the parties, Peter knew he was not going to see Sylvia for weeks. Perhaps she would leave Merriscourt for good. George may have made other arrangements. Every time Sylvia's figure stepped into the London train, the door of the compartment was shut and the train moved off – she never bothered to wave – he felt quite ill.

Drinking her tea, Dolly was looking at him reflectively.

'You're keen on Sylvia, aren't you?' she suddenly said.

'Aunt. What a word.'

'Don't bother to deny it. I know you. And I understand how you feel, she's a handsome creature.'

She never said women were beautiful.

'What do you want me to say, Aunt?'

'Nothing. I want to give you some advice.'

Her confident tone grated. He felt raw.

'My advice is this, Peter. Do and say nothing just yet. She's very taken up with Lady Chedworth and all the plans for the Season, which is only to be expected. In the next three months, with the parties and so on, she's going to meet a great many young men. She may have her head turned a bit. So bide your time.'

She looked smilingly at him, but when he returned the look, something in his face cut her to the heart. Her brightness, her lack of depth, defended her against tragedy. She was afraid of the destructive power of passion. She gave a nervous laugh.

'You *are* keen on her.'

But her advice was deliberate and given with all her affection for him because she knew he was in love. She had watched her daughter in the past drawing close to Peter and had always felt sure Elizabeth wasn't going to win. Dolly wanted Peter, whom she adored, to be happy. She didn't want him hurt by Sylvia fluttering about and upsetting him. Unless Sylvia got herself a rich husband, which was on the cards, Peter had a good chance. But he must wait until the excitement was over. At present Sylvia talked about people with names like Guy Devonshire and Jack Northampton.

Having done her duty by her nephew, who took the advice in gloomy silence, Dolly decided to tackle her daughter. Early the following morning she sent Kathleen to ask Elizabeth to share her morning tea. Elizabeth, looking tall in a camel-hair dressing gown, arrived in her mother's bedroom. The gas fire roared loudly. Dolly was propped up with many pillows.

'Sit on the bed and put your feet under my eiderdown.'

Elizabeth climbed on to the big bed in which she had been born, and which her mother had occupied since coming to Merriscourt as a bride.

'Spring's gone again,' Elizabeth said.

'It'll come back suddenly.'

Silence.

'Sylvia's in a whirl, isn't she?' said Elizabeth. 'How can she afford so many clothes? Did you see the black and white satin? And the pink chiffon?'

'She had a cheque from George.'

'How do you know?'

'She showed it to me. She thinks her godfather is rather a joke, but I think he spoils her.'

'Is he staying in Skye much longer?'

'He seems to be. It's months since he wrote me a letter although he sends messages via Sylvia. Not that one can get much sense out of her just now. Even Peter is finding that.'

'Why "even" Peter?'

'Peter might marry her.'

Elizabeth felt as if she'd been kicked in the stomach. The odd thing was that together with the intense pain there was no immediate exclamation of 'But that's impossible!' It was as if she had been waiting to hear somebody had died. And now here it was.

'How do you know? You said the point of being a deb is to get a husband. She may meet someone else.'

'She may indeed. But I have a feeling that it probably won't be anybody as suitable as Peter.'

'Suitable?'

'Property, my child. Merriscourt. Our lands. Surely it's occurred to you that your cousin is a catch.'

'No. It never has.'

It hasn't, has it, thought Dolly with the pity of a woman who in her time had held an entire hand full of tricks for a girl without a single one.

'Does Sylvia love him?' Elizabeth said, after a silence. She did not ask if he loved Sylvia.

'My dear child, I don't know anything about that. What I do know is that apart from the expense of being presented, which is using up the little money her father left, and any cheque George happens to send her, Sylvia hasn't a farthing to bless herself with. Now she is *not* a catch. So I shall be quite surprised if she finds anybody, as I say, as suitable as Peter.'

'Mother, you don't know he wants to marry her.'

'I don't miss things, my child, even if you do.'

With the consciousness of having done her duty by her daughter and her nephew, Dolly rang for more hot water.

Chapter Six

Spring came back, bringing the wild daffodils, the green finches and chiff-chaffs. Elizabeth found a grass snake nearly a yard long, a brownish green in the orchard. It slipped away, more alarmed than she was. There were primroses thick in the woods and hedges and ditches. Some of the flowers had stalks four inches long. Marchant brought a great bunch into the kitchen and put them on the table in a cream jug. All Devonians knew that a small bunch of primroses was unlucky and meant that home-farm chickens would catch the gapes; a really large bunch ensured lucky hatching and rearing.

The crimson mud on the lane leading up to Merriscourt, a squelching trap for wheels or hooves, began to dry in the thin sunshine. The sea which had thrown itself against the high beach wall in Teignmouth grew innocent and blue. Sylvia, darting through Merriscourt's lofty rooms or off on trips to London and coming back with more cardboard boxes, was as sunny as the weather.

After the first shock of hearing what her mother had told her about her cousin and Sylvia, Elizabeth had settled into a kind of controlled grief. It was as if she could hear a crying child and could do nothing about it. To silence the poor thing, or at least to mention the sobs to a sympathetic ear, she rode Snowball over to Whitefriars.

She found Topsy as usual in the stables, giggling with Josh. Both turned faces with a similar expression on them, slightly self-conscious and warm, as Elizabeth dismounted.

'About time!' said Topsy, putting an arm through hers. 'Why didn't you telephone?'

'Why didn't you?'

'Because I'm a lazy bitch. Come and have coffee and tell me the news. Is there any?'

They went into the Green Parlour where a fire burned and a bunch of primroses as large as Marchant's was on the windowsill. Before talking about her troubles, Elizabeth glanced at her friend. Topsy's broad good-looking face was relaxed. Her fair hair, she had pulled off her felt hat, was as thick as a horse's mane, a coarse glittering fairness on top, brownish glinting gold beneath. It looked burnished with life.

'You seem very cheerful, Topsy.'

'It's Josh. He does make me laugh. You, on the contrary, look rather down. I bet it's that Ashton woman. What's she done now?'

'Mother says Peter might marry her.'

Topsy whistled.

'Bloody hell. He hasn't said so, has he?'

Elizabeth repeated her mother's words. Topsy made a face.

'You used to say your mother had premonitions, or was it intuitions? But she isn't the Oracle at Delphi, Liz. Don't take any notice. You said she's all over that girl and she's probably got it quite wrong.'

Elizabeth said nothing and Topsy looked at her with love and sympathy. She was devoted to Elizabeth and admired a core of toughness in her. She hated to see the strong one struck down.

'Was I really such a fool as to think –'

'That you and your cousin would live happily ever after at Merriscourt? Nothing's ever like that.'

It certainly wasn't for Topsy with a husband nearing sixty and no sign either of marital bliss or a baby. Yet Topsy glowed.

The two girls continued to talk and Topsy set out to amuse her; she managed to make her laugh. But under the conversation she was trying to decide whether what Dolly had said was true. Perhaps she was wrong to tell Elizabeth to forget her mother's warning. She had no way of judging. Was it kinder *not* to blow on the cold ashes of Elizabeth's hope? She saw her friend was in pain, and for all their apparent merriment, she felt helpless.

In the weeks leading to what Lady Chedworth would call 'your Great Day' Sylvia and Dolly were in London a good deal. They were still staying at the Imperial and Royal, saving Brown's for the time of Sylvia's parties and later for her presentation.

Returning after three days of learning to curtsey and making the acquaintance of other debutantes, Sylvia confided to Elizabeth that Great Aunt Bessy was very tedious.

'We had Army shop during the Windsor soup and right through to the watery coffee. She goes on like a regimental mascot. You know, those goats they have marching with the band.'

'Her father and brothers were in the army and she almost married –'

'A Captain in the Blues killed before the relief of Ladysmith. Have mercy. We had *him* with the apple flan.'

'Don't be unkind. You'll be old one day.'

'I will, won't I?' said Sylvia, laughing. She wore yellow chiffon, and flicked a curl on either side of her cheeks.

'Don't make such a long face, Lizzie, I really am being bored a lot just now. There's Lady Chedworth with her "utterly"'s and "divine"'s and making one curtsey until one's knees crack like rifle shots. I should've thought the King and Queen would be frightened into fits, wouldn't you? Then there was tea at the Ritz, that was boring too. I had to meet a lot of girls who gave me funny looks because I'm not in their set.'

'Do you wish you were?'

'Of course, stupid.'

A pause.

'It's jolly hard work,' added Sylvia. 'Arranging about one's clothes. Gloves and handbags and shoes all matching *perfectly*, and during the season you change five times a day –'

'Surely not!'

'Of course. Morning. Luncheon. Afternoon. Cocktails. Ballgown. See? You'll admit it is tiring. And suppose one's hem on some dress or other is half an inch too short or too long, everybody knows you're dowdy.'

She sighed, and then said in a sweet, coaxing voice, 'Lizzie. Promise you won't be offended. But would you mind awfully if I don't ask you to my cocktail party? Lady C. has added up the numbers and horrors, we're three men short. So I must have Peter. But can't have you. You don't mind, do you?'

When her mother, Sylvia and Peter left for London on the April week of the party, Elizabeth was actually relieved. Lately her cousin had been offhand with her. He rarely made jokes or teased and sometimes, for the first time in their lives, he looked at her self-consciously. To be distanced from him, not to see that expression, was what she wanted. It hurt to be with him. So when the trio left, she and the old house breathed more easily. Outside the windows April was budding. Indoors were kindly silences.

She decided to wash her airedale, and finding him on the terrace, seized him by the collar and dragged him into the house. Bob, knowing what was in store, resisted with all his weight. Laughing and scolding, she took him up to the bathroom, lifted the big animal in her arms and stood him in a foot of lukewarm water. Bob, filled with gloom, stood slipping with his claws on the enamel while she picked up and soaped each leg, making lover's remonstrances.

'How many times have I said you're not to hunt? There's the gamekeeper and his beastly traps. I thought you were so clever, but you're as stupid as Bill. You're an awful old man and filthy into the bargain.'

A tap on the door. Marchant loomed.

'Captain Westlock has arrived, Miss Elizabeth.'

'*Who*? He's supposed to be in Scotland – damn and blast. Marchant, say I'll be down soon and give him a sherry or something.'

She rinsed the dog, lifted him out and muffled every inch, including his face and eyes, in a towel. Unable to see, he

84

didn't shake water all over her. She rubbed him energetically.

When she hurried downstairs and into the drawing room, she found George standing gazing out into the gardens. He was directly under the stained-glass windows and coloured light, ruby and gold, shone on him, turning him into a saint. He stood as straight as a figure holding a martyr's palm.

'I'm so sorry, George! I was washing the dog. What a surprise. But Sylvia's in London again. They all left this morning.'

'I wrote to say I was coming and when she didn't reply I imagined she'd be here. Unreliable Sylvia. I must ring the hotel,' he said.

When they sat down, he looked at home.

'You won't leave for London right away. You'll stay the night?'

'That's kind of you. If it's inconvenient I could always put up in Teignmouth.'

He knew very well that Merriscourt had twelve bedrooms.

'And how was the castle in Skye?'

'Small and draughty, sixteenth century, but you never saw such views.'

'Did you sail?'

'A lot. And went shooting, and fished for salmon, and climbed. We saw two magnificent eagles.'

What about Lady Priscilla, was she magnificent too? thought Elizabeth. A large damp dog padded in. Elizabeth stroked him and he growled, showing the whites of his eyes.

'Careful, Elizabeth, he could bite.'

'Bob would no more bite me than develop wings and fly. He's growling because he's jealous of you. Anyway, dogs never bite me.'

George considered asking if people did, but decided against it. It might not amuse her. In a curious way she matched this idiotic gothic house with its galleries and carvings, trees sculpted in the hollows of arches, its frieze of hunting dogs, the stained-glass girls playing the viol and the harp. She was as English as they. He had known many different women in very different settings. A girl in a sari heavy with silver, gazing at him with enormous dark eyes while she sat by a chain of lily pools. A Scottish figure, black-haired, merry and fierce. This Devonshire girl was pretty and certainly not a fool. But she had no mystery. Another English girl, Sylvia, had a good deal of mystery and very annoying it could be. You wanted to spank or hug her. You could never have such thoughts about Elizabeth Bidwell.

George's unexpected appearance delighted Garnett, who came into the drawing-room before lunch and exclaimed warmly, 'Why, my dear fellow, how very nice!'

He fussed over his visitor, refilling his glass. Through lunch he talked of Highland fishing and shooting, reminiscing about Loch Maree and Invergarry, about flies, salmon, grouse, pheasant, an exclusively male conversation to which Elizabeth did not bother to listen. She was pleased that her uncle looked happy. But when the trio were having coffee Garnett grew quiet, and after a while he excused himself and left.

When he had gone, George said, 'Your uncle doesn't look too well.'

'I know. He's overtired. He's often like that.'

'He went as white as a sheet.'

'He's never been strong, poor uncle.'

He put down his coffee cup and said musingly, 'The estate worries him. From what he's told me in the past I gather there's much to worry about. He doesn't have much help, does he? Except from your bailiff.'

For the life of her she couldn't spring to Peter's defence. Not after watching her uncle's worn face. She said she wished Ferrers was better at his work, and that her uncle hadn't employed him in the first place.

'I wasn't too impressed with him,' George said. 'But Garnett presumably had good reasons for giving him the job?'

'Oh yes. He had a reason. Ferrers' father was our old bailiff and a very good one who knew the work backwards. But Leslie Ferrers is useless. If Merriscourt was mine, I wouldn't give him house room.'

'I can see you wouldn't,' he said, looking at her with interest. 'Have you ever thought of offering to help your uncle? You'd be an acquisition.'

'He'd never allow it.'

'Hm. I know what you mean. But suppose I . . .?'

'No, George. That's kind but please don't. It would only fuss him. He'd never agree to let me do anything for the estate, and would be embarrassed to explain why to you. Because there is no good reason except that I am not a man.'

'I suppose you're right. People do dislike admitting to prejudice. It seems a pity, though.'

To her relief he changed the subject and enquired about Sylvia. Elizabeth told him about her comings and goings, and repeated Sylvia's crushing descriptions of Lady Chedworth.

He laughed. 'She'll hold her own. Nobody worsts Sylvia. And is she getting used to all the London junketing?'

'She must be. She never talks about India any more.'

'That's because the food Sylvia eats is the *plat du jour*. Yesterday's gone.'

'But it hasn't, George! Nobody can live exclusively in the present.'

'My god-daughter does. And jiminy, doesn't it suit her?'

He pretends to be detached about her, but he's not, she thought. She could hear in his voice the identical note she'd heard in her counsin's when speaking of Sylvia. Is that what my future holds? she thought. To listen while men talk about that girl. And to see in their faces the same look. The same besotted look . . .

During the sunny weeks of April the London season had started. Dolly thoroughly enjoyed it. Naturally sociable, snobbish to her finger-ends, she delighted in the luncheon parties where young girls chattered in high voices while the mothers – rather over-pleasant to each other – made plans. Dolly noticed that the expression on this or that middle-aged female face, fashionably hatted, altered for the better when she added Peter's name to their lists.

Luncheon parties, cocktail parties, grew more numerous.

She and Sylvia were out every day of the week. The season officially began with the opening of the Royal Academy, and Dolly, Peter and Sylvia were at Burlington House, gazing at portraits of elderly men in mayoral robes, or landscapes which, whispered Dolly to her nephew, 'aren't a patch on the real thing'.

On the evenings when there was a ball, a dinner party was given for four couples, often at the Berkeley or the Ritz. There was a great deal of champagne, very young men grew very talkative, and after the meal the couples went out into the springtime street to climb into one of a row of waiting taxis, to drive to whatever Mayfair house was the place to be that night. Striped awnings led from street to house, red carpets were spread across pavements. Walking under the awnings, one could already hear the band playing *Love In Bloom*.

Dolly was secretly alarmed by the enormous number of clothes needed for the season. Dresses for lunches, dresses for cocktails, every outfit with its own hat, handbag, shoes. It would be a sign of failure to be seen twice in the same outfit. Most costly of all were Sylvia's ball dresses – creations of stiff taffeta, chiffon, watered silk or – new that season – glittering silver lame which smelled metallic. Some of the dresses were clinging, almost skin-tight and bare-backed. The latest joke was of a young man describing one of these as 'she was wearing a gownless evening strap.'

The weeks were filled with shopping, invitations, new friends, late nights and mounting bills. Goerge arrived in early May to squire Dolly and Sylvia. Peter went back to Devon, but soon returned. To Dolly's surprise, it was suddenly June and Sylvia's ball was almost due.

Sylvia was as sunny as the weather. She was much photographed, wearing one of many flirtatious hats tipped over one eyebrow, or a ballgown showing her pretty naked shoulders. A whole page was devoted to her in the *Tatler* – 'one of the season's loveliest debutantes, daughter of the late Colonel John Ashton, MC . . .'

If the weather in Mayfair was fine and the roses at Brown's

hotel made the entrance hall smell like summer, in Devonshire the season was glorious. Elizabeth never remembered such a June. Gorse flamed across the moors, it was warm enough to swim from the Teignmouth beach in the early morning in a cornflower sea. When she walked with the dogs to the old quarry, it was a lake of foxgloves.

She had been invited to Sylvia's ball as a matter of course, and had bought a dress in Exeter. She was doubtful about it. It was of soft crêpe, showed her figure and was the colour of apricots. It suited her, but she had nobody to tell her so except an over-enthusiastic woman at the shop. Would Peter like the dress? Probably not. Or worse, he would not notice it.

She was dreading the ball. She wondered if the thin gruel of hope on which she had been living for weeks was going to be finally dashed out of her hands. For wasn't it at such high glittering points in our lives that destiny takes a hand?

Dolly telephoned in the morning, before she left to catch the train.

'Sylvia's ball tonight,' she said unnecessarily.

'Yes, Mother. You're coming, aren't you?'

'My dear child, debs' *mothers* don't.'

Dolly used her 'never show your ignorance' voice.

'You go to hunt balls,' said Elizabeth, irritated. 'Are you sorry to miss this one?'

'Not in the least. I am dining with Aunt Bessy. Now, I hope you have packed everything.'

'Of course. Dress. Shoes. Handbag.'

'And your *petticoat*. Did you get one to go under the dress?'

Elizabeth said a meek yes. She was not deceived into thinking her mother was concerned about her for any other reason than that, as Dolly's daughter, she must do her credit.

'Go to the hairdressers when you get to London. I don't want you looking like a birch broom in a fit. You should see how often Sylvia has her hair done.'

Elizabeth travelled to London on a hot bright day of early summer when the sun streamed in a flood through the train window. Arriving at the sedate luxury of Brown's she was told that all her family were out. She was relieved. Blessedly alone in her room, she took a long time to bath and dress in the apricot crêpe which clung about her rounded figure. She made up her face and brushed her hair which was not newly-crimped into waves and curls; she clasped a narrow gold bracelet studded with seed pearls round her wrist. She was putting on more than soft clothes and gold bracelets; she was slowly girding on an armour like that worn by her ancestors clanking into battle with stout hearts concealed under patterned steel. Yet armour had joints and people had died, hadn't they?

When she went downstairs, the first person she saw was George Westlock; the sight was extraordinarily welcome.

'My dear Liz. We're the first. Come and have a drink.'

'An orange juice would be nice.'

'Not champagne for the great occasion?'

'Not quite yet, thank you.'

They sat down together.

'You look very beautiful,' he said.

'Thank you, George.'

She supposed it to be one of those perverse compliments, because his thoughts were on someone else who *was* beautiful.

'Did you know Sylvia has insisted on a programme dance, of all the damned things?' he said, smiling. 'I remember the little cards only too well from dances at Sandhurst. The best-looking women had every dance filled days in advance.'

'Mine will be empty.'

'Just you wait. It'll fill like magic. Ah, here they are.'

There was Peter, casual in tails, Dolly in soft grey silk – and Sylvia in a sheath of silver, turning every masculine head in the crowded lounge.

Elizabeth saw her mother's swift appraising look at herself and the switch of her eyes to the vision beside her. And knew that her cousin, if questioned, would not have known if *she* was wearing sackcloth.

Sylvia, her pale cheeks slightly flushed and her eyes too bright, burst into a description of the house where the ball was being given.

'Did Aunt Dolly tell you, Lizzie? It's a shabby old place called Malcolm House on Chelsea embankment. *Of course* it belongs to a relation of Lady C's (a rake-off as usual), and she says the mulberry tree outside was part of Sir Thomas More's orchard.'

'It's propped up like an ancient man on a crutch,' from Peter.

'The house has five creaking staircases, a secret passage, and thundering water pipes,' put in Sylvia.

'But the ballroom is lovely,' proclaimed Dolly. 'Very long, with a little stage at the end for the band. And there is a beautiful conservatory.'

'For proposals of marriage,' said George, and Sylvia burst out laughing.

Peter finally turned to Elizabeth and told her that Malcolm House was reputed to have a real ghost. Not an old nurse or a screaming scullery maid, but a cat which heralded good luck, not bad. It darted across rooms at dusk and vanished under tallboys. If someone saw it and excitedly peered under the furniture – no cat.

'I shall spot it and catch it by the tail,' Peter said, 'to make sure the good luck is mine.'

'Don't you dare,' said Sylvia. 'I want it.' She looked in the tiny silver handbag shaped like a heart and said, 'Oh, Aunt Dolly, have you got Lizzie's programme? I don't seem to have it. I'm afraid we never sent it to you in advance.'

'It wouldn't have been much good if you had. Unless Marchant gave me the supper dance,' said Elizabeth.

Peter and George laughed but Dolly made a face; she disliked what she called familiarity about the lower orders. She handed Elizabeth the minute programme, with its dangling pencil on a silk string.

Soon it was time to go. Dolly said goodbye to them. Sylvia and Peter left in the first taxi, and George and Elizabeth travelled to Chelsea together.

'Sylvia's on her high horse tonight, isn't she?' he said.

'She does look gorgeous.'

91

'She's like an actress. She blazes when she is on stage.'

Malcolm House was larger and lovelier than Sylvia's description of it. It rambled away from a stone courtyard where the mulberry tree, like some revered great grandfather, stood propped but leafy, its gnarled branches reaching to the upper windows. Lady Chedworth, in yellow satin and a topaz and diamond necklace, was receiving the guests in a very narrow hall which somehow managed to accomodate a miniature chandelier, a perfect but small-sized grandfather clock, and a row of tiny oil-paintings.

'Sylvia, at last. Come along, now, half a hundred people are asking for you.'

Sylvia in a flash of silver vanished up the winding stair towards music and voices.

The ballroom was crowded. There must have been over two hundred people, carefully divided into even numbers of young men and girls; the band was the season's most fashionable. 'Goodnight, Vienna, you city of a million memories,' sang a young man with patent-leather hair, imitating Jack Buchanan's sweet huskiness.

Tall young men whose names she did not know asked Elizabeth to dance. As they skilfully led her into the crowd of dancers, their conversation was strangely similar.

'Are you going to Bunty's on Thursday?'

'Have you seen the new Jessie Matthews film?'

'Don't you think Sylvia looks ripping?'

Sylvia did. As should happen and rarely does, she was by far the most beautiful young woman at her own ball. Elizabeth saw her glittering like a diamond, surrounded by young men arguing about whom she should dance with next, laughing as she consulted the programme on its silver string round her wrist. She had a kind of light round her so that you couldn't stop looking at her, thought Elizabeth. She saw Peter dancing with Sylvia now and then. Twice he came over to dance with Elizabeth. He danced in silence – much better than she did.

As the second dance ended he said; 'Are you enjoying yourself, Lizzie?'

'Of course.'

He did not even know that she was lying.

It was long after midnight, the music went from swooping waltz to quickstep, the laughter grew louder, champagne still circulated. The supper dance was over. Lady Chedworth, unknown to the youthful guests, had retired to a small study to take off her satin shoes. As for Elizabeth, she noticed how she was avoided by every one of the girls at the ball. Not a single girl, in a bouquet of lovely young women wearing the fashionable colours of a bunch of sweet peas, chattering and flirting and hanging on to the arms of their escorts, addressed a single remark to her. At the start of the evening Sylvia asked her to sit at her table, but Sylvia herself was never there. And when Elizabeth, finally deserted by the last of the young men asking if she were going to Bunty's, went back to the table it was empty.

Sylvia was on the ballroom floor in the arms of a dark young man with dark eyes. They were dancing a rumba as if they had been partners for the season. There was no sign of her cousin or of George. Elizabeth had a sensation of near panic. She never should have come. Across the room she suddenly caught sight of Peter and was about to spring up and go across to him, but he was on the dance floor, the music ended, and he went to claim Sylvia.

Feeling she couldn't sit another minute at the empty table, Elizabeth stood up. She threaded her way between the tables, left the ballroom and went down a corridor where dim lights shone. Seeing some girls appearing round the corner, she dived into the first door she came to.

It was a small low-ceilinged library. A single lamp burned. The room smelled of dust and of very old leather. Of the passing centuries. The presence of the books was the first welcome thing she had sensed tonight. Perhaps I shall see the ghost cat, she thought, and sank down into a chair. Faint, faraway, she heard the music. 'The party's over now, the dawn is very nigh' sang a distant voice. I wish it were . . .

When the handle of the door turned, she started.

George Westlock looked in. He entered the room and shut the door behind him.

'Sensible girl. You've escaped. So have I. Parties are only bearable if one knows everybody.'

He sat opposite her in the dusky lamplight.

'How's that programme going?'

'Empty. No. Someone called Guy. Or is it Gerry?'

'Mine,' he said, consulting it, 'has an indecipherable scrawl too. Joan? Jill? Shall we tear them up?'

'Oh, *could* we?'

'At once. And I've another idea, even better. Get your wrap and meet me in the hall. Don't talk to a soul. Especially not if his name begin with a G. Now hurry.'

When she came down the stairs he was by the open front door. A footman in livery said, 'A taxi, sir?'

'Thanks, but no. We'll walk.'

George tucked Elizabeth's hand under his arm and they crossed the road and walked away from the old house which shone with lights and echoed with voices and music. They walked along the embankment. The river looked black.

'Matthew Arnold called society barbarians,' he said.

'They were enjoying themselves.'

'But we weren't. I found them rather worse than our Anglo-Indians. At least we pretended to look after new-comers. But tonight was not for you and me, Lizzie. Sylvia was relishing every expensive minute. Hello, here's a piece of luck.'

Incongruous, haunting as the figure of the ghost cat, a vision was slowly approaching them. It was an open horse-drawn cab coming very slowly along the embankment, the horse clip-clopping, the driver jogging in his seat, his whip tied with blue ribbons. George hailed him.

'You're a welcome sight. Will you take us back to Brown's Hotel?'

'Was on me way to Malcolm House, sir.'

'Exactly. Which is where we've come from,' said George firmly. Elizabeth grinned, wondering which young man, bound for Bunty's on Thursday, had ordered this romantic vehicle. George helped her up and the carriage set off on its ambling way through the quiet streets, waking them with the mild sound of hooves. George, beside her, tucked her arm comfortably under his.

She could have been happy. If she had not remembered her cousin hovering to dance with that silver girl from whom, it seemed, neither she nor George could ever escape, no matter how enchanted the night journey.

After Sylvia's ball, and a week crammed with other less glorious evenings, with telephone calls, cocktails, last-minute panics over the right clothes, suddenly it was the day of her presentation.

George, Peter and Dolly were all at Brown's to see her leave for the Palace. There was Sylvia in white satin, her train bordered with satin shells, the three feathers fixed at the back of her fair hair, a small veil floating. Lady Chedworth arrived, magnificent in beaded blue and carrying an ostrich feather fan . . .

Peter, but not George, was to join her at midnight when, after making her curtsey to Royalty and being their guest at the Palace for what Lady Chedworth said was 'a scrumptious little buffet, my dear', there was a final ball at Grosvenor House.

Early next morning Dolly slowly drank tea and turned her thoughts over in her mind. She lay comfortably in bed, very pensive. It was obvious from the start that Sylvia had been one of the best-looking of the year's crop of debutantes. She had had great success and whatever party she attended, she was surrounded by young men. Dolly had not missed resentment in girlish faces at her adopted niece's triumph. Once or twice, she had actually believed that Sylvia was going to come to her with dramatic news. Two young men were very much in evidence. Luis Guerrero from Venezuela, who, said Lady

Chedworth 'is rolling, my dear Mrs Bidwell', and young Viscount Tremayne, whose family owned most of Essex. Even Dolly buried in Devonshire had read about *him*.

If Peter was jealous and troubled about Sylvia's successes, he never showed it. Dolly admired his easy, unmoved charm during those hectic days. Supposing Sylvia does get a proposal from one of those two young men, she will accept, of course, thought Dolly. I shall have to brace myself to see the poor boy very unhappy.

Dolly was eager to see Sylvia this morning and hear the whole story at first hand. She wanted to be told about curtseying to the King and Queen, to hear the Palace described and to share, vicariously, an evening in society. She looked forward to a tap on her bedroom door. But there was no sound from Sylvia or Peter either. When she went downstairs she was told that her nephew had gone to his club. Sylvia slept late and then sent a message to say she had left to have her hair done. She was away for hours, and Dolly grew disappointed.

Honoria Chedworth telephoned.

'Swimmingly. It all went swimmingly. I must congratulate you on the choice of Sylvia's frock, a little masterpiece of simplicity. By the way, we must have a teensy chat, Mrs Bidwell. Shall we say at cocktail time this evening, here at my house?'

Dolly knew what that meant.

After thinking about it, she decided to go and see if Sylvia had returned. She hadn't seen her but it was worth a try. She was very surprised to find her sitting pouring scent from a bottle into a spray. As Dolly came in, the girl's hand jogged and costly scent filled the room.

'Oh *Aunt*. You've made me spill it. You might knock first.'

'That is not a polite way to speak to me, Sylvia.'

'Sorry.'

Sylvia's hand was shaking, her eyes swollen with tears. Who had she seen? No proposals of marriage after all. Only half sorry for her, Dolly had a moment of amusement.

'Lady Chedworth rang.'

'What does *she* want.'

'To be paid, naturally. Will you give me the cheque? I remember that you settled the amount with her beforehand.'

'She can wait for her money.'

'Sylvia. She certainly can't. You must pay her.'

'She can wait.'

Dolly made her disapproving long upper-lip face and walked out of the bedroom without a word. She went down to the lounge. Peter was by the open window, reading the *Field*. Glancing up, he gave her a smile.

'Hello, Aunt. You look bright. That's because you didn't stay up until nearly five.'

She went straight to the point.

'Something very embarrassing, Peter. Lady Chedworth has asked me round this evening. She wants her cheque, of course. Sylvia won't give it to me. She says Lady Chedworth can wait.'

He couldn't help laughing.

'Sylvia's the limit. But she mustn't let the old – sorry, Aunt – whistle for the cash. It wouldn't do at all.'

'You tell her. Perhaps things are done differently in India.' Dolly was sarcastic for once.

'What makes you think I can persuade her to stump up?'

She saw he rather liked Sylvia's bad behaviour.

He came back twenty minutes later, put his hand in his pocket, and produced the cheque.

'She's worn out,' he said tenderly. 'It's high time we took her back to Merriscourt.'

Dolly took a taxi that evening to Lady Chedworth's small house behind Harrods. Honoria answered the door herself, saying that the maid was out. The maid, thought Dolly, is a daily help; so much for all the airs and graces. Dolly measured social position by the size of the staff.

As Honoria accompanied her up the stairs to the drawing-room, two young girls came out, just about to leave. Honoria drawlingly introduced them but Dolly did not catch their names. They were identical twins, pretty, redheaded and shy. She heard Honoria talking to them as she saw them out.

'Tomorrow at eleven punctually, and I'll go through the plans with you both.'

We take the Paddington train, thought Dolly, and she still rides the merry-go-round.

She had only been in Honoria's drawing-room once before. It was ludicrously Chinese. The sofas were covered in black satin patterned with pagodas, there were three Buddhas placed on tables in various corners. Fat-stomached, slit-eyed, greenish-brown, they nodded at her. The least movement set them slowly nodding their heads in antique approval for minutes at a time. Everything in the room belonged to the Buddhas. The red lacquer furniture. The screens. Even a snuffling Pekinese on a carpet embroidered with blue and yellow flowers.

Honoria returned briskly.

'We must drink a cocktail to Sylvia's success. Last night every eye was on her. I even think,' lowering her voice, 'the King noticed the child.'

They talked for a while about nothing in particular; Honoria again commented on Sylvia's looks.

'She's a lovely young thing. Divine. Billy Northampton said to me last night that she was quite the little film star.'

Did Dolly hear a valedictory tone?

'Sylvia has asked me to thank you for everything you have done for her. She is very grateful. May I leave this?' said Dolly, delicately placing the folded cheque on a lacquer table beside her.

'I'm glad she was happy about everything.'

Honoria wandered over, picked up the cheque and to Dolly's private amusement, opened it to see that the amount was correct. She poured a second White Lady.

'How is the child? Tired after all the excitement, I am sure.'

I'm never going to meet this woman again, thought Dolly, so what does it matter what I say?

'Sylvia seems upset. Not herself at all. Lady Chedworth, you've had so much experience in these mattters. Is it usual for a girl of Sylvia's looks and success not to – well – to put it bluntly, not to get one or two proposals?'

Honoria was unsurprised.

'My dear Mrs Bidwell, you are right. A marriage market, that's all it is. I myself, years ago, became engaged at the end of my Season. Of course, things are changing. Girls are getting jobs and so on . . . well, some do although many parents, and I so agree with them, disapprove of what verges on vulgarity. Sylvia was certainly a great success. But. The big but. She has no money.'

'Colonel Ashton –'

'Of course, of course,' interrupted Honoria, dismissing Sylvia's dead father as an irrelevance. 'I could not help seeing that Sylvia had her eye on Luis Guerrero and he was very attracted to her. South Americans do have a certain fascination, don't they? But the Guerreros are Venezuelan millionaires, I'm afraid. And Luis is quite under his mother's thumb. They're going back to Caracas shortly. Money, my dear Mrs Bidwell, marries money.'

There was a religious silence.

'Then there was Charley Tremayne,' continued Lady Chedworth. 'He was running after little June Blackford until Sylvia appeared. But June, d'you see, is wealthy. Father dead . . . big estates in the North and so on. What I am saying is that perhaps I should have warned you not to let Sylvia's hopes rise. However. She seemed a young woman who knows what is what, so I did not think it necessary.'

It was Honoria's revenge for the reduced fee.

Draining her second cocktail, she added pontifically, 'The more seasons go by, the more girls who come under my wing and then make their way either to St. Margaret's Westminster or back to their homes, the more I realise an undisputed fact. Money marries money. A little money marries a little money. And so on and so forth.'

*　　*　　*

99

It was late summer when her cousin broke the news – but Elizabeth had known for weeks. He came looking for her and found her swinging in the orchard. Inslow, who thought it daft, put up the old swing for her every spring and took it down every October. She was creaking to and fro, dragging her feet in the grass as Peter came between the trees towards her. He sat down and leaned against a tree. Creak went the swing. How happy he looked, she thought. It was awful to see.

'Lizzie. You've guessed.'

'Of course. Just waiting for you to tell.'

Pushing with her feet she swung higher. Her legs were bare and she wore her old school sandals.

'Sylvia says she'll have me.'

'So I should think.'

'Oh, there were scores of other men proposing, Liz. When we were in London it was ghastly – I kept thinking I'd lost her.'

'But she chose you.'

Punch-drunk with love he had not gone deaf, and at her tone he laughed.

'You're very rude.'

'Aren't I?'

She concentrated on her smile's frankness, knowing the danger of it being too bright.

'I'm so glad for you, Peter.'

Just for a moment she wanted to call him by some dear name, a thing she'd never done in her life. At this moment of parting she wanted to say – what? That his figure stood in her thoughts always, as if against an open door through which light shone. That Merriscourt's heart and Devon's, the orchards and farms, blue sea and red earth and richness, would always be Peter.

All she did was make a friendly grimace. Creak went the swing.

'Sylvia says you must be her only bridesmaid,' he said. 'And I've told her *I* shall definitely choose your shoes.'

But he forgot.

100

Peter was intensely, alarmingly happy. He was convinced that the emotion which made him shiver with desire and delight must stay for always. How could it not, since Sylvia was to be his lover and his wife. Never before having looked ahead further than a week or two, now he could see a whole calendar of the years scrawled with her name. He was so happy that he loved the world, and when he knocked at his father's study door, the smile he wore bordered on stupidity.

Garnett was mildly surprised at seeing his son, and dumbfounded when he heard the news. He was the only person at Merriscourt – even the blushing Kathleen had suspected it – to whom the engagement came as a bombshell.

'My dear boy! My warmest congratulations! She's charming. Charming. My warmest, kindest congratulations.'

He leaned forward to grip his son's hand.

Peter's brown eyes swam.

'And you'll both live here?' said his father.

Peter stammered that Sylvia and he had talked . . . Speldhurst had been empty for ages . . . if his father could see his way . . .

Garnett's face lost its smile.

'It would have been agreeable to have you both here but I understand. Yes. Speldhurst could be made into something, I daresay. We must ask Ferrers.'

We'll do no such thing, thought Peter.

There was a pause. Garnett sat at the desk with its piles of papers, playing with an ivory paper knife. Peter remained standing, attentive and respectful. Just then, he might have been the son Garnett needed.

'Now that you're to marry, my boy, there's something I should say. I hope you'll buckle down a little and do more for the estate. We could do with your practical head,' he went on innocently. 'There's much to be done. And you must always remember that Merriscourt will be yours one day. Perhaps sooner than you think.'

Filled with his own happiness, Peter chuckled.

'Of course I'll work harder, sir. You must not say things

like that, though, you'll be with us for many years yet!'

So, thought Peter as he left the study, I've told all the family now and it wasn't as bad as I thought. His aunt, of course, had been delighted, behaving as if she were responsible for the match. He had dreaded telling his cousin – but that had been easy, after all. Now he went to the butler's pantry to look for Marchant.

The old man received the news with deep respect which Peter, usually perceptive, did not see was assumed.

'It's very good to hear,' he said. 'Miss Sylvia will cut a fine shine as a bride.'

He'd known about it even before Dolly.

Sylvia refused to choose a ring from among Peter's mother's jewellery which Garnett offered to have brought back from the bank for her inspection. It was a kind thought, she explained, but she'd somehow always had this silly romantic idea of a modern ring. Square cut. She and Peter went to Aspreys in Bond Street and returned with a very fine diamond.

Showing the ring to the Bidwells' friends, laughing and talking all day long, Sylvia filled Merriscourt with her happy presence. She and Peter also spent hours at Speldhurst, their future home. It was the single house on Merriscourt land which had not been built for farmers or their workers – a pleasant place built in the 1830s, with a Regency air, of grey stone. Its only frivolity was a front door, pillared, with an Adam fanlight. It was 'large enough' said Peter, accustomed to twelve bedrooms. Speldhurst had six. The floors were of good polished oak, the garden mostly lawns and shrubberies and some land let out for grazing.

The trouble was that Speldhurst had been uninhabited for years. A great uncle of the Bidwells had lived and died there and once it had been let to a youngish middle-class family whom Garnett disliked because they demanded repairs. The tenants moved, with relief, and Speldhurst went to sleep in the way of deserted houses. The trunk of the wisteria, climbing up the front of the house, grew as thick as a man's arm.

The lawns were coarse. The shrubbery a wilderness. All must be civilised again.

Visiting the house with Peter and Sylvia, Elizabeth thought it a gigantic task; but slowly, with a good many workers, the house began to show its possibilities. Peter had taste and Sylvia an eye for colour.

Autumn day followed autumn day. Inslow, with an under-gardener, toiled outside; plumbers and decorators inside. Vans arrived. At last Speldhurst was ready.

All during the time of the Indian summer Devonshire was ripe and sunny and golden, and the lovers were like the bees in Keats' poem who believed warm days would never cease. Peter wanted to be married at the end of September. Then, surely the invitations could go out in October? Early November? But Sylvia delayed as this or that was not complete and in the end the date was set for the last week in November. Suddenly, with the fall of a curtain, the slam of a door, autumn was gone. The leaves came down, winds blew, it rained for a week. The morning of her wedding day was so dark that Ada had to dress the bride by electric light. George, who was giving his god-daughter away, sheltered her under an umbrella as they ran to the church through the rain.

Great Aunt Bessy Bidwell had arrived in Devonshire for the wedding, it was her first visit to Merriscourt in ten years. The old lady, over eighty and bright as a button, sought out Elizabeth directly the reception began and asked her to find George Westlock. She'd met him at the Bloomsbury hotel a year ago. He was a relative and such a dear, she said.

Sixty years before, in another world when women wore muslin and beribboned bustles, Bessy's favourite sister Kitty had married George's grandfather. Kitty had died in child-birth but to Bessy she was as real and beautiful as today's bride.

Elizabeth emerged from the crowd, bringing George who, in morning dress and a white carnation, had as always trans-formed his clothes to Army uniform. He and Bessy shook hands, smiling warmly.

'How nice to see you again, my dear boy. Come and talk to me. What a pleasure to see my darling sister's grandson once more. Did I tell you that you resemble her?'

They sat down together.

There were over a hundred and fifty guests, the great rooms buzzed with talk, and Elizabeth, in simple white crêpe to set off Sylvia's magnificent satin sheath and long train, thought she had never talked to so many people in her life. When Sylvia at last disappeared to change into going-away clothes, Topsy discovered Elizabeth sitting behind a screen, drinking her first glass of champagne. She felt tired. Topsy, unfamiliar in velvet, sables and the Rolles emerald earrings, gave a stableboy's wink and sat down beside her.

'I haven't seen you for weeks. I've been talking to your *other* cousin.'

'Who's that?'

'What a giveaway. George, of course. Distinctly attractive and the sort who likes women. How can you resist that sexy look in his eyes?'

'Very easily since the sexy eye's on Sylvia.'

'Oh, I daresay he gets led by the nose,' said Topsy, peering round the screen and waving her empty glass at Marchant, who refilled it. 'She'd see to that. But whatever you say, he can't have been mooning after her all that much because I've been hearing things. It seems there's a big affair in George Westlock's life, which explains all that over the sea to Skye stuff. His heart's in the Highlands, his heart is not here. And now,' said Topsy, draining her glass, 'another ten minutes and you'll have the place to yourself.'

'Shut-up, Topsy. Someone will hear.'

'Why should you care? And are you sure everybody likes her that much?' demanded Topsy, not bothering to lower her voice. 'Another thing. Don't you dare tell me you're going to miss Peter, or I'll brain you.'

Chapter Seven

It became, on the newly-married couple's return from their honeymoon in the South of France, an accepted habit for them to lunch at Merriscourt every Sunday. They always arrived late. Dolly listened for the car, and when the two-seater which Garnett had given them for a wedding present drew up in front of the house, she was the first to hear it.

'There they are!'

She trotted out to be kissed. Elizabeth in turn was given a tobacco-smelling peck on the cheek by Peter who sometimes, for old time's sake, tugged her hair.

'Well, Lizzie? You haven't come round to help Sylvia decide about the garden yet.'

'I'll ring,' said Elizabeth who was postponing the visit.

She sometimes felt as if in the last year she had been in a kind of deadly gymkhana of the spirit, doomed to go over a series of jumps high enough to break her neck. First had come the suspicion that her cousin did not love her. Then the pain, small at first and steadily growing, as she watched him with Sylvia. Finally, she had lost him. Elizabeth had taken the highest jumps, had not fallen and had ridden back after the show with a ribbon pinned to her pony's harness. Peter had known all that. He'd simply looked away.

He was so happy. It showed in everything. In his voice, his laughing voice. In the way he looked at his wife perched on the arm of a chair. The expression in her cousin's eyes filled Elizabeth with awe. Nobody in their senses should be as fond and uncritical, as indulgent and positively doting as he was. But who said he was in his senses? Love had punched him in the jaw and he still staggered. As for Sylvia, the sexual experience of married life, thought virginal Elizabeth, had not changed her a jot. She was the same beautiful chatterer who, on arriving, immediately started talking to Dolly about clothes, laughing and using a new expression, 'I'm a silly thing, aren't I?' Elizabeth didn't think so.

It was January, Topsy was in Northamptonshire for the hunting, and Elizabeth was lonely for the first time in her life. Her uncle and her mother had their own preoccupations. Dolly visited the vicar. 'Your uncle will have to do something about the pews. They are riddled with worm.' Garnett, in his study with Ferrers, coped with a trail of complaining tenants.

Elizabeth's subdued air was not lost on Ted, who telephoned her and took her out a good deal.

'You are seeing too much of that young man,' said Dolly.

'Oh, Mother.'

'You can do better than that.'

Elizabeth never succeeded in getting Dolly actually to be pleasant to Ted. When Elizabeth came home after being out with him, and gave her mother the unopened box of Terry's chocolates which Ted always bought for *her*, Dolly scarcely thanked her and never asked if she had had a good time. How snobbish Dolly was. 'The Ansteys really are very common,' she said to Elizabeth. Her daughter groaned inwardly.

Uncomplicated and amiable as he was, Ted could scarcely miss the chill in Dolly's voice when he came round to collect her daughter. Elizabeth never let him arrive without being ready to receive him and pour him a sherry, for Dolly never would. She was ashamed of her mother, and admired Ted for shaking Dolly's hand so warmly and making hopeful jokes.

Before Peter married, he and Dolly enjoyed teasing Elizabeth about Ted.

'How's Heartbreak House?' enquired Peter. 'He's smitten, poor beast.'

'He looks like a dying duck in a thunderstorm when he's with you,' from Dolly.

Elizabeth merely laughed, pointing out to Peter how often Ted beat him at tennis.

'That's because his arms are as long as a chimpanzee's,' said Peter. But he liked Ted. Dolly didn't.

Although the Ansteys were recent arrivals in South Devon, they soon became known because of their wealth. The navy-blue Daimler, noble enough to contain royalty, drove down the hill from Dawlish to Teignmouth, and drew up at the station every morning to drop Harold Anstey, and collect him in the evening from the Plymouth train. Ted, on the other hand, did the sixty-odd miles every day in his fast open Alvis.

Elizabeth had not known Ted for long before he invited her to meet his parents at Broad Oaks, the house in whose garden she and Topsy had trespassed as schoolgirls and which the Ansteys had rescued from vacancy and mildew. Elizabeth had never seen anything like the now-occupied Broad Oaks. It was altered out of recognition. They had built a whole mock-Tudor wing, added a garage, created tennis lawns and built a conservatory. Indoors, Broad Oaks had become an overblown version of a house in a Plymouth suburb. Plum-coloured velvet curtains; sofas for six people, covered in chintz bursting with delphiniums and cabbage roses. Giant standard lamps and grand pianos nobody played. On the turn of the stair was an enormous vase covered with dolphins and tritons. The flowers in the garden resembled those in a municipal park.

Harold Anstey, as tall and broad as his son, had a heavy face, a rumbling voice, and curling grey hair. His wife sometimes called him Curly. Lilian, who had been red-headed as a girl, dyed her frizzy hair tortoiseshell and over-powdered her large kindly face. She was fat, her big low-slung bosom hung with pearls, and when she met Elizabeth she opened both arms and gave her a hug.

Before Peter's marriage Ted had become part of Elizabeth's life and the happiest part. They drove to dances, went swimming in summer and in winter to countless Hollywood films. They liked to sing in the car driving home.

'Sweet Heartache, which aches without any pain,

I'm glad you're back, Sweet Heartache.
I'm in love again,'

sang Ted in his pleasant voice.

When Sylvia saw Ted at Merriscourt, she made no effort to
be charming, she took her cue from Dolly. But Peter liked
him from the start, and they enjoyed talking knowledgeably
about cars. He was very welcoming to Ted and the two young
men got on well, yet once when Elizabeth and Peter were
alone, he said, 'Something I've meant to say. You won't decide
to marry Ted Anstey just because nobody else has hove into
view, will you?'

He had lost his instinct of knowing how his words affected
her. He didn't know he made her feel ice cold. That night she
dreamed she was walking up the aisle in bridal dress, and
when the man at the altar turned round – it was Ted. She
woke shivering.

She did like him. How could she help it? He was her faithful friend and admirer. She did not enjoy his kisses, but
they were so chaste they could not upset her. Sometimes he
reminded her sadly of how much he loved her and how he
longed to make her his wife. Poor Elizabeth's replies were
threadbare; she heard herself saying the sort of empty stuff
Victorian girls must have used.

Now Peter was gone, she saw Ted even more. And missed
her cousin more.

Coming in from the garden on an early spring afternoon,
she left her wellington boots in the scullery and walked
through the kitchen where Cook and young Kathleen were
making scones. The kitchen range glowed. Bill and Chloe lay
toasting in front of it.

Beyond the kitchen was the butler's pantry, the door ajar,
and she could see Marchant's stout figure, he was cleaning the
silver. Elizabeth liked his pantry. It was filled with valuable
china, with sets of Regency trays inlaid with the brass 'B', and
shelves of beautiful glasses, from brandy glasses right down to

liqueur glasses small enough for a doll's house. When she went into the room, it smelled of silver polish and methylated spirits.

'Hello, Marchant. You're busy.'

'It worries me when the silver looks dull, Miss. And the devil finds work for idle hands.'

She lingered. She was fond of him and knew he was fond of her. She was not sure he approved of her just now.

'Does the devil attack you often, Marchant?'

'He's universal. Take your eye off him and he'll pounce. He's got long claws.'

She sighed, leaning against the door. She wore an old brown jersey and a skirt which had seen better days. I'm burned if you'd think she was the lady of the house, he thought. Dresses like a village girl. With Mister Peter gone, things are that shabby. *He* wouldn't have let her go about like that. Very strict on the look of things, he is. Now it's a poor come-along. No wine served. And what does the Master drink? Barley water.

'You're none too cheerful nowadays, Miss Elizabeth,' he said, smothering the silver tea-pot with pink polish. 'Not the same, is it, without the young gentleman? You didn't ought to mope, though.'

'I'm not moping. Honest.'

'Begging your pardon, we're busy and you aren't,' he said. He was cleaning a silver tray, his brush going into its deep knobbly patterns. The dust made him sneeze.

'I always have lots to do,' she said defensively.

'Tell you what I think, Miss Elizabeth. You'd enjoy getting a job.'

'Oh Marchant.'

'It isn't Oh Marchant at all. Young ladies do get jobs these days. I've seen it in the *Daily Mail*. Don't know exactly what at. In offices, flower shops, that sort of thing. It'd keep you busy, though.'

He looked up at her.

'You just think on it, Miss Elizabeth.'

Leaving him in the pink dust, she went to her room and changed for tea. Brushing her hair, she reflected about Marchant's words. She suspected that he was teasing her. Despite a reverence for the gentry, it would amuse the old man to turn her into a worker like himself, Cook, Ada and Kathleen.

She spoke to her mother the same evening. Dolly looked dubious, but it was not in her nature to discourage people, and her daughter's face looked bright, for a change.

'Certainly I've seen in the papers that girls work occasionally in Mayfair. Art Galleries. Constance Spry. There was something in the *Mail* last week about a Lady Somebody working in an antique shop.'

The *Daily Mail* was not only read by Garnett and herself but, before them, by Marchant, and after them by the entire staff until it was reduced to tatters.

'A secretarial course would be practical, Mother.'

'Really? Is a secretary quite the thing?'

Elizabeth remained hopeful. The more she thought of Marchant's idea, the more she liked it. It would get her away from the house for part of each day. It would exorcise Peter's ghost while his physical self lived happily at Speldhurst. And if learning shorthand was difficult, all the better.

The two women agreed that she must ask her uncle who would, of course, have to foot the bill for her training. Next day Elizabeth went to his study. He was not at his desk, but standing by the bookshelf, a very old guide book of Devonshire in his hand. He turned round.

'I am so sorry. I didn't hear you come in. Sit down, Elizabeth. I won't keep you a moment. I'm just looking at a most interesting paragraph about the free peasantry who colonised the waste land in Devonshire between 1150 and 1350.'

His voice, dry, courteous, was indifferent. He continued to read and she sat down, looking at him in silence. His back was turned to her, and she saw that it almost had a hump. She usually saw him sitting at meals, or in his car, and now the shape of his back shocked her. It was bent like a bow.

He closed the book and sat down at his desk facing her. His face was grey.

'Are you quite well, Uncle?'

'Perfectly, thank you.'

He destested talk of his health.

'Well?' he said impatiently.

If only, she thought, he could be like other elderly men she had met, the fathers and grandfathers of her friends. A strong, kindly, approachable, even a comical sort of man. How she might have loved him. But there was the rub. One had to go on tiptoe with Garnett. It had always been like that. As a child she'd been told 'Don't make a noise, it tires your uncle.' 'Don't ask him *that*.' What Dolly and the nursemaids had meant was don't ask him anything.

Well. This time she was going to.

She took it at a run.

'Uncle, I would like to get a job.'

He did not appear to have heard her. She repeated it.

'A job!'

His incredulous tone actually made her laugh. That did not please him.

'Truly, Uncle, I would very much like to. I could learn something useful. Of course I didn't go to University, and I'm quite untrained, but I could take a course in shorthand and typing.'

She went on to say that she'd telephoned a secretarial school in Exeter, it was not expensive. And it seemed that a trained secretary could earn as much as twenty-five shillings a week. When she'd finished the course and had a job, she could pay him back for the fees in instalments. She spoke briefly, in a business-like way.

Garnett Bidwell listened with an expression which was almost a glare. At the mention of repaying him he interrupted.

'You're saying that your dress allowance is too small, is that it?'

'No, no, of course not!'

It seemed wise to say no more. Dolly had warned her not to

111

press too hard. 'If you knock a nail in too often, you loosen it,' said Dolly.

So Elizabeth sat, looking reasonable.

A pause.

'I'm sorry,' he said.

'You mean you don't approve.'

'I mean there's no question of you getting a job as you call it. Where do you get such expressions? I certainly will not allow it. Young women of your position remain at home until they marry.'

'But some girls get j –, go out to work.'

'Indeed? I know of none. Please do not refer to this again. Ring for Marchant, if you would, since you are near the bell.'

Marchant did not exchange a look with her when he arrived with a salver and a decanter of Madeira. But he knew.

Elizabeth slammed her bedroom door so hard it made the room shake. She threw herself on her bed in tears of rage. Girls of your class stay home until they marry. My God, what's changed since Victoria was on the throne? Uncle is awful. Awful. Prejudiced and stupid and selfish, selfish, selfish. He stopped Peter going in the Army when Peter longed for it, and now he stops me doing some footling job which would make me happy and he needn't even know about. He's a bad-tempered unimaginative old tyrant.

She was angry with him for a week. Dolly counselled tact and acceptance, but her daughter felt neither. She scarcely answered her uncle's morning greeting and when she met him in the grounds, she walked the other way. She had a spiteful satisfaction in her own resentment.

Ted thought it very funny.

'Class. That's what it's all about.'

'Oh shut up.'

'That's the spirit,' he said, guffawing.

Garnett did not notice that his niece was still angry with him. He went about his life in his usual querulous way. One March day when he was tramping to an outlying farm with Ferrers, the two men were caught in a heavy downpour. The rain bucketed down, turning the ground into a lake of mud. The elderly man was drenched to the skin. When he got home, Dolly, shocked, sent him straight to bed with hot whisky and lemon. The following morning he had a high temperature. Later, pneumonia set in.

Merriscourt was hushed. Servants went on tiptoe or wore carpet slippers. Dolly never left the house, sat with the sick man for hours on end, leaning against the back of a tapestry chair, ready to give him a drink or ring for the nurse whom she replaced as much as possible. Dolly would spring up, to stoop and listen to what Garnett faintly asked for. Oxygen cylinders arrived, and the nurse gave him oxygen through a little glass mask like a filter. The gas made a hissing sound.

Dolly never wanted to leave the sickroom: she was a born nurse, quiet, patient, concentrated, gentle. But she looked exhausted and Elizabeth forced her to give up her vigil for an hour or two. Then Elizabeth sat in the chair in the big shadowed room, lit by a low, never-quenched fire.

Garnett slept, his straight yellowish-grey hair sprayed on the pillow like dead grass. His pyjamas, blue and white flannel, were buttoned up to his scrawny neck. In all her life of twenty-two years, she'd never seen her uncle in his pyjamas before: Garnett's modesty was total. It is strange, the girl thought, leaning back and listening to his breathing, to think that from that sick old man's loins my cousin came.

Peter often sat with his father, but he decided that Sylvia shouldn't. She'd had influenza, he said, and must keep away. Sometimes Peter and Elizabeth were both there, one on either side of the bed, saying nothing, united in the beginning of dread.

But his son was not with him, and nor was Elizabeth, when Garnett died. Only Dolly. The nurse had been asleep.

Dolly was prostrated by his death. She had occasional migraines and this was the worst Elizabeth could remember. Poor Dolly could do nothing but lie in bed with a wet flannel on her head. The nurse looked after her.

The morning after his father died, Peter found Elizabeth in the study. She was staring at the little guide book Garnett had been reading on the day she had asked if she could get a job.

A History of the County of Devon. It had been on his desk all the time since she had spoken to him. It made her want to cry.

'Lizzie?'

Peter came over to her and took her in his arms. She leaned against him. They said nothing for a while.

'I wish I'd been with him,' he said at last.

'How could you have been? He died at half-past four.'

'I should have stayed here.'

But she let him off.

'Uncle would have been frightened if he'd known you thought he might die.'

She felt his body relax. They drew apart.

'Do you know what Marchant did this morning?' he said in a more natural voice. 'He told me when I came in. He went out to the beehives to tap three times on them and say "Father's dead". He says other people in the family would die at the end of the year if he hadn't done that.'

Elizabeth remembered that Marchant had told her about the power of bees when they had been children.

'There's another custom. Turning the hives towards the coffin when it leaves the house,' she said.

He looked surprised.

'Imagine you remembering. He told me that too.'

He looked at her.

'Did you sleep at all?'

'Until Kathleen woke me.'

'Syl's been wonderful about Father,' he said. 'And about the funeral too. She's so wise. She said we shouldn't ask too many people.'

She paused, and then said carefully, 'But Peter. We'll hurt them if we don't.'

He stood with his hands in his pockets by the untidy desk.

'What she means is that it's too soon after the wedding and so – well – depressing. Besides, Father didn't care for most

114

of the people at our wedding, did he? All the county acquaintances. We'll have a small funeral. Just for the family.'

'If that's what you want.'

Suddenly he put out his arms again and pressed her close. She leaned her cheek against the itchy tweed of his jacket. He smelled of Virginia cigarettes. For a moment, abandoning herself to the touch and feel of Peter, she felt safe. She said, pressing against him, 'You didn't know I quarrelled with Uncle.'

'What do you mean, stupid? You and he never had a cross word.'

She began to cry as she told the story. He took out his handkerchief and mopped her eyes and petted her.

'What a storm in a teacup, I'm sure he never even saw that you were cross, he was in a world of his own, Lizzie, you know that perfectly well. Now stop being a noodle and stop crying or I shall cry too, and a fine pair we'll make.'

Dolly managed to get up for the funeral, looking dreadful, her face pinched and dark rings under her eyes. Great Aunt Bessy looked less frail. Peter had not sent a telegram to George Westlock, saying he was in Skye and it was much too far to ask him to travel. Elizabeth privately disagreed. She knew George would have wanted to be there. Sylvia was in black as all the Bidwell women were. The servants wore black armbands, and Marchant was a monument of dignity and grief. He had loved Garnett. As the coffin was carried out of the house, Marchant intoned very loudly, 'Turn the bees!' And Inslow hurried away to obey him.

When the funeral was over, Peter kissed his aunt and cousin and his old Great Aunt, and said goodbye. The women went to their rooms.

Nobody mentioned that Merriscourt belonged to Peter now.

Elizabeth sat down on her bed, glad to be alone. We're to part, old house, she thought, I shan't be with you any more. I can scarcely bear to think about it. Will you miss me? The house did not say. It rustled about her. There was a patter of dog's paws and a scratch at her door and when she opened it, there was Bob. He never came to her room, but now he walked over and leaned against her, as horses sometimes do.

Dolly's migraine, with poor Garnett dead and buried, left her. She sent Kathleen to fetch Elizabeth the next morning early, to share her morning tea.

Propped against her pillows, Dolly had a faint colour in her cheeks.

'Your Great Aunt says will you drive her to the station for the twelve o'clock train. I begged her to stay longer, but she prefers to get back.'

'Of course, darling.'

'Well? And how did you sleep?' asked Dolly kindly.

'Like a log, I'm ashamed to say.'

'Your uncle wouldn't have wished it otherwise. I've been thinking. When Bessy has gone, you and I must see Peter soon to talk about the double move.'

Her mother's recovery was quicker than seemed possible, thought Elizabeth. But Dolly had always been one for action.

'You mean that we'll be going to Speldhurst? Doing a swap?'

'Naturally. Sylvia will be sorry to leave her pretty new house, but it's an ill wind, my child. They have Merriscourt. We have Speldhurst, freshly decorated and ready for us,' said Dolly with a little laugh.

'I never thought of that.'

'Didn't you? I did. When they first decided on Speldhurst. Of course I never thought your dear uncle would die for many years, but I do remember thinking that when he was eventually taken, Speldhurst would do nicely. For us both, supposing you hadn't yet married, and when you did –'

'For you by yourself.'

'Exactly.'

Elizabeth saw it was a neat solution. Why did she feel it was too neat?

'I don't think we ought to talk about the move for a day or two,' Dolly said thoughtfully. 'Poor Peter is dreadfully upset.'

116

'He seemed quiet and resigned to me.'

'That's odd. When he kissed me goodnight he took my hand and his was trembling. It was damp with sweat. Poor boy. Poor boy.'

The idea of her cousin shaking and sweating like a frightened horse surprised Elizabeth. When she and Peter had been together in the study he had twice taken her calmly in his arms. She was mystified. She and he no longer shared the communion of thought, no longer instinctively understood each other, and she had not realised the depth of his grief. She felt she had done him a wrong .

There was no sign or sound of him or Sylvia for the following two days. The mourning house slowly returned to normal and Marchant asked Dolly if he could have the study cleaned and tidied.

'The Master has left it,' he said, as if Garnett had taken the London train, 'in a bit of a muddle.'

'Yes, Marchant, of course. Pull out the furniture, I'm sure it's all very dusty, and the papers can go into a big basket until Mister Peter has time to go through them with Ferrers.'

Dolly knew that desk and its burdens.

She expected her nephew (possibly not with Sylvia) to come round any day. But the curious thing was that three days went by after the funeral without a sign. He telephoned once when Dolly and Elizabeth were both out, but left no message. Elizabeth began to think her mother was right – her cousin was struck down with grief, poor Peter. Her own reaction in little was his in great, he was suffering from conscience. He feels guilty, she thought. She did not like the idea of Peter in his pretty new house with his pretty new wife being unhappy about the way he'd treated his dead father.

Marchant came into the drawing-room one afternoon, days after the funeral, to say Mister Peter had rung again and would the Mistress and Miss Elizabeth go to Speldhurst this evening for a glass of sherry. The thinness of the invitation struck Elizabeth: a meal was not mentioned. It must be another proof of the way Peter was feeling.

117

'Good, we can make plans for the double move,' said Dolly, who was getting to like the idea.

'You're very philosophical about losing Merriscourt, Mother.'

'One must face facts, my child.'

Her optimism rather bothered Elizabeth. Dolly might have her intuitions, but there were times when she did not face the facts, and what was colder than the fact of relinquishing one's dearly loved home?

'Well, I can't pretend not to be miserable,' Elizabeth said, running her hands along the carvings above the fireplace. She knew every head, every tree, every branched antler on the leaping stags.

'Speldhurst is going to be very nice,' said Dolly comfortably.

'But it isn't home.'

'You've always been so sentimental about Merriscourt.'

Yes, thought the girl, that's what I am. Losing it will be like waking up to find somebody has amputated my legs. I'll always feel Merriscourt is mine. The nerves will remain and the ghost legs go on hurting for the rest of my life.

'It's all for the best,' said Dolly. 'You'll soon see it as I do. We'll need fewer servants, and dear Garnett will have provided us with the means to keep a small establishment.'

'Probably too small.'

'Elizabeth, you are talking nonsense. Do you mean to imply that Garnett will not have remembered me as he should do in his will? I ran his house for him from the moment Richard was killed. And Merriscourt, after all, *was* mine. Had you been a boy, you would have inherited. Garnett never forgot that.'

Elizabeth said nothing. She was trying to imagine a life spent away from the old, elaborate, ponderous beloved house.

It was dark and very chill when Elizabeth drove the Hillman up to Speldhurst. The house shone with lights, and the door was opened by Sylvia's brand-new housemaid in a over-smart cap and apron edged with lace and threaded with ribbons.

'The Master and Mistress are in the drawing-room, Madam,' she said in broad Devonshire, speaking like a parrot. She looked as if she'd be more at home in a farm dairy.

Peter and Sylvia were sitting by the fire, and Peter stood up to kiss them. Sylvia, wearing black, put out a thin hand.

'How pretty the house is looking,' remarked Dolly, admiring the draped yellow and turquoise curtains, the deep-pile carpets, the ornaments and the silver-framed photograph on the piano, showing Sylvia in her debutante's feathers and veil. 'You must feel so cosy here.'

She literally spoke without thought, forgetting everything, and simply enjoying the house in its newly created freshness.

There was a pause which, thank heaven, thought Elizabeth, her mother did not seem aware of. She had walked over to look at the photograph. 'I must have one of these. It does you justice, my child.'

Peter pulled a chair to the fire for his aunt. Elizabeth sat further away. He remained standing. Something was wrong. Dreadfully wrong. She could see it, smell it, it was in the air like the bitter smell of fungus under trees. Peter had scarcely touched her face with his cheek when he greeted her, and had not looked at her once.

Dolly, her small hands lifted to the fire which made her diamonds wink and blaze, turned to Sylvia and Peter with a bright, interested face. She said right away, 'Well, now, my poor dear Garnett is gone and you are the heir, Peter,' looking at him with a loving eye, 'so Elizabeth and I must pack our traps. You must give us a little time, of course. Moving out of Merriscourt can't be done in a week.'

She gave a little laugh. Elizabeth was watching Peter. He still stared at the ground.

'It seems such a pity, Sylvia dear,' continued Dolly, 'that you took all this trouble and will be leaving your nice house so soon. But you'll have the comfort of knowing how much we'll enjoy the fruits of your labours.' Dolly was comfortable with clichés. 'And you'll want to do one or two things to Merris-

119

court, for young people like things done their way. Luckily we don't need to spend a shilling here. It's delightful as it is. A double move!'

She again gave her little laugh running up the scale.

'Shall we set a date? Had you one in mind?'

Peter walked to the piano, picked up the photograph of Sylvia and put it down again. Then he turned and faced them.

'Aunt. Elizabeth. We're very – we're truly sorry, but I'm afraid you can't move in here. Of course we see it would be convenient but the trouble is there's poor George Westlock.' He began to speak faster. 'He's badly in need of a home. Sylvia owes George so much. She owes him everything, in fact. She doesn't like talking about it, but after her parents died she had literally nobody. And George was wonderful. He brought her back to England and looked after her – he did everything for her. He paid towards her London season too. I believe he's left himself practically penniless. Now Sylvia feels it is her turn, and her duty, to do something for him. She looks on him as her next of kin. So. Well, we thought you might make a go of Kiln Cottage. It is empty and will need some repairs which of course we'll pay for. But we know you will understand about George.'

Sylvia broke in.

'I feel so sorry for him. It's sad, you see, because Daddy always said he was a born soldier. If only he could get back into the Army. He never should have given it up as his career. But he's a bit old now . . . a broken life. It is rather sad,' she repeated and sighed.

'Very sad,' said Dolly automatically.

'Of course there's no hurry about you leaving Merriscourt –'

'No hurry at all,' from Peter.

'Take your time, Aunt Dolly. You'll want to make some plans.'

'And we'll help in any way we can,' put in Peter.

Not once did he look at Elizabeth.

'If there's anything we can do, just name it,' said Sylvia prettily. 'And now we have got boring old family business out of the way, you must try a glass of Madeira. Peter brought some from London months ago. It was wickedly expensive, but it does taste like velvet . . .'

When his aunt and cousin were gone, Peter went slowly back into the drawing-room. Sylvia was lying back with a grey taffeta cushion behind her head. She raised her eyebrows questioningly.

But he was not looking at her. He went over to the mantelpiece, put both hands on it and bent his head, staring into the embers of the dying fire.

'That was awful.'

She said nothing. He repeated, 'It was awful, Syl. Did you see my aunt's face? I thought she was going to faint.'

'Oh Peter. We've discussed this over and over. We've worn it out. You surely aren't going back on it now.'

'No, but –'

'But George needs a home, doesn't he? Admit that he does. What's he got for all that he's done for me? You don't expect me to sit still and see him living in some dreary London lodgings when I think what would have happened to me without him. You can't be as cruel as that.'

He still did not look at her, and she stood up and came to him, standing behind him but very close. For relief from the pain, he turned round and took her in his arms. The anodyne worked. She had a way of melting into his arms, all scent, all softness and from the moment he touched her he wanted her. It was Sylvia who ended the embrace.

'Darling, darling, don't be mizz over this family stuff. People always have this sort of trouble, don't they? You know I'm right really. I promise we'll make the cottage comfortable for Aunt Dolly and Liz. I'll help. I'm good at things like that. You're so soft-hearted, my darling. I think that's what I adore about you . . .'

When they made love he did forget. For a while.

121

Chapter Eight

Neither Dolly nor Elizabeth could eat at dinner. Marchant said, 'Just a taste, Madam?' and 'It's very light, Miss Elizabeth.' But the food went back to the kitchen scarcely touched.

Putting down the tray, Marchant said to Cook, 'Something's in the wind and I don't like the feel of it.'

He was the onlooker who wanted to be in the middle of the game.

With Marchant out of the drawing room it was not necessary to pretend. Elizabeth looked at her mother. Dolly's face was haggard, she seemed, literally, to have become ill. She lay back on the sofa. A wave of hot licking rage went through the girl, scorching the green plants which grew in her soul, and she said in a harsh voice filled with bitterness, 'How could he?'

'She made him.'

'We're his family.'

'That never counts when a man is keen on his wife.'

Springing up, Elizabeth began to walk about. She sat in the corner by the now dark stained-glass windows. Then she stood up again.

'How much money have we?'

'Whatever Garnett left us.'

'Perhaps he didn't leave us anything. He wasn't bound to.'

'Elizabeth, don't use that tone about your uncle.'

'For God's sake, I'm not speaking ill of the dead! I'm facing the facts. He could have left a ridiculous will. He was a muddler. Even suppose that lawyer pointed it out, Uncle probably left every damned thing to Peter. It would be just like him. The easy way out – a will with no details. He probably said to the lawyer, "My son will do what's right".'

'Yes. He could have said that.'

It alarmed Elizabeth to see her mother's spirit and vanity and liking to be right all, all gone. When she heard the weakness and apathy in Dolly's voice she felt she could strangle Peter.

'So,' she said loudly, 'let's face the worst. How much have we actually got?'

'Your grandfather left me two hundred a year and the house in Streatham, which is let. It brings in fifty pounds.'

There was a pause.

Dolly was frightened. For her whole life men had looked after her. Her father. Her lost husband. Garnett. And she'd believed Peter would do the same. It was as if she had put her arms round her beloved nephew and he had slid a knife into her stomach. She bled. It was love pouring away.

She looked across the room at Elizabeth, who had gone back to the corner under the stained-glass windows, and sat with her head against the panelling, her eyes shut. Her face was set. Dolly wondered, trembling, what the daughter she had bossed and patronised, loved and scarcely admired, was going to do.

Elizabeth was not bleeding. She was young, vigorous and furiously angry and anger made her hot. Her outrage and bitterness with her cousin were far far stronger than with the selfish beauty he had married. Anger removed everything else. It was a flame on an alloy from which the gold emerged, bubbling.

What shall we do, she thought. What *can* we do? Does Peter actually think we'll beg him for some disgusting small sum in which to eke out our existence in that dilapidated old cottage? I haven't even a skill I can sell. I'm trained for nothing. If I'd thought two years ago about getting a job, I could support Mother and myself. At least we'd have some money apart from her poor little income. What *do* girls of my class without means do?

The answer was waiting. It was as if she were back at school and the class teacher had walked to the blackboard and chalked up in large letters:

MARRY.

She didn't stir. Dolly was nervously stroking the head of the spaniel. The room was very quiet.

Marry Ted? thought Elizabeth. The idea of marriage without love made her slightly sick. She imagined sex with Ted, bearing his children, life spent with that kindly hearty presence, that big burly body, that lack of comprehension. He offered her devotion. He did love her. She should be grateful.

And then for a moment she let emotion rip and remembered with searing inward sobs how she had lain in Peter's arms in the orchard, how they had kissed and how he'd lifted her up and put her in his lap. She had loved him so. She used the verb in the past.

She went to her mother and took her small hand.

'Don't look like that, darling. It's going to be all right.'

'What do you mean?'

'I shall marry Ted.'

Looking at her mother, she wondered curiously if Dolly had thought of that solution, and saw that she hadn't. There was nothing in Dolly's face but a dreadful blankness. She let her hand lie in her daughter's. She was not demonstrative, only pecked instead of kissing and rarely touched anybody but Peter. Now she gave Elizabeth's hand a convulsive clutch.

'Are you sure? You're not, you're not very keen on him, are you?'

'If you mean am I in love with him, darling, I'm certainly not. But he's a dear and I'm fond of him and he loves me. We can make a go of it. And he's rich.'

'I thought you'd do better than that.'

'Mother. We aren't in a slave market,' said Elizabeth.

But we are, she thought.

Dolly's migraine, usually a visitant bringing pain and vomiting but rarely coming twice in a year, returned with a

124

vengeance. It was a week since the funeral, and Dolly was again prostrate in a darkened room.

Peter telephoned twice. Elizabeth told Marchant to say her mother was unwell and that she was out. 'And if he telephones again,' added Elizabeth, 'tell him, Marchant, that Mother and I prefer to be alone for a while.'

Bursting with curiosity, the old man looked at her. The look said, 'I never heard such a thing in my life. Not see your cousin? Come on, tell your old friend.'

Avoiding his accusing eye, she went out of the house to the stables.

Snowball, snuffling and sending out a cloud of warm breath into the cold early spring air, trotted leisurely down the lane. Beads of moisture hung on the black thorn hedges. It was very still and Snowball's hooves did not ring out, but were muffled by a thin mud. Elizabeth rode the three miles until she reached a row of small cottages. Standing apart from them and set back from the road was Kiln Cottage.

There had been a pottery there in Tudor times which Garnett had sometimes talked about. 'I ought to do something about the old place. It has a certain historic interest.'

Old Mrs Widgen, a farmer's widow, had lived there since long before the 1914–18 war. A little old crone in black with a grey knitted shawl pinned round her shoulders. People in the village said she was a witch. When she had died Elizabeth had been about eight years old, and the cottage had been empty ever since. Its thatch had grown green with moss, its gate and fences had rotted into the grass . . .

She dismounted, looped the reins over the gatepost, and went into what had been the garden, and was now a wilderness of dead weeds. The house must have been pretty once upon a time. Part beamed, part old Elizabethan brick, its windows peered out from under the thatch like eyes. It was larger than the village cottages, and its garden had once been rich with hollyhocks and lupins. There had been a beehive. The farmer and his wife were respected by the labourers who worked for them. All had been busyness then. Ploughing, planting, harvesting, hedging and ditching, barns to repair, hoeing, planting again. The steady march of the seasons. Nothing was left but the rotting house and wind rustling in the dry-stalked weeds.

Peter could never have come here, or Sylvia either. She supposed they had gone through a list of Merriscourt properties.

She stood silently looking at the place.

Was Peter mad?

She rode home, and telephoned Ted at the Anstey works.

'So *there* you are!' cried a warm voice. 'It's days – and I didn't like to bother you. How are you bearing up?'

'Better. Could we meet?'

'I'll say. Tonight? Shall I collect you at home?'

'I'm going to be in Teignmouth,' lied Elizabeth. 'What about the hotel at six?' She did not want him to come to the house. She needed to be free of Merriscourt just now.

'Okay. See you in the bar. I *am* so glad you rang.'

Late in the afternoon, after a long walk with the dogs in the woods where she saw some coltsfoot, she went to her mother's room. It smelled of eau de cologne. A fire burned, as it had done for poor Garnett. The spaniel lay on the bed, and Dolly wore a wet flannel across her eyes like a blinded soldier. The room was not warm, but when Elizabeth took her mother's hand it was burning.

'Darling, don't *you* get ill.'

'I've been holding my hot water bottle.'

Elizabeth stood, tall in a dark tweed coat with the collar turned up.

'Mother. I'm going to Teignmouth this evening to meet Ted.'

'Elizabeth,' the voice was weak, 'don't do anything rash.'

A sardonic look crossed the girl's face; she was thinking of a roof of rotting thatch.

She bent and kissed Dolly.

'Leave things to me.'

It was the first time in her life she'd said such a thing.

126

She telephoned for a taxi since Ted would have his car. The big smelly old Morris which did station duty came for her. The driver gingerly negotiated the muddy lane. It was rather cold. As they reached the edges of the town, the rows of small houses shone with squares of light. She looked from the taxi window as every house went by – warm, snug, weatherproof, safe.

As she went through the swing doors into the hotel she had a sudden stab of sharp alarm. Supposing George Westlock was here. She hadn't set eyes on him for weeks, he had not been at the funeral, she did not know if he was still in Scotland. But she suddenly felt sure he was in Devon – talking to Sylvia about Speldhurst. What am I going to do if I see him?

There was no sign of a square-shouldered soldierly figure. Ted, always there before her, was alone in the bar. He sprang up.

'Lizzie, come and sit. You look very pale. What about trying a cocktail? I'm drinking a Sidecar. Like to risk one?'

She smiled and said no, she would be safer with some sherry, please.

'What a coward you are,' he said caressingly.

That, she thought, is what I'm not.

When they left the hotel it had grown colder and the night air struck her a little blow. The Alvis was as cold as the night, although he'd put up the hood. He wrapped her in a fur-lined rug.

'Tuck it round your feet. Such thin shoes.'

'Peter bought them for me.'

'Why am I never allowed to buy you things?'

Bending over, he kissed her cheek awkwardly. She responded, turning her face to him in the dark car and putting her arms round his neck. He kissed her on the mouth. The kiss did not make her melt or cause her heart to beat, she simply felt, as she always did, fond of him and quite, only quite, glad to be close. She said after a moment, 'You love me, don't you?'

'You know I do.'

'How much?'

'Don't tease, girl.'

'Tell me.'

'I adore you. Only you. You're the one for me. Sometimes just looking at you I feel my heart is going to break.'

It wasn't like him to say that.

She leaned closer, pressing her cheek against his. She smelled of jasmine scent. He touched her hair which fell across her forehead.

'I wish to God you'd marry me, Lizzie.'

She spoke, then, in a soft sweet voice.

'Do you?'

That was it.

Her mother received the news of Elizabeth's engagement with trance-like indifference. Elizabeth began to be seriously worried. The migraine finally ended and Dolly was up and dressed but she scarcely spoke and never went out of the house. She looked as if she were gravely ill. Her voice was so weak, her face so white, she ate nothing, and it was the apathy which most frightened Elizabeth. Where was the spark, the bossyness, the interest in life? Ted came to Merriscourt, bringing Dolly boxes of chocolates and bunches of spring flowers. He was shy and hearty, kissed her and called her 'future mother-in-law'. Dolly made a feeble attempt at congratulation and Elizabeth was grateful that Ted was too happy to notice how much her mother had altered.

After the message given to him by Marchant, Peter did not ring again. That, thought Elizabeth grimly, was to the good. It gave her time.

A few days after she'd accepted Ted, she rode Snowball to Whitefriars to see Topsy, having telephoned in advance.

'I want to talk, so try not to be in the stables for once.'

There was a giggle.

'Okay, but Josh will be annoyed.'

Topsy was looking out for her and the moment Elizabeth rode up the drive the front door opened and there was her friend in the jodphurs and yellow sweater which were her permanent costume in odd weather.

'Coffee's coming and David may peer in. The County

128

Court's late today. Don't worry, I won't let him stick around.'

'Why not?'

'Silly question. Is mourning going to stop you hunting, Liz? We've been out three times this week. You never saw such a turnout. Farmers and brewers and horse dealers. Three people came down across Tanners' Brook. I saw a groom dragging the water and he brought up a stirrup leather and an iron next day. He said "Master's hoss went in here." Too loyal to say Master went in too and floundered about like a whale.'

The girls sat down, and Topsy suddenly said, 'What's that ring?'

It was an emerald set in diamonds. Ted had produced it from his pocket two days ago.

'Well. It's an engagement ring.'

'I can see that. Who on earth – good grief, *it isn't Ted Anstey?*'

'Afraid so.'

'Liz, you are mad. What in the name of –'

Words failed her. She stared.

The maid came in with coffee, which gave Elizabeth a respite from the accusing blue eyes. When the door shut again Elizabeth spoke. She told Topsy briefly what had happened. At the news about Speldhurst Topsy went red with anger and began to stutter but Elizabeth leaned forward and gripped her hand.

'Don't. Don't. Don't say anything about either of them because you can't say a thing I haven't said and thought until I felt my head would split. But that's what happened. I rode over to see Kiln Cottage –'

'Falling to pieces?'

'Worse. So I'm marrying Ted and Mother, Ted says, can have whatever she likes, a house of her own, or a wing of ours. Whatever she likes.'

Topsy was silent for a moment. Then, 'I'll get David to help.'

'Topsy, please. I didn't come here to –'

'Don't be a fool, I know that. But David could do something. He'd give you and your mother a house where you could live rent free. There's The Lodge, I know it's hideous and in bad repair but we could smarten it up.'

Now in full spate, Topsy talked herself into the Bidwells making their home near Whitefriars. The Lodge was an ugly red brick house Elizabeth knew well, not as dilapidated as Kiln Cottage but still a cast-off old place which nobody wanted. Topsy, as generous as Ted in a different way, added to the offer of The Lodge an announcement that she would sell some old jewellery her mother had left her, stuff so old-fashioned nobody in their right mind would wear it, and that might bring in a bob or two to make the house attractive.

When the long speech ended Elizabeth said, 'No, Topsy. No. Thank you but I couldn't and I won't.'

'You mean you're fed up with being offered wrecks to live in. I don't blame you.'

'I mean I'll make a go of it with Ted.'

'You mustn't,' said Topsy. For once she was serious. 'I know what I'm talking about. It's true Daddy sort of forced me to marry David and I never put up any resistance, I was so *feeble*. But with me it was different because truly I didn't care. All I thought about was doing what Daddy wanted. And David's a nice old stick in some ways. But you won't be able to carry it off.'

Elizabeth fidgeted with the ring. It was heavy and slightly too large and kept slipping round the wrong way.

'Lizzie. Listen to me. How can it be right to marry Ted Anstey when you're still in love with somebody else?'

'I shall never love Peter again.'

'Oh balderdash. Love isn't like that. Hell, why am I arguing with you? Your mind's made up and you're as stubborn as a donkey. I could murder that bloody cousin of yours.'

'I came to tell you about Ted,' Elizabeth said, after a moment's silence, 'but also about something worse.'

'For God's sake, what could that be?'

'I'm scared about Mother. I think she might die.'

130

She described Dolly's listlessness and apathy. Nothing could rouse her. She was like a Victorian woman in a decline.

'She loves Peter,' Topsy said.

'As I did.'

Topsy noticed the past tense.

'Topsy, I can't just sit and watch her fade. She got over my father's death.'

'Not the same. Tragic, but not the same. Firstly, she was young. And then, she was *made* a widow by the war and women accepted such terrible things. And then she had your uncle to look after her, and Merriscourt and everything.'

'She's got me.'

'Sorry to be crude, but she needs a man. She's that sort of woman. Ten daughters marrying ten Ted Ansteys wouldn't do it. Why not see the vicar? He's a widower. He'll bring a touch of sex into the sickroom.'

Elizabeth thought the solution ludicrous.

'Don't put on that maiden-aunt face, Liz. I can't get you to live at The Lodge but I can tell you something you ought to know anyway. Your mother only listens to men.'

The following day, unwillingly, Elizabeth went to call on the vicar. She told him as little as possible about the break with Peter and a good deal about her mother's health. Mr Spencer, a long-nosed man with the face of a lawyer, was interested; and he liked Dolly Bidwell.

The cure was extraordinary. The stricken creature slowly began to recover. The telephone from the vicarage rang, and Mr Spencer arrived to be closeted for hours with Dolly. Dolly quoted him to her daughter.

'The vicar thinks I ought to go to London for a spell – stay with Great Aunt Bessy. He says I need a change.'

Pale and rather shaky, there was a glimmer of the old Dolly. 'Mr Spencer sometimes comes to London. He suggested we might go to a theatre.'

She never once spoke of Peter. He could have been dead.

There were signs of him everywhere. The books he had not taken to Speldhurst. The riding crop with the broken strap. A

131

pair of wellington boots in the scullery cupboard. Some silver cups Sylvia had laughed about ranged on a bookshelf in the drawing-room.

It was Topsy, during this curious limbo of a time, who raised the subject of Peter. Elizabeth had not seen him or Sylvia since the evening branded on her memory as if by a red-hot iron. On her mother's too. Both women were scarred.

Topsy rode over to Merriscourt and found her friend in the poky study, packing books into a near-mouldering cabin trunk.

'Rumour has it you've found a house.'

'Topsy, you hear everything. Yes, it's nice. Holcombe Cottage. Do you know it?'

'Of course I do. Off the Bovey Tracey road. Lovely and thatched and a ripping garden. Old Miss Eames lived there. Mad about irises.'

'That's the one. Shall we drive over and see it when you're free?'

Topsy said she'd liked to. There was a pause and Elizabeth added in a practical tone that Ted was going ahead with the details of the purchase and in the meantime her things were being sent to Broad Oaks. The Ansteys were storing them in their second garage.

'Vans appear and bear things painlessly away.'

'Is it painless?'

'Not very.'

Another pause.

'And have you told your cousin when he can take possession?'

'I wrote a line to Sylvia, giving the date and saying about my wedding. I told them it was to be private and I didn't ask them. No reply.'

She knelt on the floor, opened a Revelation suitcase and began to pack more books. They were dusty and she sneezed. She opened one.

' "Deare friend, sit down, the tale is long and sad", George Herbert.'

132

'Lizzie, turn round, stop making that mess. Doesn't anybody here dust your books? Apparently not. The tale *is* long and sad or it will be if you don't see Peter before you go.'

'I can't.'

'You have to.'

'Would you say the same to Mother?'

'That's a silly question. Your mother if forty-five and not twenty-two. She isn't a young forty-five either, and has just been punched in the jaw by the man she's loved since he was a child. You're a different matter. You must see your cousin for your own sake.'

'I'm fine.'

'Of course you're not. You can't marry Ted feeling the way you do. Peter did you a wrong. Tell him so or it'll go bad inside you. Tell him straight out and then forgive him.'

Elizabeth shuddered.

'No.'

Topsy scratched her nose, and asked for tea.

Unexpectedly, uncomfortably, while Elizabeth was still thinking about what Topsy had said, Peter rang. His low voice made her feel she was going to be sick.

'Lizzie? I thought we should meet. Shall I come to Merris –'

'No, not to the house,' she said, speaking fast and almost involuntarily. 'In the orchard. We'll be alone there. At six.'

'But it's dark then.'

'Bring a torch.'

She slammed down the receiver.

The weather had been changeable and there was a frost when she went out of the house and through the rose garden. Her mother was out at the vicarage. Nobody was about. She had forgotten her gloves and as she walked her hands were very cold. She plunged them uselessly into her pockets. Stiffened against the wind, every muscle ached.

Peter was late for everything, she thought, as her eyes grew used to the gloom and she made her way gingerly across the grass through the bare orchard. Uncut grass lay in mats like dead hair. This time she was wrong; a thin pencil of light shone under the tree where her swing hung in summer. She saw a dim shape.

'Liz? It's freezing, can't we –'

'No.'

She went nearer. He had placed the torch on the grass and the light threw a glimmer on both of them. Her heart thudded so hard against her ribs that she thought he must hear it. She found it difficult to speak.

'Listen and don't interrupt. And don't touch me – 'She started back as he moved. 'What I've got to say must be said and when it's over you can forget it. And me too.'

'Lizzie, don't be –'

'*Shut up and listen.* What you did to us was filthy. Despicable. You *know* how disgusting it is. You *know* how Mother feels. Don't imagine I don't realise you tried to dissuade Sylvia and argued and told her one doesn't turn out one's family and give one's home to a stranger. Of course George Westlock's a sort of relative, and he's her godfather, but what's that? My mother brought you up. *She loved you.* How did either of us love anybody capable of doing what you've done? All right. I've finished. You're madly in love with Sylvia and under her spell as if she's a sort of witch. But whatever your passion for her, and I'd loathe to hear about it, you disgust me.'

Silence. Her heart knocked. She felt exhausted and sick.

'Everything you say is true, Liz.'

'What the hell does that mean?'

'Nothing. I can't ask you to forgive me. But I do. Perhaps you'll understand one day.'

She made a noise of savage scorn.

'When I'm older? When I'm crazy about a man as you are about her? Don't fool yourself, I shall *never* understand. I can't be your enemy. I'd like to be, and at present I hate you for having made Mother ill. Oh yes, she's been ill. I thought she might die. Going on hating you would be a kind of hideous satisfaction like lighting a fire and throwing hate on it to keep warm. But it's no good. It won't last and anyway you're my flesh and blood. In the future we'll behave normally, I daresay. When I get back from my honeymoon. I don't care about any of that. What's important is for you to make it right with Mother. She's better but it's too soon. Not now. Do it later.'

'I'll do anything.'

His voice was so low that she could scarcely hear it. Her eyes were used to the dark now and the starlight seemed like broad day. She saw the patterns of the bare apple branches, the matted icy hair of the grass and Peter's round face. He was bareheaded and wore an old coat which had belonged to his father, the collar turned up.

'So. I've had my say.'

'I'm glad.'

She turned to go back to the house, which dimly shone above the slope of lawns.

'Lizzie.'

'Yes?'

'Don't sound so hard. You hate me now, I know, but – but time goes by.'

'How true.'

He ignored the cruel voice.

'Are you marrying Ted because –'

'What do you think? Would you rather I threw myself on Sylvia's mercy? Much good that would do me.'

'I'm sure he'll make you happy.'

'Oh yes. And all's for the best in the best of all possible worlds. How handy. I don't want to talk to you any more. You and Sylvia can have Merriscourt next week. And when Ted and I get back, and Mother's living with us, everything will calm down. I suppose. I wanted to see you tonight to tell you what I think of you. If anything was a sin, that was. I bet you pay for it in the end. I'm told one always does.'

She suddenly turned and began to run.

It took him by surprise. He shouted 'Lizzie.' But it was to the air. The empty frozen air.

PART TWO

Summer – 1936

Chapter Nine

The stout lady in green silk sat in a deck-chair on the lawn. The canopy of the chair was up but she had not adjusted it, and strong Devon sun glared down on her freckled face. Her hair, gingery and touched-up as she called it, was frizzled into girlish curls on her forehead. She fanned herself with a copy of *Country Life*.

'There you are, son. Give your old ma a kiss.'

Ted Anstey bent over her. She looked up fondly. He wore his navy blue business suit and the old school tie which Lily Anstey revered. His father had been to a board school, and Lily's respect both for Curly, because he couldn't, and Ted because he could wear a certain pattern of tie was immense.

Broad Oaks basked in the afternoon light. The Ansteys had lived there now for over three years and the additions to the house, bow-windows stuck onto a simple frontage, the Tudor-style wing and new garage, no longer shocked the eye. The house was like an ill-dressed but wealthy woman, it looked prosperous. Lily had thought its name annoying when she discovered there wasn't an oak in the sprawling grounds. She made the gardener plant some oak saplings. He was disagreeable over that. 'They'll not settle,' he kept saying. And was turning out to be right.

Lilian sat waiting for her son and her tea. She was a happy woman. Happy in her husband whom she'd loved since their marriage in far-off Edwardian days. Curly had been quite poor, but had promised her great things and kept his promises. Of course they had had worries. After a successful start and much prosperity during the war when his workshops were used to make small munitions, after the excitements of

Anstey garages spreading across southern England in the 1920s, and showrooms for selling new cars, the 1930 Depression had struck Curly and the country a fierce blow. During the next four years he had come home at night with a face dark with anxiety. He'd had stomach-ache about work. But now in 1936 prosperity was back, both for England and Harold Anstey. Business grew as you watched. Curly had never looked better.

There was just one thing needed to make life perfect, and it astonished Lilian that there was no sign of it. That handsome, friendly, upper-class daughter-in-law of hers was still childless after over two years. Why?

'And how's Elizabeth?' said Lilian, when Ted rejoined her.

'Blooming.'

He waited. Sure enough, she said, 'Hasn't fallen yet?'

This was her curious phrase for getting pregnant. When they were alone she always asked it. How he wished she wouldn't.

'No, Ma, and when she does you'll be the first to know. Not every woman starts a baby just because she wants one. It can take time.'

'I was only six weeks before I fell with you.'

'You were lucky.' He wondered how many times they'd had this conversation.

'Oh well. We must be thankful you married such a nice girl. Good-looking. Smart as paint. And one of the county too. I get asked to them – those – vicarage parties.'

The maid whose name was Dorrit and whom Lilian bullied, came across the lawns with the tray which she put down on a garden table. Lilian issued a few sharp orders. Had she made the doughnuts fresh this afternoon? Not from the village shop, were they? Dorrit's pink face looked stormy. She was not, thought Ted, going to last – but when did Ma's maids ever last? She chivvied them. Drinking his tea, he waited for the right moment to introduce an uncomfortable subject. It was for this that he'd left the works early and driven the sixty-five twisting and lonely roads as fast as the Alvis

140

would bring him. He wanted to speak to her alone; he managed her better without his father there.

Lilian loved her son as much as Dolly Bidwell had once loved her nephew. But in any clash of wills or opinions, Lilian deferred to her husband. She was a wife in a million. She darned and sorted socks, ironed shirts because the maid did not do them the way Curly liked, cleaned his shoes with her own hands, and was always at home, expectant, when the Daimler drove up and Curly came into the house. He would collapse into a large armchair and talk about work, and Lilian would listen in rapt silence. She knew he was a brilliant businessman. He could push and shove, and he liked to win, but above all he had vision. He'd made money in the war, true, but he'd seen when peace came that the whole attitude to motors had changed. All the prejudices disappeared 'like cavalry on the battlefront' Harold said. Cars weren't rare any more. The war had been a marching war, he said, but millions of men had ridden in motor transport, and hundreds of thousands, including women, learned to drive. Cars were going to be popular, and no longer only the property of the rich. More people would buy cars, and would need to have them serviced. So the Anstey showrooms and garages began.

Ted had none of Curly's vision or push. He wasn't clever; at school he excelled in games. He seemed to have no sense of danger and when he was in the rugby team at school Ted had more broken bones, concussion, large cuts and purple bruises than any other boy. His tennis was ferocious. He drove fast and well. But in friendship, filial love and work, he was as meek and stupid as an ox. The only rash thing he'd done in his life was to marry Elizabeth Bidwell.

He'd been staggered when she said yes. She was not only wonderfully attractive, she was upper class, lived in an ugly old place covered with gargoyles which had belonged to the family since the year dot. She was above Ted but he'd won her. What a triumph. His parents agreed with him. On the night he came bursting into the house with the news, the first thing Lilian said was; 'Now, Curly, how much shall you settle

141

on the boy?' Followed by, 'Tell you what. We must buy you a nice comfy house.'

What a blessing money was, Lilian often thought, reaching for a lizard-skin handbag in which she kept bundles of clean pound notes and crinkling white fivers. She loved giving money to her son. Now she also had a daughter-in-law, and when Elizabeth visited her, Lilian dived into her handbag, said, 'buy yourself a little something' and winked. She then stuffed money into Elizabeth's pocket. The first time this happened Elizabeth had laughed and protested, but she saw at once that that wouldn't do. Lilian was hurt. Now with her pockets full of money, all Elizabeth did was kiss her mother-in-law and be grateful. Lilian was like a duke in a Shakespeare play who presents a bag of coins to his page, saying, 'Spend this for me.'

Mother and son finished their tea, shadows on the grass stretched long fingers, birds whistled, and the two strolled up a path between lavender hedges loud with bees. Broad Oaks, enriched, enhanced, resembled its owners now. It had grown stout and generous. Big French windows, windowsills wider than other sills, beams painted shiny black and double the size of those used by Elizabethan workmen. The lounge had three settees, huge flower pictures in white frames and as many as six bowls of sweet peas, freshly picked each morning from the garden.

Lilian sat down on one of the settees.

'What's been happening at the works? Didn't Curly say you have to go to Italy again? Seems only yesterday you were there. Does that mean you won't be coming to Sunday dinner?'

'I'm afraid so, Ma. Dad's interested in the new Fiats, they're making damned great motors which can take seven. He thinks we might sell some, with business looking better.'

'Yes, thank goodness. It's all been such a worry,' said Lilian. 'Your Dad's a different man these days.'

They talked for a while, and Ted finally came to the point.

'Lizzie may be going to London for a day or two while I'm

in Milan. To see that old aunt who lives in Bloomsbury. Remember her, Ma? You met her at the wedding.'

'Bessy Bidwell? Of course I remember her. She gave you the lemonade set. Cut glass.'

'Lizzie's very fond of the old dear,' he said, hoping he sounded casual. 'Always writing to her.'

'It's arranged then? Her going to London?' said Lilian sharply.

'Yes. She telephoned her aunt yesterday.'

'You could have asked me first.'

'She has to see her relatives now and then.'

'Your father and I are her closest relatives.'

'Ma! She has a perfectly good mother –'

'Away since I don't know when.'

'That's true. She's staying in Sussex, but they write and ring each other up all the time. And then there's Peter and Sylvia.'

'Don't talk to me about them. Much good they've done for your wife or Dolly Bidwell either.'

Knowing nothing, Lilian had inklings.

'Oh, Ma.'

'No, Ted, it's no good you thinking you can get away with that. I don't like that Peter Bidwell or his wife either. However, if Elizabeth won't come to Broad Oaks while you're away, she won't, and we'll have to put up with it. Tell her,' added Lilian with meaning, 'I'm hurt.'

The worst was over. She was soon pouring Ted a tankard of beer and asking if he planned to take Elizabeth to the hunt ball. It was true she'd been offended at her daughter-in-law choosing some gaga old aunt instead of herself, and Bloomsbury instead of the cornucopia of Broad Oaks. But she was never cross for long.

When Ted was leaving, he hugged her, lifting all twelve dumpy stone of Lilian off her feet. When he set her down she looked round for the lizard-skin handbag.

'No, Ma, not a farthing.'

'Don't you be cheeky, what makes you think I'm giving you anything?'

143

She produced a five-pound note and pushed it into his jacket pocket.

'You're the giddy limit,' he said, bursting into loud laughter. She stood at the door, waving, as he drove away.

Marriage, said the old country poem,

was much like a Devonshire lane.
In the first place, 'tis long, and when once you're in it
It holds you as fast as a cage does a linnet;
For howe're rough and dirty, the road may be found
Drive forward you must, there is no turning round.

Elizabeth agreed. She had a good practical Devon head and settled down to make her marriage a success, to be fond of her husband, be a good wife, and enjoy the novelty of money. Ted believed she had accepted him suddenly because of grief at losing her uncle, followed by a realisation that she loved him, Ted, after all. Previous to the night when she'd agreed to be his wife, Ted had always had something faint and uneasy in his mind which told him Elizabeth was in love with her cousin. He tried to get rid of the notion. First cousins didn't marry, did they? Medical men said that was in-breeding, and you could have kids that were a bit funny, a bit loony even, if you married somebody related so closely. In some of the villages he had seen children who were not quite right in the head, and Lilian had said 'in breeding' in the voice of somebody who knew what she was talking about. But soon his doubts had vanished, for Peter had fallen for that good-looking blonde. And Elizabeth had accepted *him*. What luck for me, thought Ted. What damned good luck.

Elizabeth was also deeply conscious of her good luck. Ted was a good, loving husband. He was touchingly generous and it almost hurt her to see how good he'd been to Dolly at the time of their marriage. Still shocked by Peter's treachery, Elizabeth had burst into tears when Ted suggested building an extra wing on their new house for her mother. Or should he borrow some money from his father, and buy Dolly her own house?

But after the wedding Dolly showed a surprising independence. The long talks with the vicar had restored her self-esteem. Thanking Ted with a touch of patronage, she explained that she was going to London to stay in Bloomsbury for a while with Great Aunt Bessy. When she heard this, Elizabeth went privately to London, saw the solicitors, and made over her own small inheritance from her uncle to Dolly, on the proviso that Dolly should not be told.

'It seems I'm not as poverty-stricken as I thought,' Dolly confided later. 'How grateful I am to dear Garnett for another little nest-egg.'

Without the expense and worry of an unmarried daughter, Dolly queened it at the hotel to an admiring audience of elderly ladies. Later she went to stay with her old friend Maud Entwistle in Sussex, discovering in her late forties the charm of a little travelling. She found she was a social success. Away from the great old house, poor ailing Garnett and her over-fondness for the nephew who betrayed her, Dolly blossomed. Elizabeth was glad – but piqued.

As a wedding present for his son, Harold Anstey bought the couple Holcombe Cottage, which had nothing cottagey about it. It was medieval, half timbered, half brick, with barley-sugar Tudor chimneys and a good deal of 1910 embellishment by Edward Lutyens. Its previous elderly owner, the lady who wrote poetry and grew irises, had been a sentimental gardener, and the gardens in all but a brief winter season rioted with great bushes of old-fashioned flowers. Other romantic additions made by the poetess were a fish pool where goldfish became every year fatter and darker and where red waterlilies grew, a sundial with the bronze figure of a child and a frog, and pergolas that in summer hung with Dorothy Perkins roses like fat bunches of pink grapes.

In Holcombe's low-ceilinged rooms and bee-haunted bird-visited gardens, Elizabeth finally understood the expression 'comfortably off'.

Ted had few surprises; he was the man she had thought him, hearty and good-natured and as lavish with money as his mother. He preferred men to women, beer and cider to sherry and wine. He loved her and in a way neglected her. He liked men friends, country pubs, and the feel of a tankard in his hand. Sometimes after a couple of hours in a favourite pub near the estuary at Shaldon, he came home rather drunk. She disliked the stupid look on his face, and his kisses smelled of beer. Drink made him amorous. But unlike the porter's description in Shakespeare's superstitiously feared play, it did not take away the performance – he was not made impotent by drink. His lovemaking was always the same, over in five minutes, leaving her with the feeling that she had been raped.

The only trouble in their marriage was that. Sex. A short word, thought Elizabeth, and a short subject. She'd known almost nothing about sex when she had worn her white satin nightdress on her wedding night. Ted, taking her, called her his little virgin. So she had been even in thought, except for her yearning for her cousin – and to remember that was not to be borne.

Ted would never talk about sex. The big masculine man who won at tennis, who liked trying his strength at the fairground, the male creature with male jokes and male friends, was more shrinking than a convent-bred girl on the subject of lovemaking. He never spoke a word about his previous sexual experience, and when once she asked him to tell her about it, he blushed a dull red and said it must never be spoken about.

When he wanted her, he wore a most ridiculous expression. He lay in bed while she undressed, with a little-boy face, calling her silly names. 'Ogle Pogle.' Things like that. It always meant sex. Then there would be a brief unsatisfying mating. Is that all there is, is that really all there is? she thought. But what was the use of the question. She pushed it out of her mind which, in any case, had another and different anxiety. After more than two years of marriage, she had not yet conceived.

If I can't enjoy sex with him, at least we could make a baby, she thought. I'm healthy and so is he. She knew he wanted one as much as she did, but it was another subject he wouldn't talk about. Everything tender, hurt-able, soft, private, must be hidden. She had no idea what he felt about painful intimacies; he fled from them to become the hearty beer-drinker with the loud laugh.

Sometimes she wondered at her capacity to be content with Ted Anstey. Where was her passionate love for her cousin? Where indeed? She did not hate him as she'd done on the night in the freezing orchard. Two years of marriage had changed her; she had recovered, and forgiven Peter. But her feelings for him were not the same. Love must have care and food, exercise and sun. Her love for her cousin had grown thin, poor thing. It should have been given a tonic. Benger's Food, Dolly used to say, did wonders for invalids; Elizabeth's love for Peter would have needed tinfuls of the sweet cloying stuff.

Peter and Sylvia were away, no doubt deliberately, at the time of Elizabeth's wedding and did not return until she was on her honeymoon, and Dolly had left for Bloomsbury. The move from Merriscourt was well organised by the Ansteys, and both Elizabeth's and Dolly's possessions carefully crated. When Elizabeth and Ted took over their new home, Dolly telephoned to say 'take what you want from my things, my child, I don't need them.' But Harold advised her to leave her mother's possessions in store.

'You never know. She'll be wanting them one day.'

He rather admired Dolly .

It was a couple of months before Elizabeth set eyes on her cousin. She used to think it extraordinary as the spring of 1934, her first married year, went by, to realise that a few miles away the big bunches of primroses were brought indoors at Merriscourt for good luck, and that Inslow for the first year since she was born would not put up the swing. That Marchant would serve tea. And Peter sprawl in the drawing-room.

Topsy talked about the Bidwells occasionally and never charitably.

147

'David and I went to cocktails the other night – guess where! To Speldhurst, to the sexy George. Your benighted cousin and his wife were there. He never uttered and she never stopped. Sorry, I know you don't want to talk about them. I can mention George, though, can't I?'

'Don't be stupid.'

'He still is very sexy-looking,' said Topsy thoughtfully. 'One doesn't exactly know why, but he is. The eyes? I wish I knew. Anyway, he rattles about like a pea in a box at Speldhurst. It's much too large for one man. It's all marvellously tidy, it might be the officers' mess, he practically lines up the drinks at attention. What a fancy-looking place for one ex-soldier.'

'Perhaps he'll marry.'

'Perhaps he won't.'

There was to be the usual vicarage garden party at the end of May, and although neither Topsy nor Elizabeth mentioned it, they both knew the Bidwells would be there. Even Sylvia would not be able to avoid making an appearance because the vicar, Mr Spencer, wouldn't let her get away with it. Elizabeth decided to go. Meeting her cousin again had to be done. It was like the prospect of the first flayingly cold swim in Teignmouth at this time of the year.

When she arrived on the afternoon of the party at the vicarage the sun was warmly shining, and there wasn't a flower in sight. Only green buds, for the spring flowers were gone, and the summer ones biding their time. The first person she saw was Marchant. He was in charge of the bran tub. Elizabeth ran up to him – they beamed at each other. The old man looked as if he couldn't get enough of the sight of his Mistress's daughter in her black and white checks, wearing a straw hat with long velvet ribbons.

'This is a brave good day for me, Miss Elizabeth.'

'Dear Marchant. Me too.'

'Have a pennyworth. Never know what you'll pull out of the tub, do you?'

Something in his eyes, the way for a moment he looked beyond her, made her guess. She turned and saw Peter and Sylvia on the terrace. She felt slightly faint.

'Come along, Miss, dig deep and see what the king will give you.'

She was unwrapping a package containing a wooden spoon when a voice not as lazy as she remembered said, 'Lizzie?'

'Hello, Peter.'

Of the trio who walked across the grass, leaving Marchant coping with a crowd of children, Sylvia was the natural one. Peter said little and Elizabeth had to turn away from him to listen to Sylvia who was chatting vivaciously. She wore white organdie and a drooping crinoline hat from under which she peered, smiling.

'Your hat's topping, Lizzie, I love black and white. I bet you bought it in London. Isn't mine dire? Peter chose it and I told him it would make me go cross-eyed. Where's Ted? I need to ask him about the car, I broke down *four times* on the way to Exeter.'

She described being rescued by two men, one enormous, one smaller than she was, 'a sixty year old tot'. The large one was covered in spots and she was certain it was chicken pox. She made her listeners laugh, and when Ted appeared, he laughed too. It was the old club of admiration – but one member was missing.

'Where is your godfather?' asked Elizabeth, thinking she might as well meet them all while she was about it.

'I tried to get him to come but he kept stalling,' said Sylvia. 'It's all because of that horrible-looking bird.'

'A peregrine falcon,' translated Peter. 'George is training one.'

Elizabeth, surprised and curious, asked questions. Peter explained that a village boy, apparently a daring cliff climber, had managed to steal a young falcon from its nest on the cliffs: a dangerous operation. More by luck than judgement he'd stolen a bird which was nearly fledged but had not left the nest.

149

'George heard about it and offered to buy it. It seems he did some hawking when he was in Mespot,' said Peter. 'Did you know, Liz, he was liaison officer to a sheikh? He told me the Arabs have a tradition of hawking, they use the birds to hunt bustards . . . well, now he's busy training his own bird which is almost full-grown now.'

'Hideous thing,' said Sylvia.

'Syl hates it,' said Peter lazily.

'Because *it* hates *me*. It has eyes just like a devil's and George spends all his time with the beastly thing. I believe the only reason he lives at Speldhurst now is because of that bird.'

Was there a tremor in the air when the house was mentioned? Elizabeth wasn't sure. Her cousin looked at his wife as if she were an entertaining child.

'You should see her in the fields when George lets the hawk fly,' he said. 'She practically dives under the hedge.'

'So the feud's over at last,' said Topsy, arriving at Holcombe the following day. 'Intriguing. What did it feel like, talking to them?'

'One moment of panic, then perfectly natural.'

'How was she?'

'More beautiful than ever, and happy, I should guess.'

'Oh good. I was worried about that,' said Topsy with heavy sarcasm. 'And your cousin?'

Elizabeth thought for a moment or two.

'Do you know, I didn't find him changed at all. Why did I think I would? It was rather an anti-climax. After all the drama. I really did *loathe* him. I could have killed him. And there we all were drinking tea with the vicar, and somebody put on a wheezy old record of *You're Blasé.*'

'You're bored When you're adored, You're blasé,' sang Topsy, laughing.

The girls were in the garden, Bob the airedale, Bill the mongrel, sitting on the grass nearby. Chloe the spaniel had left Devon with her mistress and become a dog who travels in trains.

Elizabeth mentioned George and the falcon, and Topsy said David had called at Speldhurst once and seen the bird – he had said it was magnificent.

'George is doing okay, isn't he? Country life. Hawking. And that nice big house. One does wonder how he pulled it off.'

'You're not saying *he* engineered it?'

'Perhaps.'

'But it was all Sylvia. It couldn't have been him!'

'Oh, I don't know . . .' said Topsy airily. 'Men are odd about property, look at the way Daddy went on. They're possessive. Grabbing's a better word. Maybe George always wanted to keep a hawk and live round here, and there was Speldhurst – just the thing. By the way, you remember that rumour I told you about? The affair in Scotland. I hear it's all over and done with.'

'Poor Lady Priscilla.'

'Yes, that was her name, how *did* you know!'

'Sylvia mentioned her living in Skye. And my mother met her once when George was very young.'

'So, you do see,' said Topsy. 'The Hieland lassie and George have parted by the loch. "Farewell, there's a bonnie great house awaiting me in the South." You can't help admiring George. He manages his life so neatly.'

Disturbed, Elizabeth said nothing.

'Then back he comes to Sylvia. He would, wouldn't he? You've always thought he was rather in love with her . . .'

Topsy peered at her friend.

'Hell. Now you're taking me seriously. I was only advancing one or two bitchy theories. Take no notice of me, Liz. I talk too much. Anyway, what do you care? Holcombe is a hundred times prettier than Speldhurst, and you wouldn't mind if George had fifty houses. It's all in the past. Golly, I must rush or Josh will be annoyed and he's such a bore when he sulks.'

Elizabeth raised her eyebrows.

'Does that matter?'

Topsy looked at her with a bland, laughing face.

'Oh, but I like Josh in a good mood, not a bad one.'

It was Peter, wandering into the spacious bedroom which for so long had been his aunt's realm, who opened the subject. Sylvia was sitting at her dressing-table painting her face. She had changed for dinner into black silk and pearls, and was carefully putting on the dark red lipstick, the colour of clove carnations, which this year was the newest fashion. She looked absently at him in the glass as he bent to kiss her neck.

'You smell expensive,' he said.

'I am.'

'I've noticed.'

'Worth every penny, wouldn't you say?'

'So far.' He pressed his face against her bare shoulder; the dress had shoe-lace straps.

'Do stop, darling, that tickles.'

He sat down on the window-seat and looked at his shoes, a habit of his. He had also changed, he was wearing a dinner jacket. Black and white suited him. Sylvia often reflected with satisfaction on how well her husband wore his clothes, she was not sure why it was that he made other men look like nothing; except George, of course.

'How did you think it went? Meeting Lizzie,' he said, after staring at his shoes for inspiration.

Sylvia began on her eyebrows, and remarked that Lizzie looked fine and that silk dress was topping.

'Ted,' she said, underlining it, 'is obviously generous.' She enjoyed flicking Peter and waited for him to rise, to exclaim, to object, but this time it did not work. He spoke absently.

'She's come on,' he said.

'I thought Ted looked rather good too. He's the open-air type, I bet he plays a marvellous game of tennis. Let's ask him round.'

'Them round, you mean.'

'Peter, don't be stupid, of course I mean both. As if we'd ask Ted without your cousin. As I say, let's ask them round.

We should have done it ages ago, I suppose.'

'We couldn't possibly.'

Sylvia raised her fine eyebrows and swivelled on the dressing-table stool to look at him.

'You can't be talking about all that old trouble with Speldhurst. Look how it turned out for the best. I told you it was a storm in a teacup. You take things so seriously. Now,' said Sylvia, spreading out a hand as if describing places on a map, 'there is your blessed cousin married to a man with the best teeth in Devonshire, your aunt setting the pace in London, and my godfather boring us to death with those horrible birds of prey. If you ask *me*, we should have given George a hovel, then he couldn't have taken up anything so ghastly. Let's tell him he can't have Speldhurst after all, shall we? That'd take the smile off his face.'

She came across the room to Peter, knelt between his legs and put her arms round his waist. She looked up with a face as innocent and impish as a child's.

'You're not going to be broody, are you, darling? I don't enjoy it when you're broody. It doesn't suit your style one bit. Now, let me see, how would you look if I made you shave off your moustache?'

She put a finger across his upper lip and studied him, her head on one side.

'Not nearly so sexy.'

After the first meeting in May 1934, Elizabeth and Ted began to see a little of the Bidwells, and a sort of friendship was re-established. Ted, naturally sociable, was pleased. He had always liked Peter and once again they talked about cars. Sylvia was charming to Elizabeth and often commented favourably on her clothes which she saw were expensive.

Now and then the Ansteys were asked to dine at Merris-court. The first time this happened Elizabeth was sure it would upset her, but it did not. The house was changed. The little blushing Kathleen was gone, new servants were about, the food was more elaborate and Marchant approvingly served the best wine in the Bidwells' Georgian glasses. Elizabeth thought her old home even smelled different: less of beeswax, flowers and dogs, more of French scent and Egyptian cigarettes.

There was never an occasion, during the following two years, when they went to Merriscourt without George being invited. She had grown fond of George, particularly after the night he had taken her home in the horse-drawn cab. They'd been friendly together. But the fact was that Topsy's theory stuck and she found herself looking at him differently. Had he caused that cruel family division, was he capable of such selfishness? She wondered if anybody could actually know what anybody else *was* capable of doing. Could she have imagined ever that her cousin would do what he did? And although her wound was healed, Dolly's was not. She never spoke Peter's name – it was as if he had died to her. Sometimes, glancing at George, Elizabeth was certain it had all been caused by him. He was tough and her cousin must have been the poor besotted pawn.

And her feelings for Peter were changed, too, as Merriscourt had changed – they had a different smell. They were wavering and faint and sometimes they evaporated altogether. There were times when she thought he knew that. But they were rare.

It was very hot on the afternoon when Ted drove to break the news to his mother that Elizabeth was going to London. She had spent the afternoon under the trees in the garden, reading, after having had an early chilly swim in Teignmouth after breakfast.

The Holcombe gardens, like those at Merriscourt, were on one of the country's innumerable hills which sloped and climbed, and even lying on the grass with cushions was uncomfortable. There were no woods near the house, and the shade of the crab-apple tree was thin. Bob panted. Bill lay as if felled. Elizabeth's thoughts went to fly-haunted ponds, to quarries and sand-pits in deep shade, to the long leaves of now dead bluebells and the bridle path through the hazel woods. It was so long since she and the dogs had been there. She felt a moment of homesickness, not for the house but for the woods themselves, the log which in autumn was covered in crimson fungus, the trees she'd climbed, swaying from high branches and singing.

When she stood up and called the dogs they recognised the tone and pricked up their ears.

She parked her blue Austin Seven by a gate leading to a clover field. The dogs knew it well, leaped from the car the moment she opened the door, pushing her aside and scrabbling to squeeze under the gate. Across the field was the short cut through the woods to Merriscourt, which she and Peter took as children sometimes when they were late. Once, when she was about eleven, she had climbed the gate in a hurry, jumped from the top bar and landed in a heap, putting out the cartilege in her knee. Peter carried her on his back all the way home, and afterwards the place was called Agony Gate.

The dogs rushed into the clover and vanished, and she followed slowly, looking about, hearing the sound of bees, smelling the grass and sweet clover. Bob galloped up to her and disappeared again. At the edge of the woods she caught Bill and put him on the lead; as of old, he must not be allowed to hunt. Bob reappeared, and they went into the shadow of the trees.

It was a pain and a pleasure to be on Merriscourt land again. The hazel trees were in full leaf and she saw clusters of unripe nuts. There were the thick rosettes of broad primrose leaves, flowerless now, and in sunny patches the spikes of pink foxgloves which Devonshire people call Flopadocks. The place spoke. Its voice was old and faint and she had to listen carefully; it sounded cracked and ill, as her love for Peter was. I'll come again, she promised the voice. I'll walk here in snow, and bluebell time, and in the autumn. Looking through the trees, she was sure the trunks had thickened. And did martins still nest in the sand-pit?

'Why, Elizabeth!'

It was George Westlock standing right in her path. He was

dressed in white flannels and a blazer, incongruous, sporting, his fair hair plastered back as if he'd brushed it a moment ago.

'Hello,' was all she said. She whistled for Bob. She could scarcely bear to bring herself to look at him. On the occasions when she met him at Merriscourt, she rarely spoke directly to him. And here he was, spoiling the afternoon.

'Aren't you a long way from home?' he pleasantly said.

'Yes, I am.'

'You know these woods like the back of your hand, of course. I've told Peter they need to be thinned. By the pond there's a real mess, and has been since old Inslow was laid up.'

'What is wrong with Inslow?' she asked sharply.

'Didn't your cousin tell you? Broke his hip, poor chap. Fell eight feet into the quarry. He's still very lame and it hurts him to walk. Your cousin and Ferrers will have to do something about the woods. Want to take a look?'

'No, thank you.'

'Are you sure? You might have more effect on Peter than I do. Merriscourt's always been your baby.'

'Not any more.'

She didn't want to stay. Didn't want to hear about the woods decaying and Inslow's broken hip.

'I must go.'

'You're in a great hurry, Elizabeth.'

'I have to get back.'

'But weren't you walking *towards* the house? Were you coming to call? We've been playing tennis which is why I'm in flannels, but Peter and Sylvia have gone out. Didn't you see my car by Agony Gate?'

His use of the old name made her furious.

'I saw a car. I had no idea whose it was.'

'I often park there and walk across the field. Peter's idea. Last week I saw a hare.'

'I wasn't going to the house.' She stopped to pat Bob.

'A walk in the woods? May I come too?'

There was nothing for it.

'I'd rather you didn't.'

156

He made a curious grimace. And remained standing in her path.

'Out with it.'

'What do you mean?'

'You know perfectly well. You make it only too plain when we meet that you have changed your opinion of me. You dislike me now. I've wanted to ask why, but your husband's always there, so how can I? Then I've thought, she's has a perfect right to dislike me if she wants to. Who am I to expect anyone, let alone a pretty woman, to want my company. But we *were* friends, Elizabeth. Something happened. What was it?'

She hesitated. She was blunt and she had a sudden quite violent desire to tell him what she thought of him. Topsy's theory had stuck all right. There he stood, doubtless on excellent terms with himself. She wanted to hit at that pride.

'Spit it out,' he said.

But she only said, 'I don't want to talk to you.' She suddenly felt she couldn't bear to open the healed wound.

He put out his hand and actually stopped her walking by. He held her arm.

'Let me go.'

'No, Elizabeth. You're going to tell me what this is about.'

'I'm not going to. Let me pass.'

'I'm afraid not. Have you any idea how absurd this is? It's been going on now too long – the moment you see me your whole face changes, you even try not to look in my direction and if I speak to you you scarcely answer. People have noticed it, I might say. Sylvia thinks it an enormous joke and rags me about it. I don't think it funny at all. Just tell me what the hell is wrong.'

'No.'

'That's a pity because we'll stay here until you do.'

She tried to pull away, he gripped her more firmly, and Bob gave a long threatening growl, showing his teeth. Elizabeth knew her dog and the noise alarmed her.

'If you don't stop grabbing me Bob will bite you, and that

wouldn't be at all funny. Very well. If you must hear, you must. You won't like it.'

He let her go. The dog, fur up, continued to threaten.

'Shut up, Bob, it's all right,' she said, stroking him until the growls died away.

'Yes, it's true,' she said, looking straight at George Westlock, 'I do dislike you. I didn't at first. You're related to the family and I was willing to be friends. But after what happened I changed.'

'What are you talking about?'

'Don't pretend you don't know.'

'For God's sake!' he exclaimed angrily, 'I do *not* know. What happened?'

'You took Speldhurst.'

'*I did what?*'

'You took the house where my mother and I were going to live. When Uncle died, and we had to leave Merriscourt, did you imagine we weren't certain we'd go to Speldhurst? It belongs to our family. My great uncle lived and died there. You knew, because Sylvia tells you everything, how little Mother and I inherited from my uncle. We had almost nothing. So what happened? Peter coolly told us that you were to have the house. Poor godfather George needs a home,' she said savagely. 'What did you think *we'd* do? Oh, Sylvia was most thoughtful. We could have Kiln Cottage, it would be so cosy. It certainly would, the roof fell in a few months later. Are you surprised I don't like you? You took away our home. *You*. A single man with no family calmly moved in, and as far as you were concerned we could go to hell.'

She had talked fast, her cheeks flaming, and she suddenly stopped. For what seemed to the excited girl the time a man needs to think of a lie he was silent. She was too taken up with her anger to see that he looked even angrier. He was very white.

'None of that is true.'

She gave something like a laugh.

'You're *there*, aren't you?'

158

'Yes. I was glad to have the house. But I didn't know I was taking it from you and your mother.'

'I don't believe you.'

'Believe me or not, I don't give a b – a damn. You prefer to think it, don't you? You enjoy casting me as the enemy.'

'So you're putting *me* in the wrong!'

'I am simply telling you the plain truth. I did not know, and would not have dreamed of taking the bloody house had I been told. I heard your mother was leaving for London and that you were getting married.'

'That's a lie. All that happened afterwards. When we were homeless. After they'd said Speldhurst was yours.'

They glared at each other. He was markedly silent. Finally, he said, 'I repeat that I did not know anything about this. Sylvia didn't tell me the truth. For whatever reason, she behaved wrongly.' He stopped and then said, 'Is that why you married so suddenly?'

She blushed deeply for the second time.

'Do you imagine I'd marry the first man who came along merely because of what you did?'

He stepped towards her, she backed away and he took hold of her hands, gripping them so hard that she gasped aloud. The dog growled loudly.

'Elizabeth I refuse, I simply refuse to take the blame. I'm damned if I'll be Sylvia's scapegoat. Ask your cousin.'

'I couldn't talk to him about it again.'

'Did he tell you it was my idea?'

'No. It was only afterwards that I was sure –'

'I engineered it,' he said and dropped her hands.

He looked grim.

'I suppose Sylvia wanted to help me. She's always been excessive – she must have persuaded herself it was the right thing to do. She probably guessed you were going to marry Anstey. Oh, Sylvia, Sylvia . . .'

His face lost its flinty look.

A feeling of exhaustion came to Elizabeth just then. She had misjudged him. She did believe him, after all. But there it

159

was as it always would be, that tone, that expression in a man's face when he talked of Sylvia. You could no more fight her than wage war upon a fog. She pervaded, floated, obscured, possessed.

'Well?' he said. 'Shall we call a truce?'

He stepped aside to make way.

'Yes. I suppose so.'

She walked off, with Bill dragging on the lead and the big airedale close at her heels.

He stood watching until her figure disappeared into the trees. Then he went in another direction, walking fast until he reached the old quarry. It was overgrown with brambles, hidden beneath them, its deepest part now a sea of intertwined branches thick with white flowers and fierce with thorns. He sat down on a tree trunk. What Elizabeth had told him had shocked and angered him more than he wanted to show. He'd been quick enough to cover that up, knowing that Elizabeth did not like Sylvia – he could scarcely blame her. And the ugly fact was that Sylvia had told him some barefaced lies.

He remembered very well because the news about Speldhurst had come as an unlooked for solution to his problems. He had been wryly thinking of where to live, and realising the limitations of an Army pension and a meagre private income, when Sylvia had telephoned him. It was some days after Garnett's funeral.

'Georgy? I'm coming up to London to have a frock made. Would you like to buy me a champagne cocktail at the Ritz?'

'In memory of your deb days.'

'I don't see why I must say goodbye to the Ritz just because I'm *out* now. Six tomorrow? Don't be late. I have some ripping news.'

'Don't tell me I'm to be a grand-godfather already.'

'Don't be horrid, of course you aren't.'

The following day was foggy and when he arrived he turned into the golden radiance of the Ritz with relief. But the fog had managed to creep in even here, to hang in the distance

160

at the end of the long main corridor in a smoky haze.

Sylvia, having insisted on punctuality, was late. She came into the bar wearing dark brown velvet, a little circle of mink on her blonde head, and carrying a muff pinned with Parma violets. She kissed him. When the waiter brought two pink cocktails, she picked hers up and looked at George over the rim of the glass.

'Lovely.'

'The cocktail?'

'That first. You second. Now, George, as I told you, I have some good news which I've been dying to tell you. I've got a house for you!'

Her kittenish face brilliant with the pleasure of giving, she told him the details. He was astounded.

'Speldhurst! You can't mean that Peter suggests –'

'Oh, it was my idea.'

'I'm sorry, of course, of course, but how can it be Speldhurst? Surely Aunt Dolly and Elizabeth will move there since they're leaving Merriscourt and you and Peter take possession? Speldhurst is close by, and belongs to the family.'

Sylvia was light as a souffle. Oh no, she said, there was no question of that, George could put it right out of his mind. Aunt Dolly was probably coming to London and even if she didn't, Peter had found her just the thing, a little place – George didn't know it – in which Peter was planning to make some expensive improvements. As for Elizabeth, hadn't George heard the big news? She was marrying that rich Ted Anstey.

'So there's Speldhurst sitting up and begging for its new owner.'

He had continued to ask questions. How charming and glib her replies had been.

Why had she done it? Had she got her knife in the two Bidwell women although she never showed it? Or was it that Sylvia, feline to the tips of her dark red finger-nails, preferred a man about?

He sat for a long time, so still that a grey squirrel stopped nearby, twitched its tail and in a leisurely way climbed a tree beside him. George was thinking about Sylvia's duplicity. Should he tell her he knew? Have it out with her? What good would that do – it was all old and forgotten, and Elizabeth had accepted the truth. So nobody cared.

Except me, he thought. There was grimness and regret in his face.

Chapter Ten

Spending money still gave Elizabeth a feeling of pleasurable guilt. When she arranged to go to London, she protested because Ted said she must stay at Brown's in Mayfair, rather than at the respectable, stuffy old Imperial and Royal. But when she arrived at Dover Street and was shown into a charming bedroom, she was pleased. Perhaps being rich suits me, she thought. She had already arranged for her great aunt to dine with her at Brown's.

Elizabeth loved Bessy. The old lady, now in her early eighties, was garrulous and almost entirely fixed on the past, but there was something graceful and tender about her. In her worn face Elizabeth could see the beautiful woman she had been. She had the Bidwell eyes with little flaws like freckles; her manner, with its leisurely charm, used to remind Elizabeth of Peter's.

The old lady arrived in antique glory, kissed her with great affection, and droned on through dinner about the family. She spoke of her parents, brothers, uncles, sisters. All were dead, but they lived in her imagination and in her listener's too. Now and then, making an effort, Bessy enquired after 'dear Ted'. Whoever a Bidwell married became 'dear'. Dear Ted had joined Dear Sylvia, who to Elizabeth's certain knowledge never set eyes on Bessy from one year to the next.

Bessy enjoyed the evening: it was a luxury to talk to a close member of the family about Merriscourt, where she had spent part of her girlhood. She told stories she believed her great niece had never heard and which Elizabeth took pleasure in hearing again. She talked of her sister Kitty, a Victorian ghost who often haunted Bessy's conversation. It was strange,

163

thought Elizabeth, to think that that long-dead Kitty had been George's grandmother.

'I remember the evening when she broke the news to me that Gervase Westlock had asked Papa for her hand,' said Bessy. 'How happy she was. She danced the polka all round our bedroom.'

The conversation then turned to George. How was he? One could see there was a lot of Bidwell in him, said Bessy.

When, after coffee and refusing with laughter to have a crème de menthe, Bessy finally decided it was very late and she must go home, Elizabeth walked with her to the door.

'Dear Ted is very naughty,' murmured the old lady. 'Do you know what he did? Sent me such a big present for my birthday. I loved the beautiful book you sent me, dear, and the card with that pretty verse, but Ted's present quite shocked me. Of course I know *you* were really responsible.'

Bessy believed that anything kindly done for her must come from a Bidwell; it couldn't possibly be the action of a mere in-law.

Elizabeth protested truthfully that the little Morocco writing-case, gold-initialled and beautifully fitted, was entirely Ted's choice. He loved things made in expensive leather. But she knew she was wasting her breath.

As the taxi drove away, there was a flutter of a thin hand from the window.

Wandering back into the lounge, Elizabeth looked at her watch and saw it was only half-past ten, an absurd time to go to bed. Here she was alone in a great unfamiliar city. Beyond the glass doors, down the warm streets, breathed a curiously exciting life. She heard it like music. Girls in billowing ballgowns walked down Dover Street by the side of young men in evening dress. There was laughter, and the slam of taxi doors. The windows of the lounge were wide open, and a night breeze blew in, dusty and warm, with a sigh of distant traffic. She went across the room to retrieve her little pearl-covered handbag.

A man was sitting nearby, his chair turned away from her;

all she saw was a roundish dark head and two extended legs.

'Peter!'

'Liz!'

Springing up at her voice, he came to her in a bound and took both her hands. They exclaimed at the same moment, 'What are you doing here?'

Explanations were simple. Peter had come up to his tailors, and when Elizabeth mentioned Bessy Peter groaned aloud, saying – if only he'd known. He had just returned from his club, but could have dined with them. How was Bessy? He must see her tomorrow. Why hadn't he thought of it sooner?

Why indeed, thought Elizabeth. Who reminds him now?

'Let me look at you,' he said, making her sit down facing him. 'Black suits you. You should always wear it.'

'How could I possibly in Devon?' she said, smiling.

'Sylvia does sometimes.'

'*She* looks good in everything.'

'She does, doesn't she?'

She wondered if she imagined that the doting note was gone from his voice. He called a waiter and ordered coffee, a brandy for himself and a quarter bottle of champagne for her. He was extraordinarily glad to see her, and different in every way from the Peter she met at Merriscourt. He told her about a new dog he wanted to buy, a red setter, very temperamental. He asked when Ted had left for Italy, and was interested to hear all about the Fiat factory. He talked about Holcombe; he said nothing more about Sylvia.

Elizabeth was trying to get used to being alone with him. She suddenly realised that she hadn't seen her cousin by herself since that dreadful night in the orchard. God knows what she had said to him then. She didn't remember anything but the torchlight and the cold.

Apparently neither did he.

'It's so good to see you, Lizzie. I couldn't believe my ears when I heard your voice. It really *is* good to see you.'

She didn't say 'but we meet sometimes at Merriscourt.'

The coffee came, and the champagne, and Peter, sprawling

in the old way, asked about her mother, regretting that he hadn't seen Dolly 'since I don't know when. Do you know I actually wrote to her last Christmas,' he added, impressed with himself, 'and she never even replied.' He laughed, saying she must be as bad a correspondent as he was. Elizabeth realised, with a moment of pain, that her cousin had no idea that Dolly had never forgiven him.

Peter asked about Topsy, had she bought that new horse? There seemed no end to the things he wanted to hear. An hour went by. Girls and young men left the hotel or returned from wherever they had been. Elizabeth was smiling at one of Peter's feebler jokes when he suddenly said, 'I'll tell you what. We'll go dancing.'

'Peter, it's nearly midnight.'

'Don't be silly, Liz. I know you used to say you were the lark and I was the nightingale. Let's both be nightjars and sing into the small hours, shall we? I know a good place to dance. When did I last dance with you? A hundred years ago.'

'You said I wasn't very good.'

'I'm sure I was right.'

They walked out into the warm street. As they went down a kind of passage, carpeted and covered with striped awning, Elizabeth confessed that she had never been to a night club. The foyer was decorated with a vase of lilies four feet high, the scent so heavy that they waded through it.

'What's Ted thinking of, not taking you on the town?' Peter said. 'One must see a little life, Liz. It makes for that sparkle in the eye.'

He signed the members' book, explaining that this meant they were temporary members of this, the Lily Club, and so could have a drink. Some law or other, he added vaguely.

She was surprised when, on entering the ballroom, they walked into pitch dark. A band was playing *These Foolish Things* and as her eyes grew used to the dimness, she made out a smallish floor crowded with people, many with their arms round each other.

They were shown to a table in a far corner, lit by a blue-night light.

'How romantic,' said Elizabeth, laughing.

'Yes. It is.'

He stood up, lazy, graceful, and led her on to the floor. The music changed. What did they play then? She did not recognise the music or ever remember it, but once, years later, she heard it on the wireless and thought she was going to faint. Peter pulled her close, not as if they were dancing but into an embrace. They began to move, pressed close, among the dancers in the dark. The music wrapped them round as his arms were doing.

And as she leaned against him, the poor sickly love woke up as if she had shaken it by the arm. It woke and grew and burgeoned until it filled her entirely. Everything about him was so familiar, so dear, so known and unknown, even the smell of Peter was the same – she'd known it from childhood, a scent of his skin and hair, something like no other creature in the world.

'Dear Liz.'

They went on dancing. How weak she felt. Her conscience told her it was wrong. Everything I want is wrong and what we're doing is wicked, cruel. She tried to conjure Ted into her thoughts as people once believed they could conjure good or evil spirits. She couldn't even recall his face.

The music ended with a little roll of drums.

'Shall we have a drink?'

'I don't think I want one.'

'You. You never drink.'

Putting his arm round her waist, he led her back to their table. She was vaguely aware of other couples leaning close by the dark blue glow of the night-lights, kissing and laughing. Why does sex make people laugh? she wondered. I suppose just because they are happy. But she couldn't laugh.

Peter ordered her an ice. He put out his hand and touched her cheek. 'It's hot in here. Your cheek's on fire.'

She leaned against his hand.

'Liz. Beloved Liz. How I love you.'

'So you should. I'm very nice.'

'Yes. You are. Nice is a crazy word. You're wonderful.'

'Am I?' She was beginning to be frightened, not by the darkness and the music which had begun again, not by being surrounded with lovers, not by Peter's round face which she knew so well or the voice whose tone she seemed not to know. It was herself who frightened her.

'Yes,' he said. He put her hand to his mouth and gently bit the top of her fingers. 'You're wonderful. Strong and wonderful. God, you can hurt me, though. You did once.'

'I know.'

'I thought I'd die of it.'

There was a curious silence. She said slowly, 'Perhaps we all thought we'd die. Wounding each other. Like the end of *Hamlet*. Bodies all over the place. Poisoned pearls in the wine.'

She had let him off as she used to do. She knew by the convulsive way he held her hand that he realised it.

'Let's dance again, Lizzie. Have you ever danced until there were holes in your slippers?'

'You're quoting Mother. She always said *she* had.'

'That's what we'll do. Tonight we'll wear your sandals out and tomorrow morning I'll buy you a new pair.'

They danced. But only so that their bodies could touch, their arms, shoulders, the length of them pressed more closely than they'd ever done before. When she looked up she saw his pale face full of desire. She was no longer the virginal cousin sitting embarrassed on his lap. She wanted him as much as he seemed to want her. During the dance he bent in the dark and kissed her.

'Your mouth is cold.'

'Is it?'

'Do you know what that means? I suppose you don't . . .'

She thought again – everything I want is wrong. I must never hold you in my arms. Loving you can never do me good. This is dangerous. Dangerous.

The last dance was at half-past four and finished with the roll of drums. Some of the dancers had gone long ago, but she never saw them leave. They traipsed in silence into the street. Elizabeth had no cloak to collect. It was warm as milk as they wandered out hand in hand. The dawn was paling the sky.

They never said a word until he tapped on her bedroom door, a towel round his neck.

She opened the door in silence. He shut and locked it.

She managed to say, 'Why the towel?'

'My alibi.'

They half laughed as they began to kiss. Then, still kissing, they moved to the bed.

'Oh Peter, should we?'

'My dear one, it isn't that we should. It's that we must.'

She hadn't known anything, anything about sex, she thought. She'd never imagined it could be like this. He took her slowly and lingeringly, gently, excitingly. He stopped making love to her, lay looking at her until she begged him to go on. She didn't know what she said, how she felt, she abandoned herself to bliss. So long, so violent, so gentle, then flaming up again like fire. When they separated at last their bodies were wringing with sweat.

Wrapping his arms round her, he fell asleep.

It was Elizabeth who woke first, with a start, groped for her watch and saw in the faint light from the line between the curtains that it was after seven.

'Peter. Wake up!'

He opened his eyes drowsily, looked at her and grinned. All the past, she thought with a rush of feeling which made her eyes brim, was in that smile. How insouciant he was. How could he be?

'You must go.'

'Not yet . . .'

'You must.'

Her whisper was tense and he sat up and yawned and stretched, looked at her and said, 'Mmm?'

She did not reply. She climbed out of bed and he lay studying her naked back with its long curved line of the spine, the narrow waist and swelling hips. She was more beautiful naked than when she was dressed.

He reluctantly climbed out of bed too. She had already pulled on a nightdress and was holding out his dressing gown, as she used to hold his coat at Merriscourt when they went for a walk. He knotted the belt, draped the towel round his neck and smiled, showing white teeth in his mischievous round face.

Elizabeth couldn't wait for him to go. Suppose somebody saw him. She was in an agony of nerves.

He refused to be hurried, but towered over her, putting his hand under her elbows.

'We must do it again, Cousin.'

He'd used that name when they were making love. Never before.

A rush of love, of woken desire, of passion, ran through her. Dragging herself out of it she managed to say, '*Go!*'

'Little fusser. Kiss me.'

He gave her a long, open-mouthed, remembering, sweet-tasting kiss.

'That's better.'

He left, closing the door quietly.

She went back to bed.

A bell woke her. She swam upwards out of sleep and felt blindly for the telephone.

'Still asleep, lazybones. Imagine that.'

'And imagine you being awake early,' she said in an imitation of her old self.

'Well. I suppose it is quite early. Only quarter to twelve.'

She sat up as if stung by a wasp.

'*What* time?'

A lover's conversation followed. He asked about her plans. She said she was going home this evening. But must she? he said. What about Aunt Bessy? Could she get out of that by any marvellous chance? Elizabeth lay, waves of happiness drenching her like glittering light. But she wouldn't change her plans. How she wanted to – but she'd promised, and, and . . .

'Why home tonight?'

'The in-laws are meeting the train.'

Propped up with pillows, a newspaper and his breakfast tray beside him, filled with the well-being that sex always brought like a second gift, Peter smiled.

'You're a truthful soul. No tricky alibis for you. Okay, I'll take you out to luncheon and deliver you to Aunt Bessy's. I don't promise, but I might join you and Bessy for tea, which means I could take you to your train.'

When he rang off he had a long bath.

Being with Elizabeth had shaken him a little. He preferred to think it was only a little. Their sex had had a beautiful sense of familiarity, as if he'd come home from a long journey. Something else too. The bitter, at times excruciating remorse was gone at last. Sitting with his cousin last night when they had first met, he knew he hadn't really *seen* her for nearly three years. There she was, the sweet companion of the past, with her face slightly like his own, her freckled eyes, her mouth curling upwards, her curiously moving voice. It was as if until now Sylvia had put a mask over his eyes. And because he and Lizzie were by themselves, and Sylvia's sorcery weakened by two hundred miles of distance, he was able to rip off the mask. And see his cousin again.

Bathing, shaving, dressing, he reflected about her. She was a marvellous lover. Should I feel guilty about having her? How can one feel guilty with a woman who wants it as much as Lizzie does. She and I owe ourselves some joy. It was going to happen for us ever since we grew up. We must do it again.

He went down into the lounge and deliberately chose the chair where he had sat last night. He ordered coffee. Leaning his chin on his hand, itself the epitome of idleness, the little finger heavy with the Bidwell signet ring, the nails perfect ovals, he thought again of what it had felt like to take Elizabeth that first time. They had made love again afterwards, how often? Three times? He didn't quite recall. But he did exactly remember her ashen face and how she'd felt, moist and delicious, like beautiful feathers against himself. We must do it again. He did not once think about Sylvia. It was ill-bred to bring his wife into his mind while he was enjoying the thought of his lover.

Looking up, he saw her walking towards him, a beam of sunshine momentarily lighting her like a searchlight. She wore a clinging yellow and white silk dress and was carrying a saucer-shaped straw hat. The dress outlined her figure, her flat stomach and strong hips. For the first time in his life, he saw she was beautiful.

'Peter. I can't believe you're actually ready before me.'

She tried to sound normal and met his eyes brightly.

He would not allow the shall-we-pretend-it-didn't-happen look.

'I adore you,' he said, waving for another coffee cup.

She sat down rather suddenly. She was about to speak but he put his hand over hers and pressed it and, as he'd known it would, touching him silenced her.

'Now listen, Coz. I haven't grown up with you and known you since you were born without also knowing what you're about to say and the answer is stuff and nonsense. Do you really imagine we can pretend we didn't go to bed? And that it wasn't gorgeous? It's no good looking at me in that charming way, I'm not going to let you escape. Yes. I accept that you must catch that blasted train and I won't fuss you by inventing dotty alibis which you wouldn't be able to carry off anyway. Okay, Lizzie, go you must. But I've got you *now*. And until we go to Bloomsbury. That's an eternity. It's half past twelve. We needn't see Aunt Bessy until quarter to five. Four and a quarter hours, my darling, is an eternity. Now. Coffee first. Then I must decide where to take a beautiful woman to luncheon.'

She gave in. Her conscience which must soon take command was gagged and tied, she simply abandoned herself to being happy. It was like being drunk, she supposed, although she had never known what that felt like. Peter took her into St. James's Park, tucking her hand into his arm and now and then pressing the hand against his side. Everything he did seemed to her hungry body to be about sex. The way he looked at her. The way he touched her bare hand, through the little circle where her suede glove fastened. The way when they sat down in the park, he moved so that they just touched. They had luncheon at the Ritz. She remembered nothing about it. At the end of the meal he said, 'I think you're a wee bit overtired after such a late night, don't you?'

Her face made him burst out laughing.

'Oh Liz, you're worth a fortune, why have you always been so easy to tease? I think we *both* need a rest before tea. We must be fresh for Aunt Bessy, mustn't we?'

They returned to the hotel, simply crossing Piccadilly and walking up Dover Street. Elizabeth couldn't say a word. Sex lay ahead of her again. It seemed almost dreadful, almost fearful, the thought of taking off her clothes in daylight, not in the maze of the secret dawn, and lying down and waiting for Peter to take her again. As they turned the corner of the stair and walked down the corridor to her room he saw her look round, the whites of her eyes showing, it reminded him of a scared animal. A horse. A dog.

'Don't be scared, my love. Hotels in the afternoon are always dead. Never a soul about. I discovered that in my misspent youth. Where's your key?'

The sun was brilliant, and the chambermaid had pulled the satin curtains together. The room was shadowed.

'Undress. I shall watch you.'

'I can't.'

Yes, he said, pulling off his jacket and sitting down on the bed, yes, she very easily could . . .

He stood on the station platform, and Elizabeth let down the window and they simply looked at each other. The train hissed, there was the bitter smell of steam. Passengers going by began to hurry. He looked at his watch.

'Two minutes.'

He leaned towards her and kissed her.

'You look wonderful. Even Aunt Bessy remarked on it. What was it she said? "You have a glow." I wonder why?'

There was a piercing whistle. The porter waved his red flag and the train began to move. Peter put up his hand and took

173

hers and she said, '*Oh my darling* –' as their hands were pulled apart and the train moved faster. She leaned out of the window, waving, and he moved into the middle of the platform to watch the little yellow-clad figure vanish at a turn of the rails.

'All I can say is that *I* don't know why she isn't expecting,' complained Lilian Anstey, dressing for the works dinner. Her husband gave two of these a year, and this was the July party; it meant a long drive to Plymouth and back, with Lilian waking and nodding on the journey home. Harold was looking for his cuff-links, his pearl studs and his black socks, and was scarcely listening to her.

'Where are my damned socks?'

'Surely they're in your top drawer where they should be, Curly?' said Lilian in a sympathetic voice. She had discovered when a bride that if Curly lost anything to wear, a habit of his, it was only necessary to sound concerned. One did not have to budge. She studied her over-powdered face and added lipstick. Her sapphire and diamond earrings swung, pulling down the lobes of her ears. She didn't like the feel of the earrings but they had cost Curly a lot of money, and she didn't like the soapy taste of lipstick either, but nobody was going to say she was out of date.

Muttering, Harold went into his dressing-room.

'Found your socks, dearie?'

'Yes, but I can't fix this blasted stud.'

'Curly, you're as helpless as a baby.'

Standing up and pulling down her diamanté embroidered dress, she wobbled towards him. Her fingers, flashing with diamonds and like small sausages, were neat and clever. She made delicious pastry and dumplings as light as air, and now fixed her husband's studs, re-tied his white tie and patted his curly grey hair. She looked him up and down.

'You're still a handsome man, there's no denying it. And,' she went on, returning to flop down on the dressing-table stool, 'you haven't yet said what you think of Elizabeth still not being in the family way?'

174

'Young people now like to take their time.'

Lilian pooh-poohed that. Ted was longing for a baby. She knew her own son, didn't she?

'You don't think, her being upper-class and all that, she *can't*, do you, Curly?'

'Shut up, Lil, you're talking rubbish, and find my silk scarf.'

While this conversation was going on and the Anstey chauffeur was backing the Daimler out of the garage, and 'the girl' in the Broad Oaks kitchen was rejoicing that Lilian was going to be out, Elizabeth and Ted were also dressing. Holcombe had nothing as grand as a dressing-room for Ted, whose burly body was sometimes too big for the low-ceilinged old rooms. He always retreated into the bathroom to dress, giving his wife what he called elbow room.

She fastened the little buttons at the neck of her white satin evening dress and looked at herself in the long mirror. She had hung it there, taking Dolly's advice when they had been furnishing Holcombe before Dolly went to London.

'Always have a full-length looking glass, my child. Otherwise you won't see what you look like. Particularly to be sure your stocking seams are straight. They never are.'

'That's because I walk with a wiggle,' Elizabeth flippantly said.

'It's because you're slapdash. In your appearance as in everything else,' Dolly had said. She was by then quite recovered from misery and back to her old form. 'You must always remember to think things out, my child.'

Elizabeth recalled that with irony. She had thought everything out. She had thought out her escape from threadbare gentility, and she'd helped to rescue her mother. When she became engaged and asked the solicitor to settle her own small inheritance on Dolly, she also went to see her great aunt. She wanted Bessy's advice. She explained about her mother's lack of money, and wondered if she might approach Ted? He was so generous. Would it be all right to ask him for help? Bessy was shocked and decisive. The idea of a stranger, for so she

175

called Ted then, helping a Bidwell was not to be considered. She, too, saw the solicitor. Dolly never discovered that the considerable increase in her income had not come from Garnett after all . . .

Perhaps the best of Elizabeth's achievements had been to think out how to love her husband – in a way.

But now for the first time she could think nothing out. She'd fallen in love. Violently and passionately, helplessly and uselessly. At school in her last year they had studied Nathaniel Hawthorne's *The Scarlet Letter*. It told the story of a girl in Puritan America who, after guiltily sleeping with a man, was forced to wear sewn on her back for the rest of her life the red letter 'A' for Adulteress. Is that what I wear on my back now? thought Elizabeth.

She had done Ted a great wrong. She had betrayed him. She owed him everything and conscience said she had committed a sin. Yet she could not feel sorry. She despised herself and felt the guilt until she remembered Peter's body in her own, and then she knew a curious sense of triumph. All their lives until he married she and her cousin had shared a mute conversation, reading each other's thoughts. But there had been one secret thing which had never been said. The conversation had stopped as if in death on the winter night when she and her mother went to Speldhurst. Now it had begun again. And after Peter lay with her and entered her, the secret thing was spoken at last.

Elizabeth had not seen him alone since they had both returned home. They behaved, when they met in the usual way with Sylvia and Ted, in a relaxed fashion. It astonished her that such a thing was possible. She had been afraid of their first meeting; but Peter made it easy, as he made everything easy.

It was strange to be able to hear her cousin's thoughts again. When he looked at her across the drawing-room at Merriscourt, she felt the old sensation; it was as if another part of herself sprawled there, lit by the rainbows from the stained-glass window.

If the thought of seeing Peter again after they'd made love alarmed her, she was more frightened still at the prospect of sex with Ted. She'd been sure that she would feel a revulsion against him. Yet it had not been like that. Because she now knew the bliss of being sexually satisfied, she forgave Ted his brief, brutal mating. It isn't his fault, she thought, and how dare I blame him when I've been unfaithful?

She finished dressing for the works dinner, and put on some Worth scent Ted had given her. He padded out of the bathroom, looking big and clumsy in white tie and tails. She always thought he looked his handsome best in tennis flannels.

'Could you push my shirt in at the back a bit, Lizzie?'

She did as he asked. When he turned, the sight of that broad masculine back, solid and strong, moved her. She surprised him by putting her arms round him and leaning her cheek against him.

He gave an embarrassed laugh.

Chapter Eleven

Taciturn old Inslow, the Merriscourt gardener for thirty years, appeared at Holcombe Cottage one summer evening and offered to do a little work 'when I'm free, like'. Elizabeth accepted with gratitude. He must have heard that their gardener had retired – the village bush telegraph still worked, even though she was no longer a Bidwell. Now in the evenings, she saw a familiar figure working in the flower-bed.

Summer was hot and dry. Inslow watered the garden every night for more than an hour, and the scent of wet earth floated into the house through windows which were never shut. But by noon next day the flower-beds looked as if they'd had no water for a month.

After Ted left for work very early every morning, Elizabeth drove down to Teignmouth. It was scarcely half-past eight, there wasn't a holidaymaker in sight along the dark red sands, and she swam alone in the chilly sea. By the time she was home, the sun had begun to beat down and the dogs panted in the shade.

One dazzling morning she spent an hour in the garden picking an enormous bunch of flowers for the church. She put the flowers in heaps on the lawn. Lupins, thorny yellow roses, delphiniums, fat pink peonies, bunches of Mrs Simpkin white pinks.

Whistling for Bob, the mongrel Bill was in the kitchen hanging about for scraps from the maid, Elizabeth left the house. From Holcombe to the village church the lane was long, high hedged and too narrow for two cars to pass, which fortunately was a rare occurrence. If one appeared, the other had to back for half a mile. Marriage, Elizabeth remembered, was like that old Devonshire poem about the lane. One must ride ahead and she supposed that must officially be Ted, though she knew who was the stronger of the two. Like marriage, too, there was no escape from the lane and you simply went on until it stopped.

Her thoughts worried her. Do I mean I don't want to stay married to Ted because Peter and I made love? That's wrong and it's stupid too. Peter belongs to Sylvia. Because of what we did nothing has changed.

But that wasn't true for *she* had changed. The triumph of having Peter as her lover was beginning to be replaced by something that felt like being ill.

The high-banked hedges were buzzing with hidden insects and tangled with flowers, pink and yellow and misty scented white. Curling bracken too. How painful it was to pick; when she and Peter had built their cubbyhutch in the woods they had used bracken for the roof and walls, and as they'd wrenched and dragged at the bracken stems, their fingers had streamed with blood.

At last the lane ended, opening out into a space by some cottages and the wall of the churchyard. A little stream rushed across the road here in winter and somebody long ago had put two diamond-shaped stepping stones in the middle. They were believed to bring good luck if you stood, oné foot on each diamond, without getting your feet wet. But the stream now was almost dry mud, which she and Bob gingerly crossed before going through the gate into the churchyard.

Telling her dog to wait in the porch, she pushed open the door. She expected to find Mrs Rye who cleaned the brass, or Miss Hennock who practised the organ. But the church was empty. The ancient benches made by village carpenters centuries ago when faith was absolute stood in rows, waiting for the return of the faithful. Flies buzzed along the windows. Through the open door floated the sweet smell of flowering grass.

The church was so old. Sad, too. There were three broken pedestals where statues and a stone crucifix had stood, but they had been smashed in Cromwell's time. The angels' heads round the capitals of the pillars had been knocked off. Everything ornamental and graceful had suffered. Somebody in Devon, the official destroyer, had made a clean sweep of all things in the churches which he considered idolatrous. Passions used to be strong for religion then.

The crumbling place moved her. It was nothing to do with her own family, whose church near Merriscourt was still prosperous. There were no Bidwell memorials here of sleeping Tudors, their feet in shoes with rosettes, rows of children kneeling below them, some with skulls under their arms as if holding school satchels. This little place was deserted, as much of Devon was.

Going into the dusty sacristy, she put the flowers in two buckets of water and scribbled a note to the vicar or Mrs Rye to say there were lots more if they were needed. Signed, E. Anstey.

As she was leaving, she turned to look back, noticing how worn the church looked, small and scarred by time, nothing quite straight. The rustic benches were out of the true, the paving stones laid unevenly with hollows made by the feet of villagers shuffling, century after century, into their places. Long before the Reformation, before Bidwells came to Devon to grab land and grow rich, the Latin Mass had been chanted here where, on Sundays, hymns were sung now in broad Devon. She stood musing. Against the sweep of the years she, too, felt small. I must not see Peter for a while. I must try and avoid him, she thought. It's the only way to be myself again. Like the benches, she was out of the true.

At the church door the dog was waiting patiently. He wagged his tail as she came out into the sunlight. She looked across the grassy churchyard, blinking in the brightness. Standing by the gate, arms folded, grinning delightedly, was Peter.

'Lizzie. I was driving to Holcombe on the off chance of finding you and I caught sight of old Bob by the church door. Elementary, my dear Watson. I've come to invite you to

180

luncheon. Do say yes. We badly need some help.'

She was so glad to see him she scarcely knew what to say. But couldn't help inwardly laughing at his appearance five minutes after her resolve. She noticed the 'we'. That meant Sylvia. She said she would love to come to luncheon.

Peter settled her into the car, with Bob upright on the back seat. The airedale disliked cars slightly less than boats. As a very young dog, he'd been taken in a rowing boat by Peter and Elizabeth across the bay to Shaldon. He had hated it, standing, back bent and face like a fiddle, until he could jump out on to the sand.

'Pimm's on the lawn and cold luncheon,' said Peter, turning into the drive.

'It sounds delicious. Specially the Pimm's. Ted never drinks it.'

'Don't you, though?'

'Home-made lemonade instead.'

'Why not a Pimm's or two?'

'Now you don't think I'd drink alone.'

'I thought I'd cured you from being a prig,' he said, giving her a look she pretended not to understand.

Like Holcombe, like the old church, like the county, Merriscourt slept in the sun. They went into the hall and the dog disappeared towards the kitchen, home again. Elizabeth heard a distant sound of endearments. It was Marchant.

'Let's go into the garden,' Peter said.

Although she came here quite often now, it was usually at night, and it was a sort of shock to see how large the gardens were, and how open, after the jumbled mass of flowers and shrubs at Holcombe. The lawns sloped away towards the rose garden, and under the group of ash trees were new garden chairs, a swinging sofa-thing of the kind seen in *Vogue* photographs occupied by mannequins wearing beach pyjamas and floppy hats.

Peter said she must sit on the sofa. He took a chair and stretched out his long legs.

'All this looks very expensive, Peter.'

181

'Don't remind me. It was.'

She made the sofa swing like the old swing in the orchard.

'One of your extravagancies?'

'One of Syl's. I sometimes tell her she spends money like a drunken sailor,' he said amiably.

A blackbird, unalarmed by humans, hopped boldly across the grass.

'Where is Sylvia? Getting dressed?'

He laughed. 'Even my wife, Lizzie, is in full rig by one o'clock. No, she's gone to Speldhurst to meet some of George's friends from her father's old regiment. He keeps in touch with them, and Syl relishes being the only woman in a dining-room full of men.'

'Shan't I see her, then?'

'It depends how long we can persuade you to stay.'

Marchant came across the lawn with a silver tray of tall frosty glasses decorated with pieces of borage feathery with lilac-coloured flowers. He greeted Elizabeth.

'Miss Elizabeth – I should say, Mrs Anstey.'

'I still like hearing my real name, Marchant. How are you?'

The old man and the girl looked at each other, each seeing changes.

'Luncheon will be in half an hour, sir. Hope you've an appetite. Cook has made a chicken pie.'

Summer, thought Elizabeth, sipping her drink. Peter and Merriscourt were part of it. Summer made spells. This was the last place she should be. How happy she was. Why did women always want to plan and have stakes in tomorrow. There was today. There was now.

She asked him idly, wondering if he'd invented it, why he and Sylvia needed her help? He said it was Sylvia's idea to convert one of the box-rooms into a place for ping-pong.

'She's a pig at ping-pong. You never saw anything like the way she slams the ball, it hits one in the eye. The box-room she's picked out is in the east wing, and perfect for the game. But it's full of stuff that I think you and I really ought to look through.'

'That sounds like work.'

'Oh, Syl will decide on most of it. But there's a trunk full of papers she couldn't possibly cope with. Let me fill your glass. Lovely Pimm's, mm?'

Luncheon was uncannily like meals in the past. Chicken pie, with Cook's pattern of pastry leaves. Marchant bringing in the tall jug of home-made lemonade. Raspberries from the garden. They had coffee on the lawn again, and of course it was Elizabeth who finally said, 'If you mean it about the trunk of papers, we ought to do it now. I have to go at five.'

'Is it so late? Okay, slave-driver.'

The particular box-room he had talked about was at the end of the Jacobean wing, reached through a trap door in the ceiling, a ladder fixed to a wall nearby. Hooking the ladder, Peter went up first and pulled her after him. They clambered in through the trap to the attic.

Surprisingly lofty and long, although only with skylights in the roof, it had been a refuge to the children years ago. They'd used it for hide and seek and, in her case, for fits of the sulks. Peter's collection of birds' eggs had been safe there, so had her mess of foreign stamps, both kept away from the tidying hands of nursemaids. Once both children swore they'd seen a ghost: it turned out to be a dressmaker's dummy, stored in a corner unknown to them, under a sheet. Now they stood again in the dust-smelling place, the skylights throwing light through the cobwebs. Elizabeth thought – if there are ghosts, they are of Peter and me.

She looked about. A Victorian rocking horse was nearby, one of its legs missing. There was a fifty-year-old pram. Trunks, which Sylvia had left open, were full of mildewed books. Riding boots and plimsolls, tennis racquets with broken strings. A sewing machine. In a far corner there was a pile of games, ludo, snakes and ladders, draughts and dominoes. There were Army blankets which had belonged to Garnett. Framed religious engravings of the saved and the damned. A heap of red brocade curtains.

'What an impossible mess.'

'Syl says it must all go. Here's the trunk.'

They squatted on the bare boards. The trunk was of leather so old that it was rotting into soft flakes. When Peter opened it, they saw it was full of packets of maps, tied with string and scrawled with a name.

'John de Cartaret Bidwell.'

'Peter! They must be some of my father's maps from the war.'

'Fascinating. Look there. He's marked a route through Normandy. And here, he's ringed a château. Perhaps he stayed there. Maybe it was turned into a barracks or a hospital.'

They turned over the maps, and found letters tied with ribbon, stamped H.M. Forces. They were from her father to his brother.

'My dear Garnett,
A curious week. From where we're stationed, the ground trembles with grey convoys of motor lorries bringing up ammunition from the dumps. Over all and taking no notice, sail a flight of German aeroplanes. They're more elegant than ours or the French. They're at a height where we can't reach them with our guns. All is bustle and action here . . . streams of wagons, great logs due for the dugouts, ammo convoys never stopping day or night . . .'

Peter had read the letter aloud. He stopped.

'Do you think Aunt Dolly would like these?'

'I don't think so.'

He looked very surprised and she said, 'She doesn't keep much from the past, Peter. You know she doesn't.'

And she thought – she hasn't even kept *you*.

She collected the maps, separated the letters, and decided to keep those herself. Peter said he'd have the maps. At the bottom of the trunk were packets and packets of postcards of France, and photographs of men in uniform, laughing into the camera.

'Do look, Lizzie. That dog is just like Bob. I expect everyone of those poor fellows is dead.' She took the photograph

184

from him and looked down at it, and he said huskily, 'Lizzie.'

He pulled her to him and began to kiss her, opening her lips with his tongue and kissing her until she could think of nothing, nothing at all. She faintly said as he drew away, 'Peter, we can't,' but he took no notice. He undid the buttons all the way down her thin dress, and peeled it off, and looked up and down at her breasts beneath the satin petticoat, her long legs – he reached up and pulled down the satin straps and undid her suspenders. She could no more have stopped him than have killed them both.

They lay on the heap of curtains and made love for a long time. It was not strange any more, and in consequence more exciting. Sometimes he shifted so that she was above him, astride him, and he could look up into her face. How beautiful you are, she thought, you are like a god . . .

At last their climax came and they lay glued together until they fell asleep.

She drove home ten minutes before Ted arrived back from work. She just had time to park the car, change into fresh clothes, hers smelled of dust and lovemaking and were crushed and dirty, and brush her hair. Her body ached with pleasure. Peter's fierce lovemaking still made her body tingle.

She went into the drawing-room – it seemed small after gothic spaces.

'You there, Liz? God, it's hot. Is there any lager in the fridge?'

'I'll get some.'

When she came back carrying the ice-cold beer in his pewter tankard, he was lying in a chair, fanning himself with the evening newspaper.

'There's a sight for sore eyes.'

'The beer?'

'You and the beer. You look very pretty tonight. Come to think of it, you're a very pretty girl and I must say I take the credit. I like that dress. Turquoise, isn't it?'

That night he made love to her. She had climbed into her own bed and a minute later he joined her, pulling up her

185

nightdress and rolling on top of her. Very soon, grunting, he finished. He said, 'Was that nice?' as he always did, and not waiting for a reply, went back to his own bed. He fell asleep at once.

She lay wide awake, looking into the bluish dimness of the room. I must give up Peter, she thought. I must never do it with him again. That way madness lies.

Peter telephoned her the following week, but it was Ted who answered. He came out into the garden where Elizabeth was squatting by the rockery, picking the dead heads off a mass of yellow flowers.

'Your cousin rang. He said not to bother you, he only wanted to tell us that he and Sylvia are going to the South of France tomorrow. For a few weeks, he said. Lucky devils. They do themselves proud, don't they? We won't see them for a bit. Pity. Peter wants to talk about buying a new car.'

Blessedly interrupting Elizabeth's thoughts and forcing her to think about somebody else, Dolly rang some weeks later. Dolly said gaily that she wanted Elizabeth to come to London for a night.

'I have something to discuss,' said Dolly, her voice full of news.

'Can't you tell me what it is, darling?'

'Of course not, or I wouldn't ask you to come up. Can Ted spare you? Tell him I know he'll do it for *me*.'

Ted had a soft spot for his mother-in-law, he admired her as his father did. He readily agreed to Elizabeth being away. Not longer than a night, he hoped? She must be back to come to the tennis tournament on Saturday. Ted, one of the most popular members of the club, was on his way to winning the trophy.

London was stuffy and gritty. It had lost the fresh new-season air it had worn on one exquisite night at the end of May when Elizabeth had danced at the Lily Club. These were the dog days now. Looking from the taxi window at empty Bloomsbury with its ponderous hotels and shabby eighteenth-century houses, Elizabeth wished she was back in Devon. But she was glad to be seeing her mother, and the six weeks since Peter had been gone had been a permanent struggle to keep her body from aching for him. She must fix her thoughts on Ted. Ted.

The person who would have cheered and amused her, Topsy, was in Scotland.

'They do nothing but shoot things,' she wrote to Elizabeth in her scrawling writing. 'They don't know what *to do* with the pheasants in great heaps in the kitchens. By the way, guess what! I met someone who knows your second cousin once removed. She told me more about the affair in Skye. He's by way of being a lady-killer, they say. Well, he didn't kill us, did he? Back 27th. T.'

When Elizabeth entered the huge, tiled Victorian relic of the Imperial and Royal, with its polite and aged servants, its antique shuddering lift, she saw her mother immediately. Dolly was sitting with Great Aunt Bessy and both women appeared to be talking at once, nodding and apparently not hearing a word the other said.

Dolly saw her daughter and lifted her cheek to be kissed. Elizabeth thought her mother looked very well; her small face was tanned from the hot summer, her hair without a thread of grey, fashionably dressed. She wore pearls and a blue and white silk with real Wedgewood buttons, which Elizabeth had not seen before. Elizabeth also kissed Bessy, whose worn face was lit with its customary expression of relaxed benevolence.

'You two have much to talk about. No, Dolly dear, I shall not stay. Very kind of you but no. You must speak to the child alone. I'll take myself off for a little nap before dinner.'

The old lady moved away with a regal wave.

Elizabeth looked at her mother enquiringly.

'Yes,' said Dolly. 'I have a surprise. I have already told Bessy my news. Do you remember my speaking about Maud's doctor?'

Maud Entwistle was Dolly's oldest friend; they had known

each other in their flighty Streatham days. When Dolly ascended to the glory of becoming a Bidwell, she never lost touch with Maud, a sardonic woman from Leeds, now a widow with what Dolly described as a long pocket. It was with Maud, in her spotless and capacious Sussex house, that Dolly had been staying for months.

'Isn't his name Doctor Hoskins?' ventured Elizabeth. She had begun to believe the unbelievable.

'That's right, my child. Christopher Hoskins. He has an extremely good practice in the district. Maud swears by him. She says,' quoted Dolly, 'he has diagnostic flair. Well, Christopher lost his wife many years ago, and he has often come to dinner with us . . .'

Beckoning to a waitress for some sherry, with a face of positively girlish satisfaction Dolly announced that she and Doctor Hoskins were to marry. It had been, she coyly said, a whirlwind courtship. She did want Elizabeth to meet him soon, such a dear man, Elizabeth would not be able to help liking him. While Dolly talked on, Elizabeth digested the news. Her mother showed her an engagement ring of large diamonds.

'Christopher says I must have all my old half-hoops redesigned.'

During dinner, with Bessy as gentle audience, Dolly talked of a quiet Sussex wedding, her future husband's plans, her eagerness to help with the busy practice. Elizabeth listened. Her mother had thrown off the past like a dress she was tired of and which no longer fitted. She never mentioned Merriscourt or Devonshire. And, as had been so for three whole years, did not once speak of Peter. She was a woman whose talent was simply for the present. Elizabeth envied that. How could I have thought for a moment she would want my father's old maps?

The following day her future stepfather came up from Sussex to lunch with the three ladies. He took unadulterated female company in his stride: Elizabeth guessed that was how Christopher Hoskins took life. He was tall, handsome, late fiftyish, half Irish, with a long face, green eyes and thin crinkly grey hair. His manner was intimate, as if inviting his hearers into a secret. It must be very popular with his women patients. He treated Dolly as if she were a girl. He was tender, bantering and concerned. He asked her questions about the length of time she had spent shopping, and listened with what Elizabeth considered a saint-like good nature to her mother's replies. Elizabeth never felt she could talk to Ted about buying clothes or new fashions. It seemed an unnecessary burden of female-ness to dump on his manly shoulders. Not so Dolly who spoke of the colour of autumn coats, the new styles in hats, 'all with veils, Christopher,' and the question of flat-heeled shoes. 'So unfashionable, do you agree?'

'My dear, you have such pretty feet and high heels exactly suit them.'

King Edward and Queen Alexandra were still on the throne, apparently.

Elizabeth caught the afternoon train. She settled in a corner seat, looking out at the blessed sight of fields, a flash of the Thames, punts, willows. She was still marvelling at her mother. How strange, how painless, to forget yesterday. I wish I could. *I will.*

'I thought it was you! Josh said it wasn't,' cried a laughing voice. The door of her empty first-class compartment was pushed open and there stood Topsy, dressed in navy blue and white, a tiny hat tipped over her thick golden hair.

She came over and sat down facing Elizabeth.

'What fun. Shall we pull down the corridor blinds and say one of us has measles? Then nobody would dare.'

'Topsy, you can't.'

'Josh and I always do,' said Topsy, tugging down the blinds. 'Perhaps I could dot my face with lipstick. I did once.'

Delighted to see her friend, enthralled at the story of Dolly, firing questions punctuated with bursts of laughter, Topsy was in high spirits. Scotland had been a bore, but dear old David liked it. But do you know how many birds he shot? Two hundred and sixty-seven.

'I said, do you promise to eat them all. He was a bit offended.'

'Your father always liked shooting, Topsy.'

'That doesn't mean I have to have it all over again. Anyway, David's in town. He's gone to Purdey's to order a gun. They call it "building" you know. Once when we were engaged he took me into Purdey's and spoke to the big cheese and said, "Thompson, I want you to build this boy a gun." '

'I quite like that. But you don't look in the least like –'

'Quite. David likes calling me a boy for some odd reason.'

'Did Thompson build one?'

'Yes, he did, and it cost David the earth and he made me use it, but somehow I managed later to escape the dreaded task. Actually, I gave it to Josh.'

'I hope David doesn't find out.'

'Josh could say he was cleaning it for me. He's on the train, actually.'

'But I thought you said David was –'

'No, no, silly. Josh is on the train. I wanted to pay for him to travel first class, but he said somebody from home would be certain to spot him. "They wouldn't like it if I was with the bettermost folks," was how Josh put it. You are going to say what was Josh doing in London. He came up to see me. We went to Tattersalls. Lovely, the horses were. We had a lot of fun. Josh does make me laugh. Did I tell you what a demon driver he is in my car?'

Topsy leaned back, pulling off the straw hat which had made a mark across her forehead. She lit an Abdulla cigarette. The smell of Turkish tobacco, scented and heavy, reminded Elizabeth of Topsy smoking at school, during a winter run of hare and hounds. Her friend was regarding her with a quizzical expression, twisting one eyebrow.

'Topsy,' said Elizabeth as the pause lengthened. 'Are you sure it's quite right to treat Josh as if –'

'As if we sleep together?'

'I never meant that!'

'Oh, but I did. I do. That's what he is. Lady Chatterley's

lover in person. And that's a very comic expression on your face, Lizzie. Do stop looking as if I'd slapped you in the belly with a wet fish. Certainly Josh and I go to bed together, if you can call the stables a bed. As a matter of fact, he's rather good at it.'

'Topsy, you can't mean to tell me –'

'For heaven's sake! I *do* mean. I *do* tell you. Josh and I have been lovers for ages and it's a surprise to me you didn't notice, particularly when you came over one day and we'd just finished. In the nick of time, actually. I thought people could tell by one's eyes or something. Josh says they can. Anyway, there it is. It suits us.'

Elizabeth digested the story. Shock on shock. Her mother to be remarried. Topsy and a groom.

'I don't know why you're so shattered,' continued Topsy. 'My late lamented father shoved me into marrying poor old David, you never approved, you were a true friend. You came round and begged me not to. I believe I said it didn't matter.'

'Something like that.'

Topsy gave a large shrug.

'I was wrong. David's a dead loss in bed, I mean, embarrassing. One, two, three and that's it. What am I supposed to do? Grin and bear it? He hoped his pathetic efforts would make me preggers but they never have and a jolly good thing too. If I were, how could I have my rough and tumble with Josh? You'll just have to get used to this, Lizzie,' she added kindly. 'I won't bring him to Holcombe to dine, I promise! I can't tell you what he looks like in a dinner jacket – there was an old one of David's (from when he was young) in the house and once I made him try it on. He was all knobbly wrists, and as for his neck! When I think how he looks in breeches . . . anyway,' she added, with another more quizzical look, 'you can wipe that disapproving look off your face. You are *not* the one to preach. Who went to bed with her cousin, I'd like to know?'

Elizabeth blushed crimson.

There was a moment's silence filled by the sound of the train. De-de-de-*de*, de-de-de-*de*.

'It's no good pulling yourself together and swearing you never, Lizzie, because I know you did. Now you're going to ask if my spies are everywhere, and the answer is my spies are my own eyes. *You* may not be able to see when people have been at it, but I can. When I came to Merriscourt one evening before we went to Scotland, you and Peter were by the window, and I saw at once it had happened. I knew by the very way you were both standing. As for your face, well, if I'd been Sylvia, I'd have slapped it. Ted, like David, is fortunately as blind as a bat. So. How's the affair going?'

Elizabeth drew a breath.

'I've stopped it.'

Topsy didn't laugh, or ask why. She regarded her, her head on one side.

'Quite right. An affair, I mean a real affair, wouldn't suit you. All those arrangements . . . is Sylvia going to be out? Is Ted away? Dispiriting. Okay for me and Josh because we think it a lark, but you wouldn't. Anyway, supposing Sylvia found out . . . poor old Peter.'

There was another of their silences.

'I hope you've noticed that I didn't ask what Peter was like in bed. Anyway, I saw it in your face. Lucky old you.'

A few weeks later Elizabeth discovered that she was pregnant. She went to the doctor who confirmed it, and drove home in the soft rainy evening, wondering how Ted would take the news. She herself was somewhat stunned. Ted had continued his brief lovemaking, of course, and she had indifferently submitted, sometimes thinking it strange that he did not seem to notice her lack of interest. Her body still longed now and then for Peter. But Topsy had been right. The lies wouldn't do and in the end they'd destroy even her cousinship with Peter. It didn't bear thinking about. I shall have to put up with it being over although it lasted so short a time, she thought. Pregnancy now gave her the answer.

She made up her face, put on some of Ted's favourite scent and waited for his return. He had been in good form recently

192

because he had won the tennis tournament with some brilliance, and later had bought himself a new Alvis, even more showy and handsome than his first. He loved the car, spoke of it as 'she', and bought Elizabeth a leather driving cap so that he could take her out, the hood down, in the winter.

He came into the house, shouting as always, 'Liz? Supper ready? I could eat a horse.'

'It will be about ten minutes.'

'Time for a beer.'

He was pouring it into his tankard, tipping both tankard and bottle carefully to avoid too much froth, as she came into the drawing-room. She sat down. He drank with relish.

'Sit down, Ted.'

'Give us a mo.'

He finished off the drink, smacked his lips and sat.

'Well? What's the trouble?'

'Guess what. I saw the doctor today. Ready for a shock? I'm expecting a baby.'

She had never seen anybody so pleased. He sprang up with a loud laugh, rushed to her, seized her and pulled her to her feet. He swung her round.

'A baby! You clever, clever old thing. You're just – well – I don't know what to say!'

'You're clever too,' she said, with some generosity.

Chuckles.

'*What* is Ma going to say! I'll ring her –'

'Ted, not right away.'

'You don't think I can let her wait. She'll be so tickled. I just want to hear her – oh, I must phone!'

Chapter Twelve

Reaction to Elizabeth's news was varied. Lilian, loud and triumphant, took her daughter-in-law to Exeter and spent too much money on a cot decorated with organdie frills, pure silk baby dresses, nightdresses for Elizabeth, and was only prevented from buying an elaborate christening robe when Elizabeth mildly said the Bidwells had a family one.

'Made of cotton and going yellow, I daresay,' said Lilian, who knew things like that.

Harold Anstey gave Elizabeth a kiss, and his son a rise in salary.

Elizabeth telephoned her mother in Sussex, now busily preparing for her wedding.

'Is Ted pleased?' asked Dolly. Her voice had a tinny sound.

'Mother, what do you suppose? He's going on like a dog with two tails.'

'Some men don't enjoy their wives expecting a child.'

The conversation then changed to tea-sets, and the prices at Midhurst compared to those in London. The coming grandchild did not get a look in.

Ted was noisily amazed when Elizabeth said she would not call round to see her cousin and Sylvia, newly-returned from the South of France.

'For Lord's sake, why not? He's your closest relative, not counting your Ma.'

'We're having dinner with them on Sunday. It can wait until then.'

'What an odd girl you are. I should have thought you'd trot round on that pony, bursting (ha ha!) with the glad tidings. Hey, did you ask the Doc if you can ride?'

'No, I didn't, and of course I can. Mrs Fulford hunted until she was eight months.'

'Oh, did she, well just you ring the Doc or I will. And don't run up and down the stairs, and keep that dog out of your way. You nearly fell arse – sorry – head over heels last night when we were going to bed.'

'You're turning into an old woman, Ted Anstey.'

Although she laughed at him, she was touched. And her own state interested and absorbed her. Even during the first days when there was of course nothing to show in her slim figure, she noticed that pregnancy affected her state of mind. It blurred and hazed things. She, the practical energetic one, felt lazy. She, the guilty one, felt innocent. Her cousin did not yet know, and when he did, it would part her physically from him. He would see her in a different way.

Her new serenity, keeping her calm and telling her lies, said it was good to forget they had ever been to bed. All she had left of the passion which had shaken her to the roots was a swooning acceptance that, after all, they *had* made love. I'll always remember it, she thought, and fell asleep.

She was woken by the telephone on her beside table.

'Lizzie? I've been ringing for ages. Were you in the garden.'

'No. I'm here . . .'

'You have remembered that you're dining tonight? You haven't forgotten?'

Sylvia's light voice was urgent. She never usually sounded like that.

'I rang to ask if you could be a little early. Are you coming before Ted? I wish you could. I want to see you alone.'

For a moment a thrill of fear went through Elizabeth, then, listening to the reproachful tone, she knew she was wrong.

'It would be nice to talk to you on my own,' said Sylvia.

Elizabeth decided it was rather convenient to go to Merriscourt by herself before Ted arrived. She had not been looking forward to her husband's booming announcement of her pregnancy. He was, as her mother used to say, a bit much.

He was in fact too much. Too loud, too positive, too hearty, too big. There were times when his size irked her: he always seemed to be just where she was about to walk or move. She had to edge her way past him.

She had imagined his loud, 'Have you heard about Liz!' She had wondered how Peter would take it. The physical facts – Ted making love to her, Peter in bed with Sylvia – were full of unthinkable pain.

Now it would not be quite such an ordeal as she'd feared.

The old house lay in an October mist when she drove up in her little car. The door opened at once. Marchant had been waiting for her.

'Hello, Marchant, are you well?'

'Trouble with the knee again, Mrs – Miss Elizabeth. My old war wound. Doctor says it's getting on nicely, meaning it's going from bad to worse.'

Elizabeth said how sorry she was and did not believe a word. Walking with the mincing steps of a fat man, Marchant opened the drawing-room door, intoning,

'Miss Elizabeth, Madam.'

Sylvia was stretched on the sofa where Dolly used to sit presiding over the tea-table. Sylvia had discarded her shoes, pushed cushions behind her head, and did not get up but held out a languid hand.

'I'm glad you're early. Tea? Or would you prefer a cocktail.'

Elizabeth chose tea and Marchant bowed and left them. Sylvia patted the end of the sofa, saying that Elizabeth must forgive her for not getting up, but she did not feel too bright.

'Peter's awful when one isn't well. He keeps saying "let me ring for Ada" in an accusing voice. One sees only too clearly that he's bored.'

Elizabeth made polite noises and did think that her cousin-in-law looked rather unwell. Not the usual golden girl. She wondered if Sylvia drank too many cocktails.

Tea arrived, Marchant threw a proprietary look towards

the erstwhile daughter of the house, and Elizabeth pretended not to see. She was certain he thought that she ought to pour out.

The two women, one as fair as a lily, the other glossily dark, exchanged commonplaces. Bob, who had come with his mistress as a matter of course, pattered across the parquet.

'Don't let him sit on the chairs, please,' said Sylvia, and 'go away, you stupid animal,' giving the dog, who had sniffed at her in a friendly manner, a push. Bob philosophically fell to the ground and put his chin on Elizabeth's foot.

Sylvia put down her tea cup, twisted her finger in her hair for a moment, and blurted out, 'Liz. I'm pregnant.'

Elizabeth burst out laughing, saw the frown of offence on Sylvia's face, and managed to say, still laughing,

'Oh Sylvia, I'm sorry to laugh but – so am I!'

Sylvia did not know whether to be pleased or put out by the trumping of her ace. She decided to be pleased. It would, she said, be much more fun to have someone to share things with. One couldn't talk properly to a man about morning sickness and – the conversation became technical. Elizabeth found herself being asked questions she could not answer, and given facts she'd rather not know. Sylvia was set on wringing the last ounce of drama out of her condition. Elizabeth's dreamy peace, which had silenced both love and conscience, seemed very dull in comparison.

Sylvia went upstairs to change for dinner, returning in grey chiffon and the Bidwell pearls. She talked about clothes. 'How shall we bear smocks?' Ted arrived, heard her news, and was hearty and twinkling. At last, when Marchant had rung the dinner gong a second time, making it reverberate through the house, Peter came down the staircase and into the room.

Elizabeth saw that he had just had a bath. She knew that fresh, damp-haired look. He came over to kiss her cheek and for a second, no more, her body longed for him.

'I've heard your news,' said Ted. 'Now you must hear ours.'

'Your cousin's preggers too, darling,' interrupted Sylvia, stopping Ted in mid-boom.

'*Lizzie*? Really?'

He laughed. He congratulated them both. He was easy and smiling. She did not hear a word. A string had always united them, a string which he had cut and later reknotted, which tied them together and through which they could have that mute and beautiful conversation from her nature to his own. It broke so violently that she almost groaned aloud.

Ted had always liked his wife's cousin. Liked him with a mixture of disapproval – what did the chap do with himself – and respect for a man who sprang from a class which Ted felt above his own. Sometimes he and Peter went out together. They got on well.

Peter was a worldly, seasoned, idle man and Ted an unsophisticated busy one – but neither was complicated or unhappy and both loved cars.

Cars were Ted's profession. He never admitted it to anybody but secretly he had always longed to be a racing motorist. He loved fast cars, low-built, graceful, powerful, costly. He was a car snob and this snobbery, unconscious and unmistakable, earned Peter's respect. Ted knew so much more about cars than he ever would.

There were over forty different makes of British cars now, and some fashionable American ones. The Prince of Wales drove a Buick, which Ted said was a 'drawing-room on wheels'. But the luxury cars were the Rolls Royce Phantoms, the Lagondas and Ted's own car, the Alvis. Alvis had been performing brilliantly in many sporting events from trials to the races in the banked concrete bowl at Brooklands where Ted's dreams centred. Ted owned a new Alvis 20. The car, with a powerful and finely-tuned engine, good handling and beautiful lines, was a pleasure to look at. It had long swept wings, huge lamps, a low-slung body; it was hailed as one of the best British sports cars of the year, and there was not a young man in Devon who didn't envy it when it drove by.

Harold Anstey did not approve of Ted's choice. Cars, he said, were to get you to places in comfort, like his capacious Daimler, and to earn good money when sold in the Anstey showrooms.

Peter was dazzled by Ted's Alvis. He sometimes telephoned him at the Plymouth works, officially to talk about cars, but actually to be invited out in the Alvis which its owner was glad for him to drive. People in Teignmouth often saw the big strong-shouldered young Anstey, the slimmer aristocratic-looking Bidwell, driving fast down the empty roads.

Three years ago Peter had been obsessed by his desire for Sylvia Ashton. He had wanted her, dreamed about her, eaten and drunk Sylvia. There were times when he felt if he did not win her, he would go mad.

The passion to possess was the strongest emotion in Peter Bidwell's nature, it attacked him rarely but when it did he could think of nothing else. He had wanted, and got, Sylvia. For a night and a few days he had wanted to possess his cousin and in that, too, he had conquered. Now divided from Elizabeth by the repugnant barrier of her pregnancy he was restless and he developed a new desire. He loved Ted's black and silver car, looked forward to driving her, feeling her answer to his hands and knowing the latent power similar to riding a powerful hunter.

'You certainly fancy the Alvis,' said Ted, pleased.

'I certainly do.'

For Peter to lust after the car meant determining to have one. Soon after learning his cousin was carrying a child he telephoned Ted at the works.

'About the Alvis.'

Ted laughed.

'I'm not ringing to ask if I can drive her again. I've been looking at my bank balance and I think I could just about manage one. Can you help at all?'

'I should just think I could.'

They met at the hotel that evening to drink and talk. Ted

was encouraging, and Peter more eager than Ted had ever seen him, bombarding him with questions. Where were the Alvis cars manufactured? Had Ted any acquaintances who could help?

'Hold on. The Alvises come from Coventry, and I happen to be going to Brum, as a matter of fact.'

'Where's that?'

Ted guffawed. 'Sorry, old boy, Birmingham. I'm going to Br – Birmingham at the end of the week and Coventry is only a doddle away. Want to come?'

Peter accepted with enthusiasm. They ordered drinks.

'My own Alvis,' said Peter slowly.

'What does Sylvia say about it?'

'Oh, she likes the car we've got. The Morris my father bought us.'

'So we're going on the trip alone?' said Ted, winking.

The two young men boarded an early train for London a few days later. It was scarcely eight in the morning, and they breakfasted as the train rocked and thundered by the greyish October sea and dramatic red rocks, rushing in and out of tunnels. Neither Ted nor Peter mentioned the pregnant wives left behind: there was a boyish conspiracy of freedom as they lingered over coffee and cigarettes and then made their way back to the compartment. They had it to themselves, fresh, polished, the seats pinned with spotless lace antimacassars. Filled with food and lulled by the train's song, Ted slept.

Peter read *The Field*, and looked out of the window. The red earth was gone now, replaced by black ploughlands and flattish countryside. He was thinking about Sylvia. Why hadn't he told her the true reason he was going to London and the Midlands? It was ridiculous to use the alibi of visiting Savile Row. He'd been in London a few months ago for that, little guessing it would lead to that exquisite meeting with his cousin. The trouble was that he lied to Sylvia from boredom. He was going to do what he was going to do, and arguments were tedious. In that he resembled his dead father.

He had learned many things about the girl he'd married,

200

things one only found out – not from having a woman in one's bed but as the centre of one's life. He loved her still. There was something outrageous and spoiled, delicious and catlike about Sylvia. She was without conscience. She was simply her wicked, selfish and utterly desirable self. But he was as selfish as she, and had no intention of allowing her to rule him. He would have his own way whenever he was so minded.

He didn't like lying but it had to be done. There was something else too. Sylvia's lunatic extravagance worried him more and more – she spent money like a drunkard in a cellar full of bottles of brandy. Alarmed by the overdraft at the bank, fretted by the bailiff, Peter often attempted to face her about money. All she did was weep and sulk. Remembering those conversations, he noticed that she never promised to mend her ways but always said that *he* should. She meant he must sell some land. Once he'd caught her looking through the list of Merriscourt properties. She had started as guiltily as a boy in the jam cupboard.

It was her relentless attitude to money which made him decide he'd have the Alvis. He had a few hundreds in a separate account, money he had been given by Garnett on his twenty-first birthday. He was going to be the extravagant one this time. He wanted that car.

Ted woke, yawning with a mouth, thought Peter, as large as that of a hippopotamus, showing his thick tongue and excellent teeth.

'I've been asleep.'

'Close on an hour.'

'Lord. Did I snore?'

'Now and again. I kicked you on the shin.'

'Oh, did you. Well, well, soon be in London.'

'I hope,' said Peter casually, 'the Alvis isn't going to cost the earth.'

He had actually not talked of the price, so determined had he been not to be baulked.

Ted looked at him sideways.

'Don't know what that means. Are you backing out?'

'Of course not. It's just that, frankly, I have less than a thousand. It was a coming-of-age present. My father left it in gilt-edged, where it still is.'

'Gilts are pathetic.'

'Are they? Safe, though. Anyway, that is what I'll spend on the Alvis.'

'Why use the nest-egg, old chap? Take it from your current account.'

'Mm.'

On an impulse Peter began to talk about his wife. He had few intimate men friends, although he was popular. The only deep friendship in his life was with Elizabeth, and she had been his conscience. He had never talked about money to a soul except his bank manager and his solicitor. He never even discussed it with Aunt Dolly. But he liked and trusted Ted who had a kind of extra dimension because he was married to Elizabeth. He was a relation of sorts. So he described to Ted his anxiety over Sylvia's uncontrollable extravagance. What could a man do?

Ted was amazed.

'My dear fellow, I never heard of such a thing in my life. Put your foot down.'

'I can't. Nobody could.'

'That's tosh. Tell her she can't have things. Stop the joint bank account. That's a mistake if ever I heard one. I'd no more give Lizzie a joint account than jump off Dawlish cliffs.'

Peter said drily, 'You could give her your entire fortune. You could trust her with your life.'

'Oh, trust,' said Ted with contempt. 'I don't trust anybody and neither does Dad. Only fools trust people. You have to be certain-sure, as they say in Devon. I tell you, you must simply put your foot down.'

Peter's silence was of disagreement. He looked out of the window again. The suburbs were creeping up. Handkerchief-sized gardens, gimcrack summer houses, lawns on which a mower stood, waiting for its owner to come home by the local train.

'So,' said Ted cheerfully, 'that's my advice and believe me, it's right. But to return to the Alvis, you've got that bit of cash safe. I take it Sylvia doesn't know about that?'

Peter shook his head.

'So when you come back with the car, there'll be nothing she can do about it.'

'Exactly. But I've been wondering,' said Peter casually 'not à propos the Alvis but just to help us out a little, if you could see your way to lending me something, Ted. Nothing big. A few hundred. It would be very good of you, and I'd pay you later, of course.'

Ted had guessed what was coming. Any fool could have seen it. Like his father, Ted was often approached by people needing cash. 'The trouble with us,' Lilian had said, 'is that we *look* well-heeled.' Such requests had made Ted's skin as thick as his father's.

'The fact is,' he said, while Peter leaned back, looking rather as if he were the person conferring the favour, 'I never lend money. Sorry, old boy, but it's a rule I never break and nor does Dad. Lending money means losing friends, an old saying but true. We'd quarrel in a month if I lent you what you ask for. Anything, in fact. Loans are no good except from banks. Try Lloyds.'

'I might.'

Peter was silent for so long that Ted said, for his heart was kind, 'That Ferrers chap, your bailiff, does a good job, doesn't he?'

'Adequate. I don't like him and nor does Lizzie.'

'But he manages the estate, brings in the rents and so on?'

'He's a pompous bore.'

'But he does the job,' persisted Ted who saw, faintly and unmistakably, on Peter's roundish self-indulgent face, a look of the old wicked upper classes of the past. 'What I was going to say was that you've got Ferrers, whom you pay, running the estate for you and you don't like being involved, Lizzie once told me. So why not work for us?'

Peter looked as if he didn't understand.

Ted leaned forward, his broad hands on his knees.

'You love cars. You understand 'em and they interest you as much as they do me. You're just the sort of chap, too, whom people like. You'd take to our business, you couldn't help it. Cars all day and every day. Think of it. You could escape from Ferrers complaining about the crops, or whatever he talks about, and put your mind to carburettors. You haven't seen round our works, they're as good as a picture. Let me speak to Dad. He's met you, but he doesn't *know* you. And think,' ended Ted, 'how you'd feel at having a real salary coming every week.'

He leaned back.

'Well? What about it?'

Peter burst out laughing.

'It's very good of you, Ted, but –' he was laughing quite genuinely as at a good joke, 'but I couldn't, I'm afraid. I really couldn't.'

He looked at Ted with a face of amusement, of unconscious patronage. He had no idea how rude he was being.

Chapter Thirteen

Nowadays Elizabeth had begun to like being alone. Ted was away, the maid had cycled off home after tea, and she was by herself with the dogs as company. She had been sick this morning, and was glad that Ted hadn't been there with his somewhat overwhelming sympathy. Now she felt well, and lazy.

It was the end of October, but there had been no autumn gales at all, and this evening it was getting dark much too soon. She wondered if the storms, like distant giants, were on their way. Looking out, she saw that the sky was a curious colour, an uncanny underwater green. From the window which was ajar she noticed the birds had stopped singing. Perhaps they were waiting for the thunder.

Although she enjoyed her solitude, she was looking forward to Ted returning from the Midlands. Now that she was pregnant they were getting on so well. Elizabeth knew, for Sylvia had confided in her, that Peter was frankly bored by his wife's condition, and often annoyed her by saying wasn't exercise a good idea? Ted, on the other hand, never stopped telling Elizabeth to put up her feet, not to carry this or lift that. He cross-questioned her when he came home, to be sure she had rested. He was always making her cups of tea.

He had telephoned from Birmingham this morning, saying he wouldn't be home until late, and might not be back until tomorrow. He'd ring again.

'I'll surprise you. Your cousin's here.'

'*Peter!*'

'He's decided he wants to buy an Alvis. He didn't admit it to Sylvia, because he thought she'd kick up a fuss. However, he broke the news to her just now,' said Ted, with an ironic note he rarely used. 'By the by, he sends his love.'

Oh, does he, thought Elizabeth.

She leaned back against the cushions, thinking of Ted and Peter. The well-being, the protective cloak of pregnancy, wrapped her round, and she did not even worry that her husband and her lover were spending two days together. She was simply, idly, glad that they got on well.

The telephone broke the silence.

'It's your Ma-in-law,' said a facetious voice. 'Coming round to have a bite with us, dearie? Roast lamb just the way you like it.'

Elizabeth explained that Ted was ringing again and that she was a wee bit tired.

Lilian sounded disappointed. She liked the young about, and enjoyed it hugely when Ted brought his tennis-club friends to play on the grass courts at Broad Oaks, followed by a big and noisy dinner. Lilian had a number of young friends whom she energetically sought out. She hunted Elizabeth incompetently, unsure whether to use aniseed, a snare or a lasso. She tried expensive presents, stuffed the girl's pockets with money, had woman-to-woman chats, coffee and dough-nuts. She bought her *Vogue* and a fox fur. The traps and snares were partly affection and partly possessiveness. Elizabeth was fond of Lilian, but wary.

Extracting a promise that she'd see Elizabeth at Broad Oaks tomorrow, Lilian rang off. Elizabeth dozed, and was woken again by the telephone.

'Lizzie? It's your hubbie, still in Brum. We *are* staying another night. The fact is, we're off to Northampton this evening. We had a good time at the factories, Alvis, Riley *and* Triumph. We stayed longer than we meant. Then we had a stroke of luck. A chap I know suggested we might go to Feeley's in Northampton. They've got an Alvis, only one, which came in last week. It's supercharged, and Feeley's sold it only a month ago to a chap who's had to go off to Malaya. They say it's a car to make your mouth water. A snip. Peter's very keen. I never saw a chap so set on anything. We're catching a train in a mo, and going to put up at the station hotel. Home tomorrow night, then. Okay?'

'Of course. Are you enjoying yourselves?'

'I'll say. I've done some business for Anstey's, and Peter and I had a slap-up lunch. None of your red-tea-in-the-canteen stuff. He does himself well.'

'Oh, I know!'

She sounded so relaxed and good-natured that he blurted out, 'You're a trump. That's what you are.'

He had been listening to Peter talking to Sylvia, poor chap.

Yawning, Elizabeth walked out through the French windows into the garden, thinking about Peter buying that expensive car. She stood idly picking dead heads off a rose bush. The old feeling of concern came faintly back: one could see from the look of Merriscourt, and the look of Sylvia, that the Bidwells were spending money like water. How could Peter possibly afford an Alvis? It isn't my problem any more, she thought. Odd to remember that . . .

Just then there was a long threatening growl of thunder. The greenish aqueous sky turned black. A great drop of rain fell on her bare arm.

She scurried back into the house, preceded by both dogs dashing for cover. They were only just in time. As she slammed the windows the rain began. There was a crash of thunder.

She sat down on the sofa and both dogs came to her like nervous children. She stroked and petted them. A vivid flash of lightning lit the garden, followed by louder thunder, sounding very close. The rain pelted, and the branch of a rambler rose outside the window beat against the pane like a whip.

The storm went on for an hour. The thunder moved away, and just as she and the dogs began to relax, back it came with forked lightning and renewed downpours of heaviest rain. Elizabeth began to wish that she had accepted Lilian's invitation. It would have been cosy at Broad Oaks – and talk would have drowned the elemental noise of the storm.

It was almost nine o'clock when she decided that she must eat; the dogs had been fed an hour ago. She had little appetite, and went out to the kitchen to lay a tray and boil an egg. As she was making toast she switched on the wireless. Ted lavishly had two, one of which he had kindly rigged up for her on the kitchen windowsill. Both wirelesses resembled their owner, they were on the large size. The kitchen wireless, shaped like a church window, had the loudspeaker covered in with stretched brown silk and decorated with carved wood flowers. She turned it on to listen to the nine o'clock news.

The affected, measured voice of the announcer was reading an item about the Spanish Civil War, which was now in its third month. Like most of the people she knew, Elizabeth felt the conflict to be very far away and unlikely to spread. Yet the war seemed to be dividing people into two opposing sides. Fascism against communism, Italy and Germany against England and France, Catholics against atheists. She was too selfishly wrapped up in her own life to do anything but merely listen, but she'd heard Ted and his father strongly on the side of the left, and David Rolles on the right.

Picking up her supper tray, she was on her way to the drawing-room when she froze.

'An item of news has just come in to Broadcasting House. There has been a train accident near Northampton . . .'

'Oh God!'

She went almost deaf with fright, but heard, 'crash of a passenger train with a goods train . . . carriages thrown down an embankment . . . some casualties feared but at present no details . . .'

Putting down the tray very carefully, and trembling from head to foot, and she rang the local police.

She had to wait. She was passed from one officer to another. She sat quietly, trying to control the trembling. At last a sergeant came to the telephone and gave her the number of the Northampton police.

'The number may be engaged a lot, Madam, but just keep on trying.'

As she rang off she heard a loud noise. Someone was hammering at the front door. The bell didn't ring once, but continued without stopping in a long shrill peal.

When she opened the door Sylvia, drenched to the skin, rushed in.

'*They're in a train crash. Did you hear? They're in a crash. They may be dead.*'

'Sylvia, calm down. Yes, I did hear. You're soaked! Come into the sitting room and I'll switch on the fire. I've been on to the police.'

Sylvia looked wild. Her hair was plastered to her head, her thin dress, one of Sylvia's chiffons, glued to her body. How long had she been out in the rain?

'What did they say?'

'Sylvia, you really must take off your things.'

'How can you be so calm? Don't you realise they may be –'

'Stop it!' exclaimed Elizabeth loudly, seeing by the strange look in her face that she was going to have a fit of screaming. 'Stop it and sit down and I'll get a dressing gown. Why are you so wet?'

'I don't know. Marchant was out and I couldn't open – open the car door –'

'Now calm down, *please*. Take off those wet clothes, what good will it do for you to get pneumonia? I've got the telephone number of the Northampton police, our local police said to ring. But we may have to hang on for ages because other people will all be telephoning too. You ring this number. I'll get my dressing gown.'

But when she came back down the stairs Sylvia hadn't moved. She sat staring. She looked slightly mad. Elizabeth, suddenly angry, made herself speak soothingly. It was like talking to a horse or a dog. She helped the girl to strip and wrapped her in the dry gown. Then she sat down and rang Northampton.

It was literally nearly an hour before she could get through. At last she did. They were hurried but kind. Yes, there was a derailed coach. More, there were four, on the line outside the town. Yes, police and ambulances were already on the spot.

'My advice is for you to ring the hospital. They'll know more than we do. St Mary's General. I'll get you the number.'

Throughout the long time it had taken Elizabeth to get through, Sylvia did not utter a word. She sat pulling at the dressing gown, her arms crossed on her breast, hunched like an old woman. She was staring into space.

Inside Elizabeth's head was a nightmare of horror and an almost unbearable desire to *know*. Surely soon she would be able to talk to somebody who would tell her that Peter and Ted were safe! But she controlled herself in a kind of frozen calm. Sitting very still she thought – I won't ring the hospital yet, I will wait. She tried to imagine the hurry and urgency, the ambulances arriving, the telephones shrilling, the staff intent on one thing only – to save life. I won't ring yet.

Then she wondered if she should telephone her mother or Ted's parents, none of whom could have heard the news or they would have rung by now. What would she say? That hundreds of miles away there had been a train accident, and that she did not even know if Ted and Peter had been on that particular train. What good would it do to upset them now? Perhaps have Harold driving through the night? I must do this alone, she thought, and for a moment forgot Sylvia was there.

The storm had stopped. At last she spoke.

'Sylvia, I'm going to ring the hospital. I didn't think it would be any good ringing sooner.'

'In case they hadn't brought in the corpses.'

'*Shut up.*'

'We have to face it, though,' muttered Sylvia.

'We'll face nothing until we find out. Be quiet.'

When Elizabeth got through to the hospital, she was trembling.

'St Mary's General? My name is Mrs Anstey. I think it's possible that my husband Edward Anstey and his friend were on the Northampton train which crashed earlier this evening. He rang me at six to say he'd be taking a train about that time.'

'I'll get Sister.'

A very long wait.

'Sister speaking.'

As Elizabeth repeated what she'd said Sylvia sat with her eyes fixed on her, completely still.

'I see,' said a matter-of-fact voice. 'You mentioned that your husband had a friend with him?'

'Yes. My cousin Peter Bidwell.'

'Could you please describe both men.'

A wave of terror went through Elizabeth. Sylvia is right, they are dead. Their bodies have been pulled out of the wreckage and brought to the hospital and somebody is going to identify them from my description.

Without looking at Sylvia, and using a dry careful voice, she began. Her husband was six foot two, heavily built, dark and clean shaven. Peter Bidwell was also dark, he had a round face and a black moustache; she even mentioned his cleft chin. Still she couldn't look towards Sylvia. And all the time she kept seeing bodies lying on marble slabs, faces grey and streaked with blood.

'Could you wait, please.'

Waiting had a death-like quality. She felt she couldn't breathe. She heard the noises of a hospital, echoing footsteps, voices. She sat pressing the receiver to her ear so hard that her ear began to ache.

'What's happened?' asked Sylvia, shuddering.

'They've gone to find out.'

'Oh God. Oh God.'

'Try to be calm. Remember the baby.'

'What does that matter? Why are they taking so long?'

'Stop asking. *I don't know.*'

At last a voice said, 'Hello? Hello?'

'Sister. I am still here.'

'Mrs Anstey?'

'Yes.'

'Both the men you have described have been admitted. Mr Anstey and Mr Bidwell. One of them will telephone you later.'

211

'Are they both alive?' she burst out, terrified that the nurse would ring off.

'Yes. One of the two patients is not seriously ill. As I said, he will ring you later. I must go.'

The long level sound of buzzing replaced her voice.

Putting down the telephone, Elizabeth repeated word for word what the hospital sister had said.

Sylvia's eyes were huge.

'They mean one of them may die.'

'I think she could have meant that.'

Sylvia was silent. Elizabeth put out her hand and felt for Bob's furry head.

'One of them may die, Liz. One of our husbands may be dead while I'm talking. *Which?*'

They waited all night long. The rain had stopped long ago and a ringing silence followed. The lights in the sitting room burned: it was damply, strangely cold. Elizabeth lit a fire and kept it going with logs. She put her mind to doing physical things, to using her hands. She laid the fire carefully and piled it the way Dolly had taught her. She made more tea and forced Sylvia to eat some toast. She went to the window with her dog companion, to watch the dawn come up over the trees. She had never been awake for a whole night, and remembered, with unbearable pain, when she had danced in her cousin's arms and how dark the night club had been and how, when they wandered home, the dawn had begun to pale the London sky. And what had followed.

Kneeling down to feed the fire, she remembered how it had felt to be taken – at last – by the man who had been her life. Then she thought of Ted who had saved her from poverty, and heard his loud laugh, and felt his arms catch her and lift her off her feet when she told him she was having a child.

Which? Which?

The Sister had said 'seriously ill', not 'is going to die'. Was it a hospital euphemism? Perhaps whichever of the two men was badly injured would pull through; both were so young and strong. Why was it, then, that all through the long night she never once felt the sweet fellowship of hope?

At half-past four in the morning, the time when the Lily Club had rolled its drums for the last time, Sylvia fell asleep. Elizabeth covered her with a travelling rug, looking down at the pale face for a long time, feeling pity, almost love, because they suffered together.

At six, as the dawn came paling across the sky, a harsh noise broke the trance in the room. It was the telephone.

'Liz? Oh Liz, Liz, he's dead. He died an hour ago. Oh God . . .'

And she heard the dreadful sound of Ted breaking into a storm of weeping before the receiver was replaced.

Sylvia was awake. She looked terrified.

'Peter's dead. I know it's Peter.' And before Elizabeth could speak she began to scream. It was the most terrible noise Elizabeth had ever heard, inhuman, hideous, high, piercing. Unable to bear it, she slapped Sylvia hard across the face.

Sylvia gasped, opened her mouth to shriek again, saw the hand still raised and was silent.

'Don't you dare have hysterics, don't you dare,' shouted Elizabeth. 'Yes, Peter is dead and it's dreadful, dreadful, but if you scream again I shall hit you again, *I will not have it*.'

Sylvia's teeth chattered in her head.

'George. I want George. I must go to George.'

She stood up, the rug trailing and nearly tripping her, and began a ludicrous half stagger to the door. Elizabeth ran after her and pushed her bodily back to the sofa.

'If you drive in that state, you'll kill yourself.'

'I don't care, I'd be better dead, better dead.'

Wanting to shout again, Elizabeth covered her with the rug and said carefully, 'I'll drive to Speldhurst and get him. Stay here and keep warm.'

Sylvia rolled over on her side, curved into the shape of a foetus.

'I want George.'

'I'll be as quick as I can.'

213

In the east the sky was turning to lemon yellow. Elizabeth drove fast. She tried to stop herself from thinking of anything but the twisting road between the high hedges, the mud from last night's storm. I turn here. Slow down there. As she came to the road which led to Speldhurst she looked at her watch. Half-past six. George would be still in bed. And suddenly the memory that yesterday Peter had been alive hit her in the breast. Peter. Lover. Cousin. She groaned, as if in labour.

But when she turned into the drive she was in control again. It was as if there was an iron door in her soul against which she must push with all her strength or a demon would enter.

The house stood symmetrical against the lightening sky. She rang the bell. Silence. She rang again, more urgently. No reply. She tried the door handle, and the door opened.

'George?'

The over-decorated empty drawing-room was quiet. Deserted. Nobody came.

'George?'

She went to the window, which was open, and suddenly saw a figure in the fields beyond the garden. It was George, and above him a dark shape was hovering, which then soared away. She ran out, stumbling through the wet grass and fumbling with the catch to the gate opening on to the field.

'George!'

He had his back to her, and when he heard spun sharply round.

'Elizabeth – what –'

'There's been an accident.'

'*Sylvia.*'

'No, no, it's Peter.'

She poured out the terrible story and he listened with a face of horror.

'I'll come at once.'

He whistled and out of nowhere the dark shape she had seen dropped out of the sky. The hawk landed on his outstretched wrist. He fed it with a piece of meat which

214

disappeared in a swallow. Then he covered the cruel head with a leather hood, fed the bird again, and walked beside her. He tethered the hawk on a long leash on a wooden block outside one of the stables. When he removed the hood, the bird stood hunched and glaring.

They went to the car in silence.

'Peter,' he said at last. 'I can't believe he's gone.'

'Poor Sylvia.'

'You have lost him too.'

And then for the first time she began to cry.

The telephone at Merriscourt rang day after day with people asking about the funeral. Marchant answered with a grave formula, using the same words and the same tone. The funeral was to be private, only close members of the family would be present.

News of Peter Bidwell's death in the train crash had shocked the county. He came from one of Devon's oldest families, he was known and liked, and represented something they clung to. Squires who had hunted with him, girls who had flirted, scores of people who had come to the wedding and looked on the family as part of their own lives were told they were not to share the tragedy. They were surprised and wounded. To be at the funeral, to attend the solemn rites was all that was left to show a Devonian whose family had belonged here for hundreds of years that he was valued and respected and remembered.

Nobody disagreed with Sylvia's decision, if one could call a message to Marchant delivered by the parlourmaid a decision at all.

'Mr Marchant, the Mistress says to tell you she won't have nobody but the family. Nobody.'

When Marchant expostulated, Ada walked out and slammed the door.

Sylvia had been brought home after the accident by George, who had literally carried her up the stairs to her bedroom. Since then Ada had taken charge. During the following days, while the necessary and dreadful arrangements were made for fetching the coffin, and the vicar and George had travelled to Northampton and back, Sylvia remained invisible.

Ted, bruised and shocked, was driven back to Holcombe by his father, and Elizabeth put him to bed and sent for the doctor. The Ansteys came and went. They hovered about, kind and shattered and anxious, hiding the relief in their hearts that it had not been their son crushed and dying in the train.

Elizabeth went through the days in a trance. Harold Anstey, taking a look at her, rang for Dolly who had already offered a number of times to come to Devonshire, and been refused by her daughter.

'She needs you,' Harold said. 'Just for a bit.'

'When I speak to her, she keeps saying no.'

'She's no notion what she wants, Dolly, and that's a fact. In her condition, she needs her mother.'

Elizabeth was dully relieved when Dolly, wearing her old black which she'd worn at Garnett's funeral, appeared at Holcombe. Dolly brought a kind of calm. She visited Ted and sat with him, talking gently. She consulted with the Ansteys. She was at her kindest and best.

When Ted was asleep, and mother and daughter were alone, Dolly said, 'How is Sylvia?'

'I don't know. I've been to Merriscourt twice but she won't see me. Or anybody else,' said Elizabeth indifferently.

'I am sure she will see me. I was just about her age when your father was killed.'

Taking Elizabeth's car, Dolly drove the few miles to the house. It looked silent and grey. When she was in the hall, Marchant said in a sombre voice, 'I'm so sorry, Madam. But she won't see a soul. Not even the vicar.'

'Good gracious! Surely he managed to get to the poor child?'

Marchant shook his head until his jowls quivered. He had sent up a message by that dratted Ada, beg pardon, Madam, but she was getting on all their nerves since the tragedy, to say Mr Spencer was here. The mistress simply refused to see him. 'Or anybody,' he added, echoing Elizabeth.

He did not add that Sylvia's fit of hysterics had been so loud that the vicar, in the hall and deeply shocked, had distinctly heard her.

Dolly stood adrift, looking at her old friend who looked gloomily back at her. She was thinking of the girl hidden upstairs. She ought to find a way to help her – and by doing so help herself. For she was in pain. Not only for the death of the young – for a time impossible to grasp – or because Peter's death resembled her husband's, as if destiny had chopped him down with an axe. It was more, even, than that. It was because her nephew, so beloved and so cruel, had been locked out of her heart for nearly three years. She had never forgiven him. Now he was dead, all she had was the agony of remorse.

'Madam,' said Marchant, breaking into her thoughts. 'Could you maybe fetch back Captain Westlock?'

'I thought he brought Mrs Bidwell home that morning.'

'So he did. Carried her upstairs like a baby. He's telephoned every day but she won't see him either. If you went to Speldhurst . . .'

'Perhaps you're right,' said Dolly slowly.

When she left her car outside Speldhurst she was nervous. She had not set eyes on George Westlock since before the family quarrel.

'*Why, Aunt Dolly,*' said George, opening the door. 'How very good of you to come.'

He took the little black-clad woman into the drawing-room, welcoming her and sitting her by the fire. She couldn't help noticing the room's order and severity.

'May I make you some tea, Aunt Dolly?'

'Thank you, no. I'm afraid I've come with a problem.'

'What can I do?'

His manner, voice, presence were like Christopher

Hoskins'. She felt easy and relieved.

'I'm worried about Sylvia.'

'She's not ill, is she?' he quickly said.

'I don't know. She won't see anyone.'

'Indeed she won't. I have tried.'

'Marchant told me. Look, this can't go on, George,' she said earnestly, not realising she'd called him by his name. 'I've just come from Merriscourt. Marchant said there wasn't a hope of my seeing her and I want to so very much. There's nothing more tragic than losing your husband when you're young. Who knows that better than I? I want to explain to her that you learn to bear it.'

He looked at her for a moment.

'She won't want to hear that.'

He saw he had shocked her.

'I'm afraid it's true. Sylvia can bear nothing. She goes to pieces. I've seen men like that under gunfire, it's very alarming. But surely Elizabeth –'

'She won't see her either. And Elizabeth is not well. George, *you* are Sylvia's oldest friend. A relation, in a way.'

He grimaced.

'I suppose that's true.'

'How long does she imagine she can go on hiding?'

'Haven't you guessed? She wants to escape his funeral. She thinks she can stay locked up there until everything's over. Yes. It's time I went to see her. Leave it to me.'

'Oh, I will,' Dolly gravely said.

'Captain,' said Marchant, opening the door.

'Marchant. I'm glad to see you. How are you keeping?'

'Sad, sir. Sad and old.'

'And I am the same. Don't announce me.'

Marchant stood watching the springy figure ascend the staircase.

George did not know the rooms in Merriscourt well. It was a long time since he had stayed in the house, and he did not remember in the long corridor, with rows of doors, which one belonged to the main bedroom. But outside one was a table on which was a tray of tea, the cup unused, the silver tea-pot, when he touched it, cold.

Turning the door handle, he went softly in. The maid Ada, wearing black, was at the window. When she saw him she started violently, shaking her head and gesturing for him to go. He ignored her and walked up to the bed where a figure was covered with a sheet, like a corpse.

'Sylvia. It's George.'

A muffled voice said, 'Ada, I won't see him.'

The maid ran across the room.

'The Mistress doesn't want to see you, sir. You shouldn't intrude, it's too bad of you. Please go at once.'

'*You* go. Now. And that's an order.'

Turning bright red, determined not to obey, she felt as if she were physically propelled out of the room. Yet George hadn't moved. When the door was shut she heard it being locked. She stood outside, crying with vexation.

'She's gone, Sylvia. Pull down that sheet, there's a good girl.'

No movement from the bed.

'Do as I tell you.'

The voice was not loud, but it was harsh. She uncovered her face but remained flat on her back.

'Now sit up.'

Very slowly, as if she were a hundred years old, she pulled herself up. He sat on the bed and took her hand. She tried to take it away but he held it, and after some vain tugging, she submitted. Her face had the dazed look of shock. He had seen that expression in the faces of soldiers mortally wounded in battle, and was filled with a passion of pity. Her fair hair, damp and disordered, lay across her cheek. Her cornflower eyes were swollen with crying and her lips so dry that she kept having to lick them.

'Lass. You're in a bad way.'

The tears rolled down. She did not wipe them away.

'Why wasn't it Ted? Why was it Peter?'

He rubbed the small hand.

'That's a question for the vicar, not me. Who knows why one man dies and another is spared? There's no sense in it that we can see.'

'What am I to do? Who'll look after me?'

She began to rock to and fro.

'There's nobody to look after me,' she repeated, rocking and weeping. He went on rubbing and patting her hand. When he kissed it, it smelled of sweat and scent.

'Listen. *Stop doing that*, you'll make yourself giddy. Just keep still. And stop making Peter's death worse by despair. You're pregnant – don't pull away – you've got that, haven't you? It should make you grateful. Oh, I know you think the opposite just now, I dare say you hate the child. Don't bother to deny it, I know you. But it gives you something in the future. You've got a child, and Merriscourt, Elizabeth, Aunt Dolly, a life, Sylvia, a whole life.'

She whispered something.

'Me? Of course you've got me. That's a damned silly question. You've always got me.'

'Promise?'

'I don't need to.'

'I want you to,' she said, in a feeble, babyish voice.

'Very well. I promise.'

'Swear.'

'Sylvia. I swear.' He had a moment of revulsion more at the voice than at the broken creature speaking.

He released her hand and walked to the window, looking out at the garden still littered by the storm. He was suddenly conscious of the silence which was all that the dead leave behind. The cupboards must be full of his clothes. On Sylvia's cluttered dressing-table, Peter's round face indolently smiled from a photograph in a thick silver frame. His living presence had not quite gone, after all. It hovered, casual, unserious, lazy, alluring, self-indulgent, somewhere here. Was that why the girl in the bed was afraid?

'I'm going to ring for Ada and tell her to draw you a bath.

Put on some clothes, and I'll dine with you here.'

He did not add – 'and then I'll tell you that you are going to the funeral tomorrow.'

That would come later.

Chapter Fourteen

When Harold arrived back from Northampton bringing his son from the hospital, Lilian clapped her hand over her mouth to stop herself from screaming. His appearance was terrifying. His face was nothing but a mass of bruises turning from purple to green, from brown to a livid yellow. A long blood-caked scar, left uncovered to the air for quicker healing, ran from forehead down past his eye, like a painted scar on the face of an actor playing in the battle of Agincourt. He had broken a bone in his left hand and his arm was half in plaster.

Those were the surface things. It was Ted himself, his silence and grief, which cast a pall of blackness over Holcombe as if, returning, he had brought Peter's death with him.

Elizabeth scarcely had time for her own stunned sorrow. She was filled with compassion for the shattered man who, still alive, now and then muttered, 'It should have been me. Why wasn't it me?'

For his sake as well as her own she eventually persuaded him to tell her what had happened. At first when she asked he said, 'I can't'. And turned away his head and began to cry. It was an awful sound from the big man who had not wept since he was a child of ten. But one night he woke, shouting from a nightmare, and Elizabeth went to his bed and put her arms round him.

'You must tell me. You must let me share it.'

'I can't. I can't.'

'Oh Ted. I beg you.'

With stops and breaks, hesitations, turning away from her, at last he did so. She listened in silence to her cousin's requiem.

The train they had taken had been slow, it had stopped at a number of stations, and Peter and he had both complained that they'd never reach Northampton at this rate. How fast had it been going? Thirty? Forty? Not very fast, he was certain, for Peter had said, 'I wish that engine driver would put his foot down,' and they began to talk about the cars they'd seen at the factory.

And then it happened.

There was a huge shuddering crash, darkness, shrieks. Ted was hurled across the compartment, hitting his head on the window, as the whole train seemed to lean over, quite slowly at first then faster and faster, hurtling down the embankment in a terrifying fall before Ted lost consciousness. The next thing he knew was struggling free from some wreckage across his legs, and crawling and groping in the dark for Peter. There was a smell of burning and screams and strange noises. He found Peter quite close to him. He felt his face and when Peter didn't make a sound he thought he was dead. Then Peter groaned. He was pinned to the ground by something, it was a door and when Ted frantically tried to move it, it was too heavy.

'I fainted again. I remember pulling and dragging at the thing, and Peter's voice far-off and the next thing was acetylene flares and rescue teams, and the dark was split with lights and men were putting him on a stretcher. Somebody went on screaming. I can still hear it. They say a man lost his legs . . .'

It seemed Peter had bled internally. He was unconscious when he was being carried away and Ted somehow stumbled up and the ambulance man said, 'You together?' and Ted went with him in the ambulance. Peter had once, only once, opened his eyes and tried to speak. Ted bent to hear.

'What did Peter say?'

The tears stood in Elizabeth's eyes.

'That's what's so awful – I don't know. He kept repeating it in a dopey dazed way, they'd given him an injection of morphia, I think, and he couldn't talk properly. Did he say Syl, he called her that, didn't he? Or was it your name – was it Liz he was trying to mumble? Poor chap. Oh, poor chap.'

And Ted began to cry.

She had never felt so close to him as she did during the days after Peter's death. For the first time since they had married she shared every thought in his head. She sorrowed as he did, wept as he did. Putting her arms round him, she comforted him for the most terrible thing that had happened in her life.

The day of the funeral was wild with a strong wind of the kind she and Peter loved as children, they used to rush down the hill with gusts blowing them almost off their feet. Leaves danced across the graveyard. The Bidwells were no longer buried in the gated eighteenth-century crypt, and over by the wall was a fresh-dug grave. Garnett had been buried nearby, his fine headstone had not yet weathered with moss and lichen.

In the church filled with Bidwell monuments, where Peter and Sylvia had married, the coffin on trestles was covered by the family's very old heavily embroidered black pall. Mr Spencer was High Church, and four of the curious yellow candles used by Catholics burned steadily at the head and foot of the coffin.

There were too many flowers. They lay in multicoloured fragrant heaps, in wreaths and bunches which filled the church with scent. They came from all the people who wanted very much to be here, and whom the young widow had refused.

Hiding her face in her hands, Elizabeth remembered how Peter had once laughed at her when she'd said 'If only', and told her they were the two stupidest words in the English tongue. She thought them now. If only she and Peter had married, she might have been with him on that train, and perhaps she would be dead too. Lovers believed if they died together they were united for eternity. Was it true? Cousin, if I'd died with you then this pain wouldn't fill me now. She remembered her pregnancy, and supposed it wicked to long for such a thing.

Ted knelt beside her, his poor face still covered with bruises, his arm in plaster. He leaned close so that his shoulder touched hers. When she put down her hands, Elizabeth saw that Sylvia was coming up the aisle of the almost deserted church. She was in black and her hair was covered with black lace, like a Spanish dancer. She had a ghastly pallor and leaned heavily on George's arm.

Nobody but Marchant sang the hymn.

Sylvia did not go to the graveside for the last prayers. She looked as if she was going to faint, and George took her back to the car.

Ted Anstey had been brought up on a number of maxims quoted by his parents and dinned into his head. One of these was that a man must never let go. In the winter of 1936 following her cousin's death, Ted considered that his wife had let everything go. Certainly she'd looked after him when he was ill after the crash, but that was only as it should be. He'd been up and about for less than a fortnight when Elizabeth went down with a serious haemorrhage and nearly lost their child.

As with the bruises he had suffered, sorrow and shock had begun to fade from Ted's mind, slowly at first but finally leaving him. When he thought of Peter Bidwell he had a pang of sadness, but that too began to dissolve. He was once again the man he had been, cheerful and hearty, laughing loudly, drinking deeply and looking on the bright side.

His wife's near-miscarriage, totally unexpected, was something he secretly resented. She did not once say she thought her cousin's death had brought it on. But the doctor privately told him so. Dolly had already left when in the middle of a winter's night Elizabeth had woken him, groaning and bleeding. Lilian was sent for by a terrified Ted and took over.

Nothing was too much trouble for Lilian. She was sympathetic and comforting, she busied about the house, saw to the preparation of tempting little meals, and amused Ted when he came home from work. She gave the ailing girl the blessed opportunity to let things slide.

Although the most voluble woman in Devonshire, Lilian left Elizabeth in peace. She saved her talk for the kitchen where Cissie, a relative of Ada's, was given a stream of orders and criticisms which were much resented. When not nursing Elizabeth, Lilian went shopping in the Daimler. She returned with copies of *Vogue*, *Harper's*, and *Nash's Magazine*, with quilted satin bedjackets, lacy nightdresses, bags of fresh doughnuts and pots of white cyclamen. Elizabeth was too weak to be anything but grateful.

Driven home to Broad Oaks every evening by the chauffeur, Lilian enjoyed giving her husband the latest report on her patient's progress.

'She's coming along nicely but it was a narrow squeak. She nearly lost that child.'

'So you've said, Mother.'

Nobody, thought Harold, could make a topic last longer.

'It's a good thing she's got me. A bit of luck. Where's her mother? Off to Sussex and that new husband.'

'She has her duty too, Lil.'

Lilian was not interested.

'The fact is I don't know what Ted would have done if he hadn't had his old mother to turn to. He's as much good with her as a wet week.'

'I hope he's behaving himself.'

'Oh, he does his best, but if you ask me, Curly, seeing her ill just after that awful accident was the last straw. He doesn't know where to put himself.'

Ted did find a sick wife hard to bear. His sympathy dried up after his mother took the reins. He fell into the habit of staying late at the works. There were always chaps to have a pint with in the garish public house on the corner. He took the Alvis into the workshops and tinkered with it, consulting the mechanics about refinements. When he eventually arrived back at Holcombe, he retired to the garage after dinner to continue the messing and tuning.

It was a nervous time. Elizabeth was afraid of starting to bleed again, she kept imagining she had, and was later filled with shame for her cowardice. It was also curiously boring to be weak. She had never been confined to bed in her life, never

226

had more than a cold dosed away with her uncle's old panacea of aspirins, hot whisky and honey. Now the quiet days crawled by and she was a prisoner.

Lilian came into her bedroom one frosty winter morning and whispered loudly, 'Someone to see you!'

By her manner it was obvious that it was a man. Elizabeth leaned back against her pillows and asked listlessly who it was.

'Mr Westlock.'

She had a moment of panic. She hadn't seen him since Peter's funeral, and even then he had been completely taken up with poor Sylvia. Suddenly, she felt ugly and ill.

Lilian stood looking at her.

'Don't you want to see him, dearie?'

'No. Yes. Oh, tell him to come up.'

'Righty ho, but he mustn't stay long.'

Lilian showed George into the bedroom, told him roguishly that she'd be back to 'fetch him away', and left them.

He came across the room, strong and springy, and sat down beside the bed.

'Lizzie,' was all he said. And then , looking down comically at the flowers in his hand, 'I brought you these.'

'Violets. I love them.'

'I got them from the violet farm. The girl said they'll last.'

'Dawlish violets do. Look! Some big white ones.'

'She told me they're for luck.'

'Are they?'

To her miserable embarrassment she began to cry. He had taken both her hands, and she pulled one away to grope for a handkerchief.

'George, I'm sorry, take no notice.'

He said nothing, but did not release the other hand. When he finally let her go, she picked up the violets and sniffed their cold scent.

'I rather like the tears,' he said teasingly.

She dabbed her eyes. She felt a little cheerful.

'Why?'

'Oh, since you're feeling rather weak, I have you at a disadvantage.'

He stayed for an hour. Lilian appeared and officiously told him he must go, but Elizabeth protested and it was clear that her visitor was doing her good. He was given the head nurse's permission to remain. He sat and talked. About Topsy with whom he had hunted recently and 'who goes over her fences on wings', and about Sylvia 'who it will not surprise you is now spending a fortune on maternity clothes.' And about some water-colours he had found in an old shop in Exeter.

When he finally left, she was sorry.

During the weeks that followed, weeks in which Ted never sat with her, never brought his supper up on a tray to eat it with her, stood by the door saying 'Okay, then?' before going out to his garage, and never brought her a flower or a book, George came three times a week. She looked forward to his visits eagerly. But sometimes she did feel weak or just plainly ill. She never said so, afraid he would go away. But he didn't. He sat, idly talking and making her smile. Once he said, 'Is it a bit better?'

'How did you know.'

'By your eyes, Lizzie. They are very eloquent.'

He paused and added that he was only going to stay for ten minutes, and then she had better sleep.

Silence.

'I'm such a fool,' she said.

He looked at her thoughtfully. She was decked out in one of Lilian's many gifts, a pink jacket fine as a cobweb and edged with swansdown. The delicate colour emphasised her gauntness. Her hair had lost its shine.

'You're a girl in a million. But you know that, so why am I telling you?'

Lilian had her own opinion about George Westlock and his visits. Like all generous people, she recognised it, or its lack, in others. She didn't miss the flowers and books he brought her patient, or the concerned way he talked to her about Elizabeth's progress.

'That George Westlock,' she said to Harold, 'is a man after my own heart. Do you know what he is, Curly? A tower of strength.'

Which was more, she thought, in a moment of contempt for her son, than she could say for Ted.

Elizabeth's other welcomed visitor was Topsy, arriving with out of season white lilac.

'It doesn't smell so don't bother, but it looks okay, I'll put it by the mirror. Then we've got twelve bits instead of six.'

Topsy sat on the end of the bed, unceremoniously shoving Elizabeth's toes out of the way. She looked her friend over.

'Being ill suits you. Interesting, you look. And as for your hands! Isn't it marvellous how when one's ill they look so pale and useless?'

She compared her tanned broad hands to Elizabeth's thin white ones.

'May I have a ciggie? I die for one. I suppose there's no hope that baby of yours is your cousin's?'

'No hope at all.'

Topsy fitted a cigarette into a jade holder.

'What a pity. It would have been nice having a little Peter trotting about, and don't pretend to be shocked. You know very well you'd much rather it was his and so would I. I loved Peter, his head was such a nice shape.'

'Brown eyes.'

'Like Bob's.'

Hopping to another subject, Topsy talked about Wallis Simpson. The newspapers were full of stories about the woman it was rumoured the King wanted to marry. A twice divorced woman – people were very shocked. Topsy went one better. She and David had been staying in Regent's Park with some friends, the Faulkners, who knew Wallis Simpson. Mary Faulkner liked her, but told Topsy that Wallis did keep the King waiting for hours, poor man, while she had her hair done. He was bored to death, flicking through magazines.

'Imagine. Well, last week they gave a party and who do you think was there? Mrs Simpson in person. So I met her. She isn't at all beautiful, you know, but graceful, with sort of intense blue eyes. And so suave. Very very slim, absolutely no hips, I felt like a carthorse. She's so tailored, too, lovely slick French clothes. Her hair was as polished as my riding boots. It shone. She's obviously funny because the people standing round her were all roaring. Then, Liz, *what* do you think happened? During the party there was suddenly a most fearful crash. Guess what! Sombody had thrown a brick through the window. We nearly jumped out of our skins. The brick landed smack on the bar and broke at least six bottles of gin.'

'What did Mrs Simpson do?' asked Elizabeth, enthralled.

'She didn't turn a hair of that polished head. H.M., by the way, wasn't at the party. But it was quite exciting, wasn't it?'

Another, rarer, visitor was Sylvia. From the first Elizabeth had telephoned but her cousin-in-law had refused any calls. Elizabeth persevered, and later Sylvia seemed glad to talk to her. Soon, too soon for Elizabeth, the tragedy was no longer in Sylvia's conversation and nor was her husband's name. She seemed to snatch at any pleasant subject. She told Elizabeth she was sleeping well and that her health 'was getting to be marvellous. I never imagined I'd feel like this. George says I look like ship in full sail.'

It was George who asked if he could bring Sylvia to see them. Lilian was delighted.

'Families must stick together, that's how it should be,' she said, blowing dust from spotless books and pictures. She looked critically at her patient.

'Wear the oyster bedjacket, dearie. It's just your colour.'

Elizabeth submitted to being helped into one of the six bedjackets which lay gleaming in her drawer.

Downstairs, the quiet house was transformed – there was quite a party going on. George arrived with Sylvia just as Ted's car drew up, and all three were sitting about talking. Or to be exact, Sylvia was talking and both men were listening and laughing with that indulgent admiration Sylvia conjured up.

'Now, you are not to look at me, Ted Anstey, I know I'm an

absolute sight,' she said. 'George had to lever me into his car, didn't you, George?'

'She weighs a ton,' said George ungallantly.

'Well, I think you look wonderful,' said Ted, all smiles, showing his beautiful white teeth.

'Oh, you're being kind. And the awful thing is that *you* look so good,' said Sylvia admiringly. Despite her heavy figure, awkward, box-like, she looked seventeen. George smiled, happy that his godchild was happy.

'Just you look out, old chap. When she pays compliments she wants something.'

Lilian had nipped upstairs again to her patient.

'Sylvia looks magnificent!' she whispered. 'Just wait until you see her furs.'

Sylvia came into the room and Lilian, with a merry 'I'll leave you two together', returned to the men downstairs.

'I told George he couldn't come up. I wanted to have you to myself,' said Sylvia in her pretty voice. Elizabeth had a pang of disappointment. But it wouldn't be the same, would it? to see George when she was there.

'Mrs Anstey says you are much better, but it must have been so horrid for you,' said Sylvia sympathetically, sitting down.

Lilian was right, she did look magnificent, and the picture of health. Her coat was decorated with a high white fox collar which framed her face, with the little kitten's chin. And there was a radiance about her, as if lit by inner sunlight.

She talked – about Mrs Simpson. What did Elizabeth think of her? Did she admire those sort of looks? George said he thought Wallis Simpson looked seductive. George came into the conversation a good deal. George says. Thinks. Likes or hates. Insists.

'Mrs Anstey told us you are having the baby here,' she said, looking about in a friendly way. 'I envy you. George has decided I have to go to the Westlea, because it's Doctor Witfield's place and he's looking after me. I think he's an ogre. So bad-tempered. He sort of glares at me when I ask the

231

simplest question. But George says bad-tempered doctors are the clever ones.'

She did not stay long, kissed Elizabeth, and left behind her the sharp unnamed scent she always used. She hadn't mentioned Peter once.

George only stood at the bedroom door and waved, saying 'see you soon'.

But came again alone the next day.

Ted was impressed by Sylvia's glowing pregnancy. He thought her a 'great sport' he told his mother. And Sylvia had invited him to tea at Merriscourt, wasn't that nice of her? In his mind he compared her to his thin, sick wife upstairs. Although Lilian was so encouraging about Elizabeth, Ted thought she looked ghastly. And it wasn't as if she was going to be up and about. The doctor said she must remain in bed, and that to move around might bring on another more dangerous haemorrhage.

The weeks dragged by. The only excitement as far as Ted was concerned was what the newspapers called 'This Grave Constitutional Crisis'. There were scandalous rumours that the King was seeing far too much of Mrs Simpson than was proper for a woman with a decree nisi.

On December 10, Ted and his mother listened to the King's last broadcast. It was made in a slow, harsh, tragic voice. He was giving up the throne.

Upstairs, Elizabeth was asleep.

Sylvia's child was due before Elizabeth's, and one morning in late February George telephoned Holcombe with the news. She had had a son.

'Mother and child in excellent form, and tell Elizabeth we'll soon be saying exactly the same about her. And give her my love,' he said.

Lilian was jubilant.

'Didn't I say that girl looked magnificent? The baby is *nine* pounds, that's a good size, it gives him a start, see? I really must try and pop round while she's at the Westlea. If there's one thing I love it's a new baby.'

Ted heard Lilian saying the same thing to Elizabeth as he was leaving for work.

The idea of Sylvia and her son took his fancy. All through the working day it hovered in his thoughts, something pleasant, something novel. The weather was blustery, it was nearly March, and as he drove in the direction of home the rain beat against the windscreen. He slowed down. Wouldn't it be rather a lark to go to the nursing home? He was not sure why he wanted to, perhaps because his own son would soon be born. Ted was convinced it would be a boy. So this was a kind of dress rehearsal.

He stopped at Teignmouth's best flower shop and bought a dozen out-of-season pink roses. Feeling foolish, he returned to the car and took the coast road. Westlea was a big ugly old brick house, much enlarged since it had been the home of a Town Councillor. It was on the cliff road and when Ted, drawing up, got out of the car, the wind nearly knocked him over. Collecting the flowers, he was glad to rush into the dry warmth of the entrance hall.

He enquired at a sort of cubbyhole presided over by an impertinant looking young woman in brown, for Mrs Bidwell. He had never visited a maternity home before and felt bashful.

'Is she expecting you?'

'No – that is – she's a relation of my wife's.'

The woman did some telephoning.

'She'll see you. Room 37. First floor, turn left.'

Ted went up the polished stairs and along the first floor corridor, avoiding looking at two women, horrors, wearing dressing gowns. In the distance there was a noise like bleating sheep. Babies. Soon the same noise would fill *his* house, and he found himself dreading that. Why had he come, he thought, clutching the roses.

He tapped at the door of Room 37.

A voice called, 'Ted?'

In a large room, in a large bed, in a dim light, with vases of flowers lined up like soldiers on parade, lay Sylvia. George

Westlock sat beside her. They were drinking champagne.

'Ted! I couldn't believe it when she said you were downstairs. How sweet of you to come all this way to see me.'

Sylvia held out her hand and rayed blue-eyed smiles. George grinned. Ted, for the first time in months, felt at home.

Sylvia exclaimed over the roses and asked George to ring for a vase. Where was Ted to sit? George, sit on my toes and let him have the chair. And where was another tooth glass? And did Ted like champagne?

Laughing at her little jokes, 'the baby's hideous, isn't he, George? – we asked if we could send him back,' Ted was as comfortable as if he were at the Bricklayers' Arms in Plymouth. He felt welcomed. He felt easy. He had never been so conscious of Sylvia before. When they'd met while he was courting Elizabeth, and after he first married, he was far too bewitched by Elizabeth to do more than notice a pretty girl with the glamour of having come from India. Now he saw that she was not pretty at all, but a shining beauty with a strong, an extraordinary allure. He did not recognise, and nor did Westlock, that she wore the unearthly radiance which sometimes visits women just after childbirth. It was as if nature, having forced a woman to obey her, then showered her with every exquisite physical gift, with a sheen to the hair, a light in the eyes, a milky softness to the skin, a strange, relaxed, swimming beauty, heavy with a sort of sexual power. Ted Anstey marvelled at her courage – the girl was a motherless widow who had just given birth to a son, and who had nobody in the world. There she lay, ringing the bell for nurse.

'Nurse. Dear Nurse! Isn't it dreadful, we need another tooth mug.'

She told her godfather to open a second bottle of champagne.

'The doctor says I may have a very little, just a spoonful, so don't look so disapproving, George. And Ted *needs* some.'

She took Ted's hand confidingly.

'You have to see the baby, it's no good trying to escape. Poor George has promised to come every day, and this afternoon Sister absolutely *forced* him to go to the nursery to admire Dicky. That's the offspring's name, you know. Richard Peter De Cartaret Bidwell, Dickybird for short. George said he looked just like a bird, didn't you, George?'

'He's not exactly a beauty.'

Sylvia looked delighted.

Ted was taken by a prim nurse in uniform down the passage towards the sound of the bleating sheep. He knew nothing about the new-born, and would soon have a baby of his own. They went into a room where the bleating was extremely loud. Lines of cots were ranged, each occupied by a wailing shawl-wrapped creature whose name was on a card pinned at the end of his cot. Ted saw two or three monkeys covered in dark hair, and nerved himself to be introduced to yet another hideous new arrival.

'There he is. Only a minute, please, then go back to Mrs Bidwell,' said the nurse, whisking out.

Ted stood, all six foot two of awkward manhood, at the foot of the cot. The baby was asleep. A small chubby thing, deep asleep and unconscious of the racket going on round him. A tiny hand, escaped from the shawl, lay half curled, like one of the roses he'd brought from Teignmouth. Bending down, Ted noticed as men always do the miracle of that brand-new miniature hand, with its perfect finger nails scarcely a tenth of an inch wide. How wonderful the child was . . . how he longed for one exactly the same . . .

'Well?' said Sylvia expectantly. George, relaxed, was reading *Country Life*.

'He's wonderful. Nearly as good-looking as his mother.'

'You are nice, Ted. Isn't he, George? What have I done to deserve two nice men visiting me at the same time? Have some more champagne.'

Ted enjoyed himself and returned to Holcombe to tell his wife and mother all about it. They were pleased and grateful as if he had done them a kindness.

Elizabeth was particularly touched that Ted had taken the trouble to go and see Sylvia who, since the baby's birth, was so much in her thoughts. Poor Sylvia with a little son and no Peter to share the joy. It must be like losing him a second time. When she said this to Lilian, who also went to Westlea to admire the baby and chat with his mother, Lilian assured her that Sylvia 'is keeping her flag flying. We don't want her to grieve all over again, do we?'

Elizabeth wasn't sure.

It was less than six months since Peter's death and her own heart still mourned, a desolate sorrow, a loss, a hollow nothing could fill. Did it go in the end? People said so. But when? She was like somebody in dreadful pain who asks – when will the drug work? Now? In ten minutes? In an hour? But it went on and with it came a terror of remembering the times she and Peter had made love. She wondered if that was all the bliss she was to have for the rest of her life.

'Your husband's set on a boy, dearie. You'll have to see what you can do about it,' said Lilian after Ted visited Westlea. 'Did you notice how he went on? A little boy, he kept saying. He's just like my Curly. They're the kind who need sons.'

'Poor her, if she's a daughter, then.'

'Don't sound like that, dearie. Whatever you have, he'll love it. And so will Curly and I.'

Certainly Ted was affected by the sight of the fat little creature Sylvia sentimentally called Dickybird. He went to the Dawlish nursing home again two or three times, greeted with delight by Sylvia. George was not there after the first visit. Sylvia said 'He's with that awful bailiff, Ferrers, trying to make sense out of the estate.' She raised her eyes to heaven. 'Don't ask me what it's all about, Ted, because I'm a silly thing about money and George pulls such a face. I hate being depressed, don't you? Come and sit, and tell me what you've been doing since yesterday.'

He talked on for a while about the workshops.

She had a way of listening with a most attentive face.

'Dickybird will need a car when he's older. Go and look at him, and tell me if he's any bigger than yesterday. Nurse is feeding him about now, yes, it's six, and he'll be gulping his bottle like a little pig. She says he's so greedy and big. She calls him Jumbo.'

Sylvia was not breast-feeding the child. Ted had not mentioned anything so indelicate but hoped his wife would use the natural method, as he called it to himself. Sylvia, though, could do no wrong. If she was not giving breast milk to the baby, it must be because in her widowhood she couldn't. A slip of a thing. No room for milk in that flat modern little chest, he tenderly thought.

She remained in the nursing home longer than the accepted fortnight, and when George eventually drove her and the baby home, Ted – quite one of the family now – was waiting at Merriscourt to greet them with more champagne.

'Ted.'

That was how she always greeted him now.

Elizabeth had become accustomed to her husband's exaggerated praise of the new baby and thought it showed an attractive new side of his character. When Sylvia was home again, Lilian keenly suggested they should call. Elizabeth had become almost too nervous to stir out of the house, but managed to get a special dispensation from her doctor for the visit. After all, the baby was part of her family. She promised to do nothing strenuous, but simply to call at Merriscourt for a very short visit.

Like Lilian, she was looking forward very much to seeing Ted's paragon.

When they arrived at the house Sylvia, looking fresh and pretty, greeted them, offering a scented cheek to be kissed and ringing for tea. But Lilian asked at once if they could see the baby.

'Of course. You'll find Nanny Osborn in the nursery in command. George found her. Quite a treasure and do you know, she was nanny to a Russian prince in St Petersburg?'

Sylvia grinned.

The familiar room which Peter and Elizabeth had used as children had been redecorated with expensive pink wallpaper and glossy white furniture. There was a new high brass fire-guard.

A very old woman in uniform stood up as they came in. Her impassive face was pale as parchment and networked with wrinkles; a Bible and some knitting were on the table by her chair. Lilian, watching her stoop to lift the baby from his cot, thought – Lor, she'll never manage it. She glanced over at Elizabeth hoping to share the joke. But Elizabeth was not looking at her.

The old nurse knew who Elizabeth was. Bent under the baby's weight, she came slowly towards her and placed him in her arms.

Elizabeth leaned down and looked at him. Desperately and vainly she tried to see in the tiny sleeping face a trace – the faintest look – of her lost cousin. There wasn't one.

Her own child was born two weeks later. The labour was long and exhausting, the birth difficult. After all Ted's certainties, the baby was an underweight little girl. Elizabeth named her Petra.

PART THREE

Spring – 1937

Chapter Fifteen

People in Devon said the Coronation spring of 1937 was the finest they could remember. First came the primroses thick in woodlands and ditches, followed by bluebells spreading purplish lakes under the trees. Children rode by with sheaves of them tied to the handlebars of their bicycles. At the edge of streams were the shiny marsh marigolds which Devonians called drunkards because they sucked up so much water. The apple orchards were bridal.

On a rare occasion of sociability, Garnett had once remarked to Elizabeth that he saw the county as a place of blending contrasts. The crimson cliffs dropped into a bright blue sea, the grey granite rocks were dotted among yellow furze and purple heather. 'You see the finest contrasts in the deep country and we have so much of that. Did you know the word Devon has a Celtic root, meaning "deep"?'

In harmony with the season, Elizabeth also flowered. During her pregnancy she had looked pinched and waxen, but that had gone and she was her glowing self again. Petra, now three months old, was still somewhat underweight but an engaging little thing adored by her grandmother.

Lilian still stuffed Elizabeth's pocket with fivers and bought her abominable presents, the most recent being two silver foxes linked at the back and fastened in the front by the fox's mask having a jaw-like clasp which opened to grip the animal's own feet. But now Lilian had a new excuse for giving. She provided in triumph an enormous perambulator identical to one in which some royal infant or other was wheeled in Hyde Park. She arrived with silk ties for Ted, hand-smocked baby dresses, Bakewell tarts made by her cook, and a bag of doughnuts for Elizabeth and herself to munch in the back of the Daimler when they went shopping. She wobbled into Holcombe three times a week on small feet as elegant as those of a goat. Her feet were Lilian's only beauty; the rest of her bulged in costly clothes and furs, necklaces and embroideries.

She was a grandmother in a million. The baby's smallest sneeze interested her, she had a long memory and settled down to quote her own motherly experience – she recalled early teething, flushed faces, wind, vomiting and earache and had a remedy for each. The baby liked her.

Elizabeth's looks were a pleasure to her mother-in-law. Lilian repeated to Harold, 'You can just see how marriage suits her. What we need next is a brother for little Petra.'

'Don't go saying anything of the sort to *her* Lil.'

'What do you take me for?' said Lilian who dropped hints weekly.

After the baby's birth, Holcombe became very sociable. Ted liked a crowd and was an affable host. He invited his tennis club friends round. Topsy came too, observing to Elizabeth one afternoon that 'your husband has lovely muscles.' In the dry spring weather, the tennis lawn was marked up, and the young Ansteys gave weekly tennis parties. White-clad girls and young men in flannels, their sleeves rolled up, played all through warm Sunday afternoons. Lilian and Harold came too. Harold was not a bad player, surprisingly quick on his feet, and Lilian sat in a deck-chair, presiding and commenting. She brought her own maid to help Elizabeth's Cissie in the kitchen, and tea was served on the lawn. Thin sandwiches, home-made iced sponges, Devonshire splits with clotted cream, and what Lilian called 'tennis cake', covered in marzipan. The noise all during the weekends was of a ball on a racquet, a voice calling the score.

Sylvia was one of the most popular and regular visitors at the tennis teams. Things had changed between Sylvia and the Ansteys nowadays. She telephoned or called, she made a fuss of Ted and was very sweet to Elizabeth who noticed, with pleasure, how nice Sylvia was to Ted and how much he liked

that. Elizabeth smiled when she saw them together in the garden, laughing over one of Ted's awful jokes, and when she
heard Sylvia's light 'yoo hoo!' at the open window Ted would
jump up, beaming.

'Shall we play a game or two, Ted? You promised to coach
me with my backhand.'

'So that you'll beat me at the tournament, I suppose?'

Ted and Sylvia resembled each other at tennis. They both
played to win and never gave an inch.

George rarely came to Holcombe either to play or to join the
parties. Elizabeth was sorry. Now that she was well again it
seemed he had deserted her. She wondered if he was the sort of
person who, despite a tough hardy personality, was tender-
hearted. He had known how down she was and had come to
visit her often just because of that. The idea of being one of
George's acts of charity depressed her.

'We don't see anything of George, Sylvia. You have told
him how we'd like to see him, haven't you?'

'Of course. Lots of times. But he's so busy with that disgusting bird. You should see him feeding it lumps of meat,' said
Sylvia, grimacing.

Widowhood sat lightly on the swift tennis-player. There
she was, a month off twenty-four, living in a great old house
with servants to wait on her and the antique Nanny Osborn to
cope with her robust young child. To the county she was a
romantic figure. 'That poor girl,' middle-aged men called her.
'Such a dear little thing,' said the women.

She was charming to Elizabeth.

'You and Ted don't come to Merriscourt nearly enough.
Promise you'll dine next week.'

When Elizabeth asked after the baby whom she scarcely
ever saw, Sylvia laughed. 'Dickybird's huge and fat. Come
and admire him. Nanny likes you. She said Dickybird's eyes
are just like yours. Freckled.'

Elizabeth, to her own mild surprise, grew quite fond of
Sylvia. One evening when she mentioned her to Topsy her
friend said, 'Must she be here so often?'

'What do you mean?'

'What I say. Can't you get out of asking her sometimes?'

'But we're glad to have her.'

'Mmm.'

Elizabeth looked at her uncomfortably, and Topsy sighed. 'I hate to say this, Lizzie, but someone ought to. Don't forget that you lost the last time with her.'

At that moment Ted breezed into the room, Topsy sprang up to say goodbye, and left before Elizabeth had a chance to go on with the conversation.

When Elizabeth thought about what Topsy had said, she felt slightly annoyed at first. And then uneasy. Since Petra's birth she had been a little, just a little worried about Ted. She had a feeling which she couldn't exactly describe that he was changing. She had even wondered if she should mention this to him – but what would be the use? He would hide behind his loud laugh and bury his face in his beer tankard. A conversation touching on anything serious was anathema to him still. He would start back as if from scalding water. She hadn't forgotten the few pathetic occasions when during the first months of their marriage she had tried to talk about their unsatisfactory sexual life.

Topsy's ambiguous warning told her something she had simply not considered. Could it actually be that *Ted* was beginning to be seriously attracted to Sylvia? That the old drama acted out at Merriscourt was to begin all over again with a different man? Why on earth should Sylvia's fancy light on Ted, suppose such a thing to be true? Sylvia was the belle of the country. A good many young and unattached men, many of them eligible, were only too anxious to take her out and about. Her beauty, her ownership of Merriscourt, her tragic single-ness, saw to that. She was invited out far more than Elizabeth had ever been. And then there was George West-lock. The few times Elizabeth visited her old home – there he was.

During the next few days after Topsy spoke to her, Elizabeth began to notice things she hadn't seen until now.

Ted only pretended an interest in his daughter. He paid little attention to the child, and whenever he spoke about a baby, it somehow happened to be Dicky Bidwell.

'Do you know how much that boy already weighs?'

'I popped in to Merriscourt tonight, and Nanny told me . . .'

'You should just see the way he gripped my finger.'

She had always liked to hear these things. But now, with eyes from which complacence had been removed as if Topsy had peeled a skin off the iris, Elizabeth saw that Ted scarcely loved his own baby. She even doubted if he loved *her*.

He had made love to her rarely since Petra's birth. 'Goodnight, Liz,' he said, from his separate bed. No young couple slept in a double bed any more, it was exceedingly unfashionable, quite a joke. Elizabeth wondered if this was a symbol of separateness in other things. Turning on his side with his back to her, he fell asleep at once like a log or a dog. More deeply than her airedale, who dreamed and in his dreams cried a little. And if she woke, so did he.

Had she lost Ted's love, she wondered. It didn't seem possible. For a short time? For always? Perhaps it served her right. She'd married him without love, and although he had not known, he was too in love himself and too eager to make her his wife, the bargain had not been a fair one. She had married him for rescue, without a trace, a shiver, of the passion she had felt for Peter. She'd given Ted second best, and maybe he was unconsciously paying her back.

Night after spring night she lay awake in the country dark, listening to the steady sound of her husband's snores. She hoped he would not wake the baby. Petra slept on, unaware that one of her parents, for the three months of her little life, had never loved her.

Elizabeth lay thinking about what a woman could do whose husband had begun not to care for her any more. Her body did not yearn for his. He was a poor sort of lover, sexually inexpert, taking her without any kind of caress, scarcely seeming conscious of who it was who lay under him. He had always made love in the same way in a hot thudding silence, rolling off her afterwards without an endearment, except the occasional 'was that nice?' She thought in wonder of the few hours when she had lain naked with her cousin. It had not been the same act. It was as if Ted and Peter were different animals, as far from each other as a boar and a panther.

But although she had not particularly worried that he had temporarily stopped wanting her, she had even preferred her body to belong to herself, she knew now that it was a sign of something very wrong. He used to be happy to talk when they were alone. Now he read his motoring magazines, and grunted if she spoke to him. He used to tease her. Not any more. And he often returned late with a string of excuses.

Was it Sylvia?

'Isn't it boring, Lizzie,' Sylvia had once said during her debutante days. 'Why must one have men around?'

What made Elizabeth convinced that Topsy must be right was Ted's attitude to Peter's son. He was always talking about the boy. He loved the very idea of a male child, as thriving and big as Petra was small. A child no more like his dead father than the infant Hercules.

Now that Topsy had opened her eyes, Elizabeth saw that she was in danger. She knew she must stay calm, and if she could manage it, invite Sylvia less to the house. But what good would that do, since Ted went so often to Merriscourt?

It was May. The month of the Coronation. It was no time for anxieties. The glorious spring was turning into summer and all over the county and the country, celebrations were planned.

'News,' said Topsy arriving at Holcombe. 'Guess what David found in the tithe barn, covered in pigeon droppings? A maypole! Apparently the last time it was used, according to David, was for the coronation of Edward VII. He's getting one of the lads to clean it and scrub it and he says it has to be sand-papered. You'd think it was a boat. Oh, we're going to have a merry time dancing round it, aren't we?'

'You don't mean –'

Bursts of laughter from Topsy.

'Peter always said you're too easy to take in. Did you actually imagine I'd hop round the maypole with my bosom bouncing up and down like two oranges in a sack? It's for the schoolchildren. David has broken the news to a delighted Miss Mason.'

Both Elizabeth and Topsy were on the local committee for the celebrations. Lilian had been invited but decided against it. She said she'd prefer to look after the baby.

'She'll make up in cheques what she lacks in ideas,' remarked Topsy later. 'Rather a good division of labour, I call that.'

The plans were many. There was to be a fancy dress procession, a tree to be planted (the bronze commemoration plaque paid for by Lilian), a May Queen chosen from the village schoolgirls, and of course, the maypole. Topsy persuaded the committee to add a tug of war, she said it brought out the ferocity in the men. There would, of course, be the village cricket match.

On a bright afternoon, riding back to Holcombe from a meeting, Elizabeth saw Colonel Rolles' maypole. It had been erected in the middle of the green, honey-coloured, freshly-varnished, a tall slender trunk of a long-vanished conifer. Crowds of children stood about, each holding a ribbon patriotically coloured red or white or blue. The schoolteacher clapped her hands and began to sing tunelessly.

'Come along, start. Come lasses and lads, take leave of your dads. No! No! Mary and Jim, you've tangled your ribbons already!'

The Coronation had been announced as a national holiday, and the newspapers showed pictures of crowds sleeping all night in Hyde Park; some had brought camp beds. There were shots of the coach being wheeled from the Royal Stables, and handsome pictures of the famous Windsor Greys who would be drawing it in procession. In London every seat in hotel windows, houses, or the stands built along the route had been sold for huge prices. London seemed a thousand miles away to Elizabeth, going out into the garden to look anxiously up at the sky. It was pearly, with a promise of sun. Faintly in the distance she heard the sound of church bells.

She went into the house for breakfast. The baby was still asleep, Ted in the dining-room. He had begun the meal alone.

'Thank goodness, I think it's going to be fine,' she said. 'The fun starts at two. Will you drive me and the baby? Or will you turn up later? Your mother very kindly says she'll take Petra over as I have to help with various things.'

'Don't think I'll be coming.'

'Ted, that's absurd. It's a *holiday* – the big day for everybody. Of course you're coming.'

''Fraid not. I promised to go round to Merriscourt.' She said nothing for a moment. Then, quite pleasantly, 'Oh good, you can pick up Sylvia, who will be coming anyway.'

'Syl doesn't fancy it,' he said, refilling an enormous breakfast cup, a wedding present, which held a pint of strong tea.

'But that's not possible,' said Elizabeth, still calm. 'Sylvia is from Merriscourt. Everybody in the village will expect –'

'Oh, spare us the old family tradition,' he interrupted. 'Sylvia thinks it a hoot. You're going, aren't you? You're the Bidwell, as we aren't likely to forget.'

She blushed with anger and shock. He had never spoken to her like that before. His voice, his manner, were coarse. She longed to give a stinging reply but saw the danger was real.

'You really can't *not* appear today, Ted, and nor can she. In any case,' very mildly, 'don't you think you're seeing rather too much of Sylvia?'

'You jealous, then?'

'Don't be *vulgar*.' Her good resolution was gone.

He put down the cup and looked at her with what she saw, with a cold feeling in the heart, was actual dislike.

'Why shouldn't I be vulgar? I'm not your class, am I? Funny, when you come to think of it, because Syl lives in the big house and she never makes me feel like that.'

Before she could reply the baby began her little plaintive cry.

'There she blows,' he said, in a voice of such brutal

248

indifference that she almost hurled the teapot at him.

'You're not interested, are you? You have a daughter you don't give a damn about. You're disgusting.'

'You and Ma do enough drooling for the family.'

'You go on about Dicky Bidwell all the time.'

'But I like the little chap,' he said in a martyred tone. He had stopped being unpleasant. Sounding sentimental, he added, 'Poor Syl. A stunner like her. And she's got nobody of her own.'

'George looks after her. He always has,' said Elizabeth, and had a moment of envy at the thought. She remembered how he had looked after *her* once. Before Petra was born.

'Oh yes, George buzzes round,' said Ted, shrugging.

'So what do you mean, she has nobody?'

'Dry up, Liz, for the Lord's sake. I mean Syl likes me with her, and why not? Anyway,' he added, 'don't expect us this afternoon, and stop pulling that long face.'

She was dully angry as she heard his car drive away. But the noise faded, and in its place came again the tumbling sound of bells. Most of the village would be going to church. She thought – I'll go too, and take the baby with me.

The celebrations that afternoon were crowded with farmers and their labourers, with wives and children, and the county. The sun shone. The May Queen, thirteen and fattish, was crowned with white carnations and hoisted on to a horse-drawn float on which she stood, crimson with pride, surrounded by children dressed as the countries of the League of Nations. A procession followed, and village and visitors roared their applause. The children danced round the maypole to a gramophone record, successfully plaiting their ribbons. Cider drinking began with the first event and went on all day.

Topsy organised a three-legged race, and George the tug of war. In the marquee on the edge of the green the men continued to drink raw cider, while the women and children tucked into the magnificent Devonshire tea paid for by one of Lilian's cheques. The cream came from a Merriscourt farm.

Long before six Lilian pushed the royal pram across the grass to find Elizabeth.

'Little pet's tired,' she said, indicating the baby fast asleep. 'If you don't mind, I'll wheel her home and ring Curly to come and fetch us. May I have her at Broad Oaks for the night?'

Kissing Elizabeth, she trundled away.

Elizabeth's anger of the morning had gone, although there was no sign of Ted or Sylvia. She'd spent a wonderful day. Noisy, eventful, comic, above all familiar. It was as if she were a girl again, surrounded by people who knew and liked her. Her own people.

She and Topsy served and washed up the tea. When dusk fell, the crowds moved out of the marquee to gather round a giant bonfire which was to be lit by the May Queen. Topsy finished the last plate and put it on a four foot pile of china, giving a grunt of satisfaction.

The two girls, both in white, stood for a moment at the entrance of the marquee, looking at the people milling about cheerfully.

'That cider,' remarked Topsy. 'Did you take a swig?'

'I stuck to tea. I never dare say I don't like cider.'

'Nor me. But I tasted it this afternoon because Josh was smacking his lips over it. Said he'd never had anything like it, and he knows what he's talking about. One mouthful was enough. Dynamite. Everybody will be rolling drunk by tonight.'

'Perhaps that's what they like.'

'Of course it is, silly. All men do. Even your cousin was squiffy at his twenty-first, remember? Hey, that reminds me. Where was Sylvia? I thought we asked her to give the prize for the tug of war.'

'We did, and she didn't turn up.'

'Well, well. And nor did Ted, one presumes? Now, Liz, don't pretend that you mind.'

But Elizabeth did.

The fête ended in a glory of fireworks. As Topsy had remarked when they went home, hangovers the following day

250

were universal. The village green looked as dirty as an evacuated fairground and took a day to clean. The maypole, taken down from its place of honour, was carried through the village to roost once more in the barn. All over England people with headaches were climbing up ladders to take down the flags and pictures of the King and Queen.

Real summer began. Hot, high Devonshire summer, a time of happiness. But at Holcombe all that existed was an armed truce. Nothing more was said about Sylvia. Ted was more polite to Elizabeth, and that was all.

In the late afternoon of a day hotter than the rest, Elizabeth lay under the crab-apple tree. The dogs were by her, panting. The baby slept in her pram under a further tree. It was very quiet, and Elizabeth was half asleep on the bone-dry grass when a shadow went across the sun.

She looked up.

'Why, George. What are you doing here?'

'Don't get up,' he said, and sat beside her.

'I haven't seen you since the Coronation,' she said. 'You were marvellous at the tug of war.'

She had watched him shouting, entreating, urging, the sweating string of men. His team had won.

'I used to do it in India. If you don't bully, they don't pull. Your garden looks very good. Who does it? Surely not Ted.'

'I confess it . . . Inslow comes when he has some time off. It's nice to see a Merriscourt face.'

'Good for you,' he said. He looked around at the tall flowers of high summer. In a great lavender bush the bees were making a fuss, reeling and buzzing. He turned to meet her rather curious eye.

'We don't see each other very often these days. We should. After all, we're related, aren't we, Liz?'

'Your grandfather and Aunt Bessy's sister Kitty.'

'Exactly. I remember you used to say we were "once removed", but as a matter of fact, we are second cousins. And stop looking at me like that.'

'Like what?'

'Did you know I can sometimes read your face?'

'Help. How inconvenient.'

'Not for me. I like it. You're wondering why I've come. And you're not fooled into thinking it's just to remind you that I'm your second cousin. Well. You're right. I'm afraid it's nothing as cheerful as that.'

Thinking at once of Ted, she had a stab of sharp alarm.

'I can't think of a way of breaking it gently,' he said. 'I came to tell you we've asked Marchant to go.'

'*Marchant!*'

'I know, Liz, it's appalling. He's been at Merriscourt for so many years, was your uncle's batman in Gallipoli, I know it all. How loyal he is, how your family feel about him. But Aunt Dolly is miles away and has a different life now. I don't think she would be so upset by this.'

'What has Mother to do with it? Or me? We're talking about Marchant. What on earth gave Sylvia the idea she could sack *Marchant*. It's not to be considered.'

'It wasn't Sylvia's decision, it was mine.'

Words failed her.

He sighed.

'We do quarrel, you and I. First over that damned house. Well, of course I like Speldhurst, but I don't like the fact that it made you unhappy, and anyway by rights it's yours. Now it's about old Marchant. Won't you let me explain?'

She still couldn't say a word. She was shocked. He went on slowly, 'I wish you knew how I've been dreading telling you this. Anyway. Here it is. Sylvia showed me her bank statements the other day, something she's never done before – she's secretive and silly about money. I could see she was frightened. And when I saw the overdraft, I wasn't surprised. She's seriously in debt.'

'She spends too much. And then sacks our family's oldest servant!'

'Lizzie, don't be so violent. Please listen for a moment. That girl is not a competent mother, and Dicky is doing well with his old nurse – he'd certainly pine if she went. Sylvia can't afford, and doesn't need, Marchant. What entertaining does she do? She lives in that great old house of yours like a bird in a tree, and wastes money until she frightens herself into fits. She can't afford to pay for the nanny *and* Marchant. It's that simple.'

Elizabeth could think of nothing to say, nothing to suggest. She was silent for a moment and then drearily said, 'How long has Marchant got?'

'As long as he wants. But he's naturally upset. I doubt if he will work out the month.'

The month. Is that all you get in exchange for your whole life?

As if to give her time, he stood up and walked over to look at the baby, still asleep, her arm thrown outward, her mouth slightly open.

Coming back, he sat down on the grass again.

'I can see a look of Peter. Is it the nose? She's a nice little scrap.'

She was not to be deflected.

'I must go and see Marchant.'

'Best when Sylvia isn't about.'

'Really?'

Inside, she was angry again.

'You can't blame her, Liz. She doesn't understand about English servants, she was an army child. Our regiment moved about. Cantonments here, cantonments there. She never even had the same ayah for two years at a time. She doesn't understand about English servants,' he repeated.

She heard the indulgence in his voice. It stretched back across the years from the time he had held Sylvia in his arms as a baby no bigger than Petra. She had grown up, and he had fallen in love with her. The tone, tender, uncritical, did not suit the tough soldier.

'*You* tell *me* when it's convenient for me to call and talk to my old friend,' she cuttingly said.

'I'm driving Sylvia to Exeter tomorrow. Quite a jaunt. Old Nanny Osborn too, and the boy his mother will call Dickybird.

What a name. I've told her I refuse to turn her son into a canary.'

She did not return the smile.

'If I come to Merriscourt tomorrow then, I can see Marchant by myself?'

'Any time in the afternoon.'

She felt uncomfortable. She was still in the mood to blame him for the dismissal but what he said made it impossible. *She* didn't pay the old man's salary. It was an impertinence to insist any more. She wondered about the money frittered away by Sylvia who literally looked expensive. In winter she wore furs like those in Hollywood films about Russian princesses. Marlene Dietrich, thought Elizabeth, had no better furs to frame her face. How often did one see Sylvia in the same frock twice. She had taken to going abroad to stay in the South of France. Elizabeth's country life simply did not include such a thing. She had never even crossed the Channel.

Sylvia's profligacy was banishing Marchant. Her shadow fell on everyone. It had darkened Elizabeth's life, fallen on Peter, on Merriscourt, and now on Ted. And on George.

An idea suddenly shot through her thoughts – it was like a meteor, bright and sparkling, she was quite dazzled. It was the brilliant solution to everything. And to make it shine more strongly, it was simple.

'George.'

'That's nice. You never call me by my name.'

'Don't I? I mean to.'

'I like hearing it. Well, Lizzie, and what particular thing are you about to ask me? I can see it's important by the look in your eye.'

She wondered how to begin, and decided not to rush it.

'I can't argue about dear old Marchant any more. I know you've worried about it, and it's a beastly decision to have been forced on you. I can see now there's nothing to be done. I must talk to him. I shan't be happy until I do.'

'Thank you, Lizzie.'

A pause.

254

'And?' he prompted.

'Yes. There is something else, a peculiar sort of favour. But it's important to me – I'm sure you'll see why.'

'Ask away,' he said. 'But if you want me to stop her spending money, my dear Lizzie, we both know it's a lost cause.'

'No. It isn't that. It's – well – it's about Sylvia and Ted. You don't look surprised and why should you be? I'm sure every time you go to see her at Merriscourt, he's there.'

'Once or twice.'

'Don't spare my feelings, George. I know he goes there every day.'

His face was difficult to read. Was he sorry for her? She'd hate that. She went doggedly on.

'Most men fall for Sylvia and one can see why. She's very fascinating. You know perfectly well that Ted's the latest casualty. He has a real crush on her. He even has a sort of crush on the little boy, it's Dicky this and Dicky that all the time. I don't mind all that much, although as the mother of Ted's daughter I'd be a saint if I wasn't irritated. But what has happened to Ted himself is serious. He is not happy. He isn't even pleasant when he's with me. I suppose he feels guilty, or maybe he resents any time not with her. But it's getting worse, week by week. It's going to ruin our marriage if I don't do something about it. George. *You* can help.'

'You said it's only a crush.'

'Don't fob me off. Wasn't I speaking plainly enough? Ted doesn't love me any more, and as for the baby, he scarcely acknowledges her existence.'

He looked grave and said nothing.

'You can help me,' she said again.

'What can I possibly do? I really don't see –'

'You're fond of her. Devoted to her. Aren't you?'

'Naturally.'

'Well, then. What I'm saying is, can't you keep him away from her? No, don't interrupt, just listen for a moment. Cut Ted out. It shouldn't be difficult, you're much more attractive than he is,' she went on, at her most blunt and unaware of his strange expression. 'Make her see that the man who matters to her, the one she wants, and God knows it must be true, is *you*. She'd never turn you down.'

She stopped. She knew what she was asking was outrageous but she was fighting for her marriage. She hadn't been able to fight for Peter, Sylvia had been too strong and Peter lost from the start. But this was possible. Fair. Ted was her husband. George was silent for so long that she began to hope, and, glancing at him and seeing him staring away from her across the garden she thought – Topsy's right, you *are* sexy-looking and very tough. Why should Sylvia look at hearty old Ted for five minutes if *you* were sueing for her? George and Sylvia belonged together. Hadn't he brought her to England, and except for that fatal time when he'd left her at Merriscourt, hadn't he remained near her like a shadow? But there was nothing shadowy about George. He was considerable. And Sylvia was his preoccupation.

'George?'

'I'm sorry. I can't do what you ask.'

Colour flooded her face.

'You mean you won't.'

'I mean it isn't possible. I'm sorry,' he repeated.

'You don't deny he's chasing after her?'

'I'm afraid that's true enough.'

'So how can you sit there and imply *you* don't care for her! I used to think Sylvia was your whole life – I still think it. Why is what I'm asking so dreadful?'

For the first time since she'd known him, she saw him at a loss. He said quickly, 'Don't be so upset. I'd help if I could. It's bloody for you – but I can't do what you want.'

'You hang round her all the time! She's a danger to my marriage, she's breaking it up and you won't help me. She's *your* responsibility. Who brought her to Merriscourt? We didn't ask her. We didn't want her. Who landed her on us for months on end? Because of you, Peter married her.'

His face changed. He stared at her quite differently.

'Ah. I wondered when we'd come to that.'

'What the hell do you mean?'

He continued to stare at her. It was Elizabeth who dropped her eyes.

'Nothing,' he said. 'I mean absolutely nothing.'

But she knew he had guessed it all. That she had been in love with her cousin and that Sylvia had stolen him. And that after his marriage, Peter and she had been lovers. He doesn't forgive me for wronging Sylvia, she thought. That's why he won't help me now. God! I don't *understand* what he feels about her.

He stood up.

'I really must go. Look, Lizzie, I promise to do what I can. I'll speak to her and try and warn her off. She may listen. Okay? And,' he went on, as she also got to her feet but said nothing, 'you'll remember to go and see Marchant.'

'Do you think I'd forget him?'

'No. Perhaps you remember too much and too long.'

Elizabeth, leaving Petra with her grandmother, drove to Merriscourt the following afternoon. The old house was basking in the sun, every stone warmed. Many of the arched windows were open, and so were the smaller lower ones in the Jacobean wing; summer flew in and out. Elizabeth had brought both her dogs who jumped from the car and vanished through the open front door, returning home.

An elderly figure emerged. It was Marchant, moving at a tortoise pace.

'I saw the dogs. Knew you'd come, Miss Elizabeth.'

They smiled, taking each other in. He was stouter than he used to be, his chins had multiplied, he seemed to have at least four. But he did not have the air of a man struck down by misfortune. His small eyes twinkled.

'If you've come to see the Mistress, she's out.'

'I came to see you.'

'Reckoned you would. Cook's made a batch of scones.'

They went into the cool house.

'Can we have tea in your pantry?'

'Don't you want it in the drawing-room, Miss?'

'Marchant. Stop teasing.'

He ushered her across the hall. Very large white vases straight from drawing-rooms photographed in *Harper's Bazaar* were filled with flowers. But they were not the appealing summer and autumn bunches, mauve, blue and pink, or shades of yellow and russet, which Dolly used to arrange with a natural eye for variety. These flowers were rigorously separated. Dozens of red roses. Masses of blue lupins. The house wore a 1937 look.

But in Marchant's pantry the silver was still so clean that it shone with a bluish light, and the narrow table was laid with familiar rose-patterned china, most of which had been saved from extinction with black rivets.

During their rich Devonshire tea, he asked after 'the Mistress and Doctor Hoskins?' in a roguish manner. Elizabeth told him about a week she and the baby had spent in Sussex. She didn't add, but thought he was sure to guess, how Dolly had queened it as the Doctor's Wife. In exchange for her news, Marchant told tales of ancient Nanny Osborn and the large and handsome Dickybird Bidwell.

'She's too old, Miss Elizabeth,' he said, relapsing into broad Devon. ' 'Tes time she give up before she trips up and cracks 'un head open.'

'Heaven forbid, Marchant. Suppose she dropped the baby!'

'You're right,' he said, relinquishing the accent casually, like a man who is bi-lingual. 'Heaven should forbid. Do you know how old she is? She let fall the other night that she was nursemaid before the old Queen's Jubilee. That was 1896. Saw the monarch's burial, too, four kings walking behind the coffin. One way and another, Miss, she's too old . . .'

'I suppose she does seem a little elderly.'

'I told her last night,' said Marchant solemnly. 'There's a time to give up, I said. You've got to know that or it's a poor come-along for everybody else. Give up when it's time, I said. All *she* answered was she could do with a bit of help. She's a cool one. But she's wrong. The time does come . . . I've reached it myself and I can give her a good few years.'

It was neatly done.

'Dear Marchant, *I am so sorry*. The Captain told me yesterday and I was shocked. If only I could do something!'

He went as far as patting the young hand which held his own. He reflected for a moment. Well, he said, he must admit that he'd been thinking about leaving Merriscourt for many a long day. Since the old Master died. 'The fact is, Miss Elizabeth, I can tell *you* that butlering tires me. It's the standing which is hard on the back, you see.'

He looked round as if suspecting a spy, and murmured that he had put away a tidy sum. Well, smallish tidy. Never spent a farthing on himself and never, he added piously, been blessed with a wife. So, with this smallish tidy what he wanted to do was the sensible thing for his old age. Gazing at Elizabeth, he almost winked.

Sympathetically agreeing, Elizabeth was more amused than she had been for months. How often Peter had called Marchant 'the old rogue'. From the time they had been small children, he had sworn that Marchant was salting money away.

'What's he doing taking the bus to Teignmouth? And I've seen him coming out of the post office three times.'

'Old age pension.'

'Taking cash out? Don't be stupid, he's stuffing it *in*.'

Peter declared that not only was Marchant putting away his pay and anything he made on the side, but he was also a shrewd follower of form. When the fancy took him (which Peter said was not often enough) he could give you a tip for the Exeter Stakes which was certain to be among the first three.

While Marchant talked, going round and round the point like a dog circling before it finally sits down, Elizabeth listened. He made a last circle and finally plumped down with his news. He was going in with an old friend, Sergeant Timmins, who'd turned up in Devon a year or two ago. They'd known each other in the Army. Nice fellow, Timmins, Sergeant in charge of Stores, but wouldn't set the world on fire. Well, they'd been thinking of buying a pub together. They'd been over to look at *The Dog & Pheasant* along the Chudleigh road.

'Comfortable old place, the landlord wanted to sell because he'd lost his wife and was moving away . . . so, Timmins (he's by way of being a widower too, Miss, you never know when the Lord will take our dear ones from us) . . . Timmins wants to go into the business with me.'

Marchant paused confidentially.

'I've been thinking it over. Without being boastful, I'd add something. Tone, you know. Seeing things were done as they should be.'

Elizabeth did not doubt which of the two men would get the better of the bargain. She guessed Marchant's smallish tidy must be well over half, perhaps three-quarters, of the price of *The Dog & Pheasant*. It sounded as if poor Timmins would be a kind of head housemaid. She remembered a nurse she and Peter had shared, a young girl called Harper who had greatly admired Marchant.

'Born to command, he is,' Harper used to sigh. 'Anyone can see he's a born leader.'

Tea was cleared away and later the old man left the pantry and returned with a cut-glass decanter of sherry. It was the silky sherry, dark and rich, which Garnett had occasionally given to guests.

'The Old Master,' said Marchant, pouring out two schoonerfuls, 'had the tastes of a gentleman.'

'So did my cousin.'

'Now that's true. He liked things right. But you can't say Mr Peter ever relished a good sherry wine.'

Elizabeth met two eyes twinkling like stars. Her old friend was safe. He was not insulted and stricken, miserable, made ill from shock. He was leaving Merriscourt when it suited him and with a plan of his own. He was the same old rogue, the same old pirate. The skull and crossbones still flew over the butler's pantry.

Chapter Sixteen

Proper pride should have kept her away from George West-lock. But the miserable state of her marriage left no room for such a luxury. It was extraordinary how much worse, week by week, things were between Ted and herself. It all happened so quickly, since Richard Bidwell was born. Now she and Ted, who had been contented and merry, were like the unhappy couple in a cartoon, the husband glowering and guilty, the wife resentful and sharp.

She couldn't help wondering if George had talked to Sylvia. Would it help? Anyone as lovely and predatory as Sylvia was unlikely to give up a man – but George was clever with her. Or why had he said he'd try? Again and again she remembered his flat refusal when she'd asked him, in so many words, to become Sylvia's lover. How had I the nerve she thought, bitterly amused. Perhaps they had been lovers in the past, and Sylvia had ended the affair. That would explain his manner at her asking.

There was little hope that anything would come of his promise, but she wanted badly to see him. Anything was better than moping at home. It was pathetic, but she kept remembering how happy she and Ted had been, even if it was in a limited, an uncivilised way. She scarcely thought about sex with Ted, but when she did she marvelled that Sylvia after having been in Peter's bed could even bear it. Ted and Sylvia had probably been lovers now for months. Her lack of vanity suggested to Elizabeth that Sylvia must be a very much better lover with Ted than she'd ever tried to be.

Driving to Speldhurst on a damp morning which threatened rain, she realised she had not once been to this house

261

since the fatal morning when she'd gone to tell George that Peter had been killed. She wondered if he would be at home: he said he was often at Merriscourt these days 'trying to make Ferrers earn his keep'. It was curious to hear George speak about the estate as if it were his. Perhaps, since it was Sylvia's, he thought of it like that.

Drawing up outside the house, she was struck again by how unsuitably large it was for a man living alone. She couldn't imagine George being lonely, but the house probably was. It looked severe and had an uninhabited air. The wisteria winding up the front of the house was in late flower, but for whom? She rang the bell. She was unsurprised when there was no reply. Only the chirp of birds and a waiting country silence. She rang again.

And then, with an inward shiver, she remembered that other visit when she had brought the terrible news. As if re-enacting the dawn three years ago, she turned the door handle and went into the house, calling his name.

Coming out again, she crossed the garden, opened the gate and set off across the fields in the hope of finding him. The wind blew hard and she glanced upwards to see if rain was near. A speck was moving at speed across the sky in the direction of the wind – it was not flying but falling. It seemed to drop from the sky, then zoom up as if shot from a gun. The bird hung high and motionless, then down it fell again. At last, veering away, it landed on a distant tree.

'Liz?'

It was George coming out of the trees towards her. He wore a buckskin glove on his left hand, hanging with a mess of cords and straps.

'Did you see Tova?'

'Is that her name?'

'Yes. A Viking name.'

He glanced up at the tree where Tova, perched on a branch, looked back with what Elizabeth thought were murderous eyes.

'She looks rather fierce,' said Elizabeth, sounding like a

262

visitor forced to pay a compliment to her host about his child.

'I've seen her strike a partridge and split it in two,' was the parental reply. Stripping off the glove, he handed it to her.

'Like to try? Put this on. Let me fix it.'

He fitted the roughly-sewn glove, its thumb, fingers and back of double thickness, on to her left hand.

'Why not the right?' she asked curiously.

'I've no idea. European falconers always carry their birds on the left wrist. In India and Persia they use the right. Now, here's a chicken leg. Whistle.'

Elizabeth obeyed, whistling as loudly as she could while she gingerly stretched out her gauntleted hand with its morsel of chicken. Down from the tree shot the bird with a rush of wings looking – thought Elizabeth tense and stock-still – as if it would gouge out her eyes. Tova hovered, turned her wings into brakes and landed, thrusting her talons into the leather. She gobbled the chicken. She remained a moment or two while Elizabeth, enthralled and fearful, admired the huge shoulders made from folded wings. Then the hawk flew contemptuously back to the tree.

George laughed, pleased. 'Well done. I always knew you were a brave creature. Sylvia won't even come into the field when Tova's about.'

They stood watching the falcon flying almost out of sight; it returned only when George, again wearing the glove, threw something on a long string into the air. Tova snatched at it.

'It's the lure,' he said. 'It's made from a horseshoe padded and covered with leather. That's a pigeon's wing I've tied to it.'

When Tova had almost finished eating he put a leather cap over the bird's head, topped with a bunch of feathers. He did this quickly and gently.

'But doesn't she hate that?' exclaimed Elizabeth as they began to walk, the hooded bird still eating as it balanced on his wrist.

'It took patience to break her to the hood. But she gets a few more mouthfuls after it's on, and she doesn't think the hood means the end of her dinner.'

They walked back to an empty stable which he had fitted up as a hawk house, with a long horizontal perch and trays of sawdust. At the stable door was a large solid block with an iron ring sunk into it, set low on the ground. During the day, he said, if it wasn't wet or windy, Tova preferred the block. The leash was long and she moved around quite safely. At night she was indoors. When she was on the block he took off her hood. She sat there, beautiful, powerful, deckled, regarding them with enormous black eyes ringed with lemon yellow.

'She despises humans,' he said, as they returned to the house.

'Surely not you.'

'Me most of all. She can escape me any time. She uses me.'

He did not ask why she had come to see him, and she wondered with inward amusement if she imagined it was to admire his hawk. Indoors, Speldhurst was ordered and spotless. Accustomed to the mess of Ted, newspapers and motoring magazines all over the carpet, shoes to be tripped over, tools from the car on her scrubbed wooden kitchen table which became stained with oil, Elizabeth was struck by the comparison.

'Let's have coffee in the study. There's something I want to show you, Liz.'

They went into a small room which adjoined the drawing-room and as she entered it, she gasped. The walls were covered, almost to the ceiling, with water-colours. They glowed. And they were a vision of the world. Snowy mountains awesome in their vastness. The cornflower blue of warm seas. Long roads vanishing into pearly dust. Cypresses like exclamation marks. Bridges spanning wild rivers, and the people crossing them. Camel trains. The deep shade of palms, the white of deserts.

'George, they're *beautiful*.'

He stood looking round.

'People saw things differently then, don't you think? They had a feeling of wonder. Just like you,' he added. 'Now I'll

264

make you some coffee. No, don't offer to help, I would much rather you looked at the picture and then told me they are as good as those at Merriscourt.'

He returned shortly with a tray.

'I saw Marchant yesterday,' Elizabeth said.

'And?'

'And I'm not worried about him any more.'

'Because he's buying a large share of *The Dog & Pheasant*.'

'You knew all the time!'

'With Sergeant Timmins appearing when I was at Merriscourt the other morning, I couldn't escape hearing about it. Very loquacious he was. I thought he would never go.'

'Why didn't you tell me?'

'And rob old Marchant of the fun? I'm sure he made a meal of it and you enjoyed every minute,' he said, teasing her.

'I suppose I did. You're so annoying, George.'

He laughed and she wondered, then, when he was going to speak about Sylvia.

'Do you know,' he said, 'I've seen more of you this week than at any time since you were expecting your baby. And you can stop wondering how to introduce the subject that's very obviously in your mind. I saw Sylvia late last night. Very late. I wanted to see her alone.'

'You mean after Ted had left.'

'I'm afraid so, Liz. I hung about in the lane until his car drove off. Then in I went. Sylvia wasn't too pleased when I started talking about him. Not to put too fine a point on it, when I said what I thought she was bloody rude.'

'Did you ask her to stop seeing him?' said Elizabeth. How odd. He seemed to be her champion just now.

'Indeed I did. I said there was nothing more unattractive than a young woman who has tragically lost her own husband setting out to grab somebody else's. I said there were scores of single young men who admire her enormously, and I also told her that people in the county were talking (which is true), and that she's on the way to losing her reputation. That cut no ice. She doesn't give a straw for what the people here think of her.

She's still the little Anglo-Indian at heart, it would be a different story if she were in Calcutta. She'd mind there.'

'So she won't give him up when there are so many others who – *oh, why Ted?*'

He looked at her very oddly indeed.

'Don't you think much of him, then?'

'What do you mean!' she burst out. 'The point is that he is married.'

George's expression changed. His voice was more gentle than usual.

'Lizzie, Lizzie, haven't you met Sylvia's kind before? The woman who prefers another woman's man? Who needs the thrill of competing, stealing, winning? I've known scores of them and they're dangerous. A girl like you –'

'Hasn't a hope.'

He paused and then said, 'A wren with a falcon, I'm afraid.'

But she was sure he knew she'd never been in love with Ted.

'Thank you for trying. I suppose it's all up with me, then.'

She looked down at the Persian carpet. It was a glowing ruby colour and round its edge were prayers woven in Arabic; she did not see them, she was deep in her unhappy thoughts. He looked at her reflectively. There was a good deal missing from the short tale he had just told. It had been after midnight when Ted's car had finally driven away, and he, like some private detective sitting for dreary hours on the watch outside a house, had turned into the drive. Merriscourt's high windows, as if a ball were in progress, streamed with lights. Sylvia answered the door, apparently thinking Ted had come back and when she saw him she burst out laughing and ran into his arms.

They kissed affectionately.

He was fascinated by the way she looked, melting, moist-eyed, Venus *toute entière*. She had been making love. It came into his thoughts that he never remembered seeing a woman look quite as alluring as Sylvia did just then.

'Georgy, how lovely to see you, I absolutely miss you when

you neglect me. Come and sit down and talk and I'll pour you a brandy. Isn't the weather horrid? Like the rainy season. I keep expecting swarms of flying ants and elephants wallowing in the river . . . '

She poured him a drink and one for herself, burying her kittenish face in the brandy glass. She was wearing her favourite chiffon, this one was greyish and full-skirted and made her look as delicate as a night-moth. Where had those pearls come from? He didn't remember the Bidwell pearls were as large as that.

'How have you been, Sylvia? It's quite true, we haven't seen much of each other, but I'm always here, you know, stuck with Ferrers. It's you who are conspicuous by your absence.'

'Oh. One has to shop. And Dickybird takes up so much time.'

'I thought Nanny Osborn was on duty?'

'She is, she is, but a little boy needs his mother. Nanny says mothers must be with their children every day from half past four to half past five. It's the rule. So down comes the baby and we sit and stare at each other, rather.'

'Most maternal.'

'Sarcastic old thing. Why do I love you? I do, though. Best of all. Bestest.'

'That's nice.'

'*You* aren't nice, Georgy porgy.'

Those nicknames, he thought. Dickybird. What did she call the unfortunate Anstey?

She continued to chatter, enjoying the feeling which George always gave her, that she was indulged. She was enchanting and she knew it. And all the time she wore the curious allure of looking exhausted. Perhaps Anstey's good in bed, he thought, or at any rate energetic. I wonder why that surprises me. Because he clearly was not with Elizabeth. What does one know of other men's sex? And everybody tells lies.

Tiredness made her talk herself out eventually and she

267

contented herself with holding George's hand, or sipping his drink when she'd finished her own, yawning and untying his shoe laces. He knew this mood. She had been little different as a child. The more tired she was, the more tiresome she became. And the more beautiful. Her beauty astounded him.

When he knew she was paying attention, he began casually talking about Ted. Sylvia revived. She said how much she liked him, and he was a sort of relation, wasn't he? A cousin-in-law to poor Peter. She owed Ted such a lot for looking after her when she lost Peter. Ted had been marvellous.

'He's like you, George. A real man.'

'Somebody else's, though.'

Her face snapped shut.

'Sylvia. You heard what I said.'

'I don't want to talk about it.'

'I'm quite sure you don't but the fact is that Ted Anstey is losing his head over you. Don't look so pleased with yourself. I shouldn't think it much of a coup to catch *him*. Any woman who made a fuss of him could do it. He's easy game.'

She gave him a sudden angry look, stood up and flung across the enormous empty room.

'I'm going to bed.'

'Not until you hear me out.'

He disliked the role of mentor. He was in the right and she in the wrong but he never wished to judge. Tough on himself, he was surprisingly lenient with other people, and always so with women. They were to be forgiven everything. It was the softness in him that had promised Elizabeth he would help her. And the softness again which made him despise his own voice telling Sylvia she was behaving cruelly, and forcing her to listen to a lecture. She must, he said, give Ted up.

He did not say he knew they were lovers.

She sat down as far as possible from him, darting looks at him which had the same murderous quality as Tova's.

'Silly old me. I thought you'd come to be nice, and all you do is drone on about my giving up Ted. Well, I'm not going to. He's kind to me. Anyway if I told him to go he wouldn't, so

268

what's the point? I need him. It isn't,' she added pointedly, 'as if I had anyone else.'

'What is that supposed to mean?'

Sylvia got up from the distant chair and walked back to him. She climbed on the sofa and took his hand. He could smell her strong scent. He felt tenderly towards the beauty looking so tired and seductive. She made her lips, kissed free of lipstick hours ago, into a pout.

'It isn't as if *you* are willing to look after me, are you, Georgy darling?'

She leaned enticingly towards him.

He laughed. And moved away.

'I must go.'

It was Elizabeth, pulling him back to the morning light at Speldhurst and to the company of a very different girl whose face was desolate.

'I'm so sorry. I wish I could have done more,' he said. He hated to see that look.

She didn't answer and they walked to the front door. Her head drooped, she looked weary and sad. Without warning, he suddenly put his arms round her and kissed her.

Scarcely knowing what she was doing, she clung.

He let her go, and when they said good bye and she drove away she thought – he's sorry for me . . .

Elizabeth had not seen Topsy for what seemed a long time and missed her. When her friend eventually arrived in the garden at Holcombe on a fine Saturday afternoon, Elizabeth was pleased. Petra, dolled up to the nines, had been taken out for the day by her grandmother who wanted to show her off to some Dawlish cronies. It had been lonely under the crab-apple tree.

Topsy, wearing a silk dress the colour of crushed straw-berries and cream, her hair bleached by long days of sunshine, lay down beside her on the grass.

'I've just come from the tennis club. Ted is winning set after set and looking pleased with himself. Golly, this lawn's hard. Doesn't anyone water the bloody grass?'

'Inslow does when he can get away from Merriscourt. I do the flower beds.'

'Inslow's as bad as Marchant. They've always taken you Bidwells for a ride.'

'Marchant is taking nobody for a ride. He's leaving.'

'I know. With a lot of Bidwell cash, doubtless.'

Elizabeth raised her eyebrows at the disagreeable voice.

'What's biting you?'

'Not a damned thing.'

'Don't tell me you and David have been quarrelling. It's bad enough Ted and me.'

Topsy gouged a hole in the dry grass.

'I don't know if you'd call it a row. Josh has been sacked.'

'You don't mean that David –'

'Oh yes I do. He caught us *in flagrante delicto*. To be indelicate, with our pants off. Poor Josh, doing up his flies, he looked as if he'd die of shame.'

Elizabeth was speechless with interest.

Topsy went on digging a hole in the grass, her ash-blonde hair in her eyes.

'You didn't know I was preggers a couple of months ago. I went up to London to find out, and sure enough that was it. Josh was nearly scared to death, poor beast. Particularly as David hasn't been near me for three months so I couldn't palm the little bastard off on *him*. Anyway, I came back from London and Josh and I went across the country into Dorset, God knows where, to some roadhouse or other. He bought a bottle of gin. Then we stopped the car and he forced me to drink practically the whole of it. Ugh! I was so drunk. Sick as a dog and then I passed out. He got me home somehow, and we'd chosen a night David was away, so it was okay when he shovelled me into bed. The next morning magic! The curse. I thought we were all set again and told Josh to be more careful. It was all his fault. What can *I* do about that birth-control stuff? David and I never do a thing. He's always hoping his poor efforts will work. Anyway, that's what's happened. Poor old Josh.'

'And poor old David too, I should have thought.'

Topsy looked up from digging a grave in which she was burying some wilted daisies. Her face was blank.

'I did not love David and I don't now. He's nearly sixty-five and I'm twenty-seven. He had no right to marry me – no right. I know it was Daddy's awful idea but David didn't have to go along with it.'

'I suppose he fell in love with you.'

'Liz, don't be ridiculous. He's *old* and he married me. Josh is young. That's how things are – or were until David caught us at it. It's all very well for you. At least Ted is your own age.'

'And has gone off me entirely.'

Topsy's expression slightly altered.

'I'm sorry. One doesn't have to ask why.'

'You did warn me.'

'But what could you do once she'd got her claws in him?' said Topsy and repeated that she was sorry. But her concern did not last. She dug away at the dry grass, her fair hair falling across her face.

'I came round to say that David's taking me to South Africa next week. He's got some farms there which have to be visited and I've been informed I must go with him. He was very controlled when he caught us in the stable, I'll give him that. Me doing up my blouse and Josh slinking off like a dog you've just whipped. David merely told me to go into the house. I expected him to knock me down.'

'I bet he wanted to.'

'No he didn't. I would have liked him better if he had.'

Topsy made an effort to shake herself out of her selfish trance, talked about South Africa and then about Petra. With no children of her own, Elizabeth's daughter interested her. After a while she actually laughed; since schooldays she had had the capacity to pull herself to her feet. Like Elizabeth she came from sturdy stock. Finally she said,

'Bother, I have to go. David's been quite unpleasant about punctuality. I have to be on the dot for meals now, and there are other ways I have to toe the line. Sex has hove into view. It has occurred to him that if Josh wanted it, so does he, and now it's every night. Golly. Another of his ideas is that I have to wear low-necked frocks for dinner so I can wear that damned great turquoise and gold necklace which belonged to his mother. So elderly. All gold bits hanging about. Well, Lizzie,' she said standing up, 'I won't be seeing you for a while. I realise I am in no position to give you advice, but still keep your beady eye on Sylvia.'

'Too late.'

'I don't agree at all. There's this house, for instance. She did you out of Merriscourt, and Speldhurst as well. One asks oneself what next. So sit tight at Holcombe and don't give up an inkwell.'

When she was in her white rakish open car, she roared the engine.

'So long, Liz. Next time we meet I shall be back from Cape Town. A long sea voyage . . . I wonder if it is true what they say about ship's officers?'

Chapter Seventeen

Coronation year, thought Elizabeth as she looked at the bare trees, was nearly over. 1937 had brought a joy to the country, united under a new young king and queen. From one end of England to the other the bells had pealed, strings of flags criss-crossed, people snatched at a reason to be happy. But now the holly trees were heavy with berries and the year almost gone. Old habits die hard. When Inslow came to the house, bringing a new rosebush, she asked him to cut her some holly.

'You'll not want much here, Miss Elizabeth,' said the old gardener, his face wearing a sardonic look as he surveyed Holcombe's modest rooms.

When she thought of the coming Christmas, Elizabeth doubted if she would see her husband at all except at Broad Oaks on Christmas Day. For almost the entire year she could not recall a single weekend which he'd spent at home with her and the baby. He was simply, crudely, absent. Not even bothering to lie, he drove away and returned after she was in bed, slightly drunk. How did Sylvia bear the smell of cider or beer which exuded from him? He'd moved out of their double bedroom months ago, saying that she had complained of his snoring. He slept now in the spare bedroom upstairs.

Their marriage scarcely existed and she only put up with it because of Petra. The little girl had an elfin face, an enchanting sing-song voice and the Bidwell freckled eyes. She was a mixture of daring and timid, but it was the second of these qualities which showed when her father was about. She was afraid of him. Ted took little notice of her. But Elizabeth still thought it a momentous and dreadful step to rob a child of her father. How horrified the Ansteys would be. During the year she had tried to drop hints to them. When she went to Broad Oaks with Petra, and Ted was never with them, she expected his parents to ask where he was. But their love for their son and their own comfortable marriage made them blind.

On a chill winter morning during Christmas week, Ted was as usual locked in the bathroom, not only to have a bath but also to shave and dress. When he came down to breakfast he ate standing up, his wrist watch on the table. He invariably slept late and she never woke him.

'Ted.' She was at the breakfast table, the baby in her high chair, as he walked into the room.

'Two minutes,' he said, picking up some toast to butter, and drinking the tea she had poured for him.

'Ted, I want a word.'

Petra, the moment he walked in, was transfixed and refused to eat.

'Darling,' said Elizabeth in a low voice, 'you're being silly.'

'Talking to me?' he said.

'No. To Petra. I only want to remind you, Ted, that your mother's giving a pre-Christmas tea party this afternoon. Quite a celebration. She says will you please be on time.'

'Can't manage it.'

'Don't be ridiculous. I asked your father and –'

'I don't give a f- farthing who you asked. I know my own business. And I can't spare the time to come arsing about at a kid's party.'

'Charming.'

'My God, you're hard. Have you any idea what your voice sounds like?' he shouted. He was unused to her showing her feelings. 'No wonder I don't come home when I'm married to a stone.'

She was unmoved. The insulting voice at least told her that she existed.

'So you won't come?'

'How many times have I got to tell you? I can't. I work. Remember?'

He walked out of the room and the door slammed so loudly that the old house shuddered.

So did Petra.

The party that afternoon was on the Broad Oaks scale, with tables laden with rich food and an expensive present for each child guest. Nannies, parents and grandparents arrived with children of various ages, from six down to babies in arms. Dicky Bidwell had been invited but did not appear. Petra, in white organdie and a pink satin sash, sat on the floor with a vast book of pictures, beaming at little girls nearby. The afternoon was coloured like a circus; there were red jellies and pink ice-creams, yellow balloons and blue streamers. When the visitors finally left, and the maids were clearing up, Lilian carried her granddaughter up to bed. There was a room at Broad Oaks always kept ready for the child.

Harold had not been expected to attend the party; Lilian had let him off from paper hats. When he arrived home from Plymouth, he found his daughter-in-law by the fire. He asked in his old-fashioned way how the party had gone? When he talked of such things, children, clothes, or when he listened to Lilian doing so, he had a sort of Olympian kindness just verging on boredom.

Lilian bustled in, plumped up some cushions and remarked that Elizabeth, who had not lifted a finger, must be tired.

'Just you sit there, dearie, and I'll get you a sherry. And Curly wants his whisky and soda.'

Teetering on Louis heels, she came across the room to her husband. Her magnificent jade necklace, a gift from him, swung as she moved. She looked so happy. Elizabeth felt she held a hammer which was about to smash that happiness into hits.

It was after dinner that she did it.

'Mr Anstey. Mrs Anstey,' she began. She never could manage 'aunt' and 'uncle'. 'I have something to tell you. It's pretty horrible and it will be a shock. But I think Ted and I should get a divorce.'

Lilian gaped. She was speechless.

Harold said slowly, 'What is all this about?'

Before Elizabeth answered, Lilian drew breath and launched into a stream of expostulations. What stuff and nonsense! Had she and Ted quarrelled? Why, she'd never heard of such a thing –

Harold stopped her in mid-flood.

'Shut up, Lil, and let the girl speak.'

Elizabeth told the story without spite. She said that in the last year their marriage had grown from bad to worse. Ted had changed completely. If they had not noticed it, it must be because Ted had gone on pretending things were all right. But at home it was impossible. The truth was that he did not care for her any more, and had never cared a pin for Petra. She was sorry, but it was true. He was very unhappy. And so was she. Living like this was impossible.

Lilian looked as if she were going to cry.

'Is it Sylvia Bidwell?' Harold asked.

'How did you know!'

'Seen them together. Hoped it didn't mean anything.'

Elizabeth realised that he had known for months.

'But he's never shown the slightest interest in that girl –' burst out Lilian. Harold was not listening. He looked at Elizabeth.

'Is he sleeping with her?'

Lilian gasped. She had never heard him use what she called crudeness except in the privacy of their bedroom.

'I haven't any proof, Mr Anstey, but he doesn't come home until very late.'

'Does he sleep with you?'

Lilian blushed all down her neck.

'No. Not for about a year.'

'Some men –' began Lilian, but he stopped her, pressing her hand.

'Leave this to me, Lil. You and I can talk later. Have you told my son you want a divorce?'

'No. I wanted to speak to you both first.'

'Why?'

She saw how he must be at his work. Uncompromising and hard and kind, if it was possible to be all three.

'If I say anything to Ted he'll shout and make a scene. And in any case he won't talk sense. He'll listen to you.'

'Do you want me to try and patch things up?'

'Mr Anstey, it's too late.'

Lilian rolled and unrolled a lace handkerchief. He lit a cigar, and finally said, 'A shocking thing, a divorce. A disgrace. I never thought such a thing would happen in our family.'

'I know. And I agree. But we can't go on as we are. He is miserable and making me so. He has even started to hate me. Yes, Mrs Anstey, it's true. I'm sorry to hurt you but it's true, I can see it in his face. He hates me because I am in his way and he wants to be with somebody else. As for poor little Petra, she's afraid of him. He never addresses a word to her, but when he speaks to me his voice is so loud that she starts to cry. The only child he even mentions is Dicky Bidwell.'

'Ted always wanted a boy,' muttered Lilian.

Harold Anstey looked angry.

'Hold your tongue, woman, that's quite enough. Very well, Elizabeth, I will talk to him in the morning. A divorce. What a dreadful thing.'

The morning after the children's party, with Petra safe at Broad Oaks, Ted appeared as usual to snatch some breakfast while standing up. She looked at him dispassionately as he stood eating and reading the newspaper. He was handsome still, but had begun to run to fat. She tried to imagine the coming interview with his father, but couldn't. It was so long since Ted had been pleasant to her that the idea of him alone with Harold, polite and reasonable, filial and affectionate, was beyond her imagination. She thought – I used to be really fond of you. I looked forward to you coming home in the evening. But love needs care. It must be watered and pruned, fed and sheltered. She'd had the same idea when she believed her love for her cousin was dead. But Peter had never left her, he had only absented himself from felicity awhile. Ted was gone from her heart, as he was gone from her body.

When he drove away without saying goodbye Elizabeth whistled to the dogs to go for a walk. The telephone rang. She was surprised to hear her mother's voice.

'I'm coming down this afternoon. Meet me at the station, would you, Elizabeth? I'll be arriving at four thirty-five.'

In answer to Elizabeth's question her mother said, 'Yes, Harold Anstey rang. A terrible shock. I simply don't know what you can be thinking of. But we won't talk about this now. I'll see you this afternoon.'

Winter had set in across the fields and woods. There was a cold and drenching rain. The dogs, who had been out in the garden, sat in the back of the car when she set off for the station, their coats smelling like a stable.

She wished her mother was not coming: Harold Anstey should not have interfered. But he was accustomed to taking the reins, and by confiding in him last night she had put them in his hands. She knew he was on her side. But she didn't want elderly attempts at mending her marriage. Harold, Lilian and Dolly would not succeed; they'd be hurt and would look foolish. It would all be a waste of time and emotion, and thinking how her mother and Lilian would chew it over, Elizabeth felt worn out in advance.

The train was punctual to the minute, and there, stepping on to the platform out of the smoke, was the familiar neat figure, trim in a suit of broadcloth, her shoulders looped with a string of sables. Doctor Hoskins must be doing well.

'You don't look too bad,' remarked Dolly, as they drove out of Teignmouth. 'Goodness, those dogs smell. Don't you bath them now I'm not there to remind you?'

Elizabeth had slowed at the crossroads and her mother added, 'No, we are not going home yet. We are seeing the Ansteys.'

'Mother. I saw them last night, as you know.'

'Yes, my child. But we have to talk as a family.'

Dolly, although concerned, was also rather puffed up with

278

the drama. She had seen little of her daughter since her own marriage, although they wrote to each other regularly, and telephoned sometimes. She liked to talk of Elizabeth's 'comfortable circumstances', and to boast a little to her Sussex friends about the wealth of the Ansteys and the nature of that good sort, Ted. Now it was all going up in smoke. She was shocked and fascinated.

'I'd much rather not see the in-laws again,' said Elizabeth.

'I'm afraid we must. Harold wishes it.'

Harold was home early, an unheard-of occurrence. He had left the works after lunch. There had been a great deal of comment about this after he had gone, from colleagues, secretaries and men in the workshops. Everybody decided that at the very least Lilian had crashed the Daimler and was at death's door.

Lilian kissed Dolly when they arrived at Broad Oaks. She had been crying. She took them into the drawing-room where an enormous log fire blazed, saying that Dolly must be very cold and worn out. Train journeys, to Lilian, were like going to the Pole.

'Petra's as good as gold. The Whittakers have taken her out to tea with little Bobby. I hope you don't mind, Elizabeth? Mrs Whittaker's so fond of her and Bobby follows her about like a puppy. He simply loves her.'

Dolly enquired about her granddaughter, and was shown a number of photographs. Harold drank his tea. He waited until the older women stopped talking. Their conversation resembled the hard cheerfulness at a funeral, each woman taking up the subject from the other and returning it with a determined smile.

Harold put down his cup and addressed the meeting.

'I saw Ted this morning. He was very frank, I'm glad to say.'

He looked from under his bushy eyebrows at Elizabeth, and she saw that Ted must have attacked her; she wondered with bitter curiosity what crimes he had produced of hers to explain his own defection. Whatever he had said had had its effect.

'It's too late for anything to be done. Much too late now. If you'd both come to me earlier . . .'

279

'Harold's right,' declared Dolly. 'You or Ted or both together, you should have told him the trouble months ago. It was wrong of you, Elizabeth.'

'Ted intends to behave like a gentleman. He says that Sylvia Bidwell must not be named in the divorce. He will give you evidence of another kind. When the decree goes through, he and Sylvia are to marry.'

'I shall keep Petra.'

'Yes, yes, he agrees.'

Oh does he? thought Elizabeth, her heart swelling with indignation. She wanted to speak out. To tell them, not the plain, guarded facts of yesterday, but the truth of what Ted was like. Then, looking at the three older people who were all looking at *her*, she couldn't do it. They were intent on cobbling something together. They were like people gathered round some precious, torn vestment. She supposed it was life they were trying to mend.

Lilian, again on the verge of tears, asked Elizabeth as she and Dolly were leaving if she could keep Petra for a few days. Elizabeth said of course, and was given a convulsive hug. Then Lilian hurried back into the house, and Harold walked with them to the car. He opened the door for Dolly, shut it firmly, walked round to the driver's side and tapped on Elizabeth's window. She wound it down.

'I want you to know that you and the child will never be short of money. Rest assured of that. Don't thank me –' as Elizabeth was about to speak, 'I know what's right.'

The thought of her husband coming in to the house at midnight, and appearing at breakfast with his unpleasant face, made Elizabeth feel uncomfortable as she was driving her mother home. But almost the moment they returned there was a telephone call from Ted's secretary to say he had been held up, and would not be back tonight.

Elizabeth drew a long breath of relief.

Alone with Elizabeth, free of the dominant presence of a king of commerce, Dolly's manner altered. She had always been a chameleon, it was what had made her such a success

280

with Garnett, and now clearly the devoted wife to her Sussex doctor. After supper, and having asked some loaded and derogatory questions about Ted, Dolly remarked, 'You're better without him.'

'But this afternoon at the Ansteys you said –'

'I hadn't heard the full story then. It's clear that he's no good to you, my child, and you must make a new life of your own. Thank God Harold is in charge of the money. You'll be well off.'

'And I've got Petra.'

Her mother gave an ironic smile.

'She's a dear little girl, but don't dedicate your life to a child. She won't thank you when she's older. Make a life of your own. You're still young, and quite handsome,' added Dolly, in the voice she had used long ago, of a woman who knew how to catch men to one who did not.

After Dolly returned to London the following day, Lilian telephoned to ask Elizabeth to have luncheon and tea with her at Broad Oaks. Thinking there would be some chewing-over, Elizabeth would dearly have liked to refuse. But Lilian brushed aside excuses with such determination that she found she had to accept.

As it happened, there was no chewing at all. Lilian had invited some local friends to luncheon, two girls and their mother who had known Elizabeth for years, and the afternoon was a pleasant one. Elizabeth did not return to Holcombe with Petra until after dark.

The moment she went into the house she understood Lilian's invitation. Ted's raincoat had disappeared from its hook in the hall. So had an enlarged photograph of his school rugby team, hung over the chimney piece. When the baby was asleep, Elizabeth went into her own room, and up into the room where Ted slept, and saw everything of his was gone. Drawers and cupboards had been emptied with a thoroughness quite unlike him. In the drawing-room, silver cups, cigarette boxes, his pewter tankard with the glass bottom, even his books – Kipling, Sapper, John Buchan – were removed from the shelves. Ted lived here no longer.

She went through the house. He had forgotten a second tankard in a kitchen cupboard. She threw it into the dustbin. She looked for her album in the bureau, and tore out their wedding photographs. There was Ted in his morning dress, smiling down at her in her bridal satin. And there were the other inevitable photographs. Ted with his parents. Everybody so happy.

She went upstairs to the linen basket, found a dirty shirt, and that went out into the dustbin too. Then she opened the windows to let in the sharp air of the winter night. It was very cold.

Harold Anstey was right. Divorce was a dreadful thing.

The next day she drove to Speldhurst. Just as she was always sure of finding Topsy in the stables, she guessed that her second cousin would be in the barn with the falcon. He was busily feeding the bird, and training her to hop on to his wrist. When he looked up, his concentrated expression changed and he smiled with pleasure and surprise.

'Lizzie. How good to see you. I'll be with you in a moment. I must just put her back and collect any of her moulted feathers.'

He carefully picked up a few deckled feathers and put them in his wallet, then spoke for a moment to the bird who stood listening, curved head on one side.

'One has to keep any feathers. They can be grafted on to the stump of a broken feather if need be. A fiddling process. But the fact is, Liz, if you fly anything as fierce and fragile as Tova, you have to find out about everything that can help.'

'George, you astonish me.'

'Oh good!'

The wind was icy as they went from the stables into the house. That was cold too, and he took her into the little study where, in all the wonderful water-colours the Eastern sunshine flooded incongruously, captured on a chill English wall. He switched on the electric fire and she sat down on the rug to warm her hands.

'What can I do for you, Lizzie?'

'I came to tell you something.'

He looked enquiring.

'I am divorcing Ted.'

'Are you, by God.'

He was silent for some time. She had come because she was sure the news was going to hurt him. He would lose Sylvia all over again. But when she looked anxiously up at him, all she saw in his face was thoughtful self-possession. He looked as he always did, attractive and strong and in command. If he *is* wounded, she thought – and he must be – he is not going to show me. She wished quite desperately that they were close friends. He had been so kind to her in the past. When had she ever been able to do anything for him?

'I didn't know you'd do it,' he finally said. 'Of course I saw the way things were going. And you and I have talked about your troubles.'

He sat down on the sofa, she remained crouched by the paltry fire, and he put out both his arms along the sofa top like a child pretending to fly.

'Ted left home yesterday,' she said. 'I suppose he'll move in to Merriscourt.'

'Oh no. He won't do that.'

'What do you mean?'

'It would stop the divorce being respectable. He won't cite Sylvia.'

'I don't see why not,' she said flatly.

'Because he'll behave like a gentleman, Liz. He'll fudge up something, and stay with his parents or some friend.'

'Not his parents. They are on my side.'

'I'm very glad. You're going to need your friends.'

'And I suppose you won't be one of them.'

'Now why should you say that? Of course I will.'

She couldn't stop herself saying, 'Sylvia won't let you.'

'Sylvia has nothing to do with our friendship. I certainly don't take instructions from her,' he said casually. He reflected for a moment and then said, 'I did guess she wanted to marry him. But somehow I thought you would never release him.'

'What would have been the *point* of hanging on? I hate divorce as much as anybody. But it would have been so humiliating – trying to force a man to stay when it's all over.'

He said quizzically, 'It's done a great deal, though, isn't it? Face-saving. You should see it in India. All those faces being saved, and some of them so pretty.'

'I think it's degrading.'

He raised his eyebrows.

'It can work. Men stray, and then come back.'

'You talk as if they were dogs.'

'You're a little harsh today. I'm not sure it suits you. I always used to admire the women in India putting up a good show when things became bloody for them. It was brave. And I'm not sure that a good show isn't all any of us can put up.'

She said stonily, 'You think I should have kept Ted slumping about when all he wanted to be was with Sylvia.'

'Perhaps I'm thinking Ted and Sylvia may not prove the best combination in the world. Time will tell. I should have thought you would cope with him considerably better than she will.'

Was this a roundabout way of saying he did mind losing his beloved Sylvia again? That he was wounded by it. If he was, he would never show his feelings to her, thought Elizabeth. There were times when she was sure he liked her but when it came to anything important to him, she was kept at arm's length. I don't care if Ted and Sylvia fight like cats in a sack, she thought. But I do care that I thought George might need me and I was stupidly, stupidly wrong.

When she stood up to go he protested – but she didn't want to stay. He's better with Tova, she thought. She may be fierce and fragile, as he called her, but God! she's strong. I wish I were.

Whenever she thought about it, which was a great deal, Elizabeth disliked the idea of divorce more and more. It was declassé. She knew that her mother felt the same, and so did the

Ansteys in a different way. It was like that everywhere. 1938 might pride itself on being the modern world, but some things were immutable and marriage was a vow and a sacrament – and when you broke it you suffered. Yet she was the one who had been wronged. Whatever Ted had invented against her, she knew that during their marriage she had behaved well; she had enjoyed being with him, put up with his coarse brief sex, and even managed to love him in a way. She had been unfaithful, but in a curious paradox her short-lived sexual happiness with Peter had made her kinder to Ted. But she had wronged him by marrying him to keep a roof over her head. She was paid out.

Harold Anstey took her to London to see, at his expense, a leading KC of the day. They went to chambers in the Temple, tiny low-ceilinged rooms where Elizabeth thought Doctor Johnson might appear at any moment, covered in snuff and exuding benevolent wisdom. The KC was grand, patronising, paternal and expensive. He gave her documents to sign, and showed her part of a written statement Ted had made about her failings as a wife. Her lack of sympathy, her snobbery, her coldness.

When she returned home there was a letter without a stamp which had been put through her letter-box.

'Back at last!!! Can I come to luncheon? I will ride over, and we might have a gallop in the woods in the afternoon. Do say yes. I hear S is in the S of F and you are getting rid of T.

Oh good.

Topsy.'

Elizabeth waited for her friend in a house filled with sunlight. It was February and the winter jasmine was covered in yellow stars. The dogs, angular legs upstretched, were rolling in the grass. Petra was sitting on the floor pulling off a small red shoe. Thrushes sang. Elizabeth heard trotting hooves and there was Topsy, dismounting from a tall black horse. She gave the horse an encouraging slap.

'Filthy ride, he's covered in mud. Let's put him in the stable. Is Snowball still in the land of the living?'

'Of course she is. She's only eleven.'

'Well, I feel ninety,' said Topsy. She greeted Petra, who in the way of the very young, looked alarmed. When Topsy kissed her and set her back on her feet, Petra made a tedious dive behind Elizabeth's skirt.

'I frighten her, and I don't blame her. I *am* frightening,' said Topsy, sitting down and stretching her legs in wonderfully shining boots. She, also, shone, her blonde hair thicker, her face creamier and rosier, her neck like a column rising from her pale silk blouse.

'Don't look at me like that, Liz, I know I'm fat. All the women in South Africa are. Well, they're big. Like great cabbage roses – it's the food. And the men are distinctly worth the detour as they say in the guide books.'

She looked at Elizabeth for a moment.

'Getting a divorce suits you.'

'Topsy, I can't get used to it. I suppose you heard the moment you put your foot on Teignmouth station.'

'Sooner. Great Western Hotel, Paddington. David and I were having dinner and Mrs Barrington-Clark hove into view. You know the one, a twinky little female who hunts. Bad rider, never finishes. Squeaky voice. She fancies David and he's always delighted to see her, of course. She told us about the divorce, squeaking away. Pretended to be shocked.

'Oh dear.'

'Don't be feeble. David came down heavily on your side. He said it showed the right spirit, making a clean break and I agree. You know I never wanted you to marry Ted. I did offer you The Lodge.'

'I ought to have taken it.'

'Then you wouldn't have that character,' said Topsy, pointing at the cowering Petra, 'who's waiting for me to roast her over the fire and eat her for dinner, like in Hansel and Gretel.'

'Take no notice. She's like that with people she doesn't know. Later on she'll climb all over you.'

'After eating chocolate cake, I suppose. Well?' said Topsy with brisk interest, 'when's the decree absolute?'

'Oh, months. I simply can't get used to the idea of divorce. All that rubbish about Ted going to bed with a woman in Torquay. Isn't divorcing declassé? Just you tell me one woman you approve of who is divorced. And don't count titled females in gossip columns. They're quite unreal.'

Topsy thought it over, agreeing that nobody liked divorces and thought them pretty messy. Suddenly she gave a loud *'got it!'* which made Petra rush for cover again.

'Irene in *The Forsyte Saga*. Soames divorced her. You can't say Irene didn't stay a lady.'

Irene came into Elizabeth's mind once or twice during the following months and she wished she had a tenth of that character's poise. The process of breaking up a marriage was somehow rather disgusting, although she was glad to think she need never set eyes on Ted again. Her parents-in-law were kind to her, entertained her, and spoiled their granddaughter. Lilian was as embarrassingly generous as ever.

The day after the decree absolute, Ted and Sylvia were married in a registry office in Exeter. George drove Sylvia to the wedding. She wore a pale blue silk dress with patterns of darker blue which set off her frail beauty perfectly. For a hat she had a wreath of velvet forget-me-nots, and a pale blue veil covered her face and was tucked under her chin.

She was talkative during the drive. Ted was taking her to her favourite place for the honeymoon – Antibes. George must swear he would call daily at Merriscourt and see Dickybird and Nanny Osborn.

'My dear Sylvia, I'm at the house all the time, trying to clear up various messes which I'm sorry to say, on this cheerful occasion, don't seem to improve.'

Sylvia buried her nose in a bouquet of yellow roses edged with paper lace.

'Oh, do shut up, George. You're so clever. I leave everything absolutely to you. You know you enjoy running the old place. Now. How do you feel about giving the bride away for a second time!'

Harold and Lilian had already arrived at the registry office, the Daimler was parked outside, the chauffeur polishing the bonnet. The registry office was dusty, and looked more like a shabby library than an official room for ceremonies but someone – it had been Lilian – had sent some flowers which stood on a desk. There was a row of chairs. Lilian and Harold stood, with constrained smiles. Ted, paler than usual, wore a new dark suit and a red carnation. His big boyish face altered as the vision in blue came in. Nerves disappeared. And with Sylvia came her strong resinous scent and a festive air which affected even the old clerk at the desk.

Lilian thought the ceremony rubbishy.

PART FOUR

Summer – 1938

Chapter Eighteen

Elizabeth did the expected things when she was once again a single woman. She took her daughter to stay with Dolly and her husband in Sussex, was made much of, and told by her mother that there were as many good fish in the sea. Coming home to Devon in the beginning of a hot summer, she saw a good deal of Topsy who was at present behaving with perhaps alarming docility. Elizabeth dined with Colonel Rolles and Topsy at Whitefriars, and noticed that Topsy was actually rather nice to him and laughed at his elderly jokes. And Topsy's favourite mare had produced a beautiful foal.

A surprise for Elizabeth turned out to be a dearth of friends. She was used to many local invitations, to dinners and occasional parties and balls. These dried up like water into cracked earth. People had gone over to Ted and the centre of power had changed. She was no longer married to a man who might not be very classy but who made up for it by driving an Alvis and giving tennis parties. And she was – to go further back – no longer the Bidwell cousin to the heir. She was a divorced woman in her late twenties with a prettyish cottage-house and without a man.

Petra was an appealing little child and she filled her mother's day and heart, but the company of the very young was scarcely enough. When not with Topsy, Elizabeth was lonely. When she went to Broad Oaks she never asked Lilian about Merriscourt since this would mean pretending an interest in Ted and Sylvia. She preferred not to hear how happy they were, even if the fact was disguised with elephantine tact. She did not want her ex-husband in the least, but to hear about Sylvia's triumph would make her sick.

291

And yet there was Merriscourt. I suppose things are in better shape, now that George is doing something about them, she thought. Why do I bother?

When George telephoned her on a June morning and asked if he could see her she thought she sounded too eager. After they had rung off, she told herself not to be a fool. He arrived sooner than she had expected, calling 'Liz? Are you in the garden?' in his clear, carrying voice. She came round the corner of their house in the blazing sun. Sunburned from days in the garden, she wore a blue and white checked cotton dress. He thought, with a slight shock, that she looked about eighteen.

'Lizzie. Good to see you, in more ways than one.'

They sat down in the garden. The little girl was out with Gladys, Elizabeth's new maid, who preferred being a nurse to housework.

'Let's sit under the crab-apple tree,' she said, and pulled him up a chair.

She looked at him, as he had done at her, speculatively. He was thinner, tougher, ruddier. How short his hair was. He still looked like a soldier.

Talking idly, they exchanged guarded news. Elizabeth guessed why his was censored, he was not going to mention Ted's new marriage. She enquired about the falcon.

'I still think it's an odd kind of sport. Would you call it a sport?'

'One of the oldest,' he said. 'I discovered the other day from someone at the University that the most famous book about hawking was written in 1220. Guess by whom? An emperor of Germany. It's in Latin. Great man, that emperor. A Renaissance monarch two hundred years in advance . . . he had a harem and a travelling zoo, and a bodyguard of Saracens. He was called The Wonder of the World.'

'George, I think you're a romantic at heart.'

'Ah. So you've discovered my shameful secret.'

It was such a long time since she had been sought out by a man, and it never occurred to her that he was here simply for the pleasure of seeing her. He must want something – he always came to see her for a purpose. A cloud floated temporarily across the sun, and looking up he exclaimed, 'I hope to God it isn't going to rain.'

She couldn't help laughing.

'Why, are you playing tennis today?'

He stared at her disbelievingly and she said, 'What does that face mean? It's a reasonable question.'

'Not to a man who's been in the Four Acre meadow for the last two days, working twelve hours a day.'

'Haymaking?' she said flippantly. 'For fun, I suppose, which explains your sunburn. Wear a hat.'

He went on looking at her with incredulous disapproval.

'Fun?'

'Come on, George, you can't be much needed when there are eight men working the Four Acre, as I very well remember.'

'As you very well forget. Most of them are up in the top fields. I have exactly two. I take it you're not too interested in your old home any more.'

'What does that mean?' she flared. 'How can I *not* be interested, but what's it to do with me? We've been tiptoeing about in conversation for the last half hour pretending none of it happened. That my ex-husband and your god-daughter are not in possession now. Ask *them* if you want help. Why should I be involved with the Four Acre field? I'm quite sure the hay will be brought in successfully and make Sylvia a handsome profit.'

'Jiminy. You are out of touch.'

'Oh, stop looking like that, and I don't know what you're talking about.'

'I am talking about Merriscourt. Merriscourt. Nothing there makes a profit and hasn't, as far as I can see, for twenty years. Shall I spell it out?'

He began to talk about the estate. She heard him in silence. For years she had suspected and dreaded that one day someone would tell her this. Yet she had grown up somehow believing that Merriscourt was as rich and fertile as its own land. Cottages and farms, sheep and pigs, the warm red cattle, the fields and the orchards and the woods. Of course, the cottages needed money spent on them sometimes, but they were cob built, warm in winter, cool in summer, and had stood for 300 years. What George told her confirmed every one of her old and denied anxieties. He spoke of debt and decay. She remembered her uncle's yellowish-grey head bent over a paper-strewn desk. She thought of Ferrers and his pompous, 'When the time's right, Miss Bidwell.'

'The livestock's diminishing, we need new horses for the plough, last year's harvest was poor. The rates are up. And the whole essential of estate management simply isn't working – that the tenant must have a good chance to do well for the land and himself.'

He stopped talking.

She said slowly, 'What are they going to do about it?'

'Ted and Sylvia? What do you suppose. They're right out of their depth.'

'But you're helping now. You said months ago that you are often round there.'

'Every day. Picking at the surface. It needs more than that.'

'Shall you get rid of Ferrers?'

'Do you think I should?'

'He's a conceited idiot without a brain in his head. But if you get rid of him you'll need someone else. You can't manage . . . *no, George!*'

'Yes, Lizzie. I can't take the job on without you.'

'Then you can't take it on at all.'

How dare he, she thought. He only comes here to get something. And the enemy reigned at Merriscourt.

'You must talk to Ted and Sylvia,' she said coldly.

'All they say is sell.'

'Sell what?'

'That's the point. Land, if they could get buyers. Then what? The house.'

'She couldn't.'

'My god-daughter could *do* anything. She'd get round the trustees who are a lot of muddlers. She's unsentimental and she's a spendthrift. A dangerous combination.'

Elizabeth said nothing for some time.

'I can't help you, George.'

He laid his hand on her arm. He rarely touched her. Except when she had been ill before Petra had been born and he used to take her hands. And then there had been that single, pitying kiss. The rest of their friendship seemed to be carried out at a distance of two or three yards, across which they smiled and joked, or sometimes glared. But now he laid a strong sunburned hand on her bare arm, and the dog beside her did not bother to growl or lift his head.

'I need you, Liz, and so does your home. If we let those two go on with their *laissez-faire* much longer there won't *be* a Merriscourt at all. I can't take it all on without you beside me. I need your practical head, and I need your knowledge. People don't accept me, but as a Bidwell they'd always accept you. I'd make serious mistakes, have already. But there must be hundreds of things you know, without knowing. The place is in your bones. Don't refuse me.'

She sat thinking about her old home. The shape of the house, crooked, rambling, the crowned kings, the stained-glass windows throwing rainbows on the floor. To sell it would be like making Peter die again.

'I can't do what you ask. Sylvia wouldn't let me,' she said.

'You don't know Sylvia. She has nothing to do with the estate – nothing. When she and Ted married, all the papers and files were moved out of your uncle's study into an office rigged up in the old harness room. They didn't want Ferrers in the house.'

'I don't blame them.'

'You're stalling.'

She thought for a long time. Then, 'I could come through the clover field . . .' she said.

She telephoned him at Speldhurst that evening.

'There's Bernard in the stables. He'll see me.'

'That taciturn old devil.'

'Yes, Mother used to say you couldn't get him to tell you the time. But you must explain to him, George. And I'll start in a month, when you've got rid of Ferrers.'

'I gave him his marching orders an hour ago.'

'Good! In a month then.'

'A man under notice is best got rid of. I've paid him a month's wages and he's clearing out tonight.'

'You move fast.'

'And so must you.'

When she was married to Ted, Cissie, a relative of Ada at Merriscourt, had worked as Elizabeth's daily help. But Elizabeth never liked her and when Cissie gave notice she was relieved. Old Inslow had then suggested his niece. Would Mrs Anstey take a look at the girl? Gladys Inslow turned out to be as small as a ten year old, with a slight hump on her back. She had thick blonde hair, blue eyes, a complexion of peaches and cream and looked clever. She was a great success with the local boys, and had already refused two proposals of marriage.

'She doesn't want to settle down yet,' said her uncle.

Gladys took keenly to her new job, became an overnight partisan and declared in the village that she worked for the Bidwells, just like her uncle did.

When Elizabeth asked her if she could look after Petra and the dogs rather more, and do housework rather less, Gladys was triumphant.

'I'll do it for sure,' she said. 'I'm to be Nanny, then? Mother says I'm like one already to the little pet. Can I get a bit of a uniform at Hannington's?'

Elizabeth gravely agreed.

Truthful to the point of tactlessness, Elizabeth then lied to Lilian, saying she was doing some charity work and could Lilian have Petra for three afternoons a week? Lilian eagerly agreed. It was almost too easy.

At nine the following morning, Elizabeth drove down the country lane and parked her Austin Seven by Agony Gate.

There wasn't a soul about. Making her way across the field and into the woods, she could hear summer humming and rustling. It was breathlessly hot.

Under the chapel arch the stables sprawled away from the house. Elizabeth found George in the old harness room which had not been used for fifty years. The walls had been roughly whitewashed when Ferrers had moved in, and the furniture consisted of a battered old desk, a table and some kitchen chairs. It was all comfortless and none too clean. George, speckless in khaki cotton from India, greeted her with.

'You must be earlier tomorrow, Liz. I'm cleaning this place out tonight by the way. I've laid on some help. But we can't start on the paperwork today, we're needed in the Four Acre field.'

'Still haymaking? How can I, when everybody will see?'

'Come on,' he said, bustling her out of the office. 'If you imagine that Syl or Ted will even enquire about the hay, let alone come to see who's working here, you don't understand how things are these days.'

They passed a stable where Benard was grooming a pony, a pretty little thing which must be for Dicky Bidwell. Small children loved to jog in the special basket saddles placed on the backs of ponies. The old groom gave her a taciturn nod and went on with his work.

The meadow, feathery and pinkish with its high summer grass, stretched away under the sky. It had already been mown by a tractor borrowed from a farm belonging to Colonel Rolles. The two farmworkers, bent over their task, did not bother to look up. George handed her a wooden rake.

Elizabeth had not worked in the fields since the days when as children she and Peter were sometimes allowed to join the haymakers. How hot it was. The sun beat down, and the men rolled up their sleeves and undid the buttons of shirts glued to their backs with sweat. Elizabeth's legs were soon scarlet with scratches, but her tan protected her from sunburn. She and George went at a good pace, moving their rakes rhythmically with a sideways flick in a movement she hadn't used for years.

All four workers piled and carried, stacked and worked fast. The clouds in the distance looked as if they might mean rain, and over-ripe grass deteriorated.

The sheer joy of the long day in the hay, the feeling of the house as a distant presence beyond the trees, contented her. When dusk fell they had completed the field and made the hay into a good stack. The two farmworkers stacked some final swathes, and chorused a goodnight. She knew them both, tall lanky Routen and the elderly grey-haired Walrond. They made her a kind of salute.

George walked back with her to the stable office.

'Shall we have a drink? I'll go into the kitchen.'

'Thank you, George, but I'm rather late.'

There was a pause.

'Well, if you're not staying, I'll go back to Speldhurst for a bath,' he said, 'then return here to clear up this rubbish dump. I'll see you tomorrow, mm?' He put his hand on her shoulder. 'And you be earlier.'

That was Elizabeth's introduction to working at Merriscourt.

During the summer and autumn of 1938 she worked with George in the stable office every weekday. The work was complex and demanding. Tenants' complaints, repairs, the need for a vet, plans for the following year, difficulties left by Ferrers. When a new tenant arrived, it turned out that Ferrers had given permission, months before, for the man's empty cattle sheds to be used by a neighbour for his dry cows. This brought difficulties . . .

Side by side, she and George worked, telephoned, drove round the estate, argued, agreed. Problems were like weeds, the moment the ground was cleared, new ones sprang up. She learned that the country mind was often a closed mind, and the philosophy of the farmers based on self-interest alone. 'A man must look after himself these days.' She learned a lot of things. She had only dimly known about crop rotation. Now she saw wheat and barley, oats, turnips, cabbages, clover and hay each having their turn to be planted and harvested. The work was both satisfying and frustrating, not because the job they'd taken on was too large, but because the money they had at their disposal was too small.

September was darkened by something infinitely worse than Merriscourt's troubles. The crisis. It had been in people's minds for years, as they watched the advance of Fascism in Germany. Somehow, though, danger appeared to be at a distance. Now suddenly it was here. Even Elizabeth, absorbed in her own life, was affected, and longed fearfully to believe in Hitler's claim that the Sudetenland was his 'last territorial ambition in Europe'.

Day after day the headlines in the newspapers were alarming. Then the big news came. Chamberlain left Croydon airport, on his way to Germany to consult with Hitler.

When Elizabeth arrived that morning, George silently threw the newspaper on the desk.

She read the headlines.

'Perhaps he'll manage it. To bring peace,' she said.

'I don't think so. What he may get for us is a reprieve. We badly need some time. Our rearmament at present is pathetic.'

He might have been talking about a need for some new harvester.

On a hot afternoon while Chamberlain was still in Germany, Topsy and Elizabeth went to an open-air swimming gala. It was Saturday and Elizabeth's day off. There were races, some excellent high diving, and after the prizes had been given the crowd started to move to the tea marquee. Then the Club secretary boomed over the loudspeaker.

'Will everybody please pay attention. I've been asked to make an announcement. A government announcement. It is about gas mask fitting. Will all members of the public go to the local town hall, repeat, town hall, to have their masks fitted. Times of fittings are posted up, but I can give them now. From nine until one, two until five every day including

Sunday. Will the public please make a note of these times and go as soon as possible. Thank you.'

'Golly,' said Topsy. 'I can't imagine Hitler's master plan is to gas South Devon, can you? What a waste of gas.'

'But Petra –'

'Oh, poor Liz, sorry, I shouldn't make jokes. Cheer up, I'm sure the government's making everybody toe the line for the sake of general morale. The message is really for people in cities. We country bumpkins don't need to worry.'

Elizabeth envied her childless friend.

The next day, before she said anything about it, George once again threw the morning paper on her desk. On the front page was a large picture of a giggling blonde girl gaily trying on a snout-like mask.

'*What a gas bag!*' said a headline.

'I'll drive us down to Teignmouth this afternoon, you and Petra and me. Nothing like being in the fashion,' he said.

At the town hall he somehow managed to get Elizabeth and the little girl served fast, and roared with laughter when a brisk woman muffled Petra's little face in black rubber. Emerging, the child was about to cry until she saw him grinning at her.

'I'd cry too if mine were such a bad fit,' he said. 'Haven't you anything smaller?'

'No, sir, you'll simply have to fix the little girl's with Elastoplast,' said the woman crossly.

Two days later, back came Chamberlain to a nation's cheers.

'He has saved us!' shouted the papers. 'This wonderful man, aged 69!' The prime minister's umbrella, in the cartoons, was turned into an olive branch. He was a hero.

'Mr Chamberlain,' wrote a political commentator, 'was a thousand times right to save the world's peace.'

Elizabeth put the gas masks away under the stairs. And breathed again.

But it was not over. It had only just begun.

The new year came, the last of the 1930s. Air-raid shelters

were delivered all over London, and on the wireless Chamberlain broadcast about a new scheme for voluntary service, 'to make us ready for war. That does not mean I think war is coming,' he added, sounding like a vicar or a schoolmaster.

Topsy telephoned, merry as a lark.

'I absolutely can't decide whether to choose the fire service or the civil air guard. Or drive an ambulance. David's buzzing about like a pompous bee. High up in the Police War Reserve. Imagine that. I tremble for the poor men under him.'

In the stable office, rarely talking about the crisis, Elizabeth could scarcely bear to ask George what he thought.

But on a damp March morning he said he had arranged to go up to London.

'I have to see some people in the War Office. One of these fine days I may be leaving you, Lizzie. Not just yet, but things are distinctly beginning to hot up. There's going to be conscription soon. Eventually, I think I can talk them into getting me back into the Army. Good, isn't it?'

She looked up, said nothing, and began to scribble fiercely.

'Not a very cheerful face. Do I take it you're going to miss me when I'm gone? I was hoping so.'

He was teasing her.

'There's something else I want to tell you, Liz, so kindly stop drawing cats all over my blotting paper. I'd rather you didn't come to work here while I am away.'

'Why on earth not?' she exclaimed. 'There are twenty things I can perfectly well do without you.'

'So do them when I'm back later this week. In the meantime I repeat, I would rather you were not here when I am away.'

'You can't mean you are worried that Sylvia or Ted will appear,' she said sarcastically.

He was setting his desk in order. Neat as a barracks, the office's only decoration was a big old estate map he had found, and on which Elizabeth had marked the farms in red, and painted the ponds and streams in blue.

'We have got away with it so far. But if you did just happen to come across either of them, I would prefer to be there.'

'Who are you afraid *for*?' She was still irritated.

'Them, of course.'

He was dining that evening at Merriscourt, and Elizabeth asked him, recovering her temper, if Cook was as good as ever.

'Yes, the food's excellent.' He paused and then exclaimed, 'I walk in and out of your home, and you slip away so as not to be seen. It's appalling.'

'I truly don't mind.'

'I know, but it doesn't make it right.'

To her surprise, he asked if he could come round to Holcombe later in the evening. He'd never done this before and she supposed there were things he wanted to sort out about work. He said he would arrive about ten o'clock.

Walking back across the clover field to Agony Gate Elizabeth was thinking about Ted. She hadn't set eyes on him since he left her: it was as if he had ceased to exist. His parents never mentioned him, and once when she felt she must ask Lilian if Ted would like his daughter to visit him, Lilian went red.

'He can see the little pet here any time he likes,' she said, and hastily changed the subject. Elizabeth was willing to bet that Ted rarely saw Petra, although the child spent a good deal of time with her grandparents. She was beginning to talk. 'Gran.' 'Dog.' And an imperious 'Come on.' But 'Daddy' never came into her talk after returning from Broad Oaks. Elizabeth wondered whether the Ansteys liked their new daughter-in-law. She did not think, somehow, that Sylvia would put herself out to charm them.

But Ted and Sylvia must surely be happy. They had wanted each other, and had come together easily enough. Her effort to save her marriage had been pathetic in its failure. Now the couple lived in a most beautiful house, and were even freed of its weight, since she and George had taken that on their shoulders. Ted earned a good salary, and probably by now a larger one. So the young Ansteys had money enough for themselves, if one did not include Merriscourt. George had disagreed when Elizabeth said this.

302

'That girl's bills are a nightmare. And she wants to go to Antibes again.'

'I suppose the South of France is fearfully expensive.'

'It certainly is, which appears to be its charm.'

The moment Elizabeth drew up outside Holcombe, Gladys, Petra and the dogs came rushing out to meet her, Gladys smart in her nanny's uniform.

'Mrs Anstey came round. We had a lovely tea, didn't we, Pet?'

'No,' said Petra, burst out laughing, ran into the hall and hid behind a curtain.

'She's a tease, that's what she is,' said Gladys. The telephone rang and Gladys picked it up. It was for her. Answering brusquely, she slammed down the receiver.

'Sorry, Mrs Anstey. It's that Harry. I told him not to ring. He's got his cheek.'

'Is he your new admirer, Gladys?'

'He says he is but I've told him we'll have to see about that,' said Gladys carelessly. The belle of the village then clasped her short nurse's cape round her crooked shoulders, and cycled away towards the breaking of masculine hearts.

When Petra was asleep, Elizabeth put out her light and went down to the empty drawing-room. She tried to read but could not settle. Restless, she kept looking at the clock. Well before ten she heard a car out in the drive. She ran out in haste.

'What a welcome,' said George. He shut the car door, turned round and without another word took her in his arms. He gave her a long, seemingly endless kiss. He drew away with reluctance.

'Let's go indoors.'

The lamps cast pools of light, the country dark pressed against the windows. She felt excited and very nervous, and thought – he wants to make love to me, am I going to let him? But she knew there was no question of 'let'. She hadn't made love for so long, so long, and now she was alone with this familiar man, this wary, guarded stranger. His sexuality drew her. I could almost love you, she thought.

She crossed the room to pour him a brandy and when she came back with the glass, his face seemed blurred as if his features were out of focus. She thought again, I could almost love you. But you'll always love Sylvia Ashton and God! I can't do all that for a third time in my stupid, stupid life.

Putting down the glass, he picked her up in his arms. He carried her to the sofa and lay beside her. For a while they said nothing. He looked down, taking in her dark hair and sallow skin, sunburned throat and arms, and her strange freckled eyes looking back at him.

'Give me your hand.'

She put out her hand which still wore a thin platinum wedding ring and he kissed the palm, shutting his eyes and putting it against his face. She began to tremble. She was waiting for him to take her and she wanted it and must have it, but it was so dangerous. Suppose she fell in love with him, he would make her bitterly unhappy. When he did not move, she wanted him more, imagining his muscular body in hers. She pressed closer. He understood the movement and the swimming look in her face, and at last took her in his arms.

He made love strongly, never seeming to tire. Although he gave her exquisite pleasure, from tenseness and strangeness she thought she would never reach a climax and once said helplessly, 'I can't, I can't.' But he waited inside her, kissing her eyelids, and at last she did come, and then so did he.

When they had separated, he dressed – for he'd taken her naked – and stood looking down at her.

'Your skin's the colour of that honey they sell at Hatchett's farm. What is it?'

'Heather honey.'

'Of course. You smell like that too. I wonder why. Goodnight, sweetheart, I shall ungallantly leave you. I'd stay a while but there's somebody in London who's ringing me at midnight, God help me.'

'Who? A girl?'

'Of course,' he said, smiling. 'I'll see you on Friday, mm?'

When he had gone, she gathered up her clothes, went to her

304

room, fell into bed still naked, and slept for eight hours without dreaming.

When she thought about their lovemaking the following day, she had the sensation of falling from a height, her stomach dropping, which she had not known since she and Peter had made love. It was a weakening feeling, it alarmed her. What happens next? Am I now George Westlock's mistress, like that woman he had in Skye? Like Topsy with Josh? Is that what happens to women who don't make happy marriages, that they go to bed with another man and settle for that. Sex, George's sex, was like a marvellous gift. He had taken more than her offered body, he had somehow gripped a part of her spirit, and that, she thought, will have to be wrenched back somehow. I must keep my head because if I don't I shall ruin my life. She looked at the facts; here was a man who, according to Topsy who had heard it from other people, was a womaniser. Perhaps he slept with Sylvia even now. He was critical about her, but that could be the attitude of a familiar lover of some years. And now I have fallen into his arms the first time he shows me that he wants me.

She wondered if she wished she hadn't, and thinking of his love for Sylvia with something like horror, tried to tell herself it would have been better not. But she wanted him again.

When he returned from London two days later he telephoned late in the evening.

'You are going to be in the office tomorrow morning, aren't you? Promise to be early.'

She answered nervously, and knew she sounded self-conscious.

But the next morning there was no sign of her. George was in the stable office early in the autumn morning. He hung about, looking at his watch, and finally went into the big house and asked Cook for some coffee and toast. He took this back to the office to breakfast among the files. He had news for Elizabeth, and for Sylvia too, and had decided not to tell his god-daughter until later in the day. The green baize door to the main house had been open, and he had heard Sylvia's raised voice, its tone a quarrel, and Ted's angry reply and the slam of a door . . .

As Lilian Anstey did, and for the same reasons, George rarely spoke of the married couple at Merriscourt to Elizabeth. He had seen her recovering from what she thought of as the disgrace of a divorce. His second cousin was a hardy young woman; it showed in the fearless way she rode, in her bluntness, her way of facing life. He knew and admired the nerve with which she had married, not for love but for necessity. That had taken guts and a steady head. Her heart was consequently not broken or even seriously bruised by losing Ted. But her life was. She was under thirty, all the Bidwells were gone, the home she loved was occupied by enemies, and she had few friends. He did not miss how many of her old friends now visited Merriscourt to be entertained. Even Dolly, who could have given her daughter back a solidity to her life, had left Devonshire.

He thought of making love to Elizabeth. She was exciting, and kept returning to his thoughts. He made up his mind that he'd hide from her, as long as possible, the fact that what she had suffered from a broken marriage was nothing but waste. Ted and Sylvia were a disaster.

It bored him to reflect that he had known this was going to happen, and if Sylvia had listened to him, she would not now be screaming, sulking and slamming doors. She was a spoiled idiot and Ted Anstey was a weak fool, thought George. And it was ironic that the thing which brought Elizabeth secretly to the stable office, keeping her by him day after day while they worked like dogs, was the very thing about which Ted and Sylvia shouted at each other. Money. Its lack. And Sylvia's hunger for it.

Had I realised exactly what a state Merriscourt was in, I might have dissuaded her from marrying Peter Bidwell, he thought. She would have listened to that. But, like Sylvia herself, he'd thought the place as rich as it looked.

As for her marriage to Anstey, it didn't bear looking at. Ted had begun to drink too much, no longer burying his nose in a tankard of cider but choosing whisky, drunk neat, 'like the Scots, you know', before or even during a meal, with a brandy afterwards. A loathesome combination. Sylvia often left her husband and went to stay with some new friends of hers in the South of France, returning a golden brown, and more demanding than ever. She was not interested in her son – a cat, thought George, was a better mother. And her manner to Ted grew worse. Two or three times, dining with them, he had seen the meal deteriorate into a row. It was sadly clear that Sylvia had been so busy annexing Ted from another woman that she had not – as Elizabeth had done – realised the man she was getting. Now she knew it and did not like it. She had recently set out to try and turn him into a Peter Bidwell. She made him buy expensive Savile Row clothes, forced him to hunt (he was a heavy, clumsy rider), and expected the polish that two hundred years had put on Peter in the same way that it shone on the Chippendale desk in Garnett's study. Ted drank to give himself courage. George did not doubt that he was still deeply in love with her.

When there was no sign of Elizabeth all the morning, George was annoyed and then disturbed. He telephoned Holcombe, but the bell rang in an empty house. He rang again during lunch, and in the late afternoon. Finally, not enjoying the necessity, he rang Lilian Anstey.

It was Harold who answered.

He was cordial to George. He respected ex-soldiers.

'Elizabeth? She had to go to London at the crack of dawn. The little girl and those damned dogs are here with us.'

'May one enquire why she went up?' George sounded casual. He was annoyed again.

'I'm afraid the old lady has passed away.'

'*Aunt Dolly!*'

There was a chuckle at the other end of the line.

'No, no, Dolly's right as rain. She's in London too. It's their great aunt, Bessy, the old lady who lived in Bloomsbury. Very sudden it was – not a day's illness. Passed away two days ago but the lawyers couldn't get in touch – Elizabeth seems to be out a good deal . . . she won't be home again until after the weekend.'

George was grieved to learn that Bessy had died, and remembered the fine worn face, and her delight in talking of the family. He did not enquire what hotel Elizabeth was staying in or do more than send his condolences in case she rang again. He played a lone hand and the less people who knew anything about his link with Elizabeth the better. He missed Elizabeth all through the day. The work changed when she was not with him. Her bold handwriting stared at him from exercise books and ledgers. He imagined he could smell her scent, flowery and faint, somewhere in the gaunt room.

Driving home, his thoughts were sombre. The international news had become worse since Hitler had marched into Prague. The Ides of March, people called it. He wondered what the next few months would bring, and grimaced that his life was still at peace – he, a professional soldier. I shouldn't have left the Army, he thought. Two faces came into his thoughts, one as fair as a lily, the other with little flaws, freckles, in her eyes. I always swore I'd give no hostages to fortune.

He decided to spend the weekend flying Tova. Few people could imagine what it was like to flaw a hawk. In Scotland he had gone shooting with well-trained pointers, and been impressed to see the dogs stand, drop to shot, return obediently to their master's whistle. But that could never compare to a wild creature leaving him, flying up until she was nothing but a black twinkling star in the clear air, then at a whistle and the toss of the lure, fall out of the clouds back on to his wrist . . .

Early one cold wet morning – she'd been away almost a week – he found Elizabeth in the stable office. She was wearing black.

'At last,' he said.

'My father-in-law told you about Aunt Bessy?'

'I was so sorry. I liked her. She was gallant and real. I liked her. I wish I might have come to the funeral,' he added.

'Oh George, I know. I tried. But Bessy left a letter written an age ago, long before you returned from India, saying she only wanted closest relatives. When mother and I spoke of you, Bessy's lawyer who was the executor simply wouldn't agree. A stickler for the rules.'

She gave him a rueful kind of look. They hadn't met since they had made love, and it touched him to see her look slightly shy.

'She was a darling. I was so miserable. I never saw her enough when she was alive.'

'We always say that.'

'Do we, George? She was Bidwell history. Yours as well as mine,' she said earnestly. 'It was in her head, what Merriscourt was like long ago, nearly a hundred years, and when her brothers were alive, and your grandmother, Kitty, and – and so many things. If I'd asked more, she would have told more. I wasted it.'

'I'm sure you were very sweet to her. She told me how fond of you she was.'

'Did she? I wrote to her about the divorce. It was an awful shock for her, poor Aunt, she was a stickler for the rules. I mean . . . she sort of thought how I wouldn't be allowed in the Royal Enclosure . . .things like that. She couldn't understand why I did it.'

'You went to the funeral,' he prompted, thinking she seemed very sad.

'She wanted to be cremated. Awful, that Golders Green place. No religion. Just a lot of politeness and people standing about looking at the cards on the wreaths. Mother and I were the only Bidwells. Then the lawyer, *he* was there, said would we come back to his chambers for tea. So it was tea in the Temple.'

'Lizzie. You look as if you've had a shock. You are all right, aren't you? Surely losing your old Aunt –'

'I've got something to tell you.'

Before she could finish the sentence the telephone rang. Estate problems claimed them both.

Chapter Nineteen

Elizabeth had to leave at once for the Ryecroft farm at Little Crediton. Joseph Ryecroft's little boy was ill, and his wife was away nursing her mother, so the farmer was imprisoned in the house with the child and could not get to work.

When she arrived, Joseph, all six foot three and sixteen stone, was sitting by the bed in which a small flushed figure lay restlessly asleep.

'Joseph? It's me. Elizabeth Bidwell.' She never used her married name now. 'How's Billy?'

'Sore and sick, Miss.'

She touched the boy's hand.

'He's very hot. Did you take his temperature? Don't worry, I'll do it. I've rung the doctor and he'll be here at lunchtime. Now you go, Joseph. I know you're busy, and I've often nursed my daughter with a temperature. I'll take the greatest care, I promise. Do go down.'

He hesitated, then lumbered down the stairs. She heard him riding away.

When he had gone the little boy woke and began to cry. His temperature was 101°. She washed his burning face and hands, gave him crushed aspirin and home-made lemonade. She sat by him until he slept again, then crept downstairs to make herself some tea. The Ryecroft farm had not changed for centuries. The great black pot hung on its hook over the wood fire, there was a high-backed settle, a chimney place big enough for seats inside. On either side of the long elm table were benches, used by Joseph and his workers for three large farmhouse meals a day. Drinking her tea, Elizabeth returned to the sickroom.

When the doctor came he diagnosed – not measles, which Elizabeth feared because of Petra – but tonsillitis. The boy's throat was very swollen. Gargle and aspirins, warmth and good nursing, said the doctor.

All day long until his father came back, Elizabeth was alone with her patient. She had things to think about. When he finally returned at dusk, the child's temperature was no higher, and she promised to come back next morning.

'Thanks, Miss Bidwell. Misses his mother, he does.'

Elizabeth drove home. Parked outside the house was a familiar car. Her heart turned over.

'You're late,' said George accusingly. He had opened the front door.

'I had to wait until Joseph got back. The little boy's on the mend, but I'll be needed for at least a couple more days.'

'Damn. Well, I'll put up with it. I sent Gladys home, incidentally, and I put your offspring to bed. She's a charmer like her mother.'

Since the only reply to that was smug, she said nothing. All she could think was – are we going to make love? Is that what I'm doomed to think every time I see him here? She felt slightly faint.

They went into the drawing-room and before she could offer him a drink he said, 'We must talk. But I can't have a sensible conversation unless I make love to you first.'

The lovemaking went on much longer. When it ended, he said, 'It's getting damned cold. I'll light the fire. You go up and put on something warmer.' He laughed as she collected her scattered clothes, and ran naked from the room.

Alone in her bedroom, she thought – I have a cool customer for a lover this time. So much passion and skill, so violent a taker, in a way a despoiler. She was like an invaded city, and it was she who had thrown open the gates and given up the key. But the waves that drenched her were not only the pleasure from a sated body, they were happiness. I'll never keep George, she thought. I have him *now*, but he'll be going away. And in any case, Sylvia will get him in the end.

311

Deliberately composed, she returned downstairs, wearing a new, clinging dark dress and a good deal of scent. He lifted a bottle of champagne with a 'look what I've brought' gesture.

'How lovely. What are we celebrating?'

'Light at the end of the tunnel. I've been looking through our accounts, and they are just slightly better. What's more, we have not made any mistakes.'

'Thank God for that.'

'We must also say thank Elizabeth Bidwell.'

'I only add a bit of help.'

'Don't be mock modest, Liz. Well, now. You said you had something to tell me. I have news too. Shall I get mine over first? It's short. You remember I went to London to the War Office? Well, it looks as if I shall be able to get back into the Service. Not in my old regiment, of course, but at least they'll give me a desk job. They're soon going to need everybody, even the not-so-young.'

Still in her dream of sex, she felt as if he had thrown her into icy water.

'Soon?'

'Don't look at me with that frightened face, sweetheart. It isn't just yet. But next month conscription is coming in for the twenties and twenty-ones, and later it'll be extended. There's a hell of a lot to be done. For you and me too. Idyllic as our working arrangements are, we must plan for when I'm not here any more. Though God knows, there are some big debts I don't know *what* we'll do about before war comes.'

'A war. I can't imagine it.'

'It won't be like the last one,' he said, as if to comfort her. So cool, though. She used his own tone when she said:

'Yes. We have to make plans. Oddly enough my news is about that too. You remember the lawyer took Mother and me back to his chambers? That was because he was about to drop a thunderbolt. Aunt Bessy was rich. Isn't it incredible? Mother and I always imagined she lived at the old Imperial and Royal to save money, but it wasn't like that at all. She inherited a lot from some distant relation who owned

Nottingham coal mines. She never spent any of it and – with Peter dead – has left it all to me. I should have thought it would be for Dicky Bidwell, but no. She's never been close to Sylvia, never met the little boy. In the will, she called me "the last of the line". I must have seemed that to her. George. I have over twenty thousand a year.'

She looked at him solemnly.

He whistled.

'That *is* a thunderbolt. You won't be working for poor old Merriscourt much longer. You're an heiress.'

'Don't you understand!' she exclaimed. 'Bessy left the money to me *because* of Merriscourt. I'm certain of it. I don't know how she forgot about Sylvia's son but she did, or maybe she thought as Sylvia had re-married – the point is, it is Bidwell money. Think, George, how much we can do now! You said we need clean water for the animals instead of pond water – now we'll take water up to the high meadows, make a spider-web of water pipes, put down drinking troughs! And the sheep and pigs must have it too. We'll repair every single cottage. That will stop us losing tenants. We can employ a sub-agent to buy and sell the corn and send the sheep to the markets. With Aunt Bessy's money Merriscourt will be itself again.'

Her voice had risen, her eyes shone. She waited for him to share her pleasure. He said nothing.

He rubbed his chin.

'Mm. I suppose there's a sort of justice in Aunt Bessy's money coming back to Merriscourt. But I shall only allow it –'

'Allow!'

'Certainly. Who else is going to advise you? Your mother is miles away and completely uninvolved. I'm your only other relative, and very much part of this. I repeat, I will only *allow* it if an agreement is drawn up. We must put our cards on the table with Sylvia and Ted.'

'But they'll never –'

'Lizzie, don't you yet know the power of money?'

*　　*　　*

Elizabeth continued to nurse Billy Ryecroft who, as he recovered, grew more fractious and demanding; she was glad when his large father loomed back into the farmhouse. Two days later his mother, talkative and grateful, came home. Elizabeth drove back to Holcombe where her own daughter was smugly eating tea in the kitchen with Gladys.

George, missing Elizabeth, worked late in the stable office and then telephoned through to the main house to ask if he could come in for a drink.

Sylvia was disagreeable.

'What are you asking for? Of course you can come. And as for whether I'll be in, a fat chance I have of being anywhere else.'

George walked with a springy step through the cold dusk to the big house. Lights shone, throwing pools on to the terrace. He heard one of Sylvia's favourite records.

> *There may be trouble ahead*
> *But while there's music*
> *And moonlight*
> *And love and romance,*
> *Let's face the music and dance.*

In the drawing-room, Sylvia, ethereal as fair women are when they wear black, was dancing alone in a corner by the radiogram. She danced as if in the arms of an invisible lover, her silvery head thrown back, eyes half closed. She went on whirling as he came in.

'Georgy porgy, have a drink. *Soon, we'll be without the moon, Humming a different tune,*' sang Sylvia. When the record ended she shut the lid of the radiogram, came over and snuggled up to him. He could smell her strong, clinging scent. When he had been close to her, it also clung to his clothes. Elizabeth often noticed it.

'Tell me everything,' said Sylvia. They sat on the sofa where Dolly used to preside behind the teapot. Starched Ada, one of the few reminders of the ancient regime, brought in Madeira and sherry. George missed Marchant's stout commanding presence.

'How are you getting on without Ferrers, Georgy?'

It was unlike her to ask.

'Not badly,' he said. He saw that it had been a question made from charm, not interest, and he said, 'And how are you getting on as lady of the manor?'

'I suppose that's what I am. Lady Levens came round today and asked me to join the committee for the hospital. There are ten women on the committee already. Golly! I was very polite and said I'd let her know. I shall be nice, I promise, but regretful. What gorgeous clothes you do wear.'

'This suit is ten years old, Sylvia, don't be absurd.'

'Well, I love it. I'm always telling Ted how marvellous you look. Do I have to wait ten years before he's presentable?'

'He is a handsome man and what is more devoted to you, which you don't deserve. He also seems to be doing very well.'

'Of course he isn't. I made him start hunting and he does thunder about on some days, but what a rider. Like a sack of potatoes. Isn't it funny how people like Ted look so awful on a horse? His ghastly parents came over last weekend, and his father was rather nasty. Said that Ted had to stop hunting, and be at the works at half-past eight every morning. You'd think his son was a factory hand.'

What she said was outrageous, but her voice was so light and sighing, and accompanied with so many daring looks which said – aren't I dreadful? – that it was impossible to scold. He said, slightly sarcastic, that Ted was in a very profitable business and one day he and Sylvia would inherit it.

'You enjoy money. Although you pretend to be a silly child.'

She opened her blue eyes like saucers.

'I don't pretend anything. And who doesn't like money? But Ted's got Merriscourt, all thanks to me, and he jolly well ought to live up to it. I do. I may not be willing to join old Lady Levens' committee, but I know everybody, and I entertain sometimes, and I hunt, and what's more I even found somebody to cope with the estate – I found *you*. That's not silly, it's brilliant.'

He couldn't help laughing.

But the evening did not remain pleasant.

315

Ted was late home, and they were half way through dinner when he came into the dining-room, slightly drunk. He was amiable at first, but he got through almost a bottle of burgundy during the meal and then went on to brandy. George watched with growing impatience. How well he knew the good nature which turns into aggression, he had seen it in Army messes more times than he could count. It got on his nerves. Sylvia, darting sharp looks at her husband, set out to annoy him, contradicting him, bringing George in as an ally, and adding fuel with remarks like, 'Why not drink a second bottle?'

It disturbed George to see that she was accustomed to Ted being drunk. When not baiting her husband, she kept referring to another visit to Antibes. She had some friends there with an enormous villa, a swimming pool cut out of the rocks, a yacht, they really were rich, and they'd very sweetly said she could go and stay, and bring Ted if he wanted to come. How she loved the South of France. People said that enjoying France was a sign of taste.

When they returned to the drawing-room, and coffee was served, George looked briefly down at his wrist-watch ticking away the tedious evening, wondering how soon he could make his escape. He was sorry for Ted, but why in God's name didn't the man tell her to shut up? As for Sylvia, now and then he caught a shadowed, almost a puzzled look on her pretty face. He simply hadn't the heart to blame her. He had wanted to open up the whole subject of Aunt Bessy's money and Elizabeth's generous plans for Merriscourt. But it was impossible at present.

He finally stood up to go, making a sort of joke about needing to be in the stable office early next morning. Neither of the Ansteys moved. Ted, setting the brandy swirling round his glass said, 'Forgot to tell you, Syl. We're going to Milan.'

She stiffened like a dog.

'We're going *where*?'

'I have to go to Milan to see the Fiat people. I told you weeks ago. Well, the Benedettos wrote today, and they've invited us to go on a trip. A cruise,' mumbled Ted. 'You said you like yachts. We'll be going on a damned great cabin cruiser. All the trimmings.'

'Did you say I'd go too?'

'Of course. We're both invited.'

'But I hate Milan. Last time the food made me sick. What's more, before we went you kept dinning into my head that English people must never mention Mussolini's name or they got shoved into prison. We had to call him Mister Smith, you said. You frightened me into fits.'

Ted tried to stay reasonable. He said that was only being on the safe side, everybody English did it now, and Italians were so jumpy about their Dictator. Anyway, since when did Syl ever talk politics? He tried to smile.

'The Benedettos are planning a marvellous cruise, you'll love it –'

'I'd hate it. I don't even know them, and I don't work for your father's beastly firm. I won't be dragged round Italy just because you've got to go. You're dreary and boring and no fun any more!'

She burst into angry sobs.

It was too late for George to be peacemaker. Ted's control snapped. He shouted that she was a bitch, and rushed from the room, slamming the door.

Sylvia continued to cry.

'You're in the wrong, Sylvia.'

'You're as horrible as he is.'

'Why not go with him to Italy? And remember to say Mister Smith?' said George, with half a smile. 'You need a change of scene, and the Italian coast is very beautiful.'

She dabbed her eyes and sniffed, looking quite pathetic. He hadn't the heart to leave her.

Suddenly the drawing-room door burst open.

Ted, still drunk but slightly sobered by anger, was standing there carrying a suitcase. Breathing heavily, his head down, he looked like a bated bull.

'Oh, very dramatic,' said Sylvia pettishly. 'You won't make

317

me change my mind. I refuse to go to Italy, I shall go to France and –'

'Do as you bloody well like! You're driving me mad and I can't stand another minute. I'm going to Milan and you can go to hell!'

He slammed out of the room, and a moment later they heard the roar of his car.

When Elizabeth arrived at the stable office the next morning, she was not sure how to behave with George. Now that they really were lovers, she wondered if it would change their manner to each other when they were at work. Apparently not. George looked up from some papers, said good morning, and added that he wanted a word. He was going out for most of the day, so it had better be now.

'I've been thinking about your inheritance. Were you serious about spending part of it on the estate?'

'Every penny.'

Her immediate reply displeased him.

'What about using that good Devon head of yours?'

'Oh dear. Wasn't I? Then I'll speak more slowly. I have thought about the inheritance too, and I am perfectly serious. I intend to do what I've already told you.'

'Wiser to wait.'

'Waiting doesn't pay the bills.'

'Nevertheless, I prefer it.'

She thought, he can't stop me from spending my own money. All she said was, 'Let's talk about it a little more. When?'

'This afternoon. Incidentally, Ted has gone to Italy.'

'Fiat, I suppose.'

'Exactly. So we must wait until he is back before we can settle any kind of agreement. I know Merriscourt belongs to Sylvia, entailed for Dicky, so we'll have to see the trustees. And Ted must be consulted.'

'It's all going to be very difficult.'

He glanced up, he had been fixing some papers with a clip, noticing her voice was cold.

'Lizzie, in time you will learn that money talks.'

Adding that he had to see Sylvia, he left the office.

She sat miserably at her desk. Ever since the news of the legacy, she'd thought about just this – being with George, solving Merriscourt's difficulties, planning to spend money rather than save it. She'd believed it would make them happy. The belief was gone. She began to work, but the morning dragged. She ate the sandwiches she had brought, and drank the coffee from her thermos. In the early afternoon, she kept listening for his step. All she heard was the chirp of sparrows, the snuffle or whinny of the horses in the stables. What took him so long with Sylvia? What indeed? Trying to work, stopping to listen, she thought, this is ridiculous. I think too much about it. I was right when I knew that his lovemaking would be dangerous.

She scribbled a note saying she'd gone home, and left, locking the door.

As she drove back to Holcombe, she thought how little time she had spent lately with Petra and then, a part of the guilty feeling that she was behaving like a fool in love, she remembered Marchant. He had telephoned her days ago, inviting her to see his pub.

The Dog & Pheasant, at the end of the straggling village five miles from Merriscourt, had once been two cob cottages. Thirty years ago they had been knocked into one, extended and converted into a pub. The place was popular with farmers. When she drove up, it was mid-afternoon. The pub, lace curtains obscuring every window, looked dead. Above the door, the black beam was lettered with 'Props: Isaac Marchant and John W. Timmins.'

Elizabeth did not bother to try the door of the saloon bar, but went round to the back of the building where there was a small garden and another door. She rang the bell. A ground floor window flew up and Marchant's head appeared.

'God bless my soul, it's Miss Elizabeth! That's a treat and no mistake. Come in, come in.'

The door opened and there he was, filling most of it. No

longer in butler's livery, he wore grey flannels and a cardigan, giving them a certain dignity, the cardigan buttons done up firmly across his stomach. He exclaimed at the pleasure of seeing her.

They went into a parlour exactly like every Devonshire parlour in every cottage for fifty miles. A log fire burned in the blackleaded grate. A large ugly clock stood on the narrow mantelpiece. In a corner was a glass cabinet filled with Japanese china too delicate ever to be used. The furniture was slippery and over-stuffed. There was even a tabby cat sleeping on the rag mat in front of the fire.

'I'll just put on the kettle. It's a brave sight to see you, Miss.'

They drank strong tea and ate seed cake. She admired the cottage, and was taken for a tour of the pub. Timmins, he said, lived in the village. Elizabeth had correctly guessed that Marchant paid the lion's share, since he had possession of the comfortable house. He was house-proud. His butler's skill showed in the glittering brass, the polished mahogany, the spotless flagged floors, the general air that someone with high standards was in command. Tankards hung on a row of hooks above the open fireplace in the bar.

'Customers bring their own. Cider tastes good out of pewter. Maybe you'll taste some before you go, Miss Elizabeth?'

His Devonian accent was stronger than it used to be. He was turning back into the boy who had been born a few miles away, had been soldier, batman, and pillar of Merriscourt, only to be a villager all over again.

In the parlour, he put logs on the fire.

'Jack Timmins is a good man. Of course you knew we were in the same regiment with the old Master for a spell? Did I tell you he went to India after that, Jack did?'

'Captain Westlock mentioned something.'

'Ah. Well, Jack knew the Captain in a manner of speaking. You get to know your officers, Miss. Very smart, the young Captain was. But hard on the men. They all said so.'

'I dare say they needed it,' said Elizabeth perversely, finding herself agreeing with the men.

'Mebbe so. Mebbe not. Timmins, now, didn't ought to need any pulling up. He's smart as paint. And a worker too. *And* he knows when to keep his mouth shut.'

'I'm sure that's important for a landlord.'

Mellowed by the company of the young woman he had known since she was born, Marchant was like a flower in a warm room. He blossomed. He talked about the shocking state of some of the farms, about good harvests and bad prices, about Hitler, about Chamberlain, and about Merriscourt. He'd heard that chap Ferrers had got the push from the Captain, and not before time. Looking affectionately at his mistress's daughter, he grew confidential.

'Do you know, Miss Elizabeth, I'm not certain sure that I won't tell you something which will surprise you.'

'Really, Marchant?'

'Something I wouldn't tell to anyone else. Not to a living soul.'

The words slightly troubled her. They had an ominous sound. He looked at her with twinkling eyes embedded in plump cheeks, and she had the grotesque thought that he resembled some large animal who had swallowed but not yet digested another smaller creature. She wanted to stop him saying whatever it was. But it was too late.

'It's like this,' he began.

The story started mildy enough. Timmins had remained in the army after Marchant left the service at the end of the war. Timmins had served under young Mrs Anstey's father in India – he remembered her as a little child in cantonments, learning to ride. Fancy that. Colonel Ashton was a major then, of course. There was nothing that Timmins couldn't say more in praise of *him*. Brave as a lion, a born fighter, up on the North West frontier he'd fought hand to hand . . . the old man talked on. Listening, Elizabeth lost her feeling of anxiety. The story was like those old sepia drawings in last century copies of the *Illustrated London News* – rearing horses and pennants, turbaned figures, dark and white faces . . .

'Jack knew the Major's wife too, by sight, everybody did.

Such a good-looker. But sickly, very sickly.'

Marchant, who was never ill, used a solemn note.

'One lung,' he intoned.

'Poor thing,' murmured Elizabeth, faintly bored. She knew about Sylvia's mother's illness and it was sad, but it had no reality for her. It was almost like another picture in the *Illustrated London News*.

'Them that has consumption, I'm told, is greedy for pleasure. Greedy for pleasure,' he said, pausing a moment, to add, 'The Captain was only a lieutenant then. Very close to the family.'

'Which is why he is Mrs Anstey's godfather,' said Elizabeth, who now felt the tale was destined to go on for ever. Too polite to look at the clock, she guessed it was getting late.

'Then Major Ashton was sent to the Staff College at Quetta, Miss, and the young lieutenant saw a lot of the lady. Just a boy he was. Handsome. All the ladies liked Lieutenant Westlock, but Jack Timmins said he chased after the Major's wife something chronic. The regiment couldn't help noticing. Ladies like to be amused in India, you know, and he was only a boy. A dab at polo too . . . and that,' the story abruptly ended, 'is how it was.'

Elizabeth digested it. What he said was deliberately ambiguous, but his tone of voice and his expression were not.

'You mean that Captain Westlock and Mrs Anstey's mother had a love affair.'

He looked pleased at her spelling it out.

'That's about the size of it.'

'Perhaps they did, Marchant, and it was very wrong, but the poor lady is dead and it's a long time ago. It isn't important any more, is it?'

'Can't say that, Miss, when he's here in Devon looking out for his own daughter.'

'*His what?*'

'His daughter. Miss Sylvia that was,' said Marchant, and only then saw the colour had drained from Elizabeth's face.

'Don't take on like that, Miss. I didn't mean to upset

322

you – why, you look like a ghost! As you just said, it's a long time ago. I only thought you should know because the Captain *does* look out for her and you're a friend of his now, but you're on your own and forewarned is forearmed. You wouldn't be doing nothing silly with that money your auntie left you, would you?'

'Of course not,' said Elizabeth automatically. She had said nothing about the legacy, but the village bush telegraph still worked uncannily. She was struggling with what he had told her, and did not care that he knew about the money.

'I said I'd surprise you, but I didn't ought to have upset you. But that's who the young Mistress is. The Captain's girl. Did it never enter your head, Miss Elizabeth? I suspected it when they first came from India. Of course I had no proof, but Timmins knew the ayah and she told him the whole story. Well. Once you know, you can see the likeness. Hair. And something about the eyes, though the Captain's aren't a good sea-blue like hers. Father and daughter . . . rich, isn't it? We were all taken in by that godfather story. Leastwise most of us. Your dear mother, God bless her, said to me once, "Marchant, he's a godfather in a thousand. Most godparents, she said, give the child a napkin ring and then forget all about it." Godfather!'

He shook with laughter.

That evening, when the little girl was in bed, Elizabeth went down to the drawing-room and lay on the sofa where she and George had made love. Was the story true? Or had the old man told her the old faded scandal from revenge, because Sylvia had got rid of him. Marchant said they were alike, father and daughter, and in her mind she compared them. But she saw only that their colouring was slightly similiar. How different their natures were. Thinking about George, she suddenly remembered the time when she had asked him, in so many words, to make love to Sylvia. My God, if the story's true, no wonder he looked angry. It was ludicrous.

I *must* know, she thought.

323

And telephoned Speldhurst.

'Lizzie! Why did you disappear like that? We were supposed to be working this afternoon.'

'I went to see Marchant.'

'How is the old rogue?' he said, using Peter's word.

'Fine. I'll tell you about it. Look – can you come round?'

'Now?'

When she rang off, she heard the sound of rain. She was so nervous that she could not sit down, but walked up and down the room until ten minutes later she heard the car. She went to the front door.

'You've been very quick.'

'I'd have been quicker if the car hadn't got stuck at the bottom of the hill. The wheels began to slip in the mud.'

'How on earth did you manage?'

'Put an old rug under the back wheels. Since I've been living in your part of the world, I've learned a trick or two.'

The drawing-room was filled with the noise of the rain. The dogs came in, both wet, and shook themselves, spraying George with raindrops.

'Out into the kitchen at once!'

At the rap of his voice, they slunk out.

She poured him a drink and they sat down. He leaned back, looking at her, and she thought – what a fool I am! He thinks I asked him round for us to make love. She saw sex in his face, and said quicky, 'Marchant is very happy and settled in his pub.'

'Good. I must go and see him.'

'I was there for hours. He was very talkative.' She paused and added steadily, 'He told me a very odd story.'

She had taken a chair facing him, and George was sitting on the sofa. As she had seen him do before, he spread his arms on either side. He looked relaxed, as if to say, we've got the whole night to do what I came for.

'What story's that? I bet he's full of them, told in that heathenish jargon he uses sometimes.'

'I like it when he speaks broad Devon.'

'Of course you do. Well? What's the story? I can see you want to tell it.'

Frightened, she blurted out, 'He said Sylvia's your daughter.'

There was a considerable silence.

What did she expect? Scornful laughter? Denial? Even anger. All he did was to rub his chin.

'Did he, now,' he finally said.

'*So it's true!*'

'I could deny it, I suppose. But perhaps I won't. You'd have to know one day. I don't need to ask where the story came from. Sergeant Timmins.'

The worst was over. A profound depression came to her. He stayed without moving, his arms spread out.

'Did it shock you?'

'I was staggered. I never imagined such a thing.'

'I know that, Lizzie. You thought I was in love with the girl.'

She blushed hotly, and he laughed.

'It was natural to think that,' she said, hating the laughter. 'When I first met Sylvia, she said there were many men in India like you, single men who took on other people's families because they were lonely.'

'She must never know I am her father.'

'But that's not right!'

'As I said earlier, Elizabeth, use your good Devon head. What earthly use would it be for her to know? She was very fond of John who spoiled her outrageously. It would be a hideous shock.'

'Why is it a shock to find out your father is somebody you have loved all your life?'

He shook his head.

'No. In her mind *John* is her father. She couldn't take knowing he wasn't and that she's illegitimate. She'd have hysterics and take to her bed. God, you never saw her after Fay died. It was why I brought her to England, and landed her on you all. Don't think I didn't realise it was a dirty trick. I had a bad conscience about it. But she couldn't come with me to Skye for various reasons.'

'Because of Lady Priscilla.'

He rubbed his chin. 'Dear me, you seem to know a lot about me.'

'Not very much. Mother told me about her once. And Topsy said it was Lady Priscilla you were with in Skye.'

'A married Priscilla. Are you shocked this time?'

'For God's sake, I'm not shocked at what you do!'

'I think,' he said, 'I rather hoped you would be. However, I've strayed from the point. I've been the cat who walked by himself so long that it is unfamiliar for other people to be part of my gory past. As I said, it's imperative that Sylvia doesn't know who she is. She's not made of hardy stuff like you. She seems strong and greedy but she's breakable. I remember thinking,' he said musingly, 'that you and she are like a peach and an egg. Sylvia is the egg. Round and contained and well-shaped, an entity, but when you hold it in your hand, if you squeeze ever so gently, what happens? You're a different thing altogether. Juicy and ripe, a Devonshire peach ripened by the sun, but if one bites hard, one could break one's teeth on the stone.' He looked to see if she would share a smile, but she was fixed and grave.

'You want to know about Sylvia's mother, don't you? Well. I fell in love with Fay when I was twenty-two and a second lieutenant. I was posted to John's regiment in India – my family had known his for years, and I was glad to be serving under him. But when I arrived in Calcutta he was away. Sent to the Staff College at Quetta on a course. All I did in Calcutta was to kick my heels. It was an extraordinary life for someone of my age then – 1913, Lizzie. Calcutta. The city of Palaces, the metropolis of British India. Balls at the Governor General's house for two thousand guests . . . the river smothered in ships . . . private dances in the great houses along the Chowringee. People used to say the city was as elegant as St Petersburg. Gardens . . . aviaries . . . orchids growing in the bathroom. And the gorgeous women. In the Army, you know, when there's no fighting, they invent work for the men to keep them out of trouble. Not so with the officers. All I did was go to dances, play polo, and dangle after Fay Ashton. I was crazy about her. Oh, you can't imagine how lovely she was! You think Sylvia is, I know, most people do. But she couldn't hold a candle to her mother. Fay was genuinely beautiful. People stopped talking when she came into a ball-room. And – well – she liked me. We went to bed together rather a lot. She became pregnant, but the following month John came back. It was one of those pieces of luck I used to have occasionally. Not any more. Return of husband, wife soon breaks the merry news. Family rejoicing. Will you be the godfather? I felt disgusting – but.'

'And Sylvia was officially premature,' was all Elizabeth said.

'Yes. The old formula.'

He glanced at her and said, 'I've depressed you.'

'Of course you haven't.'

'I can see that I have. You're upset. Why?'

She went on denying it but he was not a man to let go and in the end she said, 'It's just that it's sad. And you sound so detached when you talk about it.'

He started. 'Detached? I'm not detached. I *loved* Fay. She bewitched me, I couldn't think of anything but Fay, and then it all became a hideous mess. She was frightened at first, but when she knew her husband was arriving back almost at once, she was the cool one. She used to laugh about it. She was pleased to be pregnant and she had that talent, I've met it rarely, of simply forgetting what it is dangerous to think about. I was posted away before Sylvia was born, and they made me godfather by proxy. When I got back, I was one of the family again, the friend they liked to have around. Fay wanted men to dance for her. My daughter, as you've seen to your cost, is the same.'

He stopped talking. He came over to her, lifted her up by her elbows and wrapped her close. He gave her his long,

327

exploring kiss. When it ended he looked down at her.

'Lovely Liz. Shall I prove how detached I am?'

Merriscourt, apart from the servants, was empty. Old Nanny Osborn had taken the little boy for an early spring holiday to East Anglia. She had friends there.

'Of all the eccentric ideas,' said George. 'It'll be excessively cold and she could have stayed here in Devon. But I couldn't get her to listen, the old image. She said the fresh breezes would do him good. And this is where young Dicky's mother is –' he added, giving Elizabeth a postcard. It was a picture of yellow beaches and blue seas and in Sylvia's scrawl said the ballet season had opened in Monte Carlo and was topping.

'She's having too good a time for somebody who sent her unfortunate husband off with a flea in his ear.'

The revelation that Sylvia was his daughter had had a curious, unexpected effect on Elizabeth. All during the time she had not known, there had been the obvious reason why George never said he loved her. She'd imagined that Sylvia owned his heart. She knew he was attracted to herself, he was an exciting and demanding lover. But that was all. They had no exchanges but physical ones. When not locked and embracing, they were simply friends. And even at her most lost in sex, she was never going to confess that she loved him.

Using some of Bessy's money with considerable effect, they worked. And as spring went by, she grew accustomed to the thought that George would go, just as Britain was steadily adjusting itself to the thought of war as a normal background to everyday life. Steel shelters. The organising of the evacuation of children when the time came. 'In an emergency' they called it. These things, on the wireless and in the newspapers, were taken for granted.

And still Ted and Sylvia stayed away.

Lilian invited Elizabeth and Petra to Sunday lunch at Broad Oaks, and produced a postcard very much like those which arrived for George from Antibes. Custard yellow beaches and Stevens ink blue seas.

328

'I know we don't talk about Ted much now that you're divorced, dearie, but I thought my little Pet would like the card from her Daddy.'

Petra, saying 'Daddy', walked off with the card, kept it with her all day, and even clutched it in her left hand when eating. She was still holding it when they drove home.

In the mysterious way of very small children, she had recently begun to talk about her rarely-met father. He had become an invisible companion to the child. 'Daddy!' she shouted, darting into rhododendron hedges. Or 'Daddy!' waving at any empty lane when driving out with her mother. Elizabeth had attempted to replace the phantom Ted with Peter Rabbit and Benjamin Bunny but she might as well have saved her breath. She hoped Petra was not going to see the ghost when she was with her grandparents. But if she did, Lilian took no notice.

The absentees were due to return soon. Nanny Osborn came first, bringing a brown-faced and slightly taller Dicky.

'According to Nanny,' reported George to Elizabeth, 'they had sun every day. I can't believe it of the Suffolk coast where the winds come straight from Siberia. However, they look very fit, even our ancient relic of better days.'

Sylvia came next. When George walked into the big house on a morning of birdsong and the first roses, he found Sylvia, surrounded by suitcases, already bossing Ada. He was struck by her beauty – she was burned a dark shining brown, and was dressed in South of France white. Her hair, bleached by the sun, was plain and glossy on the top, and a mass of tiny curls below.

'Georgy, how I've missed you!' she cried, running over to hug him. 'Ada tells me that awful old husband of mine is still in Italy after all these weeks, calling in at every port. He's sent me a fistful of postcards. I must look at them later. I quite missed him when I got home last night, strange to say. George. I had a thrilling time. Guess who I dined with? The Aga Khan.'

George returned thoughtfully to the stable office where Elizabeth said expectantly, 'How is she?'

'Bursting with health. No telegram from Ted yet, only that heap of postcards. Did his parents say anything about his return when you saw them?'

'No. Only more cards, and how clever of Ted to be buzzing round the Fiat people.'

'We'll have to wait until he's back before we settle about your money, Liz.'

'Can I please,' she said, waving a clip of papers, 'pay these bills? My money has come through and is bulging in the bank.'

'Oh, very well. If you must.'

He had decided, he told her, that she must have a half share in the estate. He'd been to see the family solicitor, and talked to two elderly ex-Army trustees. He had also seen an accountant. George showed Elizabeth his calculations and told her exactly how much it would cost, as he put it, to pull Merriscourt through.

'I don't see how you'll swing it for me to get half, George. Dicky inherits everything.'

'The entail must be broken when he's twenty-one and in the meantime the trustees are appalled at all the bills. Sylvia will sign what I tell her or Dickybird, as she calls him, is going to inherit a few farms with the roofs fallen in, fields of what Inslow calls dashells, and a bloody great overdraft. She doesn't know how lucky she is to have you.'

'Oh George. Don't joke.'

George, as had become his custom, spent the evening at Holcombe with Elizabeth. They made love. Had supper. Made love again. There was a large full moon, and the early summer night was warm.

'Wish I could stay all night. I'd like to share your bed. Wake up with you in the morning. But we must keep your reputation unsullied, must we not?'

'Oh, definitely.'

She used just the right flippant voice.

He put his arm round her shoulders and they walked out into the moonlight to his car. A bird glided down and fluttered in front of them. It settled on the gatepost.

'Without a word, they both froze into stillness.

And it began to sing. The song rose and fell, bubbling, hoarse, ending with the last pure curlew notes. At last it fluttered away.

'The nightjar,' he said.

'Peter and I used to listen to them in the woods.'

When he drove away to Speldhurst the moonlight was so bright that it was like daylight. The fields, trees, hedges, road, had an eerie beauty. But as he parked the car he swore, for he could hear his telephone ringing inside the house. The sound broke into the exquisite night, it was ugly and urgent. He ran to the door, unlocked it hastily and just managed to reach the telephone before it stopped.

'Captain Westlock?' It was Ada, from Merriscourt. 'Oh Captain, I've been ringing and ringing. I thought I'd never get you. A telegram came. The Master's been drowned.'

Chapter Twenty

George and Elizabeth were at Merriscourt all day. No longer was it necessary for her to creep into the stable office. They spoke in low voices, both shocked and grey-faced.

Further telegrams had come from Italy, and early that morning Harold Anstey, looking as if he had aged twenty years, had come round. He asked if Lilian could have little Petra.

'Tell her to keep her has long as she likes.'

'You're a good girl,' he said, and left with his grand-daughter in his arms.

There remained Sylvia to cope with.

After the news had come last night, she had had real hyster-ics, screaming, sobbing and laughing until George had been forced to telephone the unfortunate doctor at four in the morning. He'd driven up in the dawn, and given her a strong sedative. She had slept for many hours. After tea she had rung for Ada. She refused to see anybody else.

It was Peter's death all over again.

'She's fallen to pieces. Who is going to pick her up this time?' George said grimly. They were sitting in the fami-liar old drawing-room. The French windows were open to a sunny afternoon and the strong scent of dark red wallflowers. Bob and the mongrel Bill trotted in and out, the only two happy creatures in the house.

George sighed.

'Poor kid. Two husbands dead. There are women like that. Fatal to men.'

'George, don't say that! Don't even think it! It's supersti-tious rubbish. Both were dreadful untoward accidents.'

'Nevertheless, destiny seems to take a hand. It's like good luck which people sometimes have and others don't. Sylvia has beauty, and maybe she has to pay for that. Because she doesn't use it as she should? God, I don't know. But I told you that she disintegrates when things go bad. With her mother, with Peter's death, I forced her back to life. I'm not sure I could do it all over again.'

'But won't it be easier? She didn't love Ted.'

'Since when have you thought that?'

'I've always known it.'

They had finished tea and they went out into the garden in the company of joyful dogs. Ada, who had replaced Marchant as ruler of the house, appeared on the terrace and walked towards them. 'Now what?' muttered George to Elizabeth.

'The Mistress says would you come up to her, Madam.'

'Me? Ada, you are mistaken. She means the Captain.'

'The Mistress is asking for you,' said Ada. Her voice was resentful.

Exchanging a mystified look with George, Elizabeth followed her into the house.

Sylvia was at the bedroom window. She must have seen them in the gardens.

'Go away, Ada!' she said. Directly the maid had gone, she threw herself, weeping, into Elizabeth's arms.

'Oh, Lizzie, Lizzie, you're the only one who knows how I feel. Isn't it awful? I can't believe it, even now.' And then to Elizabeth's horror she said in a shaking voice, 'I'm cursed. Everybody to do with me dies. My parents. Peter. Ted. It's a nightmare. It terrifies me.'

All the time she had known Sylvia, through the years during which Sylvia had spoiled and stolen her life, Elizabeth had rarely had a shred of affection for her. Sometimes she'd hated her. Sometimes despised her. Sometimes she had been so jealous that she had felt poisoned. But now her heart swelled. The creature holding her with poor thin arms had been Peter's lover and had borne his son. She was a part of everything Elizabeth treasured. And wasn't she, more than all

333

those things, the child of the man Elizabeth loved?

She wiped her cheeks, kissed and petted her, heard herself saying things she would not have believed, even yesterday.

'You have George. And Dickybird. And you have me.'

'*Do* I have you?'

'If you want me.'

The following day Elizabeth moved into Merriscourt. All George said was, 'You're stronger than I thought.'

Sylvia was almost too grateful. She was subdued and ate little, and was very nervous. She started and shuddered when the post arrived. She was quiet, and Elizabeth wished she would be her talkative, flighty self. Apparently she found a solace in having her cousin-in-law with her. It was the sort of sick fancy which people sometimes have when they are gravely ill. The only time she seemed content was when Elizabeth was in the garden or the nursery, playing with the children. She often said, 'You're wonderful with Dickybird.'

Elizabeth's nephew, she thought of him like that, was some weeks older than Petra and half a head taller. He was solidly built and strong. He had his father's round face, his thick hair was as fair and glinting as his mother's, his nature was his own. Petra, arriving from Broad Oaks and the capacious lap of her grandmother, was frightened by the size of the house, and more at the sight of the child thundering down the staircase towards her. As he jumped the last four stairs, Petra hid behind her mother.

'Home,' she distinctly said.

'Come and play,' said Dicky, going round Elizabeth to confront his cousin.

Petra cowered.

Dicky stood looking at her for a moment or two, and then began to jump. One, two, three, he jumped quite high, coming down with a bump.

Petra emerged slowly from her hiding place. He jumped again. She tried to imitate him, remaining rooted to the ground. Both children, one tall and sturdy, the other little and shy, burst out laughing.

334

Nanny Osborn, toiling down the stairs in the wake of her magnificent charge, said the children would like a walk in the garden, she was sure.

'Come on,' said Dicky Bidwell.

'Come on,' echoed Petra.

They marched out together.

From that moment, Dicky supplanted Petra's imaginary father. The children became inseparable. They were looked after by Gladys, enjoying the glory of working in Merriscourt. Antique Nanny Osborn sat knitting, or praying in her bedroom.

'Does you good to hear her, she's that religious,' said Gladys.

George, calling frequently at Merriscourt, and missing Elizabeth's help in the office, said that the children seemed made for each other, but he hoped Dicky did not bully the little girl. Dicky, finding a slave, was royally kind. He allowed Petra first go on her mother's old swing.

As the season ripened into summer, war grew nearer in people's thoughts. At the end of June a leaflet came with the Merriscourt post. 'Some Things You Should Know if War Comes,' said its title. It sounded oddly reassuring. In July, the first quarter of a million men were called up.

'We're more ready for war in peace than we have ever been,' declared the Minister of Defence.

'We're still in limbo,' George said. 'Lizzie, you'll simply have to buckle down and do some work with me soon. This week. Every day counts. Suppose I have to leave unexpectedly.'

'But how can I explain to Sylvia –'

'B- bother Sylvia. This *matters*.'

His sympathy for his bereaved daughter was on the wane. But she hadn't the heart either to shock Sylvia by telling her about the estate work, or by allowing George to speak about Merriscourt being made half over to herself.

Sensing that Elizabeth was restive, Sylvia repeated every day that she couldn't cope without her, couldn't sleep if she wasn't in the house, knew she would be ill if . . .

'But you have George,' said Elizabeth.

'He doesn't understand the way you do. Anyway, he's going back into the Army too. And you're so wonderful with Dickybird.'

George sighed with annoyance when Elizabeth told him she must put off, for a day, a week, more, leaving Merriscourt, and telling Sylvia about the work.

'She leans on you too hard, Liz. Don't let her.'

Now and again Sylvia locked herself in her room, and Elizabeth wondered if she was overcome with grief and fear of the future. It was hard to say. She suspected that Sylvia's sorrow for Ted was fading. What Elizabeth hoped was that the hideous idea that she was cursed was also fading from Sylvia's mind. At times she did look haunted. She was so thin. Her suntan had faded from being much indoors, she was yellowish, she ate no more than a bird. Occasionally Elizabeth saw her whispering with Ada – she always stopped the moment Elizabeth came into the room when this happened. She wondered what mistress and maid could be talking about: Sylvia had always mystified her.

The worst part of being forced to live in her old home was that she and George no longer made love.

One morning, meeting her alone in the hazelwoods, he said, 'When am I going to have you again? Now?'

He pulled her towards him. She backed away, her heart pounding.

'Sylvia's over there with the children.'

He swore under his breath, and his expression changed back to the familiar, sardonic mask. The sex concealed.

'I'll come to your room tonight when she's asleep.'

'George. I daren't.'

'Coward. Then meet me at Holcombe tomorrow. We can arrange it. Have you any idea how much I want you?'

'Lizzie? Lizzie?'

Through the leafy woodland glimmered Sylvia's pale dress.

336

The next morning, earlier than usual and very suddenly as if from a nightmare, Elizabeth woke. It must have been the rain, she thought, it was beating against her window. Summer was gone. She got out of bed and looked out. The garden was already soggy, the scene dreary, and the woods where yesterday she had met George were gloomy with mist.

There was a tap at her door. It was Ada with her morning tea. The maid entered the room, placed the tray on the bedside table, and said in a colourless voice, 'Madam has gone.'

'*Gone?*'

'Some time ago,' said Ada.

Elizabeth climbed out of bed, she had no time to see the look of stupid triumph on the woman's face, and rushed barefoot down the corridor to the old-fashioned room which had been her mother's. The door was wide, and she ran into a room which was swept bare. Every cupboard gaped. Every drawer was open and emptied. The emptiness was imposible to grasp. There was nothing left of Sylvia but her scent.

She's taken Dicky, Elizabeth thought, and ran back along the passage, but almost at once she heard the sound of children's voices. Shivering, she stood listening, and then thought – I must telephone George. A shaft of fear and pain went through her. She's gone with George. He decided it was best to clear out, as they did in India. He's capable of it. Oh God!

She ran to the landing which led down the great curved staircase to the hall. At the head of the stair she stopped in terror.

In the dim light of the rainy morning a figure was crossing the hall. Tall, broad-shouldered and pale. An apparition. Ted's ghost.

She screamed.

The phantom spoke.

'Lizzie? What are you doing here? Where is Sylvia?'

'Before you explain anything, telephone your parents.'

It was George, who had come at once when she rang. How did he manage to be dressed and to look so cool? Wrapped in her dressing-gown, she was still shivering.

'We're more than glad to see you alive, old chap. A wonderful sort of shock! But you must telephone your parents. You can imagine what it's been like for them.'

'Do I tell them Syl's gone?'

Ted looked as if he were going to weep. He was haggard and had lost weight, his flesh seemed to hang off him. She was filled with pity and curiosity. Where had he been? And where in God's name was Sylvia?

He shambled out of the drawing-room to the telephone.

George shut the door.

'You look done in.'

'Oh George, I thought he was a ghost. It was horrible. I thought he'd come back from the dead.'

He patted her hand, looking somewhat amused.

'Who did you think he was haunting, sweetheart? Not you, surely.'

'But how is he alive? And where is she?'

He produced a piece of paper from his pocket. It was a letter in Sylvia's sprawling writing.

'This was in the letterbox at home. I found it just now as I was leaving. Probably she delivered it herself. She says she is going to Antibes, which scarcely surprises me, and will I tell Ted she wants a divorce when they can get it.'

'*She knows he's alive?*'

'Exactly. She must have caught sight of him and that spurred her into leaving. It's my guess that she's been planning to leave for weeks, and that creature Ada has helped her. Sylvia must have seen him from the window yesterday, lurking about or something. She took fright and got Ada to help her to pack and decamp early this morning. I've no doubt we'll find her car abandoned at the station.'

He looked down at the letter.

'She writes, "I've found somebody in France who wants to take care of me. His name is Pierre de Noailles. I shan't be coming back. Dickybird must come and stay later, I'll be in touch. But I want you to explain to Liz that it's for the best. I *know* it's for the best, leaving him where he is. In his own

338

home. And she is so wonderful with him." '

He put the letter in his wallet.

'Don't look so shattered, sweetheart. I will have to go to France to tidy things up, and she certainly won't be able to get a divorce until the three years are over. But you, at any rate, are better without my erring daughter. Now, aren't you?'

They had no chance to hear Ted's explanation. Stammering that his parents wanted him at once, he left the house. He did not come back until after dinner, looking more like the man they knew. He'd bathed and shaved and changed into fresh clothes. He refused a drink and drank some coffee. He was very subdued.

'I wouldn't like to go through today again,' he said. 'It was hellish. Poor Mother cried so, it was dreadful to hear her sobbing like that. And my father was white as a sheet. I felt such a swine. I could have spared them all that.'

'I'm sure it wasn't your fault,' said Elizabeth.

'Yes it was. Oh, I said I'd go back and spend the night at Broad Oaks. Liz, you don't mind, do you?'

She was startled at the question spoken in a humble, husbandly voice. To her further surprise he asked about Petra and said he very much wanted to see her. She exchanged a glance with George.

They both sat and looked at Ted.

He gave a long sigh.

'Syl's lawyer has already been on to my father. She wants a divorce when the three years are up.'

'You can't be surprised, surely?' said George, with his usual lack of sentiment. 'Sorry to say this, but you'll find it's for the best.'

'*Ted*!' exclaimed Elizabeth, unable to contain herself a moment longer. 'It's a whole day and we still don't know what happened. Did the yacht go down? Did you – did you swim?'

He made an attempt at a smile.

'Nothing so dramatic. I went to Milan as I'd arranged, and then I joined the Benedettos. They had a damned great luxury yacht, eight cabins and a saloon like a Hollywood film. I still can't grasp that it's at the bottom of the sea. We hugged the coast, going south, and put in at a lot of places. Pisa, and a place called Palo, and further down to Naples, and then we stopped at Capri. They spent money like water. But I hated it all. The Benedettos and their friends got on my wick. I hadn't realised, meeting the two brothers at the factory and talking business, what complete Fascists they all were. We had Mussolini for breakfast, dinner and tea. All his triumphs in Abyssinia. Then we had the Third Reich, and how England was done for. In the end, when we were sailing down the Sicilian coast, I couldn't stand it any longer. I told them I was feeling pretty miserable about my marriage and needed to be on my own. I said I'd go on a walking tour, and think things out. They put me off at Palermo. Directly the yacht had left, I took various trains, went to Rome and back to London. I had no idea about the yacht. None at all. Every one of them drowned. So dreadful. A storm wasn't it?'

'The newspapers called it a tempest,' George said.

Ted was silent for a minute or two.

'I was so fed up. Fed up with those Italians, although I'm speaking ill of the dead. Fed up with Sylvia and our rows. And with myself. The whole shooting match. I went to stay with a chap I know in Surrey, an old school friend. It was a relief being there in peace. I knew the parents and Syl thought I was still in Italy, and I was glad to keep away. Eventually I got up my courage and came home yesterday. I arrived by the late train, wandered about outside the house but hadn't the guts to come in last night, and finally made my entrance early this morning.'

George and Elizabeth had listened in silence.

Ted looked at her.

'Divorced a second time. Christ. I never should've left you, Liz. You said not to. Biggest mistake of my life.'

He stood up, yawning, and said he must go. Was it all right if he came round tomorrow to see Petra? Elizabeth wished very much that he'd stop using the humble voice, and agreed

340

too briskly. I sound like a nurse with a patient who is having a nervous breakdown.

When he had driven away, she and George returned to the drawing-room. Both were busy with their thoughts. He said abruptly, 'Someone else has left unexpectedly.'

'Who?'

'Tova. I took her out at dawn yesterday, and she didn't come back to the lure. She simply vanished. I spent hours walking through the woods and fields. I don't doubt while I was in the woods somewhere she was sitting within a few yards, paying no attention.'

'But why? You reared her from a chick.'

He shrugged. 'She probably killed a rook, ate it in peace somewhere and spent the rest of the day sitting in a tree.'

'Surely she'll come back to you?'

'It can happen. I knew a hawker whose bird returned after a week. Not Tova. I've felt for some time that she was going to leave me. I took the jesses off her legs two or three days ago. I wanted her to know she was free.'

He thought for a while.

'What Tova wants now is to hunt alone. The pride of hard flight and blood at the end of it. Every hour she spends in liberty will make her instinct for freedom stronger. And her distrust of me.'

'Are you very sorry?'

'I suppose so. It's a curious link, a hawk and a man. No affection in it. All one feels is awe that anything so wild will come to you even merely for food.'

He looked at her.

'You have a fellow feeling with Tova. You don't want to be caught again either.'

'He wants me back.'

'Indeed he does, I heard it in his voice.'

George was matter-of-fact.

'And what shall you say when he asks you?'

She had a feeling of quite extraordinary pain. He knew she was afraid that duty was going to trap her into taking Petra's father back and the idea of doing so appalled her. But George didn't pull her into his arms and tell her it was impossible because she was his. Well. She wasn't, was she?

He walked to the window and said it was raining again.

'Bad for the hay,' she said.

'Worse if it was later. Last year you did the Four Acre field. Nifty with a rake, you were.'

'So were you.'

There was one of those silences they seemed to go in for. He came back and sat down beside her.

'Has it struck you that with Sylvia gone Ted will have to leave this house? It does not belong to him.'

'I'd forgotten. Poor Ted.'

'Don't be a hypocrite. He doesn't give a damn for the place and never has. He ought to leave right away.'

'You sound as if you're giving him the sack. What was it you said about Ferrers? When people are under notice, the sooner they leave the better.'

'I'm a hard-hearted bastard.'

'I think so.'

Another pause.

'There's something I must say, Liz, and I want you to listen. We both know – everybody knows – that there's going to be a war and it's coming nearer. And one of these days, as I keep saying, I'll have to go. So will your ex-husband, he'll be conscripted. The war may start next month, or in August or September. When it does, everything's going to change.'

'And I'll have to take on the estate by myself and run it. So it can be handed to Dicky when the time comes.'

'Very noble,' he said drily. 'Don't tell me you've forgotten that half of it is going to be yours.'

'How strange,' she said. 'That's just what Peter used to say. That it was half mine.'

He sprang up and went back to the window, remarking that the rain was getting heavier. She had half hoped he would kiss her, but he seemed to want to keep at a distance.

342

She pushed her hair back. She felt tired and her head ached. Bob pattered into the room but he did not come to her, he went over to George who bent and stroked him. George said, 'You're very pale. Would you like me to stay? It's been a hell of a day.'

'Oh. Would you?'

'I might quite like it.'

He was laughing at her.

She trailed up to her bedroom soon after that, feeling exhausted and sad. Sylvia was gone from the house which she had possessed for so long; she had taken her restless beauty elsewhere. And Ted's meek husbandly voice echoed in her thoughts as she undressed. When she was in bed she did not know if she expected her door to open.

He came in quietly. He was wearing an old dark red silk dressing-gown; it was Peter's.

'I found this in the wardrobe. Mind if I wear it?'

'It suits you.'

He locked the door and came over to her. She wished her heart didn't thud so.

He sat on the bed.

'George.'

'Yes?'

'This morning when I found she'd gone I thought you had too. I thought you'd taken her with you, like when you left India.'

'Did you.'

'You look angry.'

'Because you misjudge me. You've done it before.'

'I don't mean to –'

'Which makes it worse. Did you actually believe I would leave you for my daughter?'

'Yes.'

'I see.'

He was silent for a long moment. Oh, make love to me, she thought, don't look at me like that.

'And how much would you have minded?' he finally said.

His voice and manner hurt so that for a time she couldn't answer. When she did her voice shook.

'Why do you ask?'

'Well. I'll tell you. Because sexy as you are in my arms, Elizabeth, I don't know what goes on in your head. I used to think I could read your thoughts. I was wrong. What I *do* know is that you were desperately in love with your cousin and you lost him to Sylvia. Later, you and Peter went to bed. I knew you'd become lovers when I saw you together – it amazed me that Sylvia didn't see it too. I suppose when he was killed it broke your heart?'

'I thought it had.'

There was a silence. Then he took her hand as he had done once before and covered his face with it. The tears came into her eyes. He put down her hand and said in a low voice, 'And do you care a damn for me? Because there are times when I feel that *you* will break *my* heart. Don't you know I'm in love with you? I have been since God knows when. How jealous I used to be of poor Peter . . . how little I've ever been able to show you how I feel, except when we're in bed. You haunt me, beloved girl. You don't love me, by any chance, do you? I've sometimes thought –'

She fell, half crying, half laughing, into his arms.